NEVER TOO LATE FOR LOVE

NEVER TOO LATE FOR LOVE

FICTION BY
WARREN ADLER

HOMESTEAD PUBLISHING
Moose, Wyoming

To My Grandparents
and all the generations that came after.

ISBN 0-943972-44-2 (hardcover)
ISBN 0-943972-45-0 (paperback)

Library of Congress Cataloging-in-Publication Data

Adler, Warren.
  Never too late for love : fiction / by Warren Adler.
    p.   cm.
  ISBN 0-943972-44-2 (alk. paper). — ISBN 0-943972-45-0 (pbk. : alk. paper)
  1. Florida—Social life and customs—Fiction. 2. Retirees—Florida—Fiction.
3. Aged—Florida—Fiction. I. Title.
PS3551.D64N48   1995
813'.54—dc20   95-39354
                                                  CIP

First Edition
Printed in the United States of America
on recycled, acid free paper.

1 3 5 7 9 10 8 6 4 2

Published by
HOMESTEAD PUBLISHING
Box 193 · Moose, Wyoming 83012

PREFACE

Those who believe that life after sixty is one long exercise in decline will discover some startling surprises in these stories. They are about people who have learned the hard lessons of a long life, people who are still thirsty for living, still searching for the laughter and the joy, still striving for the glories, wisdom and pleasures of the mind and the body, still defying time and trying their damnedest to taste the last good drop of vitality before the inevitable ending.

Most of these stories were inspired by the sharp observations of my parents, who chose to leave the ever-changing and sometimes dangerous urban world of their youth and middle age to live out their final years in what they hoped would be a more placid and predictable environment—in their case, Florida. What they found there is not uncommon to most people in their latter years, who choose sunny climes for their last hurrahs.

Many of the stories are bittersweet, some more bitter than sweet. The reality is that age—contrary to the view of so many in the younger generations—enhances, rather than diminishes the urge to participate in life.

As I move into the orbit of my parents' demographics, I am more than ever convinced that age is no barrier to sex, love, passion, virtue, greed, joy, humor, laughter, wisdom and folly. These stories should offer the hope that age is not to be feared, but to be welcomed, savored and enjoyed.

Warren Adler
Jackson, Wyoming

Also by Warren Adler

The Housewife Blues
Private Lies
Madeline's Miracles
We Are Holding the President Hostage
Twilight Child
Random Hearts
The War of the Roses
Blood Ties
Natural Enemies
The Casanova Embrace
Trans-Siberian Express
The Henderson Equation
Banquet Before Dawn
Options

Mysteries
The Ties That Bind
The Witch of Watergate
Senator Love
Immaculate Deception
American Sextet
American Quartet

Short Stories
TheSunset Gang

CONTENTS

NEVER TOO LATE FOR LOVE

 When it was first organized, the Sunset Village Yiddish Club met once a week. Members talked in Yiddish, read passages from the Yiddish papers to each other and discussed, in Yiddish, those works of Sholem Aleichem and Isaac Bashevis Singer that they had read during the week—in the original Yiddish, of course.

The members enjoyed it so much that they sometimes stayed in the all-purpose room at the Sunset Village Clubhouse for hours after their weekly meetings there were over, talking in Yiddish as if the language were the only logical form of communication. Finally, the Yiddish Club had to start meeting three times a week, though most of the members would have preferred to attend every day.

There were a great many reasons for the phenomena, their club president would tell them. His name was Melvin Meyer, but in the tradition of the club, he was called Menasha, his name in Yiddish. He had a masterly command of the Yiddish language. Both of his parents had been actors in the heyday of the Yiddish stage, when there were more than twenty Yiddish theaters on the Lower East Side of New York alone, showing at least 300 productions a year.

"There is, of course, the element of nostalgia," Menasha would tell the group pedantically, his rimless glasses imposing in their severity. "It is the language of our childhood, of our parents and grandparents. To most of us, it was our original language, the language in which we first expressed our fears, our anxieties, our loves, and the language in which our parents forged our childhood. The link with the past is compelling.

9

And, naturally, there is the beauty of the language itself—its rare expressiveness, its untranslatable qualities, its subtlety and suppleness—which makes it something special, simply in expressing it and keeping it alive."

To both Bill (Velvil) Finkelstein and Jennie (Genendel) Goldfarb, Menasha's words were thrilling, but merely suggestive of the depths of their true feelings. They joined the club on the same day and, they discovered later, for the same reasons, some of which Menasha had expressed. Each of their spouses had lost the language of their forebears and showed absolutely no interest in the activity as a joint marital venture; they were more disposed to playing cards and sitting around the pool gossiping with their friends.

Because they had joined on the same day, they had sat next to each other and were able to start up a conversation on the subject of their first day at the club.

"It's amazing," Genendel said when the meeting adjourned. "I haven't spoken it since my mother died twenty years ago, yet I caught every word. God, I feel good speaking that language. It brings back the memories of my childhood, my mother, those delicious Friday nights."

"Oh, those wonderful Friday nights," Velvil chimed back, his mind jogged by the previously dormant images now sprung to life—the candles, the rich rhythm of Yiddish speech, the smells of fricassee and honey cake. He looked at Genendel as someone familiar, someone that he had perhaps known in his youth, or at least someone recognizable to his spirit.

She was smallish, thinner than his wife, Mimi, who allowed herself to run to fat. Lines were embedded in Genendel's tanned face, but when the light hit her at a special angle, the wrinkles disappeared and, with them, the years. She looked then like a young girl. When he told her this after they had become intimate in their conversation, she pursed her lips in mock disbelief and punched him lightly on the arm. But he could see she was pleased.

"Thank God you're telling me that in Yiddish," she said. "If my David would hear it, he'd think you were flirting."

"I am."

She put a hand over her mouth and giggled like a school girl. It hadn't seemed possible to her that anything could occur beyond their light-hearted banter, their kibitzing in Yiddish. She dismissed such thoughts as idle, forbidden speculation. Yet they would sit for a long time after club meetings were over, discussing their lives, their children, their fortunes. At first, their exchanges were purely factual, charged with details of their biographies.

"I worked as a lawyer for the Veterans Administration and hated every minute of it," Velvil said, "but I was frightened to death." He was surprised that he told her that. He had never referred to being frightened, except to himself, normally characterizing his long term as a civil servant merely as "an easy buck with no hassle."

What he really meant, he knew, was that he had been too scared to leave the government.

"But I had two kids, and it was safe. So we lived in Flatbush and the kids grew up and we waited out my pension. Not very exciting. My parents had greater dreams for me, but they had scrambled so hard for money that they made me paranoid about it."

"Are you sorry you stayed with the government so long?"

Why is she probing my regrets, he wondered, yet understanding the special poignancy that Yiddish could inject into such inquiries.

"Of course, I regret it. But I went through the motions for my family."

She, too, could understand that kind of sacrifice. She also had longed for other things.

"I wanted to travel," she said, lifting her eyes to his. He had all his hair, she noted, and part of it was still black. It was his most striking feature. A handsome man, she concluded to herself, feeling a faint stirring, a mysterious memory of yearning.

"Once, we did go on a B'nai B'rith package tour of Israel," she continued. "I loved it, not necessarily because of my Jewishness but because it was exotic. It all looked like a movie set. David, after the first day, didn't tour. He hates touring. And I love it. That's why we never went anywhere else."

"I love to travel," Velvil said suddenly, knowing it was true, though he had never traveled either.

"Where have you been?"

"Not very many places," he said. But it was important for him to be scrupulously truthful with her, like strangers meeting on a train who say things to each other that they wouldn't dare say to anyone they really knew. "In fact, no place. My wife would never leave the children."

Sitting in the back corner of the room after the meetings adjourned, losing all sense of time, they picked through their lives with care and detail as if embroidering a tapestry.

"I have a son and a daughter," Genendel told him. By then, their Yiddish returned to them in full force, their vocabulary amplified, dredged up from some secret place in their subconscious. They could be both fluent and subtle, the little nuances delicate but sure. "They were good kids. All that's left now is merely the loving of them."

"Yes," he responded, his heart leaping as she struck just the right chord. "I must remember that way of putting it.... Mimi thinks there should be more, extracting the last bit of tribute, making them always feel that they haven't done enough somehow, keeping that tug of guilt in force, always taut. She whines to them constantly on the phone. I tell her she's wrong, but she insists that daughters must care more. We have two daughters. I keep telling myself I love them, but I sometimes have doubts. They are not really very nice people."

"What a terrible thing to say."

"It's the truth." He blushed, wondering if she sensed the special joy of telling it. He had vowed to himself that he would never express anything but the truth in Yiddish, in this special language between them.

"Where is it written that parents should love their children and vice versa?" he pressed, the Yiddish rolling easily off his tongue.

"It is a forbidden thought," she answered, but the idea of it intrigued her. David, her husband, had always been the sentimentalist, the worrier. It was he who fidgeted when the children didn't call at their accustomed intervals.

"The Ten Commandments talk of honor, not love."

"So you've become a Talmudic scholar in your old age," she bantered, a sure sign that they were growing closer, he thought.

Finally, after it became apparent that it was getting on past the time of propriety, they said good-bye. He was conscious of his hand lingering for an extra moment in hers, followed by a light squeezing response. He walked her to the driveway and watched her as she moved into her car. Then he stood for a long time observing the red tail lights until they disappeared into the darkness.

His condominium was close enough to walk to and, after she left, he could feel the exhilaration in his step, a springiness in his legs that seemed uncommon in a man nearing his sixty-ninth birthday. He thought of her now with great intensity. He had willed himself to think of her only in Yiddish, as if she were his special possession and he had to guard her reality in the privacy of his own thoughts. He was certain that there was something stirring in him, a dormant plant, struggling for germination beneath the soil of time.

"You come home so late from those meetings, Bill," his wife would mumble as he slipped in beside her. He never succeeded in not waking her.

"We're working on a special project," he said.

"So late?" Then she would hover off, snoring lightly.

When it became apparent that three days a week was not enough time for them, Velvil suggested that the two couples socialize.

"Have you told her about me?" Genendel said, looking at him curiously. She wondered why she said it in that manner, as if they were engaging in a conspiracy.

"No," he answered. "And you?"

"I tell David about the club and its activities," she answered.

She knew she was growing tense about her feelings concerning Velvil, but she could not stop them, nor did she care to for that matter.

The couples met at Primero's for dinner. It was a Sunday, so they had to wait in line for nearly an hour before being seated. Perhaps it was the wait that soured the meeting.

"We were ahead of them," Mimi told the headwaiter as another group passed ahead of them, her lips tight with anger. She could not abide being bested.

"They were a fiver," the headwaiter said. His arrogance deserved a challenge.

As always, Velvil was embarrassed when his wife did this. He poked her in the small of the back.

"Don't poke me. He could seat four very easily at a table for five. God forbid he should lose one lousy meal," she said loudly, knowing that the headwaiter would hear.

"Mimi, please."

"You should be telling him," she snapped. "Why should I have to fight with him?"

"It's all right, really," David Goldfarb said. He was a smallish man, bald with a fringe of white hair around his pate and a benign, kindly look on his face.

"It's not all right," Mimi said, huffing and continuing to direct a withering gaze at the headwaiter. "You don't squeak, you don't get the oil."

Velvil looked hopelessly at Genendel.

"I'm sorry," he said in Yiddish.

"It's all right," she responded in Yiddish.

By the time they were finally seated, the wait and the altercation with the headwaiter had put them all in a gloomy mood, particularly Mimi, who could not let it go.

"They take advantage," she said, tapping the table with her forefinger. "You let them get away with it once, they take more advantage."

"Why don't we forget about it and enjoy the meal?" Velvil suggested. It was simply her way, he tried to tell Genendel with his eyes; she is not a bad woman, really. But he wondered if that was true.

"You like it here in Sunset Village?" Velvil asked David, who was either not very talkative or simply cowed by Mimi's performance.

"Actually, it's not bad," he answered. "Not bad at all."

"He has his regular gin game. He likes the sun and the pool." Genendel patted her husband's hand in a gesture of reassurance.

A flash of anger stabbed through Velvil. She must have seen his frown and quickly withdrew her hand.

"So you really like the Yiddish Club?" David asked after a long stretch of embarrassed silence.

"It's really quite wonderful," Velvil said, smiling at Genendel.

"It could be Greek to me," Mimi said. "It seems like an odd waste of time, keeping a dead language alive."

"It's not dead at all," Velvil said, annoyed at her obtuseness.

He suddenly realized that he was no longer rationalizing her actions.

Watching her, he felt her bitterness. Did she know? he wondered. Could she feel it?

"Yiddish is quite beautiful, really," Velvil said, watching Genendel. "She's not always this bad," he said suddenly in Yiddish. "I'm sorry it's not working out. It wasn't a very good idea."

"All right," Genendel responded in Yiddish. "At least we gave it an honest try."

"What are you two jabbering about?" Mimi said, with a mouthful of salad.

"We're illustrating the possibilities of the language," Velvil said.

"It's still Greek," Mimi said, spearing some lettuce leaves.

"Actually, I like the sound of it," David said. He was a pleasant man, very bland and eager to please. But he looked frequently at his wristwatch, as if he were anxious to depart.

When the entrees came, the conversation turned to the couples' children, a common denominator when all else failed. Velvil winced, knowing what was coming.

"My girls married well," Mimi said, directing her gaze at Velvil as if in rebuke. "But then they set their hearts on it. Bill always worried too much about security. They're always fighting among themselves, all the time, but underneath it all, they love each other. I'm sure about that. They both live in Scarsdale. Huge houses. They each have three kids, all doing well."

Not the pictures, Velvil thought in Yiddish. Please not that. He saw her pocketbook on the floor beside her, a vile time bomb.

"She's going to show you pictures in a second," he whispered to Genendel in Yiddish.

"That's not polite, Bill," Mimi said, glancing at him briefly but continuing her story without missing a beat. "Everything they touch turns to gold. One thing the girls knew was how to choose well. I taught them that." She reached for her pocketbook, took out her half glasses, perched them on her nose, and reached into the crowded interior of her bag.

"Must you start with the pictures?" Velvil said, feeling the food congeal into a lump in his stomach.

"He hates when I start with the pictures," Mimi said, taking out a sheaf of pictures and handing them over to the Goldfarbs, who took them politely and seemingly with great interest.

"I think it's disgusting," Velvil said in Yiddish. Genendel ignored his comment. He discovered why after they viewed Mimi's pictures. David Goldfarb reached for his wallet and drew out a few faded colored Polaroid prints.

"That's my son Marvin, the orthodontist. And there's Greta, who runs a boutique on Madison Avenue."

"She's divorced," Genendel said.

"Every time I think about it, I get sick to my stomach," David said suddenly. One felt his anger and frustration.

"It's her life," Genendel said gently.

"One of my daughters was on the verge once," Mimi said. "But I told her, 'Dotty, if you divorce Larry, I'll never speak to you again. You have the children to consider, my grandchildren.' That was ten years ago. Today they're still together, happy as two peas in a pod."

"What she doesn't know doesn't hurt her," Velvil said in Yiddish.

"Will you stop that jabbering, Bill? Can't you see it's impolite?"

"I'll speak as I damn-well please," he said in Yiddish, watching her irritation increase.

"See? He does it just to make me angry," Mimi said, cutting into her roasted chicken.

Genendel watched, signaling with her eyes. You'd better stop, he imagined she was saying.

Perhaps it was the stark comparison between the two women that, in the end, triggered the intensity of his emotion. But by the time they finished dinner and parted with politeness and empty promises of "getting together" again, he was certain he had spent his entire adult life in a bargain with the devil.

Turning it over in his mind—in Yiddish, of course—his wife of forty-five years seemed a gross, unfeeling monster. Perhaps I am imagining this, exaggerating her weak points, ignoring her essential goodness, he thought. After all, he told himself, he was no bargain himself, and she had put up with him all those years.

The idea filled him with such guilt that he abandoned even his most secret Yiddish thoughts, reverting to English, trying to remember with difficulty all the good things that she brought him over the years. He even forced himself to be affectionate when they finally went to bed after the eleven-o'clock news. He reached out for her and cupped a hand over a breast, feeling the hardness begin. Mimi seemed so startled by the act and the obvious reaction of his body that she did not shrug him away as swiftly as usual.

"Not now, Bill," she said after a while. He wondered what "now" really meant, thinking this thought in Yiddish.

But what the socializing had done was to trigger an awareness in Velvil and Genendel that both of them finally admitted to themselves.

"Seeing you two together only emphasized her grossness," Velvil said after the Yiddish Club adjourned one evening.

They decided to take a walk in the hushed stillness of the tranquil night. The air seemed light, with a touch of tropical scent. The path took them to one of Sunset Village's man-made ponds, which reflected a half-moon in the clear sky.

"I think you're exaggerating," Genendel responded, after a long pause. She dared not articulate what she truly felt—the sense of his entrapment, the frustration of his wife's overbearing inanity.

"Actually..." he sighed, "your husband seems like a sweet guy."

That he was, she thought, sweet, with a disposition that never registered below sunny. She had long ceased to wonder where the fire had gone, knowing in her heart that it was never there to begin with.

They simply lived together, copulated occasionally, passed the time. She shivered in the warm night, aware of Velvil's closeness and the sound of his breathing.

"You are the person..." Velvil began, stumbling, feeling the power of the compulsion to say it.

"Me?" she asked, knowing what was coming next, yearning for it, conscious that her shivering was not from the cold.

"I feel closer to you than to anyone I have ever known in my life," he said swiftly, the Yiddish floating in the air like a musical phrase. He looked at her but did not touch her. She seemed to move away from him as they walked.

"I know," she said, feeling her knees weaken.

"And you?" he asked after they had not talked for a while.

"I confess it," she said. It was such an appropriately Yiddish remark, as if a sense of guilt were necessary to embellish the mystery.

His heart pounded, the revelation of the shared feeling a caress in it-self. He wondered if he should stop and reach out for her, but he held off, as if the spiritual kinship might be lost in physical touching. Or perhaps he was simply shy, like an adolescent. He suddenly remembered the dis-comfort and frustration of his first stirrings in the presence of a female.

I am a grown man, he thought, wanting to express it some way, boil-ing down the essence into Yiddish elixir.

"You are a flower to my soul," he said, the Yiddish translatable only in the heart.

"You are embarrassing me, Velvil," Genendel said. A sliver of cloud passed over the moon, emphasizing the darkness. "We have no right," she protested, but he caught the collective pronoun. It assured him, af-firming that, whatever it was, they were in it together.

When he said good-bye at her car, he felt the courage to touch her, squeezing her hand briefly, though she withdrew it quickly.

I love her, he decided as he walked home, feeling a new sense of strength, an infusion of youth. He was surprised there was no guilt in the declaration and, when he slipped in between the sheets, next to his wife, he reveled in his private thoughts, wondering who the stranger was who snored beside him.

She stirred briefly. "I won twenty dollars in canasta tonight," she croaked hoarsely.

He hummed a response without interest, thinking of Genendel.

He hardly slept that night, knowing it would be impossible to wade through another two days without seeing her.

In the morning, he feigned sleep while Mimi rattled in the kitchen.

"If you didn't come in so late, you wouldn't be so tired," she cried when he did not respond to the breakfast call.

"Make your own breakfast," she said finally as she finished dressing and slammed the door behind her.

Jumping out of bed, he reached for the telephone book, found Genendel's number, and called her.

"I must see you," he said.

"I'm afraid," she said.

"So am I."

"We could have breakfast."

He mentioned a coffee shop on Lake View Drive to which he could walk. He knew she had the car, as her husband rarely used it.

They met an hour later, feeling awkward, hardly speaking until the coffee was served. He watched her as she peered into her cup. What was she looking at? he wondered.

"I want to see you every day," he said, in Yiddish, of course, feeling the power of his new-found courage. He never thought himself capable of exercising it. People at the next booth looked his way. He noted their deeply tanned faces and knew that their curiosity was aroused by the strange language.

"I want to see you every day," he said again.

"People would talk, Velvil. They would notice."

Suddenly, a crowd of people came into the restaurant, Sunset Village types in well-filled Bermuda shorts. Outside, he could see the parked tricycles of the Sunset Village Cycling Club, the high pennants limp on their antennae.

"We could join the Cycling Club," he decided, watching the group come in. "They meet every day. Besides, it will be healthy. Plenty of fresh air and exercise."

"They look so foolish," Genendel said, smiling.

"Who cares?"

She knew he was responding to another question. She wondered about her own caring, thinking suddenly of David, her husband, and of the hurt he would experience if he knew of her feelings for Velvil. With effort, she pushed the thought from her mind.

"All right," she said, lowering her eyes. She knew she had taken another step in the journey and felt the mystery of it, the joy.

In the Cycling Club, they practiced discretion, talking to the others as they pedaled en masse through the crowded roads, making a mess out of the traffic, prompting occasional catcalls and anti-Semitic epithets, which they ignored and laughed about.

They didn't have much time to themselves, but it seemed enough that they were together. Even in the silence, their intimacy grew. When they exchanged information, it was always in Yiddish.

"Don't you people speak English?" one of the club members asked as he pedaled close by.

"Not very well," Velvil said slyly, hearing Genendel's giggle begin beside him.

The idea had been growing within each of them for some time, but it wasn't until they had been in the Cycling Club for several months that it became clear, hitting them both with the force of a hurricane.

They were having breakfast, the entire cycling group, chattering like children, making the waitresses in the coffee shop move more swiftly than they were accustomed to. A couple sat down beside them, a large freckle-faced woman with wispy gray hair curling from under her blue baseball cap. Her husband was tanned almost black by the sun, his bald head shining like some mahogany wood sculpture.

"We're the Berlins," the woman said.

They knew instantly that she would dominate the conversation with her rapid-fire questions, a dyed-in-the-wool yenta. "I've been watching you," the woman said. "I even remarked to Harry. Didn't I, Harry?"

Harry nodded, his dark face breaking, the neat line of false teeth flashing in the brightness of the sunlight.

"I have a sixth sense about devoted couples. Tell me, how long have you been married?"

Velvil wanted to respond immediately, but shrugged instead, watching Genendel's discomfort.

"Forty-five years at least, right?"

Genendel lowered her eyes, which the woman must have taken for affirmation.

"See, I was right," she said, turning to Harry. "They are a truly devoted couple. How many children have you got?"

Velvil looked at Genendel, wondering if she could see the humor of the situation beyond her anxiety. He decided to be playful and held up four fingers.

"I figured at least," the woman said.

"She wanted to have more," Velvil said, "but she got a special dispensation from the Pope."

"You had a hysterectomy?" the woman pursued. "I had one ten years ago."

"They took the baby carriage out and left the playpen in," Harry said suddenly.

"It's not often that you meet such a devoted couple. I can tell. I've got a sixth sense about it, haven't I, Harry?"

Velvil felt the idea explode in his head, but dared not entertain it and worried that once broached it would affect his relationship with Genendel.

After the Yiddish Club meeting that night, they sat on chairs near the pool.

"Is it possible that we look like a married couple?" Velvil said, noting his own caution as he watched her face in the glow of the clubhouse lights.

"I'm afraid so," she said. "You can't fool an old yenta."

"I hadn't realized."

"I have."

"You?"

"How long do you think we can get away with it?" she sighed.

"What have we done? Have I once..."

She put a finger over his lips, a gesture to induce silence. Instead, he kissed her finger, their first kiss. He took her wrist and showered kisses on the back of her hand. She let her hand linger, closing her eyes, tilting her head. He could see a tear slip out of the corner of her eye and roll down her cheek, catching the brief glow of the lights.

"I want to spend the rest of my life with you, Genendel," he said, a lump growing in his throat, his heart pounding. "I want to marry you."

"This is madness. This is crazy," she cried. "I don't want to hear it ever again, not ever." He had never seen her so upset.

"Not ever again," she repeated. But she did not take her hand out of his. "If you dare mention such a thing again, I promise you I will never see you again. You must promise me, Velvil."

He clutched her hand, feeling the full impact of the emptiness of his future without her, not daring to precipitate her anger further. But he did not promise.

"You must promise," she persisted.

"I cannot promise," he said, after a long silence, still holding her hand.

He lifted it again to his lips. "I love you," he said. "And that is the only thing I can promise."

She withdrew her hand, stood up, cleared her throat, and wiped her tears.

"I think we better not see each other any more." What angered her particularly was that she was actually thinking the unthinkable. How would David react? Her children? The cruelty of it. She had no right. She strode forward, and he rose to follow her.

"Leave me alone," she said. "I am going home now."

"Will I see you again?" he cried after her, afraid to follow, knowing his voice was carrying too far in the quiet night. He stood rooted to the spot, watching her depart.

Genendel did not join the activities of the Cycling Club the next morning. Instead of going with the group, Velvil rode to her condominium and watched it for a long time without gathering the courage to press the buzzer and confront her. The blinds were drawn. Later, he stopped at a pay phone and dialed her number. There was no answer.

A heavy depression washed over him as he moped around his condominium, thinking he had lost her, letting self-pity clutch at him. Mimi made his lunch, not noticing his strange behavior. He did not listen as she chirped away about her friends, her card games. The incessant patter of her voice with its empty gossip increased the blackness of his mood.

"Stop eating so fast," Mimi said.

He chewed the food, aware of its tastelessness as it moved without relish or awareness down his gullet. Without Genendel, he told himself, life would be empty, the future just a long wait until his lifeless corpse was finally filed away beneath the earth, forgotten and unvisited.

After Mimi left for her afternoon game, he made an effort to calm himself, to rationalize his position, go over his options.

He was, after all, a lawyer. But contemplation of what a divorce might entail boggled his mind, made him tired. His wife's harangues would be hysterical. The children would think he was a monster. Would he hate himself later?

He did consider having a clandestine affair, but it was so foreign to his nature and his morality that he could not bring himself to accept such a possibility. What he concluded was that he could accept any pain from Mimi, from his children, from anyone, pay any price for the privilege of spending the rest of his life with Genendel. Anything was worth that.

He was tempted to phone her again but lost his courage, deciding instead to suffer through the long night and day until the meeting of the Yiddish Club. It was not an easy assignment.

Feigning a slight cold, he was able to escape from Mimi's patter by squirreling himself in bed for most of the next day.

"You're going to the Yiddish Club?" Mimi asked as he dressed.

"I feel better."

"You're acting strangely, Bill."

"I know," he mumbled, wanting to shout out at her, to tell her what was happening inside of him. Instead, he walked out into the warm night, hoping that, in a few minutes, he would once again be in the presence of the woman he loved. But the slight optimism that he felt as he walked quickly dissipated when he arrived and it became apparent that she was not coming. He listened listlessly to the speakers, walked out early, and roamed through the clubhouse.

In the long card room, he saw David playing gin. He moved toward the table and watched the game for a while, waiting for the moment to ask him news of his wife.

"Where's Jennie?" he asked casually. "Missed her at the meeting."

"Said she missed the kids. Went up north to visit for a few weeks." He poked Velvil in the stomach. "Look at this," he said, holding up the score. "I got him on a triple schneid."

Her absence made his longing more intense, and he spent his time in long solitary walks around Sunset Village. You must come back to me, he begged her in his mind.

"What's wrong with you, Bill?" his wife asked with casual but persistent interest.

"I am sad and lonely," he said in Yiddish.

"That again."

"You give me no pleasure," he said, again in Yiddish.

"This is ridiculous."

"You are ridiculous," he said in Yiddish.

"The hell with you," Mimi responded with anger, slamming the door behind her as she rushed off to the clubhouse. He savored his cruelty, yet knew that it was wrong.

After the first shock of Genendel's departure wore off, leaving him only with a gnawing emptiness, he continued to participate in the morning cycling and the Yiddish meetings. He went through the mechanical process of the activities in the hope that when she returned, she would join him again. He was certain that her life with David was as empty as his life with Mimi. Was she prepared to compromise her remaining years in the name of duty? Foreclose forever on the possibility of... love?

When she finally returned to the Yiddish Club two weeks later, he felt that the curtain had been raised on his life again, and he could barely sit through the meeting waiting for a few private words with her. By then, he had convinced himself that he would take half a loaf, to leave it as it had been. Even a few moments of her time were better than enduring the suffering of her absence.

When the meeting was over, he dashed over to her, stumbling over a chair. "Did you enjoy your trip?" he asked, stammering, unable to control the frantic beat of his heart.

"It was all right," she responded.

He imagined that he could detect sadness in her eyes.

"Would you like to take a walk?"

She nodded. He had gone over and over this request in his mind and could hardly believe that he had made it.

They walked along the familiar path in silence.

"I promise," he finally said.

"Promise?" She paused, then turned to look at him.

"I promise I won't bring up that subject again." He wondered if she understood.

"You think it's that simple?" she said, looking at him.

She touched his arm, and he felt his flesh respond with goose pimples. He was confused.

"How many more years do you think we have, Velvil?"

Her question left him speechless, as his mind groped for some kind of logic.

"I try not to think about it," he said at last.

"I have been thinking about it for the last two weeks."

"You have?"

"I spent the time with my daughter. I felt like a picture on the wall."

He knew instantly what she meant, and she sensed his understanding. She, too, had dreamed and longed for this moment, when she would reveal to him that she was, indeed, willing to pay the price.

"We are in the elephant burial ground, Velvil," she said. "We know the end is coming fast. We have to seize the present."

In Yiddish, the words came to him as poetry and he felt the power of himself. His energy surged as he gripped her shoulders and gathered her in his arms.

"It will not be easy," she said firmly, relieved at last, unburdened. "And, frankly, I don't know if I'll be able to go through with it."

"We'll give each other courage," he said.

They resumed their walk, arms locked around each other like young lovers.

"They'll think we're crazy," Genendel said suddenly. "And they might be right."

"Between us, Genendel," Velvil said, "we've been married nearly a century."

"Eighty-nine years," she said. "See? I've been thinking about it. I even thought of ways that I might get David interested in your wife. It would make matters so much simpler."

"I wouldn't wish it on him," Velvil said.

On the way back to her car, he pondered the legal problems.

Although he was a lawyer, he had never paid much attention to divorce law. He was annoyed with himself for allowing practicalities to intrude. What did that matter? Somehow they would survive it.

But it was not that easy to break the news to Mimi, and he agonized over it, sleepless, tossing and turning, unable to shut off his mind. In the darkness, he felt the terror of guilt, knowing what Genendel must be going through. He felt his courage ebb and only when the light filtered through the drawn blinds did his resolve return.

Following Mimi into the kitchen, he sat down at the little table and watched her as he gathered his thoughts. It was not that he despised her.

Hardly that, although he knew he had lost all feeling for her, except compassion. He did feel compassion, he told himself. Only because he knew that she would never understand.

"I want a divorce," he said, flat, straight-out. She turned and looked at him quizzically, coffee pot poised in mid-air, hair still disheveled from sleep. The odor of her floated across the room.

"What!?" She squinted, as if seeking comprehension with her eyes.

"I want a divorce," he repeated.

"You want a what?"

"A divorce."

She started to smile, alert to his words, but not yet understanding.

"I'm serious," he said, wanting her to be sure of his meaning, urging himself to be precise. "I want a divorce. I am in love with another woman."

"Another what?"

He surveyed her coolly, knowing she was aghast, her lips trembling. The coffee pot slipped with a clang into the sink.

"Another woman. Genendel Goldfarb."

"Genendel?"

"Jennie."

"Her?"

He imagined that he felt the eruption begin with vibrations in his toes, like the beginning of an earthquake. He had seen her like this before, once when he threatened to leave the government, and again when he at first refused to move to Florida. But this time he was girded with the image of Genendel. Watching Mimi now did not diminish his courage as it had done in the past.

"Are you crazy?" she began. "An old fart like you. And that dried-up prune. She hypnotized you. You should both be put away in an institution." She paused, sneering. "You had relations? That's it, right, Bill? I got it. Right, Bill? She put her hands on my husband's fly, right? So what did she get? Such a big deal. And she made you all hot and crazy, right?"

She rushed into the living room and grabbed the telephone, her hysteria mounting. "A psychiatrist is what you need. And quick. Forty-five years of marriage and he wants a divorce. I got a senile old man for a husband."

He shrugged and walked back into the bedroom, hearing her voice rise behind him.

"You want me to call your children?" she cried. "I'll call them.

"Are you ready for me to tell them about your shame?" she yelled at him. "I'm calling them."

"There's the phone." He pointed, surprised at his calm.

He went into the bathroom and observed his face in the mirror as she banged on the locked door.

"You want a divorce, you bastard?" she screamed. "I'll show you divorce. I'll get a knife and stick it through my heart first. You hear me, bastard? I'll put a knife in my heart first."

How absurd, he thought, feeling pity begin. Listening, he heard her walk heavily into the kitchen, opening doors, making a racket with the pots and pans. Then he heard her coming back.

"I have a knife," she said. "I have it in my hands, pointing into my heart."

He remained silent, listening. Her breathing was heavy, gasping. Tempted by the movement at the other side of the door, he put his hand on the knob, then withdrew it as if it were hot.

"Do you hear me, you bastard?" she hissed.

"I hear you," he said, turning on the tap.

"Your children will curse you forever," she screamed.

He could tell by the pitch of her voice that she had reached the outer edge of hysteria.

"And you'll rot in hell."

He knew she was dissolving into self-pity when her deep sobbing began. She is thinking only of herself, he thought, of her own humiliation, of the effect on her card-playing friends. Who cares, he thought, surprised at his own callousness, yet exhilarated by his sense of freedom.

I am no longer frightened, he told himself. I am free. He opened the bathroom door and saw her face-down on their bed, her shoulders shaking. He kicked the knife away with his foot.

"I am going out," he said loud enough for her to hear and embellished his words with a slam of the door.

Genendel met him where the cyclists gathered. Her eyes were puffy, evidence of her own pain of disclosure. He reached out and held her hand.

"Done?" he asked.

"Done." Her eyes filled with tears. "It was like feeding him poison."

"Now what?"

"I had no illusions," she said, the Yiddish between them a soothing tonic. "It is part of the price. And you?"

"I got a genuine suicide attempt," he said. "But don't worry. She's done it before."

"Have we done the right thing?" she asked, brushing aside the tears that rolled down her cheeks.

"My conscience is clear," he responded. "For once in my life, I have done an honest thing. Genendel, my darling Genendel. It was the only way."

"I hope so," she said, squeezing his hand.

"They'll hate us," Velvil said, "but that is to be expected."

They wheeled away from the main body of the cyclists and found a bench.

"Now what?" Genendel said.

"You mean practical considerations?"

"Yes."

He patted her arm, proud of his courage. He had not pondered the consequences. He had been true to himself, following his feelings.

"We'll rent a place and, if necessary, move in together now," he said, contemplating financial matters at last. "It will be no bed of roses," he said, "but we'll have each other."

"You mean live together before we're married?"

"We'd share an apartment."

"I hadn't..." She paused. "It would be difficult for me." It was against her grain, she admitted to herself.

"Well then," he said gently, "perhaps David will move out and I'll rent a place alone." He silently calculated the burden of supporting two households on his pension. If necessary, the children would have to kick in for Mimi. He knew they did but hid the knowledge from him. He had been offended by the thought of taking money from his children, as if it diminished him in some way. But that did not prevent his acquiescence, another act of hypocrisy that was part of his old life.

"I'm sure David has called the children by now," Genendel said suddenly. David always called the children in major crises.

That was another hurdle that she dreaded. Was it all worth it? she wondered, watching Velvil. Her life with David had, after all, been tranquil. Hardly anything had happened, except that they had produced children, fussed over them for a few years, and had grown old. The children were the only thing they had in common.

They simply had cohabited. Was this what one must accept of life, eschew joy or adventure or love? David would survive, she concluded. He had his friends, his gin games, his television set, and he would have to find himself another companion to cook and clean for him. In Sunset Village, this nest of widows, it should be easy enough. She reached out and took Velvil's hand, feeling the bond between them, the friendship and communication.

"It's no sin to want more," she said suddenly in Yiddish, the inflection of the language reassuring.

"We are in for some tough times in the near future," Velvil said. He was thinking how the telephone lines must be burning between his wife and their daughters.

"I am prepared," she said calmly, her faltering resolve shored up as she watched his face. "We will help each other."

By the end of the day, he had sublet a condominium and moved some of his clothes out of the place he shared with his wife. She had sobbed bitterly as he packed a small valise, wailing like a mourner at a graveside. I am not dead yet, he thought, to give himself courage, but he could not fully control his pity. In ten, maybe fifteen years, it will hardly matter to anyone, he assured himself. Such a thought bolstered his courage.

They agreed to meet at the poolside that evening. Genendel was late. When she finally came, he noted again the puffiness of her eyes and a deepening in the lines of her face, which even in the dim light seemed to have assumed a gray cast. They began to walk along the path that led around the pool.

"Your wife called me," Genendel said, her voice breaking.

"The bitch—"

"Please, Velvil. I understand."

"Was she hysterical?"

"Worse. She accused me of being a whore, of stealing her husband."

"The bitch. I hope you hung up on her."

"No. I listened. I listened to every word."

"It wasn't necessary."

"It was to me."

He was agitated. He balled his hands and hit them against his thighs in frustration. They walked for a while in silence.

"Your children will be here tomorrow," she announced.

"My children?"

"Both daughters and their husbands."

"She told you this?"

"And mine are coming too."

"How awful." He was feeling his indignation now, searching her face in the darkness for a hint of her reaction.

"I agreed."

"Agreed?"

"When she calmed down, David got on the phone and they decided that perhaps we should all meet."

"Together?" It would be, he told himself calmly, a new experience. Perhaps this was what was required. One big final meeting. He shook his head. "It is sheer madness," he said. "They'll overwhelm us. We wouldn't have a chance against them."

"What could I say?"

"You could have said no." He willed his anger under control.

"They have no right. We are entitled to our own life, to our own decision."

"I said that, but then your son-in-law called."

"Larry?"

"The lawyer."

"That one. You should have hung up the phone. He's the worst of the lot. He has ten women on the string, a miserable character." He felt fear at this effort to pry them apart. "We must resist them."

"We are going to meet tomorrow morning." Genendel's voice broke as she said it. "How could I refuse? They're our children. Our families."

"I have finished my duty toward them," he said, sensing the frustration of the impending confrontation. "I have made enough sacrifices."

"I felt we owed it to them," she said, holding back her tears.

"I knew it wouldn't be all wine and roses, but I hadn't expected this."

"Are you sorry?"

"Not sorry," she said, the tears coming now. "Confused."

"Unsure?"

"Please, Velvil," she said, then sniffled. "I've been a quiet, peaceful married lady for forty-four years."

"A vegetable."

"Yes, a vegetable. But this kind of aggravation is more than I think I can take."

"When is the meeting?" he asked stiffly.

"Tomorrow morning. In a room in the clubhouse."

"My God, it is like an innocent family affair, a family circle."

He bit his lips. "I'm not coming," he said weakly, knowing his protest was in vain.

"I promised for you."

His anger would not dissipate, and walking her back to her car in the dark parking lot, he wondered if he had lost her. She should be coming home with me, he told himself, gathering her in his arms, kissing her cheeks, tasting the saltiness of her tears.

"Are you slipping away from me?" he whispered. But she did not answer. She got into the car and drove off, leaving him lonely and despairing in the darkness, feeling the weight of his years.

During the night, he tossed in the strange bed, going over imaginary conversations with his children and their husbands, with David, with Genendel's children. In all of these fantasies, his words sounded hollow, unpersuasive.

How can an old man talk of love? Even in his own mind, he sounded like an adolescent. It was only toward morning that he discovered that the conversations in his imagination were not conversations at all. Information was transmitted to him, but not from him as he had been talking Yiddish. That idea restored his courage and calmed him enough for him to fall into semi-slumber.

He timed himself to be the last to arrive. They all looked toward him, tight, anxious faces masked with bitterness rising like steam. They had set the room up like a business conference, twelve seats around a long table. Thankfully, they left one seat empty at the far end of the table. Larry, his son-in-law, sat at the other end, looking very much like a board chairman.

Genendel was sitting between what must have been her son and daughter. They resembled her. Dutifully, he kissed the proffered cheeks of his daughters, who each mumbled something politely. Mimi turned her eyes away.

The scene was ludicrous, he told himself in Yiddish, a strange assemblage. He knew that the two families had briefed themselves in advance, had hit upon a strategy and, as he had suspected, had appointed Larry as their spokesman. Looking at the group, he was surprised at his own calm.

His eyes sought Genendel's, who lifted hers. She had been crying again, he saw, hoping he could will her to take heart. She looked defeated and he sensed her indecisiveness. We must free ourselves from them, he vowed. It is our only hope.

"We felt this was the only way, Pop," Larry began.

What a pompous ass, Velvil thought, observing him with his coat opened and the Phi Beta Kappa key dangling from his vest.

He wondered why they hadn't brought the grandchildren. It was, after all, everybody's business.

"I don't want you both," Larry began unctuously, "to think of this as any kind of special pressure. We are simply all in some way involved in these decisions. What we are discussing here are two families, children, grandchildren, and, essentially, peace of mind. We all have a genuine interest in your mutual welfare." He paused, as if he were in court, feeling the strength of his own authority.

Mimi sat stiffly, indignant and sour-faced, but assured and under control. Velvil watched as David nodded.

"We all honestly feel that if we appealed to your reason and intelligence, to your practicality and good sense, that you would conclude that this idea is detrimental to yourselves and all of us," Larry said.

"As far as I'm concerned, they could both rot in hell," Mimi suddenly blurted.

Larry turned to her in disgust. "You promised, Ma. You promised." He banged the table. "We will have none of this, do you hear?"

"They can still rot in hell." Mimi huffed and folded her arms over her fat breasts.

"If we allow ourselves to get emotional," Larry said, glaring at Mimi, "then we might as well adjourn this meeting. We are here as mature adults discussing what could become a complicated problem, one that will give us all, everyone in this room, the kind of grief that none of us have a stomach for. We've all taken time out of our lives to see if we can solve this problem."

He looked at Velvil. "Now, Pop, my understanding is that you wish to divorce Mom and marry this woman."

"I'd appreciate it if you didn't refer to my mother in those terms," Genendel's son said.

"I hadn't intended anything disparaging," Larry said quickly.

"I wish you wouldn't interrupt," Genendel's daughter said to her brother.

"You realize, of course, Mrs. Goldfarb," Larry said, looking at Genendel, "that you are encouraging an action that will result not only in humiliation for your husband and my mother-in-law but ostracism for yourself and my father-in-law."

"Now you're trying to fix blame," Genendel's son said. He had his mother's gentle face. Velvil wondered if he was sympathetic, a thought quickly dispelled. "I don't agree with what they're doing, but I don't think you can fix blame."

"She's a woman," one of Velvil's daughters interjected. "She knows that it's the woman who controls the situation. She encouraged him."

"I resent that," Genendel's son said. "Your father is not exactly innocent in this matter."

"They should both rot in hell," Mimi said, her voice booming in the room. "I still say he needs a psychiatrist."

"That's for sure," one of Velvil's daughters said huffily.

"It's that Yiddish Club," Mimi shouted. "They should close that Yiddish Club."

"This is getting out of hand," Larry shouted and banged on the table. He waited until they settled down again.

"You're all acting like a bunch of children."

"I think Mother's right," Larry's wife said. "Dad needs some help."

But Velvil listened calmly, surveying, in turn, each of the people around the table allegedly debating their fate. He looked at Genendel again, observing her calm, which gave him courage.

David Goldfarb wore a long face, the embodiment of gloom.

"You must realize, Pop," Larry said, "that you're being cruel to all of us. You're breaking up two families. Both of you are."

He was being manipulative, attempting to use guilt as a weapon of last resort.

"Are you all right?" Velvil said suddenly to Genendel in Yiddish.

"I'm not exactly comfortable, but I think I can bear it."

"You see," Mimi cried, "they're talking gibberish again."

"Please speak English, Pop," Larry said in exasperation.

"They are all idiots, Genendel," Velvil said, sure that his courage had returned. "Nothing they say will matter to me."

"I feel better now too, Velvil," she said.

He imagined he could see the gray cast to her skin lift and a healthier color begin.

"They're sick. It's obvious," one of Velvil's daughters said. She looked at him, glaring. "Will you please speak English?"

"I'll speak whatever I feel like," he said in Yiddish.

"See. Was I right?" Mimi asked, posing it as a general question to the group.

"In order to solve this," Larry said, "you've got to communicate in a language we can all understand."

"I didn't call this meeting," Velvil said in Yiddish addressing the group. He could see Genendel smiling. "I don't think it's any of your business. Who are you to preside in judgment over our lives? What do any of you know of our lives?"

"Of course," Genendel said in Yiddish. "They have no right." She looked around the room. "None of you have any right."

"What are they saying?" Larry said and stood up. "Is there anyone here who knows what they're saying?"

"I know what we're saying," Velvil said, feeling the joy in his strength, in his freedom.

And I know what we're saying," Genendel said.

This is impossible," Genendel's daughter shouted, turning to her mother.

"I didn't ask you to come," Genendel said, continuing to speak in Yiddish.

"I can't stand this," Mimi shouted, standing up. She put a hand over her throat as if she were in agony.

"See what you're doing to her," one of his daughters said, holding her mother's free hand.

"She's only acting," Velvil said. "Can't they see that?"

"They know it," Genendel said. She stood up.

"Where are you going, Mother?" Genendel's daughter shouted.

"That bitch. That whore," Mimi shouted.

"Who are you calling a whore, you fat pig?" Genendel's daughter said.

"They're a low-class family. Pigs!" one of Velvil's daughters shouted.

"A whore," Mimi cried, forgetting about her assumed frailty, pointing her finger at Genendel, then at her husband.

"Rot in hell. Both of you."

"My conscience is clear," Genendel said quietly.

"We can still make the Cycling Club, Genendel," Velvil said quietly.

"A wonderful idea," Genendel responded. She moved toward him, reaching for his arm. They stood now together at the end of the table, looking at the faces of their families.

"Please," Larry persisted. "If you will all sit down..." But neither of them was listening.

"Who are these people?" Velvil asked, as they turned and proceeded toward the door, arm-in-arm.

"I guess some people we used to know," Genendel said, as they walked out of the room.

You'd Be Surprised How We're Related

"Cousin Irma," Sarah whispered, as she looked again at the signature below the message on the New Year's card, tapping her finger on the edge of her coffee cup. "Who is Cousin Irma?"

She studied the card, the postmark, "New York City" in the center of the canceled imprint and the name "Mrs. Nathaniel Z. Shankowitz" with her Sunset Village address. She searched through the imaginary archives of the family tree, both on her and her ex-husband's side, finally shaking her head in defeat.

"Do I have a Cousin Irma?" she asked herself. It was a mystery.

When her son called from Connecticut on the Jewish New Year, she quickly disposed of the amenities and asked him the question that was on the surface of her mind.

"Do I have a Cousin Irma?"

"Who?"

"That's what I said. Your Uncle Eddie has Rebecca and Arthur and my father and mother, your grandmother, had no other relatives in this country…" She paused, shook her head and shrugged. She emitted a sigh of surrender.

"Maybe it's the wrong address?"

"No." She paused again. "Did your father ever have a cousin Irma?" Even twenty-five years of divorce did not temper the unmistakable acid tone. After the divorce, Nat had always been "your father," the tone heavy with sarcasm as if he were some terrible obscenity, which he was, of course, in her mind.

"Not that I remember," the son said. He was used to such inferences and let it pass tactfully, a posture that always annoyed her, triggering old insecurities and suspicions.

"What would you know about him anyway?" she said, feeling her own crankiness emerge. Since the divorce, he had only seen him a few times and that was soon after he had left the house. She sensed his annoyance and knew that she had, as always, gone too far.

"Well, it's not important" she said finally. "Look, I'm grateful you called, darling. Happy New Year and send my regards." The implication was clear. His wife wanted no part of her, an old divorcée with an only son. Who could blame her? She understood and was happy to get his periodic calls.

Now that she got her son's call, she would be able to report that fact to the yentas around the pool and the pity would pass on to some other poor woman whose ungrateful children hadn't called on New Year's.

"Your Barry didn't call?"

"He called last week."

"He didn't call on New Year's?"

"They had company. Her people came all the way from Chicago."

"That's an excuse?"

It was a form of torture she really did not like to hear. It was bad enough that she had been a divorcée. Even at sixty-eight, such status had its special distinctions in the pecking order of the Sunset Village yentas. A married woman was the highest order of female, with her credentials descending in the order of the condition of her husband's health. A woman with a vigorous healthy husband was on the highest rung of yenta envy. At next to the last rung of the ladder, lower than the women with the most sickly and debilitated husbands, lower than the varying gradations of widowhood, was the divorcée, further graded by the chronology of the divorce. A woman divorced beyond twenty-five years, like Sarah Shankowitz, was just short of yenta purgatory. Purgatory, the lowest rung, was the old maid, although woman's lib had provided some measure of late respectability to the condition.

If Sarah Shankowitz knew what was in store for her, she might never have precipitated the action that sealed her fate. She knew she had made a mistake in prompting the divorce from Nat, but she never confided that to anybody.

"You have your pride," her best friend Mildred had advised. She lived in the apartment across the hall and every day, when the husbands and the children had gone off to work and school, they spent the morning over coffee, sharing the intimacies of their lives. Neither of them were what might be called "liberated" women. They lived their lives as their mothers did, housewives who manned the homefront while others in the family went out into the world.

"Maybe he's getting senile early. He doesn't seem interested anymore," Sarah confided to Mildred one day. They had begun to share little secrets and, on the days when self-pity emerged in Sarah's heart, Mildred would rise to the occasion with energy and investigative zeal. Encased in fat, her big unburdened breasts resting over a bloated belly, she had an air of superior wisdom and self-satisfaction. Perhaps it was the flesh itself that gave her the illusion of solidity, but the less assertive Sarah envied her confidence and what she supposed then, her worldliness. Mildred tapped two fat fingers into a dimpled palm.

"Show me bed trouble and I'll show you marriage trouble."

"I'm not exactly Marilyn Monroe."

"How long has it been?"

"Maybe a month." Actually, she remembered, she had lied by half. "But he works so hard," Sarah had added quickly. "He comes home and sleeps in the chair." Nat was a cutter in the garment district. "It's not easy."

"That's no excuse."

"Maybe he should see a doctor. He might have just lost his pep."

"They don't lose their pep so easily," Mildred said cryptically.

"To tell you the truth, I don't really care that much about it."

"What has that got to do with the price of fish in Canarsie?"

"But you noticed?"

"Certainly I noticed." Despite her confidences, she still maintained a delicacy when it came to sex. Perhaps, Sarah thought, she had confided too much, but now that the floodgates were open, Mildred persisted.

"I make sure my Sam is always interested."

"How do you do that?"

Mildred smiled, her jowls tightening. Sarah found it difficult to think of her in that context, especially since Mildred was such a big woman and Sam so slight.

"I don't give away trade secrets."

But the matter became a constant inquiry and Sarah could not bring herself to lie about it.

"Not yet?"

"No." She would twist and untwist her fingers. Seeking something to do, she would pour more coffee, which only made her more nervous than she was.

"You know it could be another woman?" Mildred said one day, lowering her voice as if the walls could eavesdrop. It was, of course, a seed planted. That had been the farthest thought from Sarah's mind. Other women were not in the range of her experience. She had been married at eighteen, twenty years ago. Life was making a living, making ends meet, taking care of her son, cleaning the house, going shopping every day for food, talking to Mildred. And on Sundays, they would go to his mother's, Friday nights to her parents'. Occasionally, they would go out to eat Chinese food or to the movies. Other women? That was only on the soap operas.

But despite her skepticism, the idea was loose in her mind, rattling around like clicking marbles, causing her to look at Nat in some new way. She watched him snoring in his chair and could not conceive of such a thing.

He wasn't exactly Cary Grant himself, with his bald pate, pale skin and hawklike nose, although she once had thought him very attractive.

Besides, he was rarely out of her sight. Except for the twice-a-month meetings of his Veterans' group, he was always home at the regular time, tired, a bit-forlorn, but home. Of course, there was the once-a-month union meetings but those, too, were part of the regular routine. Mildred was crazy, she decided. My Nat, a philanderer? It was an absurdity. Yet the idea persisted.

Finally, one night in bed, she became mildly aggressive, moving toward his sleeping body and attempting a furtive caress. It was, of course, contrary to all the tenets of her upbringing. A woman waits. A woman submits. Nat merely gulped, shrugged her away and continued his snoring.

"He rejected me," she told Mildred the next day, having been up the rest of the night, turning a bleak future over in her mind.

"I think you got trouble, Sarah," Mildred responded, the hint of dire foreboding in her tone. She crossed her fat arms over her ample bosoms, clucked her tongue, and shook her head from side to side. Nothing more needed to be said. Sarah was an object of pity.

"So what should I do?" She felt the tears well in her eyes, and Mildred's bulk swam in the mist.

"Talk. You got a tongue," Mildred scolded, her disgust at Sarah's passivity and helplessness unmistakable.

"And suppose it's true?"

"You'll cross that bridge when you come to it."

That night after she had finished the dishes and her son sat down at the table to do his homework, she went into the living room and shook Nat awake. Startled, he opened his eyes and looked at her, first with annoyance. She must have seemed compelling, because his attitude quickly changed to alertness.

"I want to talk to you, Nat," she said, standing over him, rubbing her moist hands along the sides of her flowered housedress, stained with the recent soap suds.

"Now?"

"Now."

"So talk."

"What's going on?" She felt her courage leaving her as she assessed what she thought was guilt in his response. Maybe she should leave it alone, she thought, but the image of Mildred and her remembered sternness persisted. He didn't answer and turned his eyes to the ceiling in an attitude of exasperation.

"I'm pooped. I worked hard all day. Goldstein was a son-of-a-bitch. The patterns were two inches off. I don't need this aggravation." It seemed an overreaction at first. After all, no accusations had, as yet, been made.

"Something's going on," Sarah probed, wishing Mildred could see her, feeling her strength gather.

"There's nothing going on." He had answered too swiftly, she thought. Then he paused, looked quizzical. "What should be going on?"

"You know." She imagined her gaze was intimidating, the rebuke forbidding but clear.

"What do I know?"

"You think I'm stupid, huh Nat? Dumb stupid Sarah. That's what you think." Her hands were on her hips. "Well, I got eyes." She pointed to her eyes. "I got ears." She pointed to her ears. "I got instincts." She pointed to her head. Then she drove her finger into his chest.

"You think you're fooling me?"

The finger pressed hard into his chest and he winced. "Whaddymean fooling?" He was being defensive now, and she suspected now that he was hiding something. "A woman knows," she said. It was Mildred's line, almost Mildred's voice.

He pushed her finger away and stood up, pacing the floor, moving his fingers through his hair. She recognized the gesture. My God, I think Mildred was right, she thought, her heart sinking. It had gone too far. She watched him pacing the floor.

"All right," he said finally. "So it's true."

"Its true?"

She could not reconcile his admission to her expectations. She was prepared for a denial. It wasn't possible. She felt her knees grow weak and the blood drain from her head. It was one thing merely to suspect. But to know was hell. He looked at her and opened empty palms, a picture of abject surrender. "I hadn't meant it to happen."

"I don't want to hear it."

"You don't think I'm ashamed?"

"It's too late."

"Too late?"

"How can I live with it?"

"What can I say?"

Her strength was returning, but on waves of self-pity, white caps of anger. "I've been a good, a faithful wife. A good mother. I worked hard. I kept a clean house. I cooked. I saved." Her voice rose. Nat put a finger over his lips, his eyes looking toward the kitchen. "You disgraced me. You disgraced your son," she hissed.

Their son, hearing the raised voices, had come into the living room. Nat turned to him and pointed, in the direction of the kitchen.

"Go do your homework. We're having a discussion."

"You're making too much noise."

"Go ahead. Tell it in front of him. Sure. Talk in front of him. Why not? Let him know what kind of a man his father is."

"Go back to your homework," Nat pressed their son.

"No. Stay here," Sarah shouted. "Listen to your wonderful father. Let him tell it in front of you about his escapades."

"Would you please go back to your homework?"

"Don't. Stay!" Sarah screamed.

It seemed to go on interminably with the son looking bemused, rotating his gaze from mother to father, like a wind-up toy, fixed in one spot, with only the head being able to pivot.

"If you don't go, I'll go," Nat finally said. The boy stood rooted. Finally, Nat stalked off to the closet, got his hat and coat, and stormed out of the apartment, slamming the door behind him, shaking some bric a brac off the shelves.

"See," she said. "That's the kind of man your father is." Then she burst into tears and the confused boy went back to the kitchen.

She stayed up all night, listening for his footsteps in the hall. But they never came. Once, she put on her coat over her nightgown, went downstairs and stood in the vestibule watching for him. The streets were empty and soon the cold seeped into her bones and she went upstairs again.

"You have your pride," Mildred said the next morning. Sarah's hands shook as she lifted the coffee cup to her mouth. "Believe me, I know my onions when it comes to men." Her round fat face seemed to glow with satisfaction.

"Now what?" Sarah asked. She was totally disoriented. It was the first time since her marriage that her morning had any break in its normal routine. Her ears were still turned to the hallway. She dared not think where he had spent the night.

"He'll come crawling."

"He will?"

"Wait."

"And then?"

"Then you let him crawl. But not right away. He's got to suffer first."

"Suppose he doesn't."

"He will." She said the words with finality as she thickly buttered another piece of toast and stuffed it daintily into her puffed face.

After two days and no word, no crawling, Sarah called Nat at the shop.

"Well," she said, anger rising as she heard his voice.

"Well, what?"

"What do you mean, 'Well, what?'"

"You don't know what I mean?"

"No, I don't know what you mean."

"What's going to happen? That's what I mean."

The phone was silent. She felt him searching for words. But her anger would not contain itself. Why wasn't he crawling?

"You can go to hell," she said, slamming down the phone, running across the hall to Mildred. She was in the bathtub, a blob of gelatin stuffed into a white mold.

"I told him to go to hell," she cried.

"Good."

She stood there in the steaming bathroom, watching Mildred soap her huge belly, which looked like another whole person in the tub with her.

"Well, what happens now?" she asked, sitting on the toilet seat, clenching and unclenching her fingers.

"How should I know?" Mildred looked up at the ceiling, obviously annoyed at the violation of her privacy. Sarah started to say something, but no words came out.

"I think he's gone for good," she said after a long pause, the sense of defeat overwhelming.

"Good riddance," Mildred said, flapping water over her flesh to remove the soap from her belly.

A week later, he came to the apartment and removed his clothes. He must have been watching the front of the apartment house waiting for her to leave on her daily shopping chore. He also left a brief note: "I'll send you money every week."

That was that. Later, there were lawyers. She got custody of the son, although he was already nearly eighteen. Nat sent her money until the boy was twenty-one. She went to work for a furniture store in downtown Brooklyn as a bookkeeper and no longer found time to schmooze with Mildred, who got fatter and fatter.

When the neighborhood began to change, Mildred and Sam moved away. But by then, she had made new friends, mostly widows, divorcées like herself, and old maids. Women alone. Occasionally, she went out with other men, but she could no longer trust them and her suspicions as to their motives made it impossible to develop any lasting relationship.

"You can't just keep pushing them away," her son remonstrated.

"I should trust them? After what your father did to me?"

"You should try, at least, to be pleasant."

"I am pleasant."

"Is it better to be lonely?"

"I'm not lonely."

If she was lonely, she would never admit it to herself. Nor did she allow herself to have regrets, although she maintained a continuing high level of animosity toward Nathaniel Shankowitz, which did not soften with the passage of years.

He had remarried, her son told her, within a year after the divorce—to whom, she supposed, was the other woman. There were twinges of jealousy and anger at the time, but because it followed the pattern of Nat's infamy in her mind, it only added fuel to the flames of her animosity.

She never saw him again, nor did her son ever broach the subject, although he saw his father very briefly on rare occasions. When he did mention him again, the son was, by then, a paunchy graying man with his own family responsibilities, reasonably prosperous, with a liquor store in Flushing.

"Pa died last week," he said, shrugging, as he whittled at the fat on a slab of pot roast in his mother's apartment during his weekly Friday night visit. His wife rarely came. Sarah did not even stop chewing, although she felt the beginnings of heartburn prompted by the sudden revelation.

"You were at the funeral?"

"Of course."

She tried to put the idea out of her mind, but she could not fully contain her own feeling of elation at his dying first. It wasn't really nice to think such thoughts, she told herself, remembering, for the first time in years, their early years together. She wondered if she should have gone to the funeral.

By the time she became eligible for social security, the neighborhood had changed drastically. The apartment house was completely black and, although she found her neighbors hard-working and reasonably quiet, she felt decidedly alien in their midst. Her friends, many of whom had already moved out of the neighborhood to Flatbush or Queens, had already begun to leave for Florida and it wasn't long before her son bought her a small condominium in Sunset Village.

"You like it there, Ma?" her son would ask whenever he called, which was increasingly rare.

"Better than Brooklyn."

"You got a lotta friends?"

"Too many. They're all a bunch of yentas." It never occurred to her that she was a yenta as well.

Not long after she received the New Year's card from Cousin Irma, she got a person-to-person call from Huntington, Long Island.

"I have a person-to-person call for Mrs. Nathaniel Shankowitz from Huntington, Long Island," the impersonal voice of the operator announced.

"I'm Mrs. Nathaniel Shankowitz," she said, a note of tempered hysteria in her voice , as she did not know anyone in Huntington, Long Island.

"Go ahead, please," the operator said.

"Yetta?" It was a woman's voice.

"Yetta?"

"This is Molly."

"Molly?"

"Your sister Molly, Yetta. You don't know your sister, Molly? Are you all right?"

Sarah grimaced at the phone, then began to click the button on the receiver.

"What's that noise?" the voice asked.

"I'm not Yetta."

"But the operator said you were Mrs. Nathaniel Shankowitz."

"I am."

"And you're not Yetta?"

"No."

The confusion was obvious. The woman mumbled something about a wrong number and the telephone connection was broken abruptly. Stupid operators, she thought. It was an accepted axiom that all of the operators in Poinsettia Beach were dumb.

The day after the phone call, she got a letter from the credit department of Macy's in Brooklyn. It was one of those computerized letters, addressed to Mrs. Nathaniel Shankowitz, which carried the dire threat of credit cancellation unless the sum of $3.48 was paid immediately.

Coming so close on the heels of the telephone call from Molly something-or-other, the situation took on the air of a genuine, and most annoying, mystery. She hadn't been into Macy's in years. Besides, she lived in Florida for nearly five years by then.

"The computers are going crazy," one of her friends told her. "They got you mixed up."

But when she got a post card signed "Irving" from Barcelona, she decided to take some action. In Sunset Village, taking action meant going to the big main office near the clubhouse. She had never "taken action" before and had prepared herself for intimidation by the blue-haired lady with the big round glasses on a chain who presided over the office.

One knew immediately upon seeing her, with her imperious air and frown lines around the eyes, that she would be menacing behind her fixed false-tooth smile, the quintessential image of the jew-baiting shiksa. She was, rumor had it, the builder's secret weapon, keeping all the complainers at bay.

"Somebody's got me mixed up," Sarah told the woman, mustering her courage. The blue-haired woman looked at her through the big round frames, her ice eyes expressionless, although the smile never wavered. She said nothing, demanding, Sarah knew, further explanation by her silence.

"I keep getting strange letters and phone calls for Mrs. Nathaniel Shankowitz."

"Obviously some address problem," the woman sneered. "Have you called the telephone company or the post office?"

"No."

"Well, don't you think you should?" the woman asked, as if she were addressing a child.

"The problem is," Sarah said, ignoring the admonishment, "I am Mrs. Nathaniel Shankowitz." She detected a sudden brief movement of surprise in the blue-haired woman's eyes.

"Who?"

"Mrs. Nathaniel Shankowitz."

Surprise became puzzlement as her lip curled in contempt. It was well-known that the woman felt she was in an institution where the occupants were suffering from galloping senility.

"You're not Mrs. Nathaniel Shankowitz," the woman said haughtily.

Sarah felt her anger rise and her knees grow weak. She gripped the counter.

"You're telling me what I am?" Sarah asked.

"Not what. Who."

Sarah fumbled in her bag and brought out her wallet with the Sunset Village identification and, leaning over the counter, placed it in front of the woman's eyes.

"In black and white."

The woman hesitated, her lips wavering slightly over her tight smile, tiny evidence of her defeat. Still silent, with a lingering look at Mrs. Shankowitz she went to the resident card file and flicked through them, slowly, with disdain, as if such duties were meant for lesser souls. Then she returned with two cards in her hand.

"There are two of you," she said, as if describing two different kinds of obscene germs. "One of you has just been here complaining about a missing social security check."

But the idea of two had registered and Sarah stared at the card with the strange address under her name with disbelief. "Mrs. Nathaniel Z. Shankowitz and, in parenthesis, (Yetta)." Could it be? Could it really be?

She felt herself grow hot, her embarrassment intense. There should have been some ritual of victory now, some contemptuous gesture to the blue-haired woman who had been bested, but her strength was gone and she moved, speechless, out of the office.

Walking home, she contemplated the impending humiliation. The two Mrs. Shankowitzes. Number one and number two. They would snicker behind her back. "There goes number one." She would be an object of ridicule, talked about, ridiculed, a yenta's delight. "Shush, girls, number one is coming."

People would laugh about it at the table. Briefly, she entertained the idea that her first assumption was wrong. But logic and old memories intruded. They had been the only Nathaniel Z. Shankowitz in the Brooklyn directory. It was too much of a coincidence. Besides, she knew that Nat had been living in Queens and, once, just once, she had looked up his name in the Queens directory.

There, too, it was the only Nathaniel Z. Shankowitz. She cursed her pride now, the insistence that she be listed by her married name with the man's name intact. It seemed such a harmless little idea, but she felt some protection from it and in Sunset Village, especially Sunset Village. It had buttressed her pride. Her and her stupid pride. Where had it gotten her?

By the time she had returned to her apartment, she was in tears. The mail had come and she picked it up from the floor beneath the slot. She was too harassed to look over the envelopes and, instead, put them aside and sat on the couch, where she stared into space for the better part of the morning, contemplating her disastrous fate.

She had no alternative but to move now, she knew. To pick up and find some other place to live. But as the day wore on, self-pity turned to anger, humiliation to indignation. How dare she? She will not do it a second time. Without proof, she had firmly decided that the second Mrs. Shankowitz was "the other woman." Who else? It was she who should move, Sarah decided, as her hatred took shape again and crowded out all self-pity.

It was with that sense of new-found strength that she finally got to the mail, sometime in the late afternoon, after she had done her household chores and checked in with her various friends. Actually, she had called them in rotation more to feel out their knowledge than for any other specific reason. Assured that the cat was still in the bag, she busied her-self with the affairs of her household, which included looking at the mail.

It was check day, the third day of the month. In Sunset Village, that was more like a religious holiday with the mailman being followed around as if he were the Pied Piper. Her interest in it had been momen-tarily deflected but, remembering, had prompted her to seek out the spot where she had put the mail. The check was there, its bluish official-look-ing funny typescript peering at her from the little plastic window. But the envelope below it was exactly the same. Same name. But the address was quite different. The mailman had simply made a mistake.

She held up the second envelope to the light. Was the amount the same as hers? Or more? Surely more. That scheming woman surely had found a way to squeeze more out of the government. Sitting down, she put the envelope on the cocktail table in front of the couch and looked at it. What if she opened it? It had the same name. She knew there was a penalty for opening the wrong check. Hadn't she warned others about it from time to time. She was not a fool, she thought, rejecting the idea.

But as she sat there watching the envelope, other thoughts began to fill her mind. Suppose she simply let it sit there. Just that. Put it under the candy dish and leave it there. Who would be the wiser? She reveled in this sudden sense of power over the second Mrs. Shankowitz. For a change, she, Sarah, would not be the victim. The woman deserved it. Look what she had done to break up her marriage.

A missing social security check was one of the major disasters, next to sickness and death, that could affect their world. It was, of course, replace-able. But that took time, and the aggravation it caused was more than simple inconvenience. For those who lived from day to day, it was the fuel of life. Without it came the humiliation of borrowing from friends, or, if pride meant more than hunger, foraging for scraps among the household leftovers.

She slipped the check under the candy dish. Wasn't she entitled to in-flict such punishment? she asked herself, knowing that the missing check was already causing the woman anxieties. But look what she had done to Sarah. Considering the crime, it was hardly the punishment for twenty-five years of loneliness and humiliation. She could be honest with herself now. It was lonely. It was humiliating.

She made herself dinner and went out for her usual Mah-Jongg game with her friends in the clubhouse cardroom. But she could not concentrate. Her mind dwelled on the envelope hidden under the candy dish.

"Whatsamatter Sarah?" Eve Shapiro asked. When it came to Mah-Jongg, Eve was all business.

"I got a headache."

"You got worse than that, Sarah," Eve Shapiro pressed as she exposed her winning combination.

"You let her win, dummy," Ida Fine said, shaking her henna red curls.

"I'm not myself," Sarah protested.

"Yourself is such a big deal?"

During the night, she could not sleep, declining to take a sleeping pill. Did the other Mrs. Shankowitz really deserve such punishment? But the envelope beneath the candy dish loomed bigger and bigger in her mind as the night wore on. She got up, made herself some tea, and sat sipping it while she watched the candy dish and prayed for the swift end to night. In the sunlight, she might find her courage again, she decided, knowing that remorse was beginning to afflict her now.

In a way, she was fortunate. She had worked for more than twenty years. There were a few dollars put aside in the bank and, of course, there was always her son, although she dreaded to ask him for anything beyond the fifty dollars a month he usually sent her. But she had heard enough horror stories over delayed or missing social security checks to blunt the edge of her malevolence as the night wore on. Think of what that woman did to you, she repeated to herself over and over again, charging her resolve. But by morning, she was contrite. It was a monstrous thing to do, even to your worst enemy, she concluded. And that was precisely the case.

That morning, she dressed with care, although she had no intentions, she assured herself, of doing anything more than putting the check in the mailslot of the other Mrs. Shankowitz's apartment. That, and nothing more. Then why was she dressing with such care, running the comb repetitively through her hair, putting on faint patches of rouge, even powder. The mirror taunted her as it did every time she saw her ravaged image in it. A sixty-eight-year-old wreck of a woman. Where had her life gone? Secretly, she hoped that the other Mrs. Shankowitz was ravaged beyond her years.

The address on the check made it necessary for her to take the open air shuttle bus, and she waited patiently at the stop, checking to be sure that the check had been secured in her purse. She got on the shuttle bus and nodded politely to the familiar faces, wondering how they might react when they finally knew. She could imagine how they would suddenly drop their voices, watch her as they whispered the story among themselves. No. She could not bear that. She got off in the approximate vicinity of the address on the check and, with beating heart and a sense of dragging in her limbs, she walked down the path, following the sequence of the numbers.

When she arrived at the correct address, she stood in front of the door, rummaging in her purse, while, peripherally, she looked beyond the transparent curtains into the apartment's interior. She saw the bluish glow of a television set and the brief movement of a shadowy figure. Instinctively, she knew she was being watched, which triggered a conscious desire to leave quickly, although she felt herself rooted to the spot. The door opened before she could slip the letter into the slot, and the check fell to the ground.

"Yes?" a woman's voice said. She was a slight woman, very thin, in a seersucker house dress. She wore brown horn-rimmed glasses with very thick lenses, which made her eyes seem oddly magnified and distorted. Sarah watched her, embarrassed, unable to find any sensible words, transfixed, it seemed, by the magnified lenses. In the shock of confrontation, she had momentarily forgotten the fallen check.

"Mrs. Shankowitz?" Sarah finally managed to blurt out. In her mind, it seemed a contemptuous ejaculation.

"I'm Mrs. Shankowitz," the woman said. Although her hair was dyed brunette, her face had a gray caste, testifying to the futility of the dye job. It was Sarah's first logical observation, bringing the woman into perspective on a human scale.

"So am I," Sarah said, nodding. She had felt a sense of diminished dignity at first, as if she had been caught peeking, being a yenta. But she was recovering fast now, remembering the check, which she bent to retrieve.

"I got your social security check," she said, lifting it and handing it to the woman, whose face brightened, the lips trembling into a warm smile, although the teeth were devastated.

"Thank God," the woman said. "I was going crazy."

"We had a mix-up."

"Please. Please come in," the woman said, opening the door and stepping beside it in a gesture of hospitality. "I was going out of my mind." Sarah hesitated. "Please. We'll have a nice cup of coffee."

Where had her animosity fled? Sarah wondered, although she could not shake her embarrassment. Was she about to be humiliated? Was this the wrong thing to do? I shouldn't really, she prepared herself to say, but the words stuck in her throat as her legs carried her into the apartment. Like hers, it was the efficiency type, the smallest unit, still incomplete in furnishing.

"I'm here only two weeks. Forgive the mess." Candace Bergen was on the television tube talking about telephones. The woman flicked off the set and went into the kitchen. Sarah heard the sound of coffee cups rattling.

"They tell me the first check is always a problem. The woman at the desk says the mailman first has to get to know you. That I can't understand..."

Sarah listened, half-understanding, surveying the little apartment with an avid curiosity, knowing that something in the room was engaging her, tugging at her.

"...Frankly, she wasn't very helpful. You can't imagine how grateful I am." There was a brief pause. "You say your name is Shankowitz..."

She had seen it briefly as she came into the apartment, but apparently something inside her would not let it register. Nat's picture staring at her from a corner wall, the hawk eyes watching her, although the face was fuller, older. Her heart thumped, and she sat heavily on the couch. The woman came in with the steaming coffee cups on a little tray. Sarah continued to feel the hawk-like eyes watching her, looking inside of her.

"Shankowitz. I didn't think it was such a common name."

Sarah remained silent, reached for the coffee cup, but her hands shook and she quickly put it down again. She could tell by the woman's sudden interest that she wanted to inquire about her health, but she was holding back. At Sunset Village, one did not make quick inquiries about what seemed like obvious afflictions.

"I've been a widow for three years, so a number of my friends live here now and I finally decided to come." Sarah felt her eyes watching her.

"You got a husband Mrs. Shankowitz?"

"I had one," Sarah mumbled. "He... He died."

The woman shook her head.

"When was that?"

"A long, long time ago," Sarah said, finding little courage, abruptly changing the subject, postponing it in her mind.

"How long does it take to adjust?"

"Adjust?"

"You know what I mean. To the point where it doesn't hurt as much."

Sarah's instinct was to say "never," or was it simply the automatic expectation, the desire to hurt. Hurt who?

"Your name is Yetta?"

The woman smiled.

"How did you know that?"

"You got a Cousin Irma?"

"My God! Yes. Cousin Irma from Philadelphia."

"And a sister Molly."

"I can't believe it."

"And an Irving in Barcelona."

"My brother. He's traveling in Spain. Maybe we're related?"

"Maybe." Sarah shrugged. "Actually, I'm getting your mail, your telephone calls. I expect in a little while that you'll get mine."

"The Shankowitz girls. I could see where that could be a problem."

Yetta seemed thoughtful. She pointed a finger at Sarah. "You know, I'll bet maybe we are related. Maybe our husbands were cousins. What was your husband's name?"

Sarah continued to squirm now. She rubbed her finger joints as the pain shot through her hands.

"You'd be surprised how we're related," Sarah said. It was not easy, she thought. Thankfully, she could see the beginnings of confusion on Yetta's face, the first flush of realization.

"You're her?" Yetta whispered. Sarah nodded.

"I'm her."

"Oh my God." Yetta's hands went, birdlike, to her hair, fussing with it. "I can't believe it. I had no idea." Sarah felt the edge of indignation and stood up.

"If you think this was easy..." Sarah began, but her voice trailed off. Yetta was visibly agitated. Her face had become grayer, suddenly more drawn.

"You said he was dead a long time."

"I lied. But not completely. To me, he was dead."

"I can't believe it. We both land here in this place."

Sarah shrugged.

"What was I supposed to do? Tear up the check?"

Yetta was having a difficult time recovering. She nodded and continued to fuss with her hair. It was obvious that she wanted Sarah to leave.

"It's all right," Sarah said quietly, letting herself out of the door and walking quickly toward the bus stop. She regretted the confrontation. I could have given the check back to the mailman. I could have merely called her on the telephone. You're a dumb yenta, she told herself. Besides, what was so special about her, she thought. A raving beauty, she wasn't. And those glasses, a regular cockeyed Jennie. And a skinny merink on top of it. By the time she reached her own place, Sarah had convinced herself that she had been the better of the two bargains. But who needed her in Sunset Village?

Late that afternoon, the telephone rang.

"This is Sarah?" the voice asked. It was Yetta.

"Yes."

"I want to apologize. It was rude. You did a wonderful thing. But it was such a shock. I was stupid."

"I figured you needed the check," Sarah said, feeling an odd sense of superiority. Yetta paused.

"Look, he was a nice man. But he wasn't such a good provider. There was no insurance. No nothing. Perfect he wasn't."

"You're telling me." There were questions to be raised, Sarah thought. Old curiosities resurrected. Apparently such thoughts were in Yetta's mind.

"We'll see each other again?"

"It's a small world here," Sarah said.

"And how is your son?"

"He's fine. He called me New Year's."

"He's a nice boy. I haven't seen him since Nat died."

"A very nice boy. He calls me often." She paused. "He's very busy."

"Give him regards."

"Of course."

That night, the old life with Nat came to her again with full recall. But her image of him was suddenly different. She could not summon the same degree of enmity; the old hate had cooled. What was the real story? In the morning, she called Yetta.

"I'm going shopping this morning. Would you like to come?"

"I could use some things," Yetta said. They met on the bus and got off at the stop near the Safeway, walking together through the aisles sharing a shopping cart.

"Nat liked All-Bran," Yetta said, reaching for a box of Rice Crispies.

"I remember. He was always constipated."

"That was always his main problem."

"That and snoring."

"He always snored?"

"From the beginning."

Later, putting the purchases in Yetta's refrigerator while Yetta made coffee, Sarah said, "You had the problem with the salt?"

"My God, the salt."

"There was always too much salt. I used to say, 'I never cook with salt. Not even a pinch.' But there was always too much salt. In the pot roast. In the hamburger. In the vegetables."

"He drove me crazy."

"I couldn't understand how, if he hated salt, he liked potato chips."

"And they always gave him heartburn."

"Always." They laughed, drank coffee, made tuna-fish sandwiches.

Sarah filled her in on various aspects of Sunset Village life. When she got home, she got a call from Eve Shapiro.

"The game. You forgot the game."

"I'm so sorry."

"We were worried. We called. There was no answer. Where were you?"

"I had a problem." Sarah said, thinking quickly. There was no need to tell her the story. The Yentas would ferret it out soon enough. "Someone who just moved in from New York. They had a problem."

"Oh?" It was a signal for more information.

"They needed help with the shopping. You know. Details."

"Enough to forget the game? Who was it?"

"Someone from New York."

"A relative?"

"Yes."

"A cousin?"

"No. Not a cousin."

"A what?" Eve Shapiro demanded.

"A sister-in-law."

"I didn't know you had one."

"Yes. We weren't very close."

"You're husband had a brother?"

"Yes. But he lived in Queens. They weren't very close."

Barely satisfied, Eve's indignance would not abate.

"You should at least have called."

The next day, Yetta came over to Sarah's place to lunch.

"You got a nice place here, Sarah."

"Its not the Ritz. But its OK."

"You've got such nice things." She touched a grouping of little Wedgewood dishes.

"I went on a B'nai B'rith tour to London once."

"I never went anywhere. Nat didn't like to travel. Not that we could afford it."

"Don't forget, I worked for twenty years."

"He didn't like to go anywhere," Yetta sighed. "He came home. Went to sleep on the chair in front of the TV. Sometimes he would snore so loud I couldn't hear it."

"Then he would go to sleep and snore some more."

"I never met anyone who could sleep so much."

Sarah felt the necessity of telling Yetta what she had said to Eve Shapiro.

"I told her we were sisters-in-law." she said. "But she's such a yenta, I didn't want her to find out. They'd make a big joke about it."

"I was thinking about that."

"If we don't tell them, they won't know."

"But we're both Mrs. Nathaniel Z. Shankowitz."

"No more. From now on I'm Mrs. Sarah. I'm going to write to everybody, the mail, the phone company, the social security."

"And I'll be Mrs. Yetta."

"The Shankowitz girls."

"That's us."

"That would be something. Nat wouldn't think it's so funny."

"Nat is dead," Sarah said.

"Poor Nat."

"To me, he's not so poor."

They continued to see each other every day. Sarah introduced them to her friends and Yetta to hers.

They went to the clubhouse together, watched the shows, went shopping and sat together at the pool. Minor problems intruded only when the subject of husbands came up.

"Tomorrow is Abe's birthday," Eve Shapiro announced one day as they sat around the pool. Impending birthdays of dead husbands were special moments of self-pity. "He would have been eighty-six."

"An old man already," Sarah said.

"He was twenty years older than me," Eve responded.

"How much?"

"Eighteen, actually," Eve said. "And yours?" The question was directed to Yetta.

"Let's see." She held out her fingers, tapping each one in turn.

"Seventy-five," Sarah said quickly, too quickly.

"You know so much about your brother-in-law?" Eve probed.

"Yes, that's right" Yetta added, as if to buttress Sarah's revelation and deflect Eve's naturally suspicious nature.

"He would actually be only seventy," Yetta commented later.

"No. He was seven years older than me."

"You saw his birth certificate?"

"No. But when we married he was twenty-five."

"He said he was forty when we got married."

"And how long were your married?"

"Thirty years."

"Then he would have to be at least seventy-five. We were married twenty years."

"You think he lied?"

"Do I think he lied? I know he lied."

Yetta pondered the matter.

"Actually I lied, too, so I took off three, four years."

"What's good for the goose," Sarah said, but she was thinking of other things, the events that had, up to now, demanded a barrier of silence between them. By then, they had known each other six months and Nat had been their common bridge, their meeting place. Always, when the idea popped into Sarah's mind, she resisted, waiting for the right moment.

"Were you really the other woman, Yetta?" she said finally one day as they walked back from the pool in the declining sunlight, through the well-tended paths. The traffic around them seemed muted, the air soft. A warm breeze rustled the low plantings.

"Me? The other woman? I was a waitress in the coffee shop downstairs from where he worked. We used to talk a lot. He was a man. I was an old maid."

"He never..."

"With me? Never."

"I thought you did."

"One night, he called me at home. He said you threw him out. So I let him come in. Look, I was an old maid. I was alone. You know, when you're alone you do strange things. I wasn't a homewrecker. I was alone."

"He said I threw him out?"

"That's what he said."

"Like he was forty instead of forty-five."

"I was alone," Yetta mumbled. They walked for a while, then Yetta stopped and turned toward Sarah. "You know Nat. He was always weak, a weak man."

"Weak. That's exactly right. Weak," Sarah agreed. She could barely remember the circumstances of that night. What had she said to him? How had he replied?

"Does it matter now, Sarah? Does it really matter?"

She took Yetta's hand and they continued on their way. A few months later, they moved in together in a larger condominium and were known to everybody as the Shankowitz girls.

A Widow is A Very Dangerous Commodity

 At Sarah Gold's funeral, Zaber's smallest funeral chapel was filled to capacity. Many people had to stand throughout the entire ceremony. Murray Gold, though weighted down by grief after the loss of his wife of nearly fifty years, could not contain his surprise at the turnout. He wasn't prepared for Sarah's overwhelming popularity and, while he was secretly proud, he also was perplexed.

They had been living at Sunset Village for ten years. One of the pioneers, Sarah reminded at every opportunity—especially to new arrivals, as if there was some special status to being among the first residents. Sarah made many friends. She was both gregarious and curious, the two basic attributes of being a yenta. And Sarah was, above all, a yenta.

"Why do you have to be such a yenta?" Murray admonished her repeatedly. She knew what was simmering in every pot, and he endured her endless chattering about this one and that one, although he rarely commented. What was the use? It was enough for him to find things to do to get through the day. He had never been good at making friends, and after the first few months at Sunset Village, she gave up on him.

"My Murray is a quiet fellow," he heard her say more than once. "He reads the paper. He sleeps in a chair. He helps me with the shopping and he does the laundry."

"He doesn't like cards?" one of her friends would ask.

"He hates cards."

"He has no hobbies?"

"He sleeps. That's his hobby."

"He likes it here?"

"If I like it here, he likes it here."

To Sarah, to her friends, to himself, Murray knew, he was considered an "accepted fact." He was simply, irrevocably, Sarah Gold's husband. Most of her friends barely remembered his name. He simply followed her around, a form of appendage, while Sarah reveled in her self-actualized role of being the eyes and ears of Sunset Village. It was not that she ignored him. He was, even to her, an "accepted fact."

Other husbands played cards, pursued hobbies, watched football games, took long walks, bragged about their previous accomplishments. Not Murray. When Sarah went to her various meetings, her card games, her "yenting" sessions, Murray slept, usually in a chair in front of the television set.

"How come you didn't go to bed?" she would say when she arrived home in the evenings after her activities.

"I was waiting up for you."

She was perplexed, then she would begin to chatter about her evening, telling him about the gossip, who was sick, who bought what, who was feuding with whom, who was two-timing who, whatever, and by the time she had washed her face and put on her nightgown, he was already slipping peacefully beyond understanding.

It was true that what she liked, he liked. Nearly fifty years of conditioning had confirmed this. Actually, the converse was far too formidable for him to cope with and he finally surrendered to it. When she was unhappy, he was made unhappy. And how.

Like when the air-conditioning broke down and all her caustic entreaties brought little results from the maintenance people.

"You're the man in the house," she screamed at him. "You tell them. You march over there right this minute and tell them, 'This will not do.'" She banged her hand on the wall. "I cannot live with this. It is your duty. We pay good money for the maintenance."

He had, of course, made the usual call to the maintenance people, and they had promised to fix the unit, just as soon as they could get to it. The explanation satisfied him, although he knew he would not be able to placate Sarah.

"What do you mean, wait our turn? They're lying to you. I never saw such weakness. You go right over there now and tell them. Now. Do you hear? Right this minute." Her voice rose, in an endless mind-boggling cacophony.

"But I went..." he protested.

"You went."

She looked around their one-bedroom apartment, sweltering in the summer heat, the windows open. He was sure the neighbors could hear every word. "What kind of a man are you?" She turned away from him as if talking to someone else in the room. "What kind of a man did I marry? No wonder you never made any money. People step on you. That's what they do. They step all over you. They use you for a doormat."

"All right, I'll try tomorrow."

"Tomorrow? What about tonight?"

"They're closed tonight."

"Then get them out of bed." Again she looked away from him.

"Look what kind of a man I married. What did I do to deserve this?"

It cost him a hundred dollars, secretly withdrawn from their account, to bribe the maintenance man to fix the air conditioner on his own time. It was either that or endure her wrath. It wasn't the heat as far as he was concerned.

"You see," she said finally when the air conditioning was fixed. "If I don't push you, nothing gets done." And she was happy. And when she was happy, he was happy. Or, at least, content.

Occasionally when their son Milton came to visit, he would ask his father if he was enjoying his retirement.

"Your mother is very happy here."

"But what about you, Pop?"

"Me?" It seemed a puzzling question. "I'm happy if your mother's happy."

Milton would look at him and shrug. Later, when they thought he was asleep on the chair, he would overhear them talking.

"Is he really happy here, Mom?"

"Does he look happy?"

"I can't really tell."

"In his own way, he's happy."

Maybe that was true, he thought. She had, after all, always known what was best for him. He hadn't been that good of a provider. The Depression hurt his parents badly, and he never quite recovered from the psychology of failure, holding one lousy job after another.

Yet Sarah knew how to stretch a dollar and, with Milton's help, they bought this condominium. Better than living in Brooklyn, the way it had become, though he missed certain things. The mornings, especially.

He loved getting up early, going downstairs to the candy store for his bagel and coffee and reading the *New York Times*. Maybe things had deteriorated, but he did like walking the streets of New York, the hustle and bustle. Still, he knew that Sarah was happier in Sunset Village and if she was happy, he was happy.

What right had he to be otherwise? She set a nice table, kept the house neat as a pin. He was a small man, a little hard of hearing now, but thankful that he was able to get around. Not bad for seventy-one, he told himself.

She died suddenly. She had played cards and, as usual, he had slept on the chair until she had come home.

"Ida Katz talked all night about her heartburn. I couldn't concentrate," she said as she got into bed that night. "I told her to take a Malox or stop stuffing herself so much."

He remembered drifting away, but he heard her last words. "Malox is constipating, she told me." Then he had heard a long sigh, and the next thing he remembered, he was shaking her in the morning. But she didn't move. She was dead.

He sat in the funeral chapel, consumed with grief, his eyes puffy from crying. The loneliness that assailed him that night was terrible, although Milton had flown down to keep him company for the night.

"How can I live?" he asked his son. "She was my whole life."

He looked around the condominium. "Everything here reminds me of her."

"I don't know, Pop," Milton said, "I know it won't be easy."

"Easy? It will be impossible," Murray said, holding his head in his hands, feeling the unbearable weight of his loss.

"I should have gone first," he said. "At least she had friends here. She could have gotten along fine without me."

"That's the way it goes, Pop."

He surveyed the little funeral chapel. It was amazing how many people showed up. Mostly women. He recognized many of them from the club-house. Others had been merely shadowy figures, passing acquaintan-ces. He hadn't realized she had so many friends. The women from her regular canasta group were in the second row behind him and Milton. They were particularly solicitous.

One of them, Mrs. Morganstern, touched his shoulder and whispered softly in his ear.

"You shouldn't worry about anything, Murray. We took care of every-thing. There'll be bagels and herring and cakes for after the funeral. We'll set everything up. It'll all be perfect."

He felt her breath on his earlobe, the pressure of her hand on his shoul-der. He nodded, lowering his misted eyes as the rabbi finished the eu-logy. They were so wonderful, he thought. Sarah had that rare ability to make friends, the Rabbi said, responding to what he had told him. The rabbi had, after all, never met Sarah and had been hired for the occasion for fifty dollars. But what Mrs. Morganstern and her other canasta play-ers were doing was proof enough.

Walking behind the coffin, supported by his son, he followed it out to the hearse and got into the hired limousine, with Milton beside him. Another woman was inside waiting. He recognized her as Minnie Schwartz, Sarah's old friend from Brooklyn, who, he remembered, just moved into Sunset Village.

"I asked Minnie to come with us," Milton said.

"Thank you, Minnie," Murray said. He could barely control his sob-bing. He felt her arm entwine itself around his.

"I know. I know," she said, sniffling, blowing her nose into a bit of tissue, already moist with previous tears. "When I lost my Sam, it was a living hell, a living hell."

"I should have gone first," Murray mumbled, repeating the thought all the way to the cemetery.

It was a terrible ordeal, watching Sarah lowered into the strange Florida ground on this sunny day, the air thick with the scent of tropical plants. At the first drop of earth on the hollow coffin, a high wail filled the air as the women reacted. The crowd was almost exclusively female, and Minnie Schwartz's wail was the loudest.

"How can I go on?" he sobbed, as the big limousine headed back to Sunset Village.

"You'll go on, Murray." Minnie Schwartz said. She clutched his arm in such a way that he leaned against her bulky body. "I did and you will. Time will heal everything."

"Time," he said. "She should have had the time."

"She was a wonderful woman."

"Wonderful," he agreed.

"We'll all miss her, Murray."

Back at their little apartment, the canasta players had arranged what seemed like a lavish repast. It was traditional among Jews for the chief mourner to provide for the guests, and they had done a splendid job.

"You'll tell me later how much it all costs," he said to Mrs. Morganstern when he finally washed his hands, also a tradition, and settled into his chair. The apartment was filled with people, mostly women, all of Sarah's friends. He hadn't realized she had so many friends.

"I wouldn't think of it Mr. Gold," Mrs. Morganstern said. She gripped his hand. "Sarah was my friend."

"How can I ever thank you, Mrs. Morganstern?" he said.

"Lily," she responded.

He seemed confused.

"Call me Lily," she said. "After all, Sarah called me Lily. She was my friend." "Of course."

In the kitchen, two women did the dishes, while others puttered around, removing plates and neatly arranging additional food when the table needed to be replenished.

There was only regular seating for six in the small dining room, but additional chairs had materialized and he noticed that he was encircled by women, some of whom he did not recognize. Others arrived, whom he had never seen before.

"I'm Mrs. Bernstein," a woman said, bending over him, clutching his hand and pressing it to her breast. Despite his grief, he felt the ample softness. "Sarah was the finest woman in Sunset Village. We'll miss her."

He nodded, and the woman lingered whispering in his ear, the strong scent of perfume emanating from her skin. "If there is anything, anything, I can do. Please let me know. Will you?"

"Of course."

"I'm Harriet Berstein from across the court—222, upstairs."

He hadn't ever seen her before, he was certain. She stayed a moment longer, shook her head in a gesture of sympathy as she blinked her eyes, heavy with mascara, and passed on to the buffet table. He hadn't realized that Sarah had made such an immense impression, had won so many hearts.

"I'm sure Sarah mentioned me," another woman said, gripping Murray's arm. "I was once a model. It was a long time ago, but I showed her the clippings from the magazines." He couldn't remember, but he nodded in affirmation. "She mentioned me?"

"Of course," he said solemnly.

"I could have gone on to a bigger career, but you know I got married, had children. You understand."

"Yes," he said.

"When Harry died, I came here," she said, her voice carrying through the room. Some of the other women turned to watch. Sensing this, she lowered her voice.

"Life goes on," she whispered. "You'll learn that. You need a lesson in that Mr. Gold, just call on Rose Ginzberg." She paused.

"Better yet, I'll call you. I'm a Hungarian. You should taste my goulash."

She had so many wonderful friends, Murray thought. If only he had been a better husband.

"You can't imagine how much we'll miss Sarah." It was Ida Katz, stuffing herself as usual, her mouth filled with herring as she moved to a vacant chair. There seemed to be some rhythm in the movement onto the chairs. When someone stood up, someone immediately sat down, as if to find a place in the circle around Murray was the most coveted honor of the day. He remembered that Sarah had been talking about Ida the night she died.

"She was always so much fun. Always joking. A kind word for

everybody." She paused, concentrated on eating the last morsel on her plate. "And you, Murray. She always said such wonderful things about you."

"Me?"

"You."

"I hadn't realized."

"What a wonderful man you were... how handsome you were when you were younger. Although I don't think you're so bad now." She mumbled the compliment, as if imparting an important confidence. Did Sarah really make such a reference, he wondered?

As the day wore on and the food diminished, a few of the women lingered, tidying the apartment.

"Nothing like a good Jewish woman," Minnie Schwartz said, as she folded a tablecloth and put it in a drawer.

"You said it," Lily Morganstern responded.

"They have a certain something," Ida Katz agreed. She turned toward Murray, who was growing weary, contemplating sadly a future without Sarah. He was beginning to slip back into self-pity.

"Sarah was the epitome of what it meant to be a good Jewish woman," Minnie Schwartz said. "Knew her all her life. Didn't I Murray?"

He lifted his head and looked at her. He had barely exchanged two words with her throughout his married life, either in Brooklyn or Sunset Village.

"We were very close," Minnie Schwartz said.

It was growing late. The women gathered what they could carry and prepared to leave.

"There's herring, bread, some knishes and cakes left," Lily Morganstern said. She came over to Murray and talked quietly.

"If you like, I'll come by in the morning and maybe make some breakfast," she said. Murray nodded. Why not? Anything but being left alone.

"I'll call you tomorrow," Minnie said. She embraced Murray's head and kissed his cheek. "Time will heal everything. Believe me, Murray. Respect time."

"I hope," he said, feeling the emptiness, the panic of his impending loneliness.

"Maybe I'll be over tomorrow to keep you company," Ida Katz said.

"We're not going to play cards for the next few days." Her eyes filled with tears. "Without Sarah, it just wouldn't be the same."

"I can imagine," he said. Then the apartment was empty, except for Milton, who had been packing in the bedroom. He came out with his suitcase and looked at his watch.

"I can just make the last plane," he said.

"So soon?"

"Really, Pop. I can't take off more time. Two people are out sick. You can't run a pharmacy today like you used to. Who can you trust?" Murray nodded. Then he stood up and embraced his son.

"You sure you can manage alone, Pop?" Milton asked, his voice breaking.

"I'll manage." They disengaged and he looked for a moment at his son, but he was thinking of Sarah. "She had so many wonderful friends, your Mama. I never realized."

"She was a good mother, Pop." Milton said, picking up his suitcase.

"And a wonderful wife."

His son kissed him again and went out into the court. In a moment, he had gunned the motor of his rented car and was off.

Alone in the apartment, Murray felt his disorientation. He could not believe that Sarah was gone. What happens now? he wondered.

He walked around the apartment, touched edges of chairs, let his fingers linger over objects, trying to remember how they had been acquired. He opened the closets, looked at Sarah's clothes, still hanging neatly, mute mourners. Touching the clothes, he started to cry, sinking to the floor, seeing her shoes. It was too unbearable. He sat there on the floor for a long time, then undressed and went to bed.

It seemed he had just been thinking that he could not sleep when suddenly he was emerging out of a deep slumber, reaching beside him for Sarah's body. There were noises from the kitchen, the sound of water pouring into a pot, dishes clinking, the refrigerator door opening and closing. Oh, she was in the kitchen, he thought, although it was he who was usually up first making the coffee.

Then he remembered. Getting out of bed, his joints seemed stiffer than usual and, in the mirror, he noted the redness of his eyes. Putting on his robe and slippers, he shuffled into the kitchen.

"You like eggs?"

It was Minnie Schwartz, carefully groomed, dabs of rouge on both cheeks and a discreet line of color on ill-defined lips. Her grey hair was neatly combed with a thin white ribbon tucked under it and tied in a little bow on top of her head. Her flowered housedress was neatly starched and crinkled as she moved.

"I heard noises. I thought it was Sarah," Murray said. He felt odd, uncomfortable, seeing this strange woman potting around in Sarah's kitchen.

She held up an egg. "Scrambled or bull's eye."

"Whatever."

He could not get over his surprise. She placed a steaming coffee cup on the little table. Not knowing what to do next, he sat down. She was, after all, making him breakfast.

"Milton gave me a key," she said, breaking the eggs into the frying pan. "I told him he shouldn't worry so much about his father. Minnie Schwartz doesn't let down her friends."

"You're very kind," Murray said. It was the only response he could think of. He gulped the coffee, scalding his mouth. Before the eggs had a chance to fry, the telephone rang.

"Sit, I'll get it."

She picked up the telephone.

"Who? Mrs. Morganstern?" She grimaced and held a hand over the mouth piece. "Mrs. Morganstern." But before he could reply, she was talking into the mouthpiece again. "He'll call later. After I make him breakfast." Her words seemed unusually curt and impolite.

"It was Mrs. Morganstern."

"What did she want?"

"How should I know?" Minnie Schwartz mumbled, watching the eggs bubble. "A yenta," she said with obvious contempt. Silently, he drank his coffee. "A pushy yenta," she said.

"My Sarah was not a yenta" he said aloud, knowing in his heart that he was already beginning to idealize her. It was his own private characterization.

"Sarah a yenta?" Minnie rebuked. "Who would ever think such a thing?

Mrs. Morganstern is a yenta." She put the egg before him on the table and sat down beside him. He watched it continue to bubble on the plate.

"Listen to me Murray. Was I Sarah's best friend? Be careful of these yentas."

"Why careful?"

She hesitated a moment, putting a hand on the sleeve of his robe.

"Just take Minnie's advice. Be careful."

The admonition confused him, and rather than contemplate its meaning, he ate the egg. Minnie watched him as he ate, and he was getting uncomfortable.

"Good?"

He nodded.

"You should taste my varnishkas. Someday I'll make you varnishkas like you never tasted before. My Sam loved my varnishkas."

Actually, Murray liked varnishkas, but the idea of them seemed incongruous with the breakfast.

"I also make good stuffed cabbage. Everybody loves my stuffed cabbage. Even better than my pot roast." She nodded, moved her hand from his sleeve and patted the back of his hand. "You'll see. You'll judge for yourself which is better, my pot roast or my stuffed cabbage."

"Not as good as your varnishkas?"

"Comme ci comme ça."

He ate his egg and finished the coffee, then stood up. He wasn't quite sure what to do with the rest of his day. There were things to do, he knew. He thought of Sarah's closet. All her clothes still hanging there.

Again the grief came and his heart felt leaden. He went into the bedroom and shut his door, then sat on the edge of the bed, not knowing what to do next. He heard the water running in the kitchen, then someone was walking in the bedroom and he felt a hand on his back.

"Can I do anything more?" Minnie asked. She was whispering and he felt her breath near his cheek as she stood above him, an ample expanse of her bosom at eye-level. She grasped both his hands in her own and pressed them to her. He felt an odd embarrassment.

"I'll look in later. You just rest. Don't worry about a thing. Minnie's here." He felt his hands moving on her breasts as she continued to hold them. An uncommon stirring began deep inside of him.

After she left, he felt totally immobile, unable to make a single decision, emersed in a kind of mental paralysis. What should I do now, Sarah? he asked himself.

By the time Ida Katz knocked at his door, he had managed to dress, although he had not begun to tackle what he had established in his mind as the main job he had before him, the removal of Sarah's things. It was not that he wanted to abolish her memory, but he could not abide the idea of their being there when Sarah was elsewhere, as if she might need them.

"I thought maybe you might want something," Ida Katz said.

She was a tall woman and he had to look up to observe her features. Before he could reply, she was in the apartment.

"I think maybe I should tidy up a bit." She was holding a shopping bag that she put on the floor beside the couch as she bent to puff the pillows. "Sarah was always as neat as a pin." She removed a rag from the shopping bag and began to run it along the wooden parts of the furniture.

"I was just looking at her clothes," he said. He felt his throat catch. She straightened, watched his eyes mist, then understood immediately.

"That's the worst part, Murray," she said, shaking her head.

"With Harry, it took me weeks before I could even look in the closet. That's the worst part." She hesitated. "You show me, and I'll do it."

"What do you do?"

"I can only say what I did with Harry's. I gave them away to charity. The Salvation Army. Better that poor people have the use of it."

He thought for a moment. Yes, that was a fine idea. He followed her into his bedroom, where she opened Sarah's closet.

"You got a carton?"

He rummaged in the storage closet in the kitchen and found a folded carton, which he opened and put on the bedroom floor. Ida Katz removed each article of clothing, gently, as if to treat them roughly might be a sacrilege against Sarah's memory. She took them off the hangers and folded them into the carton.

He stood aside and watched her work, unable to bring himself to touch Sarah's clothing. "She was a lovely person," Ida Katz said as she worked. "She had wonderful taste."

The telephone rang and Murray went into the kitchen to answer it. Lifting the receiver, he stood in such a way as to continue to observe Ida Katz at work through the reflection in the mirror. It was Mrs. Morganstern. "Minnie Schwartz has left?"

"Yes, Mrs. Morganstern."

"Lily."

"Lily," he repeated.

"I thought maybe you needed something. I'm going shopping."

"I'm not sure."

"Milk, coffee, bread? Some meat?"

He did not want to seem ungrateful. Through the reflection, he noted that Ida Katz had taken an article of Sarah's and had wrapped it around her figure, viewing herself in the bedroom mirror. She stood contemplating it a moment, then refolded it and put it into the carton.

"All right. Maybe some coffee... and bread."

"That's all?"

"Well, Sarah used to make these decisions."

"I know." She hesitated.

"When you're used to a good Jewish woman..." She let the thought linger with the incomplete sentence.

"You're very kind," he said. What more could he say?

"Don't mention it." But she did not hang up, instead pausing as if she was forming an additional thought. "You know, Murray," she began. In her tone he could detect a coming confidence. "You shouldn't get too friendly with Minnie Schwartz."

Looking into the receiver, he tried to visualize Lily Morganstern's face, but it seemed to have fled his consciousness. What did she mean?

"Minnie Schwartz?" he said. It was inconceivable that she could be vested with anything less than the purest of motives. She was, after all, as she herself had said, Sarah's best friend.

"Have you ever heard me say a bad word about anybody, Murray?" Lily Morganstern protested, as if his response had actually been accusatory.

"No," he replied. Indeed, had he ever remembered any word she uttered before Sarah died?

"So what I say is for your own good, Murray. For your own good."

There was a long pause, as if in the silence, dark forebodings might be gathering. "She's too pushy. A little too possessive. You'll see. You should only be careful."

Be careful of what, he wondered, letting her ramble on without a response.

"A word to the wise." She seemed to clear her throat and with it the wire unburdened its sudden animosity. "All you want is coffee and bread?"

"I think that's it," he said, scratching his head.

"I'll bring it later."

He hung up and went back into the bedroom, feeling the compulsion to mention the call, as if Ida Katz might have been listening which, he knew, instinctively to be the case.

"That was Lily Morganstern. She's going shopping for me."

Ida Katz paused midway in her folding duties, looking upward from her bent form.

"Her?" she said contemptuously, the word ejaculating with such obvious malice that Murray was startled.

"She's not your friend?"

He recalled that Ida Katz and Lily Morganstern had seemed inseparable. They were part of Sarah's canasta game, her constant companions around the pool, sister yentas. It was inconceivable that Ida Katz could harbor ill feelings for Lily Morganstern.

"That one's a barracuda."

"A barracuda?"

"A barracuda. You know a fish that grabs on and stays there."

"She's getting me some coffee and bread."

"Make sure that's all she gets."

He seemed genuinely confused, wondering, perhaps, if she were referring to some dishonesty on Lily's part. He decided not to pursue the subject. Sarah could have explained it, he was certain, but Sarah was gone. Ida Katz continued to fold the clothes.

"I'm very grateful," he said later, as she prepared to leave.

"Just call the Salvation Army. They'll come and pick up the carton." She stood close to him and he felt her towering presence as she watched him with lowered eyes. Then she bent down and kissed his cheek.

"Remember that I'm here, Murray. If there is anything, anything." Her voice rose emphatically on the second anything. "Just call me." She started out the door, then turned for a moment. "Whatever they tell you," she said. "I was the closest to Sarah. She confided things to me." Then she was gone.

He stood watching the door for a long time, marveling at the devotion of Sarah's friends, and the goodness in his wife that could motivate such an outpouring. Maybe they had their little quirks between them, he decided, assuming that this was just one of those odd manifestations in the world of women.

In the days that followed, as he forced himself to adjust to Sarah's absence, he had ample time to observe these manifestations as the women ministered to his needs. Minnie Schwartz made it a regular practice to arrive at his doorstep every morning to make him breakfast. Ida Katz would show up in midmorning to "tidy up," and Lily Morganstern was always dropping by with items from the store. Without his realizing it, it became a regular routine. He continued to be grateful and he did admit that it chased away the blues to have a woman puttering around his now-empty apartment, but the tug of guilt was unmistakable.

"I want you to know Minnie," he said one morning, "how much I appreciate what you're doing. But I feel that I may be unnecessarily taking up your time."

"My time, Murray? I got better things to do?"

"I feel guilty," he admitted. "I mean, you've all been so nice."

"All?" He had learned to avoid any mention of the others to any of them, because their reactions were becoming increasingly inflammatory. It was a brief lapse and he regretted it too late.

"At least I'm sincere."

"Sincere?" He wondered what that meant.

She bent close to him and whispered. "At least I don't have motives."

"I don't understand," he said. She sat down beside him at the kitchen table.

"Why do you need them? I can come in and do the cleaning and the shopping. What better things can I do than that?"

"But you have your own life."

"I owe it to Sarah."

At the mention of Sarah's name, he nodded. It was a form of consent, since even beyond the grave he imagined that they might be fulfilling Sarah's wishes. Besides, he thought, it's only temporary.

Thankfully, too, his nights were filled, as each woman would rotate his having dinner at their places. And what dinners! He was being stuffed with every imaginable dish—varnishkas, pot roasts, stuffed turkeys— a cornucopia of special concoctions that left him reeling and bloated each evening.

"You like my stuffing?" Ida Katz would ask, calling attention to each preparation. He would, of course, nod politely, his mouth full.

"Better than them," she would insist.

"Marvelous."

The others, too, had their own ways of calling attention to their culinary ardor.

"Did I tell you I was a fantastic cook?" Lily Morganstern would say. "I'm a real cook. Not a Johnny-come-lately."

"No question."

But he would go home to his empty bed, still missing Sarah's presence beside him, although he was thankful that she had provided friends to take the edge off some of his loneliness.

One night, after he had taken his ritual Alka-Seltzer and was preparing for bed, he heard a knock on the door, put on his robe and answered it. A large, heavily made up woman stood before him, vaguely familiar.

"Remember me? Harriet Bernstein from across the court."

"Of course," he lied, though her presence was stimulating his recall.

"Can I come in?" Before he could answer, she had insinuated herself through the door to the inside of his apartment.

"I was away visiting my daughter for a few weeks. Then when I got back, I realized I hadn't visited since the funeral so I thought I might stop by for a minute."

He observed her taking a sweeping look about the apartment, then sat down on the couch and patted the seat next to her own, an invitation which, oddly, he obeyed.

"So how are you getting along?" she asked. He could smell the special sweetness of her scent, which filled the air around him.

"Thank God," he said, "Sarah had wonderful friends."

"The widows?" She clicked her tongue in an attitude of derision. "They come out of the woodwork," she said, jabbing him in the arm. Recoiling, he looked at her curiously.

"They're wonderful people," he said. "Sarah's friends."

"You should live so long."

"I don't understand." He was genuinely surprised by her reaction. He watched her. She was a well-kept woman, who, despite her heavy make-up, had a lively air, although her pose seemed cynical, almost contemptuous.

"It's not important," she said, pausing. "I'm also a widow. Believe me, I know."

"Know what?"

"What's happening."

"What's happening?"

Harriet Bernstein smiled, showing even, perfectly matched and obviously false teeth. She put a hand on his thigh. He let it stay there, embarrassed, not knowing what to do. An old, rarely felt feeling, stirred.

"You know, a widow is a very dangerous commodity."

"Dangerous?" He was trying to listen, but his mind seemed concentrated on her hand, which had begun to move, stroking his thigh.

"Can you blame them?" she said, lowering her voice and squeezing the heavy flesh of his thigh.

He knew his mind was trying to understand, but he was coping with feelings and reactions foreign to his recent history. Something visibly physical was happening.

"A widow's life is very lonely."

"A widower is no picnic." Would Sarah understand, he wondered?

"You were a friend of Sarah's?" he asked, the words moving quickly on waves of accelerated breathing. He felt his pulse pound. The knowledge of what was happening beneath his pajamas seemed like a miracle. He was afraid if he talked too much, it would go away.

"Not really."

It seemed better that way, he decided, as the woman's hands found the thing that had happened.

"I can tell you're a very lonely man," Harriet said, her hand deliberately probing now. She stopped suddenly in her ministrations.

"You think maybe we should go into the bedroom?" she asked.

He grunted, afraid that a single word might make it go away. But she got up and, gripping his hand, led him to the bedroom. The room was dark and he was surprised that he felt only the vaguest tug of guilt. After all, she wasn't a friend of Sarah's. Thoughts of Sarah did, however, intrude on the miracle that Harriet was making happen.

He lay down on the bed and felt the stirring of anxiety that Harriet must have sensed as she lay down beside him.

"Relax boobala," she said, the endearing term odd to his ears, since it had been so long since any endearment had been directed his way. He felt her soft touch and again the renewed sense of his sexuality.

"You see," she said. He nodded gratefully, stirred by his pride in himself as he heard zippers grating, the crinkling of her clothes, then the touch of her soft flesh.

"Such a wonderful man. Such a marvelous man," she said as she maneuvered herself under him, in a comfortable coital posture. She began a low moaning sound, as she caressed him and moved her body in a rhythmical gyration. He was not thinking of Sarah now, only of the matter at hand, his own sense of wonder at this miracle that Harriet had wrought.

"You feel good?" she asked suddenly, the moans stopping briefly. He did not reply in words, stroking her breast instead. Then he felt the climax of this miracle and lay still, listening to the heavy beat of his heart. It was only then that he remembered Sarah, but he was growing too drowsy to think about it.

A shrill sound awakened him out of a tight, dreamless sleep. He opened his eyes, disoriented, waiting for the sound to identify itself. It was a woman's voice, raucous, like the sound in a bird zoo, despotic and grating.

"Disgusting. This is disgusting." He caught words first, confused until he saw Harriet Berstein cowering under the covers beside him. Minnie Schwartz, her face red with anger, her eyes popping precariously out of her head, stood over them.

"This is the way you repay my goodness, my feeling for Sarah. In bed with a korva." It was, he knew, the ultimate expression for perfidious women, the Russian/Yiddish word for whore.

"You only wish it was you," Harriet spat back.

"I wish?" She turned to Murray. "I need him like a hole in the head." Then she stormed out of the bedroom and he heard the door slam, trembling the loose contents of the apartment.

"She's your keeper?" Harriet asked. She had gotten out of bed and slipped on her dress from the previous night. "They get their claws on a widower and they think he's their property."

He was confused, ashamed, but remembering the night before, he felt strangely indifferent to Minnie's words.

"She comes in every morning to make me breakfast," he said, getting out of bed and putting on his robe.

"Big deal."

"She was close to Sarah," he said self-righteously, as if the information could explain what had happened.

"You think she did it for Sarah?"

"For who, then?"

She had been looking into the mirror, patting her bleached hair in place, when she turned suddenly to him. She shook her head and lifted one hand, palm inward, moving it like a fan.

"Are you such a putz, Murray?" she asked. The word, ejaculated suddenly, shocked him.

"You're a man, a widower, a single. That's your qualification. You're a catch."

"Me, a catch?" He couldn't believe what she was saying, but before he had time to reply, the telephone rang. He picked it up in the kitchen.

"I don't believe it." It was Lily Morganstern's voice. He suspected what she meant and grimaced into the phone. Harriet Bernstein watching, caught the meaning instantly.

"The yenta communication system," she muttered.

"Minnie told me," Lily continued, her voice breaking. "She was crying, hysterical. I said it must be impossible. Murray Gold. Our Murray Gold, with Sarah's body not yet cold in her grave."

He held a hand over the phone's mouthpiece. "What can I say?" Then he removed his hand.

"What can I say?" he said into the mouthpiece, shrugging his shoulders.

"What kind of a man are you? After we took such good care of you." She paused. "For Sarah's sake."

"What can I say?" he repeated. He waited for her next response, not wanting to be impolite. He watched Harriet walk into the bathroom, heard water running.

"You think maybe we should talk?" Lily Morganstern said finally. Her anger seemed spent. "I don't know about Minnie, but I'm willing to forgive and forget." She paused. "I know a little something about men, especially on special occasions. A man's a man" She lowered her voice. "She's still there?"

"She's in the bathroom."

"You made no commitment?"

"Commitment." He wondered what she meant.

But she must have sensed his response by his uncertainty.

"Good. Very wise. Don't rush into things. Think it over a while. You shouldn't rush, especially now."

"Rush?"

"Anyway, I'll be over later and we'll talk."

She hung up. Another ring followed immediately. He answered it instantly.

"I want you to know," Ida Katz said, "that it doesn't make any difference."

"It doesn't?"

"From Minnie's point of view, I can understand it. But from mine..." It was, to him, an incomplete thought. But he let it pass.

"What can I say?"

"I only have a word of advice. The woman has a reputation. It's not the first time. Just don't make any rash mistakes. I personally am willing to forgive, and I want you to know that I'm still expecting you for dinner tonight."

He had forgotten. Luckily, they were always reminding him. Harriet Bernstein came out of the bathroom.

"Same time?" he asked the voice on the phone.

"Of course. I made a special stuffing. You want maybe I should get some wine?"

"I'm not a drinker."

"Just don't aggravate yourself. I'm sure you're not going to let it happen again."

He did not respond. Harriet watched him. Then he hung up.

"Another one?"

"They've been so nice to me."

"Why not?"

"I'm no big deal."

"To you, you're not a big deal. To Sarah, maybe you weren't such a big deal. To the yenta widows of Sunset Village, you're a big deal." He watched her. She held herself straight, gathering her own sense of dignity.

"A single man is hard to find," she said sadly, shaking her head. "In a few more months, you'll be so spoiled, you'll become a selfish quvetch."

"Me?" It was an idea so contrary to his own self-image that he smiled. It was the first time since Sarah had died that he had smiled publicly, although he knew he had smiled to himself last night.

"Then you'll get so fatumilt, you'll probably settle down with one of us. It's not so easy to break old habits...." She pointed a finger at her chest. "Believe me, I know."

She started for the door, hesitating.

"And you'll be a celebrity. You'll be the big story of the week."

"Me?"

"Who else?"

He wanted to call her back, to have her explain further what she meant. He went to the window and watched her cross the street, staying there long after she disappeared. I'm alone, Sarah, he implored, knowing his lips had moved. What should I do? he asked aloud. He paused, listening.

"Do I always have to tell you what to do?" He imagined he heard her voice, listening closely for any additional advice. Then the phone rang. It was Minnie Schwartz...

"I'm willing to forgive and forget," she said. "For the time being..."

"Good" he said. "I was getting hungry." He heard her mumble something, then the phone clicked dead, and he sat on his chair waiting for her to arrive.

Poor Herman

 She had first noticed him from across the huge card room of the main clubhouse, a side view, faintly familiar, but it did not cross her mind again until she sat at the little dressing table in the bedroom of her condominium rubbing off her make-up. She had always mused, daydreamed, fantasized in front of the mirror while putting on her make-up or taking it off.

Sometimes she would suddenly make a wrong dab, which would recall her to herself. That was what she did that evening, as she rubbed the cleanser a little too vigorously and got some into her eye. It was then that she realized the connection between the profile in the card room and her memory of Heshy Feinstein. The shock of recognition made her hands shake briefly and she found she could not continue efficiently with the removal of her make-up.

She looked at her face, ravaged by age—by living, she told herself. But she could not identify it at all with the vivid image of Heshy Feinstein in her mind. For this memory of Heshy was not at all lost in the mist of more than fifty years. It had been retrieved so often, an oasis of joy in the arid desert of what her life had become, that it still had retained its shimmering intensity. Heshy Feinstein! He had been the one unalterable condition of her inner life, her secret life—although once she had confided to her daughter, Helen, that there had been a man, a boy really, who had made her body ache with longing for him.

She could remember exactly because, at the time, they were sitting shiva for Herman, only seven years before. Herman with whom she had spent forty-five faithful years of marriage, of coldness, too, although her

81

children would never ever know that. Only Herman knew, because he suffered from her indifference since the first night of their marriage, from the moment of her hysterical exaggeration of her simulated virginity. What an act it had been. "It took me three days to get married," Herman had always told their friends with a laugh, although she had known in her heart that they were never really married, not in that way at least.

"I have always been a good and faithful wife, Helen," she told her daughter, who by then was impatient to get back to Chicago and her life there.

"Sure, Ma."

"Your father was a good man, a wonderful person."

"You think I don't know that, Ma? He was lucky to have such a terrific woman."

"I feel so bad for him," she said, but her meaning, she knew, was lost to her daughter. Their marriage bed had been as cold as ice. She hadn't even done her duty by him and she hoped in her heart that he had found someone to relieve his needs, some woman somewhere who could get rid of his tensions and send him back to her.

"I was not a good wife, Helen," she said. Her daughter merely nodded. They had been sitting shiva for four days and it was boring Helen, she was sure, hearing all those reminiscences of a long marriage. What else was there to do but talk about the dead father, the dead husband, and their memories of him? She dared not say to her daughter that Herman was quickly slipping from her memory, and if it wasn't for the picture of him on the piano to remind her of his features, she might not have been able to assemble them in her mind.

"Once, there was another man," she said.

"You had another boyfriend?" Helen seemed interested as they sipped coffee.

"He was absolutely gorgeous—a marvelous, brilliant boy."

"You're kidding, Ma."

"Heshy Feinstein."

"Heshy?"

"In Brownsville, in those days, the Yiddish and English was totally mixed up. His name was Harvey but no one called him Harvey except the teachers at school. He was six feet tall when he was seventeen years old and I was sixteen. He was going to Boys' High School and I was going to Girls' High School and we used to take the subway together. He lived behind us on Douglass Street, and I knew him since we were eight or nine. But it wasn't until I was sixteen that we discovered each other."

"My God. My name could have been Feinstein," her daughter said.

She ignored the remark. Her own name had been Goldberg. Frieda Goldberg. At least Herman brought her the name Smith, though God knew where that came from.

"His father wanted him to be a doctor. He was excellent in science, always doing experiments on his back porch."

"Did he become one?"

"I never found out."

"You haven't seen him since?"

"Not once. We moved to Eastern Parkway. It was only a few miles away, maybe four, five subway stops. But I never saw him again."

"Weird," Helen said.

"Heshy's father owned a grocery store and he wanted him to be a doctor."

"Do you ever wonder about him?"

"Not often," she lied, knowing that it had been the single obsession of her life.

Naturally, she left out all of the important parts, although she would have loved to confide in her daughter. But she worried that her daughter would hate her for what she did to her father. I feel so sorry for Herman, she told herself often. Even now, before the mirror, as her mind searched its secret screen for pictures of Frieda Goldberg and Heshy Feinstein.

He was shaking the pear tree in his father's yard and gathering the pears in a bucket for Mrs. Feinstein to make stewed dessert. She watched him from the little rusty swing in her own yard, making fun of his efforts, especially when one of the pears hit him on the head.

"It's not funny. It hurts like the blazes."

"Poor Heshy."

He walked over to her and nodded his head and she looked into the shiny curly sweet-smelling hair. He took her hand and put it on the lump that was growing there and she felt it gently.

"That doesn't tickle," he said. Yet she knew, at that moment, as her finger touched the hard nub of that lump that something had passed between them, and nothing was ever the same from that time on. She opened the fingers of her hand and moved them like fish in the bulrushes of his curly hair, feeling goose flesh rise on her hands and legs and a strange feeling deep inside her and in that place between her legs. It was odd how that memory never dimmed the first signal that something was happening between them, and yet there were things that happened only yesterday that she had trouble remembering.

Was it really Heshy Feinstein she had seen in the card room, or some apparition? It would not have been the first time that a stranger's face would loom out at her suddenly in a crowd and she would wonder if it was Heshy's face. Sometimes she would hide. Other times, she actually followed the person, until she discovered her error.

She could also recall, dredge up from her memories, the first sensations, the feelings, the kisses, the delicious gropings, and, of course, that first time on the old couch on her own back porch in the middle of that hot summer. It was the great mystery of her life why she could never, after Heshy, experience such sensations, that joyous release of feelings that came from somewhere deep within her. Why had it disappeared so completely when she left Brownsville? It was as if a dark curtain came down on her life and she experienced all the physical joy of a lifetime in a single year.

She could even remember the tension of their subterfuge, the ruses and, as they became more intimate, the agony of worry over the coming of her period. Heshy was as paranoid as she was, even though he was always sure to carry protection in his wallet. But even these anxieties would never interfere with the greed for each other, the joy-giving of their lovemaking. It was, of course, more than just the physical thing, and they could not hide their love from their parents, to whom it became a terrible source of concern and alienation. The harassment was bitterly frank, opening deep animosities between the families.

"My Heshy's too young," his father would remonstrate as Frieda's parents sat together watching the man's growing anger and his wife's less articulate bitterness.

"So is Frieda."

"It's ridiculous. It makes no sense. It will ruin my son's medical career if he has to worry about supporting a wife and maybe children. There has got to be an end to this."

They could hear their parents clearly through the vents in the cellar, where they had fitted themselves out a place among a suite of cast-off furniture. The cellar had a back door that led to the yard, and above them they could hear every movement and sound, every creak of danger in the house.

"At it again," he said, but she was not listening. Instead, she was concentrating on the joy that was spilling over and trying to be silent as she bit her fist and felt the suffusion of her inner pleasure and his own climactic movement. Even in the afterglow, they could not escape the sounds of their parents' bitterness.

"Somebody has to move away," Heshy's father shouted. "I can't. I have a business."

"Well, I like it here," her father yelled.

"Just keep your son away from my daughter!" her mother screamed. "She's too good for him anyway."

Whereupon they would shut out the sounds with the palms of their hands and proceed again to reach out for this mysterious thing that had brought them together.

They were, of course, being young, hardly interested in consequences. They felt they could continue to be clever in their subterfuge, and even her mother's hesitant probings about the state of her virginity were deflected, leaving her mother in little doubt that she was still intact.

"Surely you trust your own daughter. You think I'm going to jeopardize my life?" In those days, an unwanted pregnancy was a stigma from which there was little recovery. Not even a lifetime could erase the damages it would cause, and this scared them the most, especially when they knew they had tempted fate.

"I want you as close to me as is humanly possible," she cried more than once, slipping off his condom.

"My sweet, beautiful, wonderful, darling love."

But what might not have been seen was sensed, and her father soon announced that they were moving to Crown Heights, a neighborhood about ten miles away.

"It just can't go on like this, Frieda. You're too young. He's too young. Mr. Feinstein might be a horrible person, but he's right. Maybe if we moved away and you saw him less often. Maybe then."

"I won't go!" she cried.

"You'll go."

"I'll run away. We'll elope. I'll get pregnant."

She could see her father's face flush a deep red, which frightened her because she truly loved him, a gentle man who, when risen to anger, could be irrational and sometimes violent.

"I don't really mean that, Papa. Don't think what you're thinking." That calmed him. Heshy was far harder to placate.

"When are you moving?"

"Tomorrow."

"The bastards. They wouldn't even give us time to prepare."

"Prepare what?"

"To get the hell away from them. To get married. You think I can possibly live without you?"

"And me without you?" She remembered her shoulders suddenly shaking hysterically and his valiant efforts to soothe her until he too was crying, their tears mingling. Even now, she could taste the salt in them, a taste never to be duplicated in her lifetime. In the cellar, they clung to each other. They went so far to risk exposure that night—miraculously, or so she believed—they stayed together without discovery and were back in their respective rooms by morning. It was a night whose pain was to remain with her, a kind of symbol of the highlight of her life. In the aridity of her later years, she marveled at the sheer physical wonder of it, those hours together, intertwined, never uncoupling, as if a moment apart would destroy them both. They had long since explored the mysteries of themselves. No secrets of their bodies or minds escaped their mutual probings.

"I will love you forever and forever and forever." She could still hear the sound, the rhythm and timbre of his voice, strong and assured, as it thrilled her, promised her.

She had said, "They will never tear us apart. No one will ever tear us apart."

And, in a way, they hadn't because the memory never disappeared nor lost its magic, even now, as she looked into the mirror detesting the sagging lines of her face, the drooping skin around her eyes, the jowls, though she liked to think that she looked ten years younger than her sixty-eight years.

She got into her nightgown without a glance at her body, which also had run to sag and flesh, but because it was of little interest, except for the state of its basic health, she didn't care. She flicked on "The Tonight Show" and when she grew drowsy, she flicked it off again and slipped into a heavy, dreamless sleep.

But the next morning, after she dressed, made her breakfast, and cleared away the dishes, she remembered her brief recognition. When the telephone rang, she knew it was Dotty, who was wondering when she would be ready to go to the pool, their daily ritual.

"Not today, Dotty," Frieda said.

"You don't feel good?"

"I have a headache." Poor Herman, she suddenly thought, remembering the thousand times she used that excuse.

"You always have a headache," he said angrily as he tossed in the bed, turning his back to her.

You give me a headache, she wanted to say, but to her credit, she never said it. Not out loud, at least.

When she was sure Dotty had left for the pool, she went outside and, taking her tricycle, pedaled to the management office to make the inquiry that she knew was inevitable. Might as well get it over with.

"There are three Harvey Feinsteins," the middle-aged shiksa clerk with the blue-gray hair said. Her harlequin glasses hung on a jeweled chain around her neck.

There were always more than a dozen Harvey Feinsteins whenever, in weak moments, she was tempted to find him again. But she had never wished to intrude on that vast forest of Harvey Feinsteins. She jotted down the addresses and cycled over to the nearest one, where she had a card-playing friend, Toby Schwartzman, another widow. The widows held the clear majority and were a constant source of humor among the marrieds and themselves, which they bore, but privately resented. She

knocked at Toby's door, three doors down from the first Mr. Feinstein.
Toby was eating pistachio nuts and listening to Oprah.

"You didn't go to the pool?"

"I had a little headache."

They gossiped a little, talked about last night's canasta and "The Tonight Show."

Then Frieda asked the question. "You know the Feinsteins?" She
paused. "The ones in number six?"

"I know them to say hello. Why?"

It was always the "why" that she waited for, planning a strategy to deflect the skillful yenta probings.

"My daughter's cousin by marriage, Phyllis, is named Feinstein and
she says they're in Sunset Village."

"She's from Chicago?"

"No, Phyllis is from Boston."

"These Feinsteins are from Pittsburgh. He's eighty years old, in a
wheelchair."

After some more small talk, she left, satisfied that she had made only
the most casual inquiry, an important consideration in a world of yentas
that had to know even the most minute detail of every personal transaction.

It took her three hours to track down the second Feinstein, who lived
in the fancy four-story elevator condominium. She actually parked herself on a bench in front of the elevator shaft watching for movement from
number twelve, which was on the third floor just off the corner and clearly
visible on the open balcony-corridor. She had, of course, checked the
name plates on the mailboxes. "Harvey Feinstein" was clearly marked.
Seeing it caused her heart to lurch. A widower, she thought, hoping that
perhaps today was the day her horoscope predicted something of value
in her life. The sun was hot and soon she could not bear it on the bench,
nor could she bear the curiosity.

She noticed a magazine addressed to H. Feinstein on the shelf for pub-
lications above the mailbox. Scooping it up, she proceeded to go up in
the elevator and, without giving it much thought, pressed the buzzer of
number twelve. She put her ear against the door, heard stirrings, and
then her anxieties began because she had not really figured out a cover

story. She heard the door click, then open, and a small man in bathing trunks stood before her. She towered over him and looked at him, perhaps with contempt for his smallness and his not being *the* Harvey Feinstein.

"Mr. Feinstein?"

"Yes."

"I found this outside the door."

"They didn't put it in the mailbox?"

"How should I know?" she said. Then she went down the elevator, found her tricycle and peddled home.

She was sticky from perspiration when she got into her condominium. She also felt silly and decided that was enough looking for one day. She took the addresses, put them on her dresser, changed into her bathing suit, and went off to the pool, where Dotty and their friends were sitting around squinting under big hats, talking about their children and grandchildren. She lay back and dozed. Their words floated repetitiously in the air.

When she opened her eyes again, the sun had shifted, throwing long shadows across one half of the pool. Occasionally, an announcement of someone's name would blare over the loudspeaker system. They only allowed one announcement per person per day to cut down on the cacophony. Rising, she went to the edge of the pool and dipped her feet into the water, now warm from the intensity of the sun.

Her eyesight was remarkable considering her years and, being slightly farsighted, she had a longer range of vision than most of her friends. That was why from her vantage point, she was able to see the faces across the pool with uncommon clarity. Again she imagined, since she dared not believe it was actually him, that she saw him, full-face now, squinting into the sun, which was coming over her shoulder. He was standing, flaying his arms, in some personal form of exercise, a common sight.

She felt the blood surging in her heart, the beat amplified in her chest as she lifted her feet out of the water and circled to the edge of the shadows to observe the man more closely. He was bald, gray—where there was still hair. His skin was not quite tan enough to be the badge of the longtime resident, but in the way he moved, despite the thickness around his middle, she detected a familiarity, even an intimacy as she mentally stripped him of his bathing trunks and visualized the still-familiar outline of his rump and what hung in front of him. She looked around her to see if anyone had read her thoughts, then walked slowly toward the pay telephone. She found the quarters she kept in the pocket of her bathing suit and dialed the Sunset Village Clubhouse.

"Will you page Mr. Harvey Feinstein. He's out by the pool."

In the pause that followed, she closed her eyes tightly, wishing, hoping it was him, trusting in the vividness of her memory. It was, after all, more than half a century since she had seen him last. Then the name blared over the speaker system with a grating, tremulous, unmistakable sound. She saw him stir suddenly, then look about him and upward in the direction of the sound.

A woman who had been reclining near him also stirred, sitting up abruptly, a trace of fear in her face. At their stage of life, with their progeny spread all over the country, every telephone call brought a stab of anxiety. The man looked at the woman and shrugged, then searched, a hand over his eyes to shield the sun, for the phone box, which, coincidentally, was next to Frieda. She turned slightly, hiding her face, pressing downward to break the connection. Her knees shook as she felt his presence, so close that she imagined she could smell the scent of his body, another lingering memory.

"This is Harvey Feinstein," he said into the phone, the intonation clear as it was in her memory.

"Hung up, you say. Did they leave a message?"

She turned only after he hung up, watching the familiar walk or the familiar walk that was encased in an older man's body. He once was slender, lithe, had youthful energy. But it was him, unmistakably—Harvey Feinstein. She felt a gasp in her throat as if deep within her she was hungering to reveal her presence.

"It's me, Frieda," she wanted to cry out. When she got herself under control, she went back to where her friends were sitting.

"Who did you call?" Dotty asked.

"The dentist," she said, barely audible. "I've got a toothache."

"Frieda, you're becoming a kvetch," Dotty laughed.

But she had lain back and put a straw hat over her face, through which, between broken straws, she could view Harvey Feinstein with more leisure. He was sitting at the foot of the beach chair on which the woman had been reclining, talking to her and looking at the phone. His wife, surely, she thought, as she tried to gather a more complete picture of the woman, a bleached blond with a fair figure. When she stood up, Frieda could see that her thighs were starting to widen, an image that, despite her self-admonishment, gave Frieda pleasure. She did not admit, even to herself, that something else had given her pleasure, a quiver in another place, down there. The signs were quite physical, rather frightening in a woman of her years, although, from the talk of the yentas, she knew that the yearnings were still active, even actively pursued and proudly acclaimed.

"My Max, you'd think he was fourteen years old. He won't let me alone."

"You're lucky," some widow would invariably say. "Stop complaining."

"Who's complaining?" the lucky one would say.

"If he has any left over, I know somewhere he could use it."

"It's all right. He knows where his bread is buttered."

When she came back from the pool, she looked at her body in the full-length mirror, something she had not done in years, and surveyed what time had done. There was a roundness to her belly and hips, and her breasts, although pendulous, still retained, in her view, at least, a certain fullness around the nipples, which she was surprised to see were erect. There was cellulite around her thighs, but considering the shape of her peers, the only logical yardstick of comparison, she might still consider herself womanly.

The next day, she was up early and off to the bank, where she withdrew $1,500 from her $6,000 savings account and took the Sunset Village bus to the Poinsettia Beach Shopping Center. There, she bought three new dresses, two pantsuits, and a whole different line of make-up, the use of which was patiently explained by a blue-haired older woman with two-inch eyelashes. Then she went to the beauty parlor and had her hair dyed as close to its original color as possible, a kind of chestnut. The hairdresser frizzed it around the edge of her face, insisting that she looked twenty years younger.

"You couldn't make it thirty?" she joked.

"Got a young boyfriend?" the hairdresser minced.

"Seventeen."

"Sounds divine."

That evening, after she ate a salad and was feeling quite good about her willpower, she fiddled with the contents of the vials and tubes and pencils, put on her new make-up and carefully did herself up, satisfied that she had done the best she could with what she had—which wasn't much after sixty-eight years. But she did feel girlish. She felt young, and that was the important thing. She put on her new pink pantsuit over a new girdle that held her in, a little too snugly she realized, but soon her diet would be working and it wouldn't be as uncomfortable.

"Miss America," Dotty said, when she saw her.

"I'm changing my image."

She watched as Dotty surveyed her.

"Be honest," Frieda said.

"You look terrific. If I was a jealous woman, I'd be jealous."

"But you are a jealous woman."

"Then I'm jealous."

On the way to the clubhouse, they sat on the little open-air shuttle bus and she could feel Dotty's eyes on her.

"You're looking for a man, aren't you, Frieda?" she asked gently.

"What makes you think that?"

"My eyes."

Under her make-up and tan, Frieda knew she was blushing. She groped for something to put Dotty off the scent.

"I'm in my second childhood."

"One step from the home." To them the "home" was the next stop on the road to oblivion.

In the clubhouse, they found their usual card table and the canasta game began. She knew she couldn't concentrate. She surreptitiously searched the huge room, seeking out the face of Harvey Feinstein. Twice in the first hour she got up on the pretense of going to the ladies' room, conscious of the eyes of the men who turned her way, or so she imagined, since her new outfit, make-up and hair job made her somewhat of a central figure among her widowed canasta friends. She knew, too, that they were talking about her, probably discussing her strange behavior as a sign of senility, not uncommon in this place.

There was no sign of Harvey Feinstein or his bleached-blond wife in the card room, in the lobby of the clubhouse, or in any of the special club and hobby rooms that lined the corridor adjacent to the card room.

When she came back after the second time, she said, "I really can't concentrate tonight, girls. Something I ate." She lifted a palm to her chest in a gesture to validate her imaginary heartburn.

They grumbled, of course, and she could see Dotty's lips tighten though they called after her to feel better. But she wasn't listening. Her eyes were like two searchlights scanning the crowd. It had never occurred to her how much older people looked alike and how difficult it was to find one particular person in this sea of tanned faces and bright clothes. She waited in the outer lobby of the auditorium, where some live show was going on, peeking inside when someone would open the door on their way to the bathroom. She calculated that she would have to wait until the show was over before she could make a proper inspection.

There was, she knew, always the possibility that the Feinsteins had chosen to stay home that night, and she was tempted to find their place and peek in the windows to make sure and save her all this energy. Walking into the quiet, gently warm night air, thick with the scent of tropical flowers, she moved around the back of the clubhouse to the shuffleboard courts, which were heavily in use, even at this hour. It was odd, she thought, how some people pursued their leisure as if it were hard work. She hated shuffleboard and couldn't understand why people, men and women both, were fascinated by it. She planned to ignore it, giving the players only the most casual glance and deciding in her own mind that such an occupation would hardly be worthy of Harvey Feinstein—when she saw him.

Calm down, Frieda, she told herself. Her objective was becoming quite clear to her. Her heart beat faster and her knees felt a bit unsteady as she walked toward the court on which he was playing, determined to display herself, to catch his eye, to insist that she be noticed. Pausing, she looked at her face in the hand mirror under the floodlights used to light the shuffleboard courts and proceeded to a place that would put her in contact with his vision. There was a bench directly behind the court on which he was playing. Moving toward it, she slowed down so as to catch his eye as he turned to prepare himself for his shots. Across the court she could see his bleached-blond wife, moving awkwardly as she attempted a shot in her husband's direction.

Coming closer, she saw him turn and momentarily focus his eyes on her face, then move back to concentrate on his shot. He saw me, she assured herself, feeling fluttery and deliciously girlish, although she did not see any flash of recognition.

"You're terrific, Harvey," she heard the bleached blond call. "Like you played this game on cruise ships."

So he was not called Heshy anymore, Frieda thought, proud of her special knowledge. She stood behind him now, imagining that she appeared intent on watching the game and wondering quite seriously if there was such a thing as telepathy so that she might will herself into his thoughts. As she was thinking this, he turned, and she forced herself to smile slightly, a gesture miraculously returned by him but so casual as to indicate his non-recognition. His partner was a fat woman, whose chins shivered as she expended energy on her shot, her big hips and behind shaking visibly beneath her slacks.

"Not bad," Frieda said, making him turn. She could hardly just stand there watching them without making some sort of comment.

"It's only my second time," he said.

"You're a natural."

She barely understood the game and, after a while, felt uncomfortable about just standing there like a pear ready to be plucked from a tree. The reference triggered her memory and gave her a momentary twinge of pleasure. Schmuck, this is Frieda, she told him urgently to herself. Stop that stupid game and notice.

But he would not stop that stupid game and after watching a long time, she knew that she would have to catch him when he wasn't concentrating so hard.

In bed that evening watching "The Tonight Show," she pondered the ways in which she might catch Harvey Feinstein's eye. It was obvious,

although she harbored secret feelings to the contrary, that his memories
of her were too deeply embedded, so far beneath the surface of his consciousness that it would not be easy to dredge them up. She did not want
to shock him with her presence, nor upset him, nor do something that
would make him feel guilty or force his avoidance of her. Frieda Goldberg,
she told herself, might have been many things, a cold domineering wife,
a little overbearing as a mother, stubborn, independent, but not stupid.
Frieda Goldberg definitely was not stupid.

She was still pondering the method the next day as she lounged in a
chair beside the pool watching the spot where Harvey Feinstein and his
wife sat yesterday, wondering if her new bathing suit set her off well. She
imagined she had lost weight. It was obvious to her that Dotty thought
she was acting strangely.

"You want to play tonight, Frieda?"

"I'll see later."

"You've got to give us time to get someone else."

"I'll give you time."

Without seeing, she sensed that Dotty had turned away in disgust,
rolling her eyes upward to indicate to their friends that something strange
was going on in Frieda's head—which, of course, was true.

When the bleached blond walked across her field of vision, Frieda sat
up alertly to see if Heshy was behind her. It was a peculiarity of this place
for men to walk, or lag, behind their wives, and she waited patiently for
a sign of him. When he did not appear after several minutes and the
blond settled down to her ablutions—the smearing of the sun lotion,
the tying of the kerchief, the adjusting of the lounge, the placement of
the ashtray and the cigarettes beside it—she understood quite clearly
what her method would be. She would reach Heshy Feinstein through
his bleached-blond wife.

Getting up casually, she strolled slowly to the pool next to the spot
where the blond was sitting and put her foot in the water.

"Cold," Frieda squealed.

"The water is cold?" the blond asked.

She now stood over the lounging woman, being sure not to block the
sun. It was, she knew, a mark of politeness in this place.

"It warms up later. Then it gets too hot. Like pishocks."

The woman laughed. She had an even, good set of matching teeth, although the lines around her mouth were quite pronounced. From far, she looks better, Frieda thought.

"I saw you and your husband playing shuffleboard last night," Frieda said. She knew she was courting danger as being dubbed a yenta, but she hoped that the woman would take that role before she did.

"You're very good players," she added after a pause.

"Considering," the bleached blond said, "we've just been here two weeks and this is only our second time." She seemed eager for friendship.

"You like it here?"

"Wonderful. Brooklyn was getting impossible. The shvartzes everywhere. We lived in Flatbush."

"They're everywhere now in Flatbush? I lived in Crown Heights. I'm here two years. Thank God, my daughter lives in Chicago."

"You don't miss New York?"

"You miss it?"

She moved upright on the lounge, engaged at last. Frieda sat down at the foot of the chair, where Heshy had sat the day before.

"My children live there. And my grandchildren. It's not easy to break away. They both live on the Island. My boy is a dentist. And my daughter married a furrier. I figure that once a year they'll come here and once a year we'll go there. And their children will come for the holidays."

"Everyone figures that."

"My name is Frieda Smith," Frieda said, holding out her hand. "Ida Feinstein," she said, taking it gratefully.

"I'm a widow."

"I'm sorry."

"Don't be sorry."

"How long is he gone?" Aha, Frieda thought, bracing for the interrogation, a true yenta.

"Seven years."

"There's a lot of widows here?"

"You wouldn't believe it."

"I'm so lucky to have my Harvey. He was a schoolteacher in the New York public school system, in Forest Hills, which was lucky except for the long ride to Brooklyn. I used to worry myself sick. Thank God," she knocked her knuckles on the metal lounge, "he never had a problem."

"He likes it here?"

"Loves it. He doesn't like the hot sun so much. But he stays home, does the housework, the dishes, and reads. He'll come later. He taught biology. A very smart man. Not so sociable as I would like, but I'm sure he'll adjust."

Frieda caught the tinge of regret, noting that Heshy was having a hard time adjusting to retirement. It was not uncommon.

"You like to play cards?"

"I love canasta. I miss my regular game. Also Mah-Jongg. I'm sure I'll find a regular game here," she said expectantly.

"Ida," Frieda said, "you've come to the right store." She led her over to her friends and introduced her to Dotty and the others. Soon they were exchanging histories and information and Dotty was filling her in on the gossip, especially as it pertained to the new section to which the Feinsteins had just moved.

"She'd be a perfect replacement," Frieda said, after they had talked for a while.

"A very attractive woman," Dotty said loudly enough for ingratiation. She could see Ida Feinstein beam.

"Yes, I quite agree," Frieda said, turning to Ida. "You'll love it here. You'll see how the place grows on you."

"It all depends on the friends you make. That's exactly what my son told me."

Frieda made sure she left before Heshy came down to the pool. She stood up and announced that she wouldn't be playing that night.

Dotty smirked. "Can you make it, Ida?"

"I'd love it."

"Your husband wouldn't mind?" Dotty asked.

"If he minds, he minds," Ida said, flaunting what seemed like independence in this circle of widows. She paused a moment. "Perhaps he can find someone to play shuffleboard with."

Frieda was too excited to eat, and she carefully checked her make-up bottles and vials and tubes to create what she imagined was the best face possible. Why lie to yourself? she asked, putting on one of her new outfits, a bright-yellow dress that the clerk said made her look youthful. That was the way they sold goods in Florida.

She deliberately set off early for the shuffleboard courts to avoid the eyes of Dotty and the yentas who did not burrow out of their condominiums until later and, most important, to be able to flag down Heshy Feinstein before he found a partner to play that detestable game with. Sometimes a little sacrifice doesn't hurt, she told herself, climbing into the gaily colored open-air shuttle bus and looking toward the bright sunset that turned the whole western sky molten red and gold.

Picking a vantage point near the shuffleboard courts, she watched the emerging groups of people seeking the evening's play. The lights seemed to brighten as the sun went down and soon she felt her own impatience and uncertainty. Suppose he had chosen not to come? Suppose Ida had not won her battle for independence? It was past the hour when they would have assembled in the card room and she was growing impatient when she finally saw him walk through the clubhouse exit toward the courts. Standing up, she moved toward the fence. She had taken the precaution of putting her name on the list and now noted that her court would be coming up shortly—providing that the honor system of vacating the court after an hour was adhered to, which did not always happen without the use of intimidation.

She felt him standing behind her, watching the games in progress. She wondered if being close to her, smelling her, had not jogged his memory. I am Frieda Goldberg, she screamed within herself, hoping he would hear. She dared not confront him openly with such a confession, fearing rejection. Another couple was standing next to her.

"I'm looking for a partner," she said so that he might hear.

"We're already a twosome," the man said.

"A gruesome twosome," the woman said, obviously wanting to ease what she considered the pain of the other's rejection.

"I'm in the market," Heshy Feinstein said. His voice was clear, strong, and came to her over the distance of half a century. She turned and looked at him, looked deep into his eyes, which she had recognized instantly. He, however, quickly glanced at his feet.

"Perfect," she said. "My court comes up in a few minutes."

"Say," he said, "aren't you the woman who was here last night?"

"Yes."

"My wife said she met you at the pool."

"Oh?" She feigned a slow recollection.

"Ida Feinstein."

"Ida," she said, noting that he was searching her face, "a lovely woman." She paused. "You've only just arrived?"

"Two weeks," he said. She detected a note of sadness.

"You miss your work," she said softly, a trifle breathless she imagined, wanting to offer him greater understanding than he had had in fifty years.

"It's not easy. I've been active as a teacher for all those years. It'll take some getting used to."

When their court was ready, they proceeded down the line and took their sticks from the rack.

"I'm really not good at this," she said. "You're much better."

"I've only played twice in my life."

"You're probably a natural athlete."

"Yes, people have said that."

She held the stick and moved forward with her disk, overshooting the board and crashing into the wall beyond.

"Too hard," he said.

The next disk barely made it to the point of the triangle.

"I think I need a little instruction," she said.

He was a teacher and immediately began a pedantic lesson in the relationship of the disk to the stick to the muscles of the arm. He gently took her bare arm and moved it in a pushing motion. She felt the goose pimples erupt, her arm grow limp.

"Stiffer," he said.

I can't stand this, she told herself. She managed to move the disk to the lowest score.

"Now watch me." Gracefully, in a slow motion, he moved the disk across the court, knocking her disk aside.

"You're fantastic," she said, noting his concentration.

After they played for three-quarters of an hour and she was growing bored with the game and frustrated at his lack of recognition, she turned to him. "Maybe I should rest for a moment," she said. "I am absolutely the lousiest player here."

He sat down beside her on the bench and pulled out a package of chewing gum.

"No thanks," she said, thinking of her bridge.

"I've done this for years. I've still got all my teeth."

"Did you enjoy being a teacher?"

"Yes, I did."

"You didn't want to be anything else but a teacher?" she asked.

"Not really." He paused. "My father wanted me to be a doctor." She felt her heart beat swiftly again, the memory and the pain washing back.

"You didn't want to be a doctor?"

"Not really."

The anger of fifty years came rushing back.

"It didn't cause you any trouble?"

"Trouble?" He turned and looked at her, as if for the first time, almost as if the inquiry had offended him. She imagined she could hear old doors squeak open and smell the musty odor of her father's cellar.

"I have a son that's a dentist," he said, still watching her, although his frame of reference seemed deflected.

"Did you put pressure on him to be a dentist?"

"Never," he said. He continued to look at her. She hoped that the floodlights weren't too revealing and that her make-up was clever. She felt her attraction to him, untrammeled by time, the old feelings of wonder and pleasure that she had when he was in her presence, close to her.

"Do we know each other?" He seemed confused.

"I don't know," she answered, feeling at last the tug on her line.

"You lived in Flatbush, my wife said?"

"Yes."

"You were never a teacher?"

"No. My husband was a cutter in the garment center."

"I went to City College. Did you go to college?"

"No."

"We didn't meet at Rockaway, someplace at the beach. Maybe at the PTA. I used to teach in Brooklyn."

"I never went."

"Where did you grow up?"

"Brooklyn."

"Where?"

"Crown Heights." She paused, watching his eyes for any sign. Then she said slowly, "And before that Brownsville."

"Brownsville. That's where I grew up. Imagine that. What a mess that place is today. I went back once and cried like a baby."

She felt him drifting again.

"I lived on Douglass Street."

"Douglass Street? I lived on Saratoga Avenue."

"The next block."

She could sense his agitation now. Thank God, she told herself. "What did you say your name was?"

"Smith," she teased, knowing she was teasing, enjoying it, feeling the pleasure in her body, in her soul, feeling her womanliness and the wonder of this flirtation.

"No. Your maiden name."

"Goldberg."

"My God! Frieda Goldberg."

"Bingo."

She saw his lips tremble and his eyes mist slightly and the remembered little tic at the base of his jawbone palpitate.

"Frieda." He had trouble swallowing.

She moved away from him on the bench, as if to study him.

"You're not the Heshy Feinstein?" She brought her palms together and pushed them under her chin. "Heshy Feinstein. I can't believe it. I just can't believe it."

"You can't?" He paused again, then grasped her hands in his. "How do you think I feel?"

"Frieda Goldberg." He repeated her name over and over again.

"It's Smith now," she said.

"It's been lots of years." He moved his head up and down, surveying her, watching her, his face flushed quite visibly beneath the redness of his recent sunburn. She sat still, watching him, looking into his eyes, letting him drink her in, wondering what he was seeing.

"It's a coincidence," Frieda said. A new group of players came to take their court and they got up from the bench and moved toward the exit.

"Let's take a walk," he said.

She seemed to be leading him. They walked along the path that skirted the clubhouse and snaked into the pool area. There were chairs there on which they could sit in the quiet darkness and watch the clubhouse lights play against the surface of the pool.

"I've been counting the years in my head," he had said after they walked for a few moments in silence. "I'll be seventy in December," he said. "I was seventeen."

"Fifty-two years," she said, moving close to him in the quiet night, hoping he would take her arm.

When they reached the chairs, he wiped off the moisture with his handkerchief. Other couples sat in the distance. She could hear their voices.

"I've thought about us many, many times," Heshy said, his voice suddenly hoarse. He cleared his throat.

"We were something," she said, patting his hand, then moving her fingers up his bare arm.

"It took a long time for that to go away," he said.

She wanted to say it never went away. She remembered Herman again, feeling sorry. Poor Herman!

"You've had a good life?"

"Fair," he said after a long pause. "And you?"

"The same."

"Tell me."

She shrugged. "As I said, I married a man named Herman Smith. He was a cutter in the garment center, made a decent living. We lived in two apartments. One in Crown Heights. One in Flatbush. Then he died of a heart attack. Quick. No pain. I have a daughter named Helen, who got married and moved to Chicago. Now I'm a widow and live in Sunset Village with the rest of the widows." She had said it all quickly, marveling as to how swiftly it all could be said, her life. Some life. Surely there was more to it, she told herself. Was she deliberately trying to draw out his sympathy? Of course she was.

"And you?" she asked. He had placed his hand on hers, which still rested on his bare arm.

"My father drove me crazy about that doctor business. But he died a year or two after you moved away, and I had to help my mother in the grocery store. Then I went to City College and took my teaching tests. I taught for more than forty years. My two children are doing fine. Ida you met. We've been married forty-two years. Now I'm retired."

They sat silently again, his hand kneading hers now, the pool water shimmering and the din from the clubhouse washing over the air like distant thunder.

"We were something," he said. He is recalling me, she thought, wondering if he was frightened. "We never could get enough of each other."

She wanted to tell him then and there what it had meant to her, how much of it she had protected and treasured, but she held off.

"We were very close," she said. Did it seem to him that they were talking about different people? she wondered.

"Unbelievable," he said. "It was never the same again."

She felt her joy now, the validation, the thing that was alive inside of her after all those years. He bent over to catch a ray of light on the face of his watch.

"I better pick up Ida now," he said, standing up, but not letting go of her hand.

They walked toward the clubhouse through a clump of young trees. He directed her off the path and looked around him quickly. Then he enveloped her in his arms, kissing her on the lips, his tongue darting in. She felt her body turn to jelly, lurch, and she caressed his back, running her hands down to his buttocks. He pressed close to her with his pelvis, then disengaged his mouth and whispered in her ear, "It's a dream."

She felt a tingle begin in her, somewhere deep, a tremor of pleasure, something she had not felt for decades.

She wondered if he was still alive there, still needed her, and she brought her hand down to his crotch, stroking gently. She felt the beginning of hardness and knew she was giving him pleasure, but he moved away swiftly. They heard footsteps coming on the cement path.

"Are you going to mention this to Ida?" she asked as they reached another dark spot on the path. This time they paused but did not touch.

"No," he said.

"Good."

They started to move toward the clubhouse, but she hesitated.

"I'm going home from here."

"Will I see you again?"

"Of course."

She was so agitated she could not sleep, tossing and turning in her bed. The restraints of more than fifty years had simply crumbled against the force of this mysterious attraction. She did allow herself the use of the word mystery, because it was something that defied all logic—at least from her experience.

In the morning, she was tempted to call her daughter, because she dared not confide in any of her friends, especially Dotty, who would have the information all over Sunset Village as if on a streamer carried by an airplane. She was uneasy, too, about their having been seen in public together. Did someone see them last night? It was not exactly the norm to see two people embracing in the shadow of the Sunset Village Clubhouse. What she felt unmistakably was something that Herman Smith, for all his kindness and faithfulness and decency, could not produce in her and for this inability had suffered a lifetime of deprivation and frustration.

When she got out of bed that morning, she took off her nightgown and viewed herself again in the full-length mirror, inspecting every fold of her aging body, wondering whether, when compared to that image in his mind of a sixteen-year-old, it would disgust him, turn him away from her. If I close my eyes, she reasoned, I feel sixteen. Perhaps he will close his. And I will close mine, she agreed, although she had noticed that men's bodies did not seem to shatter so terribly with age.

When the telephone rang, she knew it was him and answered quickly.

"Frieda?"

"Yes."

"Heshy."

"I know."

"You knew I would call?"

"I felt it."

"I didn't sleep all night. Ida got up twice to get me an Alka Seltzer. Frieda, I can't believe it. What I feel. What I felt last night."

"Yes," she said. She knew, of course, why he had called and pondered the question. They must be very careful. Surely, this one time, she told herself.

"You can come over. Walk in the back." She gave him her address.

"I can stay till two-thirty. Ida is at the pool."

"Yes," she said.

When he had hung up, she called Dotty.

"I don't know what's wrong. I feel terrible. I'm going to nap."

"Should I come over later?"

"No. I'll be fine. Just let me sleep."

"Your friend Ida Feinstein is terrific," Dotty said. "She fits in most beautifully with our group. Her husband sounds like a big schlepp."

"At least he's alive." It was an expected reference, a wisecrack. "That's something."

She put on a brassiere to take away the sag of her breasts and she searched her drawer for a fresh pair of pink panties, the older kind. She found a pair lying on the bottom of her lingerie drawer and drew it on. Then she slipped into a flowered dressing gown. She went into the kitchen, made a tuna-fish salad, enough for two, and set it out on the cocktail table in front of the couch. For a moment, she wondered if she should put out her half bottle of Manischewitz Concord, but remembering its cloying sweetness she rejected the idea.

The rattling on the screen door came sooner than she expected, and she was annoyed with herself for not having lifted the latch because someone might see him knocking on the door. Walking swiftly to the door, she let him in. He was wearing a flowered short-sleeved shirt, white cotton slacks, and white loafers. She led him through the apartment to the living room and they sat on the couch together.

"I can't think of anything else since I met you last night, Frieda. I've been going over in my head all the things we did together. What we meant to each other. I never thought I would see you again, never."

"Neither did I," she responded. She moved closer to him and he put a hand on her knee.

"You think we're a joke?" he asked suddenly. It had been troubling him, she saw, but the feeling between them was beyond his stopping it. It had always been beyond that.

"I was going to call my daughter this morning and tell her."

"She knows about us?"

"Not really. Once I mentioned it when Herman died. But if I called her up and said, 'Helen, I met an old boyfriend and he still excites me,' she would plotz right then and there."

"How could I even tell my children? Certainly not Ida. I've never been unfaithful to Ida. Not once. What about you?"

"Not only was I not unfaithful. I wasn't even faithful."

He threw his head back and laughed, rubbing his hand up and down her inner thigh.

"I made some tuna-fish salad," she said stupidly, feeling the blood surge in her veins, the joy tickling her groin.

"There is only one salad I want," he said.

She felt her breath coming in hot gasps as she moved her head back on his shoulder, knowing her mouth was open as she made gurgling sounds. She recovered herself somewhat to begin unzipping his pants.

"You haven't got a bad heart, have you, Heshy?"

He looked down at her confused, then smiled as he helped her remove his white slacks and undershorts.

"You want to go into the bedroom?" she asked, hoping he would say no, since they had never, ever been together in a bedroom.

He shook his head.

"I'm older now," he said, surveying his still not-up-to-par member, "I need more help than I used to." He seemed to be pleading. She stood up and unfastened her brassiere. She let his hands play with her nipples while she stroked his manhood, feeling the response come, the hardness begin.

"You're marvelous, Frieda," he said. "It's been a long, long time."

"Close your eyes," she said. He did as instructed and she removed her panties and dressing gown and lay under him, bringing his member into her body. She also kept her eyes closed. "I am sixteen," she said, moving under him, her fingers instructive, feathery. Poor Herman, she thought, not to have known this. The pleasure began at the roots of her hair and moved downward until she twitched inside. It was like warm honey rolling over her in wave upon wave. She shuddered and felt him shudder and when the feeling passed, she remembered how it had been and how they had worried about her becoming pregnant.

Soon after, they dressed and had lunch, then she watched him become drowsy.

"You want to take a nap?"

He nodded and she led him to the bedroom, where they hung their clothes on a chair like an old married couple and got in between the sheets. She set the alarm clock and cuddled close to him. In a moment, he was asleep, snoring softly.

Watching his eyes twitch and the little hairs in his nose, she softly lifted the covers and looked at his seventy-year-old body, soft and bulgy. His penis, however, looked as she had remembered it, although, below, the bags seemed older, more wrinkled. She crawled down and gently kissed the head of this instrument of her pleasure. He stirred for a moment, then continued to snore.

It had not mattered after all, she thought, her going away. He never did become a doctor and all his father's dreams went into the grave with him. She would not allow herself to imagine how it might have been if they had married and had children and spent the last fifty-two years together. That would be self-pity, something that she had warned her daughter to beware of. Never feel sorry for yourself. For a moment while she was on the couch, feeling her pleasure coming, her eyes tightly shut, she could imagine herself sixteen again, with all its possibilities. It was the one memory that never withered, had withstood time, been able to be recalled at will and now, by some miracle, relived.

The alarm crackled in the room. She clicked it off and the hum of the air-conditioning unit resumed. He opened his eyes, smiled, and burrowed his head between her large breasts.

"Heshy," she sighed. He put his lips on her nipples and sucked them.

"A nosh," he mumbled.

"Want a cookie?"

They laughed and she reached down and felt him again.

"Your age again, mister?"

"Seventeen."

"I thought so."

She bent down and sucked him erect, waiting patiently, feeling the pleasure of the process. Herman had begged her to do this and she had steadfastly refused, although she had done it many times with Heshy. Then, when he was ready, she put him into her sideways and they spent a long time together and she felt pleasure, different kinds, and rhythms, many times. Then he pulled away, satisfied.

"I can't believe this is happening," he said, sitting on the edge of the bed, putting on his white socks.

"You'll never leave Ida," Frieda said suddenly, without anger, gently, a statement of fact. She knew that from the beginning.

"How could I, after all these years?"

"But, Frieda, I swear to you. It has never been like us. Never like us. I can't remember the last time..." His voice trailed off.

"Don't be embarrassed," she said.

"I'll see you again?" he said, standing up and putting on his pants.

"Can we stay away?"

"Maybe once a week," he said.

"Of course." It would be impossible any other way. She remembered how furtive they had been, the smell of the cellar, the back porch, all of that repeated now. It was all part of it, she thought. When he was dressed, she straightened his shirt and kissed him on the cheek.

"Watch out for the yentas," she said, letting him out the back door, seeing his flowered shirt fade into the distance as he walked toward the clubhouse. He seemed to move away very fast, as if he were seventeen again....

Poor Herman, she thought, puffing up the pillows of the couch.

POKER WITH THE BOYS

 The game began in earnest a month after Hymie Cohen got married. He was still living in his father-in-law's house, on the corner of Strauss Street and Dumont in Brownsville. His father-in-law worked for Silverstein's Movers, and there was always a huge moving van parked in the oversized garage at the rear of the house. There was plenty of room in the garage for a table, so they could make noise and play cards in peace without disturbing the rest of the house.

There had been games there before Hymie was married, but not on a regular basis; the routine had not yet been established. Hymie's marriage settled that. He and Muriel had agreed that Hymie would be allowed a weekly "night with the boys", though the controls were rather rigid. The "boys" were made up of the crowd that used to "hang out" around Hoffman's Candy Store on the corner of Dumont and Blake. They had all gone through public school together, played on the same team in the Betsy Head Park baseball tournaments, and shared their most profound adolescent experiences, especially after the traditional Saturday night dates. After they took the girls home, they would gather at Hoffman's for a report about the evening's events.

"I got bare tit," Solly Lebow would say proudly, his sallow face beaming with the knowledge of his sexual prowess.

"Off Gladys?" Gladys' endowments were a neighborhood legend, and anyone who could penetrate that first line of defense must have had formidable powers.

"Wow."

109

Itzie Solowey, who was small, with a big nose and a pimply face, would merely snicker. He never could attract girls, so he took refuge in a pose of superior contempt.

"Big deal," he would say.

"If I don't get stinky pinkie," Mortie Krubitch would say, patting down his shiny curly hair, "I walk."

"And did you get it tonight?" one of them would ask.

"Smell." He would put out his middle finger and pass it around like an Indian peace pipe.

"Yuk."

"And you, Hymie, what did you get?" they would ask.

Hymie, by then, was in love, and beyond sharing his experiences. He had been going with Muriel since the eighth grade. Once, at the beginning, he had told them that he had gotten her pants off and had nearly put it in. But when he knew he was in love and that her body was sacred and private, he stopped talking about it. Besides, he had never put it in. In those days, you waited for marriage. Hymie was, of course, the first of the gang to marry. He was twenty-one and because his father-in-law was reasonably comfortable by the standard then, they had a big wedding in the Brooklyn Jewish Center on Eastern Parkway, complete with a fancy "hupa" and a sit-down dinner. All the boys from Hoffman's were ushers, looking stiff and self-conscious in their rented monkey suits, as they called them.

After his marriage, Hymie spent some time with the boys in front of Hoffman's, but it was different. He was one of them, he knew, but he sensed a gulf between them.

He missed being with them, sharing the guys' talk. Life had changed.

Perhaps that was why he started the game in the first place, just to be with them. The stakes weren't that high, five and ten, dealer's choice, but he looked forward to the weekly games with great anticipation. He especially enjoyed the time over coffee and donuts—provided by Muriel—after the game, which gave them a chance to gab and catch up with what was happening to each of them.

Solly Lebow was the second of the boys to marry; again, they all trooped down to the tux-for-hire shop and stuffed themselves into starched shirts for the ushering ordeal, which netted them the usual re-ward of gold-plated cuff links.

"Now that Solly's married" Muriel said one night after the game, "can't they have it in his house sometimes?" Actually, Hymie knew that, in her heart of hearts, Muriel didn't approve of the game, nor any activity in which she did not share. The idea of separating her from the game made her bitchy at times, but he ignored it.

"How much did you lose?" she would ask when he crept into bed be-side her after the game. One time, he actually told her, and she kept him up all night with threats and recriminations. He eventually learned to tell her that he'd won a few bucks—even when he lost. Actually, he wasn't a good poker player and lost most of the time. Benny Bernstein, with his steel mind for figures and his cool rubber-lipped face, was always a win-ner. When Benny played out a full hand, he usually had the cards. But sometimes he would bluff. Occasionally, someone would reach over and grab Benny's cards before he could slip them back into the deck, which never failed to cause an eruption.

"He bluffed. The son-of-a-bitch bluffed."

"Eat your hearts out," Benny would say, sweeping the table of its chips.

After Mortie Krubitch and Blintzie Goldberg got married, they started holding the game in other houses. It had somehow evolved to Tuesday nights and it fell to Hymie to keep track of where the game would be.

"Where's the game next week?"

"Mortie's place. And the week after, at Blintzie's."

It was only after Benny Bernstein got married that the logistics of the game grew complicated, at least once every five weeks. Benny married Sheila Schwartz, whose father was a furrier and, therefore, a cut above them all economically. His in-laws insisted that Benny and Sheila move into a fancier apartment house in Crown Heights. Benny was, by then, manager of a stationery store in Manhattan and, with his poker win-nings and his excellent ability to manage money, was able to afford a better apartment.

"You couldn't move around the corner from here," Solly Lebow ad-monished. "Now we gotta take a subway."

"Look," Benny said. "I'm the one that has to take the subway most of the time. Once every five weeks won't kill you. It's only four stops, anyway. No big deal."

"Maybe we could keep playing in this neighborhood." Blintzie Goldberg said, his glasses sliding over a greasy nose. It was one of those natural afflictions from which there was no escape, and he had developed the annoying habit of constantly pushing the frames back to the bridge of his nose.

"That means somebody has to go twice," Benny said.

"Well, we never have it at Itzie's place," Mortie Krubitch pointed out. Itzie lowered his eyes in shame. He was single and still lived with his parents above their grocery store. There was hardly room for them to eat their meals in their kitchen.

"Itzie does his share. He brings us cakes."

"Stale cakes," Mortie added caustically.

"They're fresh," Itzie rejoined.

"Maybe I should drop out of the game," Benny suggested.

"And me," Itzie agreed, his tiny face flushed with anger.

"Maybe you both should," Blintzie pointed out.

"Come on guys, deal," Hymie said, and the crisis was over as the cards rained quietly onto the table.

There were times when the game was called off. A relative had died. It was a Jewish holiday. Two of the boys were sick at the same time. But beyond such acts of God, the game endured.

Even Blintzie's cheating could not shake its routine.

"He goes light, then pushes his light chips into the pot." It was Itzie Solowey who spotted it first.

"I can't believe it," Hymie said.

"Watch it next time. I'll kick you under the table."

But Hymie spotted the action before he felt Itzie's kick. Blintzie would let his chips evaporate without replenishment during a heavy bidding sequence. He would move a number of chips out of the pot to keep track of his lights. When he lost, he would merely push the chips back into the pot without making up for what he had borrowed.

"What should we do?" Itzie asked Hymie. "Tell him he's a cheat?"

"No. Let me think about it."

Throughout the week, Hymie considered the dilemma restlessly. Blintzie's actions were a major threat to the game.

"How could he?" he asked himself. "It's supposed to be a friendly game."

By this time, the weekly games had been going on about five years. Hymie and Muriel had two children, and others were beginning their families as well. Their lives were changing.

Through various recessions, money was tight, but they kept the game going by lowering the stakes. No more than ten-cent raises, three time maximum.

But the matter of Blintzie's cheating was not settled easily. It preyed on Hymie's mind for months, and he would watch with sadness every time Blintzie did it.

"Sometimes, I actually hope he wins the pot," Hymie told Itzie.

"Yeah, it takes all the fun out of the game."

"I can't believe it, even when I see it."

"Should we throw him out of the game?"

It was the inevitable question. Finally, it reached a point of no return. Blintzie lost badly one night and repeatedly went light. He got into such a rotten mood that he left early.

"What are we going to do with him?" Benny asked when Blintzie had gone.

"You saw it too?" Hymie asked.

"You think I'm blind?"

"I thought I was the only one," Solly said. "He doesn't even try to hide it anymore."

"So what should we do?" Itzie asked.

"We could throw him out of the game," Benny suggested.

"How can we do that?"

"Easy. We tell him he's a damned cheat. How can he have the conscience to cheat his friends?"

"I don't know," Hymie said. He looked around the table at the faces of his friends, knowing that, despite their brave talk, they were as confused as he.

"We could ignore it," Hymie said.

"We've ignored it for five years," Benny reminded them.

"I think we have to make allowances," Hymie said finally, looking at Benny. "We make allowances elsewhere." Benny lowered his eyes and his face flushed.

"Let's compromise," Solly said. "Each night, one of us plays watchdog. He watches the pot, calls the lights to Blintzie's attention. Not nasty. Just a friendly reminder."

"Sounds OK to me," Itzie said.

The idea seemed to work, and the threat to the game passed as Blintzie got the message.

"Maybe he didn't even know he was doing it," Itzie said.

"Maybe," Hymie agreed.

Blintzie certainly didn't serve up the only challenge to the game over the years. Mortie Krubitch nearly dropped out. It was at the height of one of the recessions and Mortie was barely able to provide for his family.

"My wife won't let me come any more," he told them one Tuesday night. "She's scared, and I don't blame her." By a strange coincidence, though, Mortie won big that night—the start of a hot streak that lasted for weeks, in fact. He never did drop out. Then Itzie Solowey nearly got drafted, but was saved by flat feet, a punctured eardrum, and a double hernia.

"No wonder you never got married, Itzie," Hymie cajoled. "You're a broken-down mess."

The once-pleasant neighborhood of Brownsville began to deteriorate, and some of the boys started to talk about moving away. In fact, Solly Lebow moved about an hour's drive away, but they all had cars by then, so it was workable.

"I think you're crazy," Muriel protested when Hymie came in at two in the morning after a game at Solly's house. "You won't be fit for nothing tomorrow."

And Muriel wasn't the only wife who protested. Things got worse when Benny Bernstein moved to Forest Hills.

"My wife is killing me," Hymie told them. "She really gets pissed off when I come in late."

"Mine too," Blintzie echoed.

"I got a bad time last week," Mortie admitted. "But I told her to mind her own damned business. I'll be damned if I'll give up our game."

"It doesn't bother me," Itzie snickered.

"Shut up and deal," Hymie shot back.

But the constant pressure from the wives escalated, and it was only after Solly Lebow came up with an idea that included the women that the pressure abated. The guys would cut the pot—which had graduated to a quarter and fifty cents with no raise limits—and use the proceeds for a weekend at the Concord. Now the women had a stake in the game, too.

It took eighteen months for them to accumulate enough money for the trip. And, in the end, it proved to be the most dangerous threat the game ever witnessed.

"This room stinks," Muriel said, after they checked in on Friday afternoon.

She sat on the bed to test the mattress, then stooped to look out of the window. The room was under a dormer of one of the older buildings. "And the view is crummy."

"It's only for two nights," Hymie said.

"It stinks," Muriel said again, her voice shrill with anger.

Hymie was embarrassed, because the bellhop was still in the room as Muriel complained.

"I'll bet we got the worst building," Muriel squeaked, turning to the bellhop. "Is this the worst building?"

"No," the bellhop said hesitantly, shifting his weight from one foot to the other. "It's a little older..." he began.

"See," Muriel cried. "I'll bet the Bernsteins got a newer room."

"We're all paying the same."

"Molly Bernstein always gets extras. *Always.*" She sat down on the bed and folded her arms. "I will not live in this room," she announced flatly, her jaw set.

"They were pretty well booked..." the bellhop began.

"Then I'll go home."

"Two lousy nights. Come on, Muriel. Be reasonable."

"If Molly Bernstein can get a better room, then I can."

Finally, Hymie went back to the desk in the main building. He was steaming when he arrived, determined to vent his anger on the desk clerk.

Benny Bernstein and Solly Lebow were there before him.

"You, too?" he asked.

"Molly is driving me crazy."

"Whose idea was this?" Solly said.

After hours of cajoling, they managed to get their rooms changed. But Muriel still was not satisfied.

"If I find that Molly Bernstein got a better room, don't expect any lovey-dovey. Not from this Jewish lady."

"I hope she has the fanciest suite in the joint."

But the rooms weren't the only problem. There was also the matter of the women's clothes.

"The fancy lady has to wear a mink stole to breakfast," Muriel pointed out as they walked back to their room.

"Who?"

"Francie Goldberg."

"So?"

"You know why? She wants to show that Blintzie is a better provider."

"Maybe she was chilly," Hymie suggested. Of course, he could never afford to buy his wife a mink stole.

"And did you see those dirty looks that Gussie Lebow gave us all? She's very hoity-toity now that she's started taking adult courses at NYU. We're not smart enough for her."

In the afternoon, the men gathered to play poker in the card room while the women tried to amuse themselves in various ways.

"This wasn't such a hot idea after all," Hymie said. "My wife is driving me nuts."

"You're not alone," Mortie chimed in. "You'd think we'd taken them to be tortured."

"I like it here," Itzie said. "I got laid last night."

"Well, that makes one of us," Hymie said.

"Deal," Benny commanded.

They never again cut the pot to provide special benefits to the wives. But the game continued.

The world changed. They grew older. They watched their children marry, celebrated their grandchildren with brisses, bar mitzvahs, and the like. And they attended the funerals of their parents. Still, the game endured. It endured Solly Lebow's first heart attack, Benny Bernstein's kidney-stone operation, Itzie Solowey's late marriage. There was a sense of pride in the longevity of the game. On its fortieth anniversary, the game was celebrated in Hymie Cohen's apartment in Flatbush. Muriel baked an anniversary cake and insisted on putting forty candles on it. They blew out the flames together.

"I can't believe it," Hymie exclaimed, looking around the table at the men he had known as boys. "Where did it all go?"

"A hundred thousand pots," Benny answered.

"Always the human calculator" Solly rejoined.

"I figure you won more than $10,000 Benny," Itzie said.

"A pleasure taking your money."

"Most of it was mine," Blintzie pointed out.

"Yours, especially," Benny said, winking to the others around the table.

Solly's second heart attack brought home the reality that the game couldn't last forever. Solly was welcomed back six weeks after his attack. He was sad and depressed. But they had missed him. When anyone was absent, the rhythm of the game changed. It was like moving a piece of furniture from an old, familiar setting.

"The doctor says I have to go to Florida, that I gotta retire." Solly announced on the night he returned to the game. There were tears in his eyes.

"That's not the end of the world," Hymie said.

"I'm gonna miss the game." Solly sniffed, as the tears filled his eyes and slid down his cheeks. Hymie felt a lump grow in his throat. He knew the others felt the same way.

The Lebows bought a condominium in Sunset Village, and the game was never quite the same.

"Now I'm getting Solly's shitty cards," Itzie said on the first Tuesday after Solly left. They all knew, of course, that he was merely offering a humorous cover for the pervading sense of loss.

"I don't see how," Blintzie said. "I'm still getting the same lousy hands."

"It's just not the same," Hymie told his wife that night. "Maybe we're getting too old. Maybe we should stop the game."

"How can you stop the game?" Muriel asked.

"Everything comes to an end," he answered, feeling depressed.

"Florida isn't such a bad idea," Muriel said. He had been thinking the same thing. The city was changing. The cold seemed more intense. Nothing was the same, and the stories of warmer days, cleaner air and safer streets were having an influence on them and their friends. Every day, they would hear about more of their acquaintances moving to Florida.

Then Mortie announced that he, too, was headed for Sunset Village.

"Gussie was mugged," he said sadly. "They took her pocketbook and she got a black eye. The kids want us to get out of Brooklyn, so they're buying us a condominium at Sunset Village."

"There goes the game," Itzie said.

"I'm sure you could get a fill-in hand."

"It won't be the same."

"It hasn't been the same since Solly left."

They tried bringing in other players, but something was missing, the ambiance gone. There was bickering.

One of the new players accused Blintzie of cheating.

"I saw him," the man said. "He went light, and he never put his money in."

"You're crazy," Hymie countered, the other joining in Blintzie's defense.

"I saw him. Don't tell me what I saw."

"Look," Blintzie said. "Maybe it was an accident. I could have forgot. I'll pay to keep the peace."

"The hell you will," Hymie said. "Who is he to accuse any of us?" he said, turning to the man. "You have your damned nerve." The man cashed in his chips and left quickly.

"We need him like a hole in the head," Itzie said when he had gone.

Still, the game endured. Perhaps it was simply inertia, Hymie suspected, because he no longer looked forward to the game, but kept playing.

"You look terrible," Muriel said to him one Wednesday morning.

"I'm just a little tired." He had come in later than usual after driving over the beltway from Flatbush to Forest Hills to play at Benny Bernstein's house.

"I think the Goldbergs are getting ready to go to Florida," Muriel said. "Blintzie?"

"Their kids live in Palm Beach now."

"He hadn't mentioned it."

"I know." Muriel said. "I spoke to Francie. Blintzie is afraid to tell you."

"It'll mean the end of the game."

"That's why he's afraid to tell you. You couldn't really play three-handed poker." They would have to bring in more strangers.

"Maybe we should go, too," Muriel sighed.

It was time, but Hymie had been afraid to broach the subject with the boys. Maybe we're getting old, he thought. Benny's hands shook now, and Itzie was growing deaf. Blintzie was going to the bathroom more frequently, sometimes in the middle of a suspenseful game.

"We're a bunch of alta cockers," Hymie told Muriel, emphasizing that perhaps it was time to head to Florida. Hymie was eligible for social security. They had saved a few dollars. Others were managing. Besides, if Blintzie was going, the game was over anyway. What would life be without it?

The week before the Cohens and the Goldbergs left for Florida, the foursome had a farewell game. None of them could concentrate though, even Benny, who for forty-two years had quietly kept his mind on every card, every nuance. He could read them all like an open book. After an hour, they gave up.

"What the hell am I going to do next Tuesday night?" Itzie said, his voice pitched higher, masking his emotion.

"You'll find some other fish," Hymie said.

"It took me more than forty years to psyche you guys out. I'm too old to start another con game."

"You think that's it?" Benny asked. His hands shook as he fingered the passive deck.

"What?"

"That it's because we're too old."

"Everything in life comes to an end, that's all there is to it. Even the game."

"I never thought the game would end," Itzie said. "God, I really never thought it would end." His eyes misted.

"I wish to hell I could persuade my wife to go to Florida," Benny said suddenly. "She won't leave the kids."

"And Sunset Village isn't ritzy enough," Hymie said.

"That, too," Benny admitted.

"I hate Florida," Itzie said. "I can't stand the sun." He paused, sniffling, his eyes lowered. "Bet Solly and Mortie will be happy to see you guys. Hell, you'll start another game down there."

"Ah, they probably have their own game already," Blintzie said.

The Cohens and Goldbergs arrived at Sunset Village on Saturday and spent the entire weekend fixing up their condominiums, with the Krubitches and the Lebows dividing their time in helping the new couples get settled.

"Some place, eh?" Solly said. "It's like they moved Brooklyn in a mass migration."

"You didn't miss it?" Hymie asked. They were sitting on Hymie's back porch sipping soft drinks.

"I missed the game," Mortie said. "I missed giving my money to Benny every Tuesday."

"You don't have a regular game?" Blintzie asked.

"Not really," Solly said, looking at Mortie.

"What he means is that we play, but its not a regular game. Not like the Tuesday game."

"Well, the game wasn't the same after you guys left." Hymie said. "We got fill-ins but it wasn't the same. And last week we played four handed.... It just wasn't the same."

"Nothing's the same" Mortie said, a shadow crossing his face. "They have this big card room, bigger than a football field. But I don't like to play there. Too noisy. Too crowded. Not like our Tuesday game."

"Today's Tuesday," Solly said.

"Funny, I lost track of time," Hymie said.

"If it wasn't for CNN, I wouldn't know what day it was." Mortie said.

"So, what are we waiting for?" Hymie asked. Out came the cards and chips and up went the bridge table.

"Deal," Hymie said, listening to the shuffle of the cards and enjoying the familiar movements as Solly's fingers worked the deck.

"There they go," Muriel said to the other wives, sitting in the living room.

"It must be Tuesday," Francie Goldberg said.

It wasn't until Benny Bernstein had a stroke that they finally added a fifth player. Somehow he had persuaded his wife to move to Florida and, luckily, the builder added a few medium-rise elevator buildings, fancier than the barrack-like apartments the others lived in. The stroke affected only his legs, and he walked slowly, with an odd halting gait. His hands still shook, but his card sense was remarkably intact.

"Well, there goes extra cash," Hymie said, as Benny scooped up the first pot.

"The shark has come home."

"God, I missed you guys," Benny said. "It was hell. And you know what I believe?" He paused and looked at each of them, in turn. "I would never have had that stroke if we had continued the game."

"You trying to make us feel guilty, schmuck?" Solly said.

"I don't care what you say. I believe it."

"Poor Itzie," Blintzie said suddenly.

"He'll be here," Benny said. "Give him time."

"But he hates Florida."

"He'll be here."

"Look at him," Hymie laughed. "We leave him alone for a few months and he becomes a fortune teller."

Itzie and his wife arrived in Sunset Village the following winter. Itzie sported a hearing aid now.

"I still hate Florida," he announced, as he sat down to play on the first Tuesday after his arrival. "The sun is about the most disgusting sight I ever saw."

"Who needed you?" Hymie said.

"You needed me," Itzie said. "The game is always better with six."

"The perfect number," Benny Bernstein said, arranging his cards and contemplating his hand.

"He's still winning?"

"Why not? We supported him for forty-five years."

"Forty-seven," Mortie corrected.

And so the game continued. They didn't play in the card room, but instead rotated between apartments. The game seemed to have come full circle.

"You should have seen Brownsville," Itzie told the others one evening. "I went back just before I came down here. I just drove through it with the windows and doors locked. It's all gone. Hoffman's is boarded up and old-man Silverstein's garage is caved in. It's all gone, finished."

"I don't ever want to go back," Hymie said.

"I cried like a baby," Itzie continued.

They noticed Blintzie Goldberg's eyes failing when he mistook the Jack of Clubs for the Queen of Spades insisting, at first, that he was right.

"You should have your eyes examined," Hymie said. He hadn't meant it to be sarcastic or sinister, but Blintzie flushed a deep crimson, protesting that there was nothing wrong with his eyes. The doctors thought otherwise. Blintzie was going blind. He had always had diabetes, but his insulin shots were becoming less effective and, as his sight got worse, they had to help him identify the cards quite often.

"It breaks my heart," Hymie told Muriel one night after he returned from the game. "Itzie can barely hear. Benny's hands shake so much he has all he can do to hold his cards, and Mortie keeps popping little white pills for his heart."

Hymie sighed and tried to go to sleep.

"But the worst is Blintzie," he continued. "One of us has to drop out of every hand to help him play his cards. We whisper his hand to him and he whispers back on how to play. He's absolutely the worst player, even when his eyes worked."

One morning, Blintzie's wife came to Hymie's and Muriel's apartment. She had been crying, and her gnarled arthritic fingers clutched a moist handkerchief.

"He can't see anymore," she said.

"That bad?"

"The worse part is that he thinks he's a burden." She dissolved into tears, her shoulders shaking. "Now he wants to quit the game."

"Quit the game?"

"He told me," she said. "Somebody has to tell him what cards he has."

"I'm not sure he knew when he could see," Hymie said, hoping the humor might soothe her. She smiled thinly, accepting the warmth of it.

"I'm afraid if he quits, he'll just give up," Francie said.

Hymie patted her arm.

"It's no trouble for us," Hymie said. "None at all."

Not a word of protest had been raised by any of them. Somehow the game got played, though Blintzie's decisions were always bad ones and none of them would dare interfere. It wouldn't, after all, be fair.

One Tuesday, near the end of the game, Blintzie suddenly groaned and his sightless eyes watered.

"There's something I got to say," he said. They had expected it, but not this quickly.

"I've cheated." Blintzie said, his fingers clutching the edge of the table. The men looked at each other. Hymie put a finger over his lips.

"I've been doing it for years," Blintzie said. "And now my conscience is beginning to bother me. You guys have been so damned good to me, so patient. I can't see a goddamned thing, and I know I'm ruining the game."

"The last part is bullshit," Hymie said.

"You've always been a blind poker player," Benny said.

"Well, you guys have been the blind ones," Blintzie protested. "It's begun to bother me and I want you to know that I didn't do it deliberately."

"The least you could do is tell us how you did it?" Itzie asked.

"That, I'll never tell." Blintzie said. The confession seemed to have eased his burden.

"All I can say," Benny said with a wink, "is that whatever you did, it couldn't have been so bad. You lost anyway. Now, if I cheated, that would be something else."

"I just wanted you to know," Blintzie said.

"Somebody deal, please," Mortie cried impatiently. "You guys are getting like a bunch of old yentas."

Benny Bernstein's second stroke complicated the game even further. It affected his hands and his speech, and he had to be moved in a wheelchair. One of the men would pick him up at his apartment and wheel him to the game while another would act as a seeing-eye dog for Blintzie.

The person who stayed out for each hand now would not only have to whisper the hand to Blintzie but play the hand for Benny, following his whispered instructions. Unfortunately, Mortie's heart condition was too aggravated by Blintzie's playing to make him an effective assistant, and Itzie was too deaf to hear the proposed options.

This meant that only Solly and Hymie could be dealt out.

"Why don't you stop already?" Muriel asked one Tuesday when Hymie returned from the game.

"Stop the game?" He looked at her as if she was crazy.

Actually, except for the hardship of playing, there was no change in the rhythm of the game. Benny always won. Blintzie invariably lost, though Benny occasionally made an error on purpose to let Blintzie win a hand. But no one ever mentioned it, and the game continued.

One Tuesday while playing seven-card stud, Benny's head slumped over his chest, a gurgle came from his throat, and he expired quietly. It came at an odd time for Benny, as he had just asked that his final raise be made. Solly was acting for both him and Blintzie, and Hymie was in the game. It was a big pot, and Hymie had just called Benny's raise, convinced that his Kings over full house beat both Blintzie's possible straight flush, which seemed an obvious bluff, and Benny's possible Jacks over full house. Hymie was relishing the possibility of winning, on the heels of three weeks of losing.

"I think Benny's gone," Solly said searching for Benny's pulse on a vein in his neck.

They looked at the slumped figure in the wheelchair. Even Blintzie's sightless eyes turned toward him. They were playing in Hymie's kitchen, and the room was quiet except for the steady purr of the air conditioner. No one stirred and Hymie had the sensation that they were frozen in a kind of eternal tableaux, like the picture of them that had appeared in the Sunset Village newspaper over the caption "Fifty Year Poker Game: Longest ever."

"My God," Mortie exclaimed. He was the first to stir, reaching into a pocket for his pill box. "Benny dead?"

There were a pile of chips in the center of the table, and the three hands lay in front of the three players.

"We better call his wife," Itzie said.

"Not until we know," Blintzie said, his eyes roaming uselessly around the table. Hymie was silent, the shock of Benny's sudden death engulfing him.

"He'd want it that way," Blintzie said.

"We owe him that," Mortie agreed.

"I call," Blintzie cried.

"And me," Hymie said.

Solly slowly lifted Benny's cards.

"I'm sure Benny would have wanted it that way," Solly said. He knew, of course, what cards were in the hole.

"Four Jacks" he called, looking at Benny's immobile face, growing swiftly gray.

"He had all the luck," Blintzie said, feeling for his cards and turning them over.

"Lucky bastard," Hymie said, his voice cracking.

They put Benny's last pot in the open coffin in the funeral parlor, where it laid overnight before the funeral.

"Who knows?" Hymie said, "where he's going, he may need the chips." He wanted to laugh, but his reflexes wouldn't respond. Even Itzie, always quick with a wise crack, could only shake his head.

They skipped the game the following Tuesday, and the Tuesday after that. Then a month went by. None of the guys mentioned it.

"No more game?" Muriel asked one night.

Hymie hesitated. "I hate four-handed poker," he whispered, turning away to hide his tears.

THE ANGEL OF MERCY

They called her "the Angel of Mercy," and there was no mistaking the sarcasm. They observed her on her daily rounds, a bent-over snip of a woman, with piano legs that made one wonder how she was able to get around in the first place, matted gray hair over which she wore a yellow bandanna, and a faded old-fashioned black dress, a little shiny with use. She wore sensible but quite ugly laced shoes, a necklace, obviously a piece of Yemenite jewelry that someone might have brought her from Israel, and she always carried her pocketbook, a heavy brown thing, by the handle so that it hung down to her knees.

Not even her closest neighbor on the ground-floor row of condominiums had ever been inside of her place, seeing it only from the outside, as the woman opened or closed her door. She caught sight of a rather overstuffed but threadbare couch and an upholstered chair with stiff doilies pinned to its backrest and arms. While she never really got close enough, the neighbor had the impression—just the impression—that the place smelled a trifle unclean, musty and old. But this could have been the impression that the woman herself gave. It was hard to tell how she might have looked as a girl, or even a middle-aged woman, since old age had shaped and gnarled her so completely. The Florida sun had tanned her deeply lined face, which looked like a muddy-colored brier, and only the fact that she smeared a deep-red lipstick too generously on her cracked lips and put two circles of rouge on her cheeks provided evidence of a still-lingering feminine vanity.

It was unfortunate that she gave such an impression, for she hardly thought of herself as eccentric, and the sick and infirm that she visited daily, sometimes five or six in a day, actually began to look forward to her visits. They, too, had formed bad first impressions and were always surprised when she first showed up, wondering, after seeing her ancient face, whether she was the harbinger of death. This, in itself, was neither strange nor morbid, because in a community like Sunset Village, death was an ever-present specter, actually a friend who seemed to be watching everyone from some balcony in the heavens, observing all the aged Jews and trying to decide who goes next.

Maybe it was something genetic, something buried in the Jewish psyche, the thing that gave the world so many Jewish comedians, but, at least here in Sunset Village, death was treated somewhat as a joke, a kind of embarrassment, like a cuckolded husband in a French farce. That was probably why a sick person, lying supine in his bed gasping for air, could actually smile when he saw this little bent-over woman appear and draw out of her huge pocketbook a cellophane-wrapped bag of candies tied with a tiny red ribbon.

"Well, it's all over now," a patient would say when she left. "The Angel of Mercy has arrived." But when she came again and the patient was still alive, she was treated with somewhat more respect and might even be offered tea and cakes, which she rarely refused.

"You feel better, Mr. Brodsky?" she would ask, parting her over-red lips in an odd grin.

"I feel wonderful, Mrs. Klugerman. I'm already in the undertaker's cash-flow projections." Mr. Brodsky had been an accountant, and the Angel of Mercy assumed that this might be a joke, so she smiled more broadly.

"Why should you make them rich?" she would say. Such a remark would provide the patient with a key to the Angel of Mercy's character and would, despite his first impression, cheer him.

Sometimes a healthy spouse, child or other relative would be annoyed at the woman's constant visits.

"She's a ghoul. I understand she spends her entire day visiting the sick."

"So what's wrong with that?" the patient would say.

"Ghoulish, that's all."

"She annoys you?"

"It's weird."

"If you're flat on your back, it's not so weird."

In a place like Sunset Village, with most of the population well over sixty and growing older, the sickbed activity was, if the term could be applied in connection with Yetta Klugerman, frenetic. There she would go, ploddingly along, using the little open-air shuttle bus to get around, visiting her wards. She never left the premises of Sunset Village. This meant that she could choose from three types of patients: the not-very-sick, the post-operative, and the terminal.

The odd thing about her visits was, from the patients' point of view, that she revealed very little about herself and her history. This was odd in Sunset Village, where everyone at that stage in life had a history. She was friendly, humorous, gentle, even loving, but when she left there was never any completed picture about her; it was as though she were an apparition.

A bedded yenta with little to do but sponge up gossip from her visitors could summon up a good head of outrage during a visit by Yetta Klugerman.

"You lived in New York?" the yenta would ask.

"Yes."

"Brooklyn?"

"No."

"The Bronx?"

"You're looking so much better, Mrs. Rabinowitz. The hip is healing?"

"I get occasionally a gnawing pain, but the doctor said it is to be expected." There would be a pause as the patient surveyed Yetta Klugerman's kindly face.

"In Manhattan?"

"Actually, we lived all over," Yetta would say and smile benignly.

They would sit for a few moments, contemplating each other, the uneven red lips poised in a half-smile.

"Your husband died?"

"I'm sure you'll be up and around in a few days, Mrs. Rabinowitz. You'll see how easy it is to use the walker."

"I'll be a walking wounded, like an old lady, ready for the home."

"You'd be surprised how many people have had your problem. They use the walker for a few weeks, then all of a sudden, they're recovered. Believe me, it's not so bad. You should see some of the cases I've visited."

The yenta would be torn between trying to discover more intimate details about Mrs. Klugerman and learning about her visitations. In the end, the stories of the other sick people won out. Nothing seemed more compelling to a bedridden patient than the ailments and mental attitude of people in the same boat.

"Mr. Schwartz lost a leg from diabetes," Mrs. Klugerman would say.

"Oh my God."

"His attitude is getting better. They'll give him an artificial leg and a cane and he'll be able to get around. Look, it's better than Mrs. Silverman."

"She has cancer?" The patient's face would tighten, revealing the impending fear of the answer.

Mrs. Klugerman would nod her head. "She has a very marvelous attitude. She said she had a full life, a lot of children and grandchildren, and her husband is alive to take care of her."

"She has pain?"

"They give her something for it. Really, it's not so bad."

"You must see a lot of people who are dying, Mrs. Klugerman."

"One way or another, we're all going to go in the same direction."

"Better tomorrow than today."

"You'll be dancing, Mrs. Rabinowitz. You'll see. I give you less than a month."

"You think I can do a cha-cha-cha with a pin in my hip?"

"You should see them."

"Next week, I'll go on the dance floor with my walker."

Because the people who got sick were older, the recovery period or the lingering with some terminal disease was longer, and Mrs. Klugerman sometimes would stretch her visits over many months. She became something of a legend. Most of the time, she learned about a sick person from the patients she visited. Other times, people would simply call her to provide her with the information and request a visit. It was one of the inevitable consequences of living in Sunset Village that if you were sick, sooner or later you would get a visit from Mrs. Klugerman.

It became somewhat of a local joke around the card tables, or the pool. Someone would complain of an ache or a pain.

"Better watch out. You'll soon be ready for the Angel of Mercy."

"Who?"

"Mrs. Klugerman."

"God forbid."

But if Mrs. Klugerman knew about these jokes, she said nothing. The initial visit always created somewhat of a stir. First, there was a shock of seeing the little bent woman at the door clutching her huge pocketbook and drawing out a little cellophane bag of candies. A son or a daughter or a sister or brother, usually someone who had flown down to act as nurse, would scurry back to the sickbed.

"You know a Mrs. Klugerman?"

"Yetta Klugerman?"

"I didn't ask her first name."

"A little old lady with piano legs?"

"The same."

"She has candy?"

"That's her."

"She's the Angel of Mercy."

"The what?"

"It's a local joke."

In the end, they let her come in, as they knew she would be persistent in her efforts. Some tried to bar her way, but her tenacity usually won out. Besides, there was a suspicion, particularly in the minds of those who had been sick, that somehow she had something to do with their recovery. Naturally, the people who had died might have had a different story.

"Laugh all you want," a former patient might tell a skeptic. "She was there maybe four, five times a week. More than my so-called friends." At this point, the patient—male or female—might glare at his or her companion, who might melt with guilt. "And I'm here to tell about it."

"You might have been here just the same."

"That's the one thing I can't be sure about."

So Yetta Klugerman became welcome wherever there was a sick person. It was well known, too, that she never went to funerals, which gave some added encouragement to those patients sufficiently uncertain about their prospects. Max Shinsky was a case in point.

He returned from the Poinsettia Beach Memorial Hospital, after his third heart attack, convinced that his faulty ticker could hardly withstand even the slightest activity. He would lie in his bed in the bedroom of his condominium, depressed and frightened that each move would be his last. Mrs. Shinsky was a woman of great courage and energy, whose loquaciousness was a legend in itself. Compulsively, every day, when she was not attending to Max, she would sit next to the telephone and call a long list of friends to whom she would outline even the most minute details of Max's illness. There seemed to be an element of salesmanship about these calls, as if she was trying to sell her friends on the proposition that her troubles far exceeded those of anyone else.

"You think you got troubles, Sadie," she would say when the innocent at the other end of the phone tried to make a cause for her own misfortunes. "I've got troubles," Mrs. Shinsky said. "What you got is aches and pains. I've got tsooris."

When Mrs. Klugerman arrived on the scene with her little cellophane candy bags, her presence was an added confirmation of Mrs. Shinsky's monumental misfortunes.

"I've got Mrs. Klugerman visiting my Max—daily," she told her friends on the phone.

"That's trouble," her friends would agree. "On a daily basis? That's trouble."

Mrs. Klugerman would arrive first thing in the morning, a sign in itself, because it had come to be assumed that the first visitation of the day was reserved for the patient who was least likely to make it to sundown, a fact that did not improve Max Shinsky's spirits.

"You had a good night, Mr. Shinsky?" Mrs. Klugerman would say, her heavily rouged mouth ludicrous in the bright morning sunlight that streamed into the room.

"Lousy," Max would say, his hands crossed and clasped over his stomach.

"That's to be expected, Mr. Shinsky," Mrs. Klugerman would reply. "It gets worse before it gets better."

"From your mouth to God's ears."

"I know what I'm talking about."

When she left, Max would shift in his bed and Mrs. Shinsky would bring him a cup of tea.

"She has to come so early?" he would ask.

"Look, I could tell her not to come," Mrs. Shinsky would reply.

"Do I have to be the first one? When she walks in the room, I begin to hear the angels singing."

"For you, it wouldn't be angels, Max," Mrs. Shinsky would say, trying to cheer him up.

He would look up at the ceiling and raise his hand. "You gave me her for fifty years. You were so good to me."

"You're making a big deal about Mrs. Klugerman," Mrs. Shinsky would say, straightening the bed. "At least she visits."

One day, Mrs. Klugerman did not arrive first thing in the morning. Max looked at the clock; it was past eleven and the sun was high in the sky, throwing different shadows in the room. Despite himself, he felt the beginnings of his own anxiety.

"How come Mrs. Klugerman didn't come?" he finally said, when the clock read noon.

"I can't understand it."

"You think she's sick herself?"

"Mrs. Klugerman? How can the Angel of Mercy be sick?"

"I'm worried about her."

"Worry about yourself."

Finally, just after noon, Mrs. Klugerman arrived. She moved slowly into the bedroom and sat down by the bed. Max Shinsky felt relieved.

"I'm surprised you didn't come earlier," he said, searching her wrinkled face, the features composed under the smudged and hopeless make-up.

"First I went to Mr. Haber, then Mrs. Klopman, then Mr. Katz. They all just came home from the hospital."

He was tempted to ask about their condition, but a sense of fear tightened his throat.

"You look better," Mrs. Klugerman said suddenly.

"Then I wish I felt like I looked."

"He's a real kvetch," Mrs. Shinsky volunteered.

"When people tell me I look better, it's time to worry," he said.

She stood for a while watching him, smiling thinly, benignly. He had never paid much attention to her before, except as an odd joke, something to be endured. Now she appeared differently, a puzzle. He wondered why she did this. Was she a little touched in the head, as everyone seemed to imply?

"You must be very busy, Mrs. Klugerman," he said suddenly, looking about him. "In this place ... all of us alta cockers." He knew he was leading up to something. He wanted to know why she did it. "I appreciate it," he said, wondering if that was what he really meant.

When she left, he discovered that his depression had dissipated.

"You think I should go outside and sit?" he asked his wife, who secretly marveled at his sudden change of attitude.

"Mrs. Klugerman made you better?" She felt a sudden elation within herself. Was such a thing possible? When she telephoned her friends that day, she felt the hollowness of her own insistence on the extent of her troubles. Could Max really be getting better?

The fact was that Max did, indeed, show signs of getting better and, despite his own lingering fears about his condition, he was able to take walks about the house and had begun to sit outside in the morning sun. Mrs. Klugerman's visits came toward evening now. He was no longer in bed, but instead was sitting in the living room when she arrived.

"I'm not coming tomorrow, Mr. Shinsky," Mrs. Klugerman said.

"You're not?" He felt his heart lurch, but there was no pain.

"You're not sick anymore, Mr. Shinsky." It seemed a confirmation of his new-found strength.

After a while, she got up and he walked her to the door, holding out his hand, which she grasped. He felt the parchment-like skin and the hand's strength that belied the little bent body and the piano legs. As he watched her, she seemed to walk directly into the blood-red sunset, a tiny figure disappearing.

She is more than what she says she is, he thought, wondering if it would seem childish to articulate his feelings, especially to his wife. But as he grew in physical strength, he pondered the riddle of Mrs. Klugerman. Occasionally on his daily walks, he would see her from a distance and would wave, but she did not seem to notice. Perhaps her eyes were failing, or had she forgotten who he was?

But the idea that she was somehow responsible for his recovery persisted in his mind and, although he resisted giving it expression, he could not subdue its power. He wanted to know more about Mrs. Klugerman and began to ask questions of others who had been sick and who had received her visits.

"She has no permanent friends?" he might ask, casually, hoping his curiosity would not seem blatant.

"Nobody knows."

"Has anyone ever seen her place, been inside?"

"I never heard of any."

"And you say you were very sick?"

"Like a dog."

"She came early in the morning?"

"At first. Then later and later."

"And the last time?"

"At the end of the day. Like I was being released from her custody."

"You felt that too?"

It was as if the idea of her strange power was floating through the soft tropical air, hovering near the surface of the minds of all those who had been sick and visited by Mrs. Klugerman. Not that the jokes did not continue—but only among those who had not been sick. The healthy ones actually laughed as they saw her plodding along on her daily rounds, clutching her pocketbook filled with cellophane bags full of candy.

"There goes the Angel of Mercy."

"Who?"

"Oh, the local ghoul."

But Max Shinsky continued to wonder and ask questions. Once he even rang Mrs. Klugerman's bell, but no one answered. The venetian blinds were drawn and he couldn't see inside her condominium, although he knew from the way it was situated that it was the smallest variety at

Sunset Village. Finally, he began to follow Mrs. Klugerman around, always at a distance, dallying about innocently while she made her daily visits, amazed at her energy. He was convinced, after a series of confrontations, that she had forgotten who he was.

"Where do you go on those walks, Max?" his wife would ask.

At first he had ignored her questioning, but one day he responded directly: "I'm following Mrs. Klugerman around."

"You keep doing that, you'll have her visiting you again." She lifted her arm and made a circular motion with her finger at her temple.

"I wouldn't dare repeat what I'm finding out to anyone but you." He felt the chill along his spine and goose pimples pop out on his flesh. "She's not just Mrs. Klugerman."

Mrs. Shinsky squinted into her husband's eyes, sighing, convinced that her troubles were multiplying again. Heart, I can understand, she thought. But the mind—God forbid.

"It sounds crazy, right?"

"Right."

"Then how come some of the terrible sick cases she visits, people that have given up, like me, suddenly recover?"

"Not everyone she visits recovers," Mrs. Shinsky said.

"That's right," he said. "It is as if she chooses who will live and who will die."

Mrs. Shinsky stood up, her lips trembling with anger and disbelief. "Now I got a nut on my hands!" she said.

"You're not going to say anything about this?" he asked, ignoring her outburst. She was a peppery woman, and he was prepared for her reaction.

"Believe me," she cried, "I'm not as crazy as my husband."

At that point, he decided to refrain from airing his suspicions. Especially now, when they were, at least in his own mind, confirmed beyond the shadow of a doubt.

Sometimes he would make discreet inquiries about patients Mrs. Klugerman had visited.

"She was so sick I thought she would never see the light of day."

"And now?" he would ask.

"It's a miracle."

Which was a word he had refused to voice, especially to himself. Whenever he saw or heard about a new sick patient that Mrs. Klugerman was visiting, he wondered: Will she choose to make that person live? Or die?

Finally, he could not keep following her on her daily rounds. Instead, he took to hanging around the court in which her condominium was located, sitting on a bench and watching her door, waiting for her return. Occasionally, he would engage a neighbor in conversation. They were all very pleasant, very polite, even talkative, but what he learned could be put into a thimble.

"You know Mrs. Klugerman?"

"I say hello."

"She has no friends?"

"I never see anybody come to her place."

"Children?"

"I don't know."

"How old?"

"Mister, in Sunset Village that's the one question you don't ask."

"When I was sick, she visited me."

"That's her business."

"A business?"

"I don't mean a business business."

He learned nothing, but nevertheless sat watching her door and the windows with the drawn blinds to which she rarely returned, except, surely, to sleep. But by then he was long gone.

One night, he awakened with a start and turned to his wife, who was a light sleeper and woke the minute he moved.

"How did she know I was sick?"

"Who?"

"Mrs. Klugerman."

"Mrs. Klugerman again?"

"Did you send for her?"

Mrs. Shinsky shrugged. "Why would I send for her?"

"Then how did she know?"

"How does she know anything?"

In the morning, he called the Poinsettia Beach Memorial Hospital, but no one on the staff had ever heard of her. If this was so, how then was she able to know the discharge date of each Sunset Village patient? He remembered that he himself had not known when he would go home until the morning of his discharge. And she arrived almost immediately upon his return.

He wanted to confide in his wife again, to reiterate his suspicions, but he dared not. It wasn't only fear of ridicule, he decided. She'd already rejected the idea of it. He imagined that he might hear her as she busily called her friends on the telephone, voice lowered, conspiratorial, as she was when she had something to impart about him and his illness.

"Max thinks Mrs. Klugerman is really an Angel from Heaven."

"You're kidding."

"He really believes it."

"Are you going to see a doctor?"

"I'm afraid if I mentioned it, he would have another heart attack."

As a result, he became more secretive, more inhibited about his confidences, more cunning in his subterfuges. At times, walking in the bright sunlight, breathing in the heavy tropical scents of the planted shrubbery, he mocked himself for his childish suspicions. It did not seem possible in this peaceful sunlit world, where everything was clearly defined. But at night, observing the mystery of the stars, a canopy for the universe, he felt the pull of other forces. The literal observations dissipated. There was more, much more, out there than met the eye and could be explained logically. Sometimes, sitting outside near the rear screened-in porch, looking up into the eternity of the twinkling sky, he felt a strange elation, as if someone had entrusted him with knowledge that he could not define or articulate. At these moments, too, he might argue with himself, or, more precisely, two parts of himself would debate the question.

I'm a reasonable man, one part would testify. A practical man. A shoe salesman, after all, must be particularly practical. As a boy, I went to shul. I was bar mitzvahed and, today, if I am not overly religious it doesn't mean that I don't think there is a God. I accept that—even if I don't indulge in heavy intellectual activities on the subject. I am not superstitious. I don't believe in ghosts. I don't get frightened at horror movies. And I am convinced that the supernatural is ridiculous. And yet—

How come I lived? How come Mrs. Klugerman knew when I got home from the hospital? How come she knew exactly when to stop coming first thing in the morning? How come nobody knows anything about her early life? How come I am thinking what I am thinking?

Sometimes his more practical side would win out, and he would go for days without giving Mrs. Klugerman much thought, spending his time by the pool or going to the clubhouse at night to watch the entertainment.

But the idea always hung over him like a morning mist, and when he heard of a death, read about it, or felt an occasional twinge in his chest, it reminded him of his own mortality, and he would believe absolutely in the miraculous force possessed by Mrs. Klugerman.

Sometimes, after a particularly disturbing night of doubt and debate with his more practical self, he would rise early and rush to find a vantage point near Mrs. Klugerman's condominium, and post himself there to await her exit. At precisely seven, he would see her open the door and leave—a tiny bent woman plodding along the neatly trimmed path while the dew still glistened on the tips of the grass. Her eyes were always slightly lowered, and if she saw him, she never acknowledged it.

As the months wore on and his less-practical self became more ascendant, his morning assignations increased until it became a kind of ritual in his life.

"Where do you go every morning?" his wife would ask.

"I love the mornings," he would respond. "Walking in them refreshes me."

His wife would shrug and turn her back to him as he sat on the bed putting on his shoes and socks.

It was only natural in a ritual so precise and rhythmical that the least disruption could become a major source of anxiety. It had, of course, become the moment he most dreaded—the moment when Mrs. Klugerman would prove to him her vulnerability, her mortality, evidence of which he feared as much as death itself.

When she did not leave her condominium precisely at seven one morning, he knew that the moment of truth had indeed arrived. He had, of course, shaken his watch to be sure of the time, reassuring himself by the position of the sun that the hour had come and gone. But even then he could think of many reasons for some delay, for even in his wildest musings he had invested the Angel of Mercy with human raiment. Whatever she was, she was still encased in a decrepit body, one in which the aging joints and muscles might interfere with the plans of the spirit, her spirit. He gave such a possibility the benefit of his growing doubt. As the morning wore on and the sun's heat became a hardship, he moved to the feeble shade of a palm tree. The morning progressed. People moved past him, eyeing him curiously as he leaned against the back of the bench concentrating on his vigil. As always, nothing stirred behind the drawn venetian blinds. And while he was tempted to ring her buzzer, he concluded that she might have left before he arrived. Perhaps an emergency case had intervened, he thought, leaving his post by the palm tree after being convinced of this assumption by his more practical self.

But when he arrived earlier the next morning, and still Mrs. Klugerman did not appear, he began to lose faith in that assumption. Finally, he gathered the courage to ring her buzzer. There was no response, nor could he see anything through the drawn blinds.

When he returned to his own condominium, he decided to enlist the aid of his wife, who, through her network of yentas, could be relied upon to ferret out all sorts of surreptitious information.

"I think Mrs. Klugerman is sick," he said casually, feeling the tension build in his chest and throat.

"That's funny," his wife replied.

"Funny?"

"Mrs. Zuckerman had a gall bladder and Mrs. Klugerman was paying her visits. Then two days ago she stopped coming."

"Stopped completely?"

"Mrs. Zuckerman decided that she was getting better."

"Was she?"

"Not really. I think the gall bladder was just a boobimeister. I think she's sicker than that."

"Something is definitely wrong with Mrs. Klugerman," he said aloud. He could feel the panic grip him, and a cold sweat begin to drip down his back and under his arms.

"You're pale as a ghost, Max," his wife said with some concern. "Do you feel OK?"

"I'm worried about Mrs. Klugerman."

Perhaps it was his paleness and the look of anxiety on his face, but Max Shinsky's wife swung into action on the telephone to investigate the disappearance of Yetta Klugerman.

"You're right, Max," she said later. "Nobody has seen her."

Later that day, he went back to Mrs. Klugerman's condominium and rang the buzzer for a long time. He also banged on the door, despite the fact that he could clearly hear the sound of the buzzer. Then he called out her name in ever-increasing crescendos.

"Mrs. Klugerman! Mrs. Klugerman!"

A door opened beside him. It was Mrs. Klugerman's neighbor, someone he had talked to earlier.

"I don't think she's home. I haven't heard a sound," she said.

"You think we should call the management?" he asked.

"Maybe she went away."

"Where?"

"To visit. How should I know?"

"All of a sudden?"

"I think maybe we should call the management," Max said and quickly walked to the end of the court and took the open-air shuttle to the management office. A woman with harlequin glasses on a chain and blue-gray hair smiled at him, showing slightly yellow teeth.

"You got a record of Mrs. Klugerman leaving?" he asked, giving her the name and address of the Angel of Mercy.

"You're the third person today that has asked," she said. "No, we haven't heard anything."

"Then I think you had better open her place."

"I'll have to talk to Mr. Katz."

"Of course," he said, wanting to add "and hurry," but he lacked the courage. He now was afraid of what he might find behind her closed door. He watched the woman with the blue-gray hair dial the phone and speak to someone on the other end.

"Yes, of course. I'll go myself." She nodded into the phone, then hung up.

"I knew he'd approve," she said.

"This happens often?" he asked, as he climbed beside her into the Sunset Village station wagon.

"When you have this many old people and lots of them living alone, you have to expect it." She seemed indifferent, looking at him through faded blue eyes, the harlequin glasses hanging over her thin chest.

"Found one last week," she said, gunning the motor and accelerating out of the parking lot. "Had been dead for three weeks. It was actually the odor that prompted our going in there." He felt his stomach turn. "Actually, it's a tremendous complication in terms of the estate. Sometimes we can't find the children or any heirs. It makes it rather difficult, considering the condominium fees." He sensed her feeling of superiority over him. Old shiksa, he thought contemptuously.

She parked the car in front of Mrs. Klugerman's condominium and searched in her pocketbook for a ring of keys. Then, perching her glasses on her nose, she observed the numbers on the keys, singled one out, knocked and waited, then inserted the key in the lock. Max felt his heart beating. Could he explain to anyone what he was feeling? The door opened and the woman flicked a switch, lighting up the interior.

The odor was heavy, but it was the familiar one of musty dampness. The bedroom was sparsely furnished, a narrow sagging bed with an embroidered foreign-looking bedspread. In the living room was an upholstered chair, with starched doilies pinned to the backrest and arms, and a little Formica table. There were no pictures on the walls, no books, no television set, no radio, no photographs. There was a battered unpainted chest, a few sparse articles of clothing, but no visible make-up tubes or vials, or medicines. In the closet, however, was a large cardboard box filled with little cellophane bags of candy. In the kitchen, the refrigerator was empty. There was no sign of food and the shelves of the cabinets contained only a few chipped dishes and cups.

"Well, that's a relief," the woman said, after he had inspected the premises. "She's probably gone on a trip. It's quite obvious that she's not living here now."

"Yes," he said, "that's quite obvious." But he dared not explore the thought further. He needed time, he told himself.

The woman went through the door before him and, as he moved the door back, he unlatched the lock in the doorknob. He closed the door after him and fiddled with it to illustrate that he was checking it.

"Make sure it's locked," the woman said as she got into her car.

"I'll walk," he said, waving her on, watching her drive to the main road. When she turned the corner, he opened the door of the condominium again and slipped into the darkened living room. He did not turn on the lights. Sitting down on the chair, he put his head back and let his eyes become accustomed to the darkness. He sat there for a long time, calm, not frightened.

"Mrs. Klugerman," he whispered, listening. "Mrs. Klugerman," he repeated, feeling the first faint bursts of elation. "I know you're here, Mrs. Klugerman." He sat there for a long time, until he could see through the thin strips of the closed blinds that darkness had come. Then he got up from the chair, walked to the door, and let himself out.

"Thank you, Mrs. Klugerman," he said as he closed the door. He was certain that she had heard his voice.

TELL ME THAT I'M YOUNG

 When Mr. and Mrs. Sonnenschein died within a year of each other, their son, Bruce, inherited their condominium in Sunset Village. He had just turned twenty-three and lived in the Bronx with Sheila, his bride of three months. The unexpected bequest gave the ever-practical Bruce an idea. Above all things, his parents had taught him the value of a dollar.

"We could live there," he told Sheila with enthusiasm, suggesting it as a stroke of rare good fortune. Bruce was a natural salesman and already beginning to make a name for himself as his company's top producer. He sold ladies' slacks in six southern states, including Florida.

"It's all paid for," he pointed out. "Best of all, it's right in the heart of my territory." He had been on only one selling trip since their marriage, and Sheila was still suffering from the trauma of that absence.

"Will I be able to see you more?" she asked timidly, kissing his hand.

"Simple logic," he pointed out. "Arithmetic. Less mileage for me. More time together for us. And you can always get a job in the area. Hell, there's big demand for dental technicians."

Sheila contemplated the idea, then shook her head in the negative.

"Everybody's so old there," she said. "Really old."

"It won't be forever," Bruce persisted, ignoring her protests. "But the money we save on rent and the appreciation on the property could mean we could afford to buy a new house in about a year." He watched her vacillate, absorbing his arguments. He knew instinctively that he was getting close to a deal.

"And you'll have all those grammas and grampas around to pamper you while I'm away." He paused again, watching her stroke her hair. She, too, had lost both of her parents.

"And when I'm on the road, I'll feel secure that someone is taking care of my baby."

"There's only one person who can take care of your baby," she said, pecking at his earlobe. After a while, he kissed her deeply on the lips, knowing that he had "gotten the order."

The day that Bruce and Sheila moved into their condominium, Mr. and Mrs. Shrinsky, their neighbors on the right, came in laden with jars and plates of food, covered with tinfoil. Later, Mrs. Milgrim, their neighbor on the left, came with a cake she baked from a Betty Crocker recipe.

"Your mother and father were my dearest friends," Ida Shrinsky told them. She was a tiny woman with three chins and scraggly over-bleached blond hair.

Her husband, Marvin, was tall and distinguished, with steel gray hair and clear blue eyes that peered out through rimless glasses. He had retired from the New York City School system, where he taught English for more than forty years.

"Why do you want to live with all of us antiques?" he asked pleasantly.

"They have their reasons," Mrs. Shrinsky snapped, embarrassed by Marvin's forwardness and the obvious touch of sarcasm.

"We're not chained to anything," Bruce said, explaining the conditions of his employment.

"Maybe it's not such a bad idea," Mrs. Shrinsky said. "You shouldn't worry, Bruce. We're right next door." She turned to Sheila. "Ask anything. Don't be bashful."

"I really appreciate that," Sheila said with grave sincerity, though she groaned silently within herself. They're so old, she thought.

"And lots of young people come to visit," Mrs. Shrinsky added. "Sons and daughters, in-laws. We'll check around." Sheila sensed the beginning of Mrs. Shrinsky's proprietressship.

"One thing we know about young couples," Mrs. Shrinsky said coyly—and Sheila imagined that she had winked lasciviously—"and that's that they like their privacy." She tugged at Marvin's sleeve and he followed her obediently out of the apartment.

"Wonderful," Sheila mocked. "I'm surprised they didn't ask if I play canasta or Mah-Jongg. Yuk."

"They build these condos with doors," Bruce said testily. "I thought they were rather considerate."

Mrs. Milgrim also was considerate. She, too, had been a good friend of Bruce's parents and, on their first meeting, insisted on recounting the events of their death, although Bruce was well aware of them.

"Can you imagine?" she said, making the traditional sound of pity— like the noise of an overeager cricket—by rubbing her tongue along the roof of her mouth. "They died within nine months of each other. He died of a broken heart, Bruce. You could just see him pining away in that chair." She pointed to what had been his father's favorite chair.

"They were very close," he mumbled, looking at Sheila, who had raised her eyes to the ceiling in a gesture of exasperation. Will I have to hear this again? she asked herself.

"So far, your idea stinks," she said to Bruce, after Mrs. Milgrim left.

"You'll get used to it," Bruce said unctuously. He gathered her into his arms and inhaled the smell of her hair. "There's a house at the end of the tunnel. Keep your eye on the objective, and it won't be that bothersome."

"When you're around, it won't be so bad." She shrugged, dreading the time she would have to stay alone.

"You play canasta or Mah-Jongg?" Mrs. Shrinsky asked her after they had been there a week and Bruce was on his first road trip.

"I hate cards. And I especially hate Mah-Jongg," Sheila replied, wondering if Mrs. Shrinsky felt the cutting edge of her polite contempt.

"They're wonderful games, and you shouldn't close your mind to them," Mrs. Shrinsky scolded with good nature.

Later, Mrs. Shrinsky came by again. "You need anything from the store?"

"No. Besides, I have my own car. I like to do my own shopping."

"So do I," Mrs. Shrinsky agreed.

Bruce had been on the road just one day when Mrs. Milgrim came to visit. Sheila had easily found a dental-technician job just five minutes from Sunset Village. Her hours were eight to four, which meant she could be home by four-fifteen.

When she returned from her first day at work, she had been in the condo for a scant few moments when she heard a knock on the door. Without an invitation, Mrs. Milgrim came in and sat down beside Sheila on the couch.

"Your job was good?"

"I think I might like it," Sheila replied, hoping the woman would leave quickly. But that wasn't to be.

"You watch 'As The World Turns?'"

"No."

"You watch Barbara Walters on '20/20?'"

"No."

"You watch the shopping channel?"

"No." Sheila smiled to herself.

"So what do you watch? Like last night, what did you see?"

On Bruce's last night before his road trip, they had made love repeatedly. She wanted to shout aloud: 'We fucked last night.' The thought seemed to have shot an idea into Mrs. Milgrim's mind.

"You gonna have babies right away?"

"Not if we can help it."

"I had babies right away, one after the other. My children are all less than two years apart. All three."

When Sheila deliberately didn't respond, Mrs. Milgrim went on. "He stays on the road long?"

"He comes home every other weekend."

"It gets lonely? You want I should come in when you get home and keep you company?"

Definitely not, she whispered. "I usually have chores to keep me busy when I get home."

"You want me to get tickets for us at the clubhouse? They have terrific shows at night."

"I don't think so, Mrs. Milgrim." She simulated a yawn. "I think I'm going to wash my hair and read a good book before I go to bed." Mrs. Milgrim was slow to take the hint.

"I always watch Jay Leno in bed. When my husband Eddie was alive, we always watched Johnny Carson in bed."

"We do other things when we get to bed, Mrs. Milgrim," Sheila said, smiling and forcing her demeanor to mask her sarcasm. Mrs. Milgrim blushed.

"I forget you're not married so long." Mrs. Milgrim stood up and stretched, and a noisy fart escaped from her. "Oops," she said apologetically. "You get old, you sometimes haven't got such good control."

When she left, Sheila sprayed the room with air freshener. She made herself a sandwich for dinner, then, true to her word, washed her hair and read until it was time to get into bed.

She put cream on her face, slipped into her nightgown, turned on Jay Leno and crawled into bed. She lay there watching him for a moment, then sprung out of bed again, clicking off the program. "Shit!" she cried aloud, admonishing herself for yielding to the suggestion.

Compared to Mrs. Shrinsky, Mrs. Milgrim, who visited almost daily, was practically a stranger. At least twice a day, once before Sheila went to work and then again before she went to bed, Mrs. Shrinsky rapped her knuckles against the door. Her exchanges with Sheila were repetitive in concept, providing kindly offers, nostalgic homilies, unsolicited advice and tragic information.

"You like Halavah?" she might say, proffering a sticky piece of the heavy candy. Sheila would shake her head.

"In Brooklyn, we used to get good Halavah," Mrs. Shrinsky opined. "Everything here is inferior, especially the food."

"I'm strictly from the thaw-and-heat school," Sheila said.

"You don't cook?"

"Not a lick."

"I'll teach you. When I was first married, my mother would come over and supervise my cooking. The first week, I made pot roast, kugel, lukshen kugel. You know lukshen kugel?"

"No."

"I'll teach you how to make lukshen kugel." The idea made Sheila slightly nauseated. Then Mrs. Shrinsky's talk would shift to other matters.

"Mrs. Klein from two courts away had a breast removed today. That was her second."

Sheila felt chills run up her spine, and her breasts began to ache. There was always similar tragic information to impart.

"You hear so much, you know. Sarah Minkoff died from it last week. And her husband can barely walk. Heart condition. I tell you the things you see. The worst sight is Marvin's friend, Sam Horowitz, with Parkinson."

A tightness gripped Sheila's insides as Mrs. Shrinsky continued her catalog of terrors. She might stop suddenly in her reportage if some other pressing matter came up. "Listen."

Sheila listened. There was the faint sound of a siren in the distance.

"An ambulance. Hear it!? The Sunset Village theme song."

Bruce and Sheila talked on the phone frequently during the week. She often dropped remarks about Mrs. Milgrim and Mrs. Shrinsky, making them sound funny, although they didn't seem funny at the time.

By the time Bruce came back for his first weekend off, Sheila had worked herself into a strange mood. They lay naked in bed passing a joint. The stereo played a Bonnie Raitt CD.

"I'm an authority on breast cancer. Mrs. Shrinsky showed me how to test for lumps," she demonstrated. "And Mr. Parkinson is not a living person. He has a disease named after him."

Bruce cupped the joint and inhaled deeply.

"And did you know that Mr. Hyman from the medium-rise in the fancy section pisses through a bag?"

"Everybody has their troubles," Bruce said, smiling.

"You know what the worst thing is?"

"Do I get guesses?"

"You'll never guess this one." She paused, her large brown eyes widening and her nostrils dilating. She wondered if she was about to laugh or cry.

"Mrs. Milgrim cuts farts—long vocal sidewinders that pass their stink into the air like poison gas."

He doubled up in laughter, and she finally decided to laugh. Keep looking at the humorous side, she told herself. It was the only way to tolerate these people and keep her sanity.

"I had a helluva week. Sold like hell."

"Take me," she pleaded suddenly. "Please, Bruce, take me with you."

"You've just started a new job," Bruce said. "And we're saving. We have a goal."

"I know. But I'd still like to go," Sheila said.

"Don't be ridiculous."

He slapped her buttocks playfully, the subject at hand obviously concluded. Maybe she was demanding too much, exaggerating, she thought. Occasionally, when Bruce was away, Mrs. Milgrim and Mrs. Shrinsky would converge on her simultaneously. To avoid them, Sheila began to develop little subterfuges, escapes, like going off to the movies after work. Sometimes she went to the Poinsettia shopping center, but how long could she shop? And watching the crowds of old people hanging around like teenagers was grating after a while. Sometimes she couldn't escape and had to endure the crossfire between Mrs. Shrinsky and Mrs. Milgrim.

"My son Harold lives in Scarsdale. He tells me his house is worth more than a million."

"My Lily lives in Westchester. The houses run a little more."

"More than a million?"

"Some even three million." The two yentas would go on interminably discussing figures. Everything—cars, vacations, clothes—had a price.

"They took a $20,000 European vacation," Mrs. Milgrim might say.

"My Jack took that $50,000 around-the-world cruise."

"You told me he didn't like it."

"Too many Orientals on the boat."

"Orientals are everywhere now."

"You can't believe where they are."

When Bruce called from Birmingham one day and told Sheila he wouldn't be home for the weekend as expected, she felt her rage overflow. Up to then, she realized, she had not conveyed to him the full extent of her unhappiness.

"Let me come up there, Bruce. I spoke to my boss. I can arrange it. Without pay, but I can do it and still keep my job."

"You're being silly. Why lose a week's pay? Not to mention the airfare. It's a waste."

"Waste?" She felt ire well up inside of her.

"It's one lousy week."

When she hung up, she was aflame with indignation. She felt trapped.

"He didn't come home this weekend?" Mrs. Shrinsky asked as she appeared at her door Saturday morning. It was more than mere telepathy. Bruce's car was not in its usual weekend parking spot.

"Your surveillance is accurate," Sheila said. Even her obvious sarcasm did not have a cutting edge.

"My what?" But Mrs. Shrinsky did not wait for an answer. Nothing could deflect her from her single-minded interrogation. "He's leaving you alone the whole weekend?"

Sheila felt a lump begin to grow in her throat. Hearing someone else say it increased the pain of it.

"He has some very important business in Birmingham."

"More important than you?"

In her tone, Sheila caught an implication that had not consciously crossed her mind. Not Bruce, she thought, dismissing the idea.

"You want to come to the pool with us?" Mrs. Shrinsky asked.

Sheila looked at the woman, on the verge of hesitation, but the prospect of spending the day in the empty apartment actually seemed even more foreboding.

"Why not?"

They drove to the pool in the Shrinsky car and found some empty lounge chairs on the sunny side.

"What a figure," Mrs. Shrinsky said as Sheila removed her blouse and jeans. She was slim-hipped and her bust was firm beneath the bikini.

Sheila smiled as she looked at the wrecked bodies around her, knowing that she was intimidating, with her smooth skin and youthful body.

"I used to have a figure like that," Mrs. Shrinsky said. Marvin Shrinsky looked up from his paperback. She imagined he had snickered silently.

She felt the eyes of the older people on her as she smeared sun oil on her body. Most of them were women, probably widows, the predominant population.

"This is your daughter?" someone asked Mrs. Shrinsky.

"My neighbor."

"She lives here?"

"Next door."

"By herself?"

"Her husband's on the road."

They talked together as if Sheila were merely an object.

"How come they live here?"

"The parents died. Left them the condo."

This seemed to satisfy the women for a few moments. Sheila tried to ignore them, lying back in her lounge chair and squinting into the sun.

"They have children?"

"Not yet."

"He leaves her for a long time?"

"Usually he comes home every other weekend. He was supposed to this weekend, but he didn't come."

Sheila undid her straps and lay on her stomach. She tried not to hear their chatter, but it was impossible to shut it out. Finally it faded, disappeared, and she realized that she must have dozed. Awake again, she felt someone watching her. Lifting her eyes and holding up her palm to block the sun, she saw that Marvin Shrinsky was observing her carefully. Retying her strap, she sat up.

"Where is Mrs. Shrinsky?"

"Over there with the other yentas," he pointed with his book. Occasionally, Mrs. Shrinsky and her companions would look toward them. She sensed they were talking about her.

"You're an object of some curiosity," Mr. Shrinsky said.

"Who cares?" Her nap had made her irritable and she was feeling sorry for herself.

"And all the alta cockers have been walking past with their eyes falling out of their head."

"Well then, consider me a geriatric therapist."

He smiled, his eyes washing over her. She wondered how old he was. It was impossible to calculate age in this place. Everyone seemed so nondescript, uniform. Actually, they all looked alike, she decided, one big blurred image.

"You like it here?" she asked suddenly. She had been thinking it, but had not intended to ask.

"What's not to like?" he said, but he had turned his eyes away. "I'm here," he sighed, then he opened his paperback again and began to read. She lay back and concentrated on letting the sun wash over her skin, feeling its heat penetrate her. She wanted to cry. After a while, they left the pool and headed back to their condos.

"Marvin wants to take you to dinner with us," Mrs. Shrinsky said after they parked the car.

"Really, I'm tired." Sheila protested.

"Well, if you change your mind ... Primero's has a special until six o'clock."

Inside her apartment, she took a shower, then, as she dried herself, she suddenly felt the terror of being alone. The bleak emptiness of the apartment made her shudder with desolation. I won't feel sorry for myself, she vowed, slipping on slacks and a blouse. But her resolution was not enough to muster the courage to cope with being alone. Hearing the Shrinsky's leave their apartment, she ran after them.

"Might as well," she said, getting into the back seat.

Primero's was crowded, as the people from Sunset Village piled in to get the discount that was offered for those seated before six-o'clock.

"Tell them, Marvin," Mrs. Shrinsky urged. "We were here on time. We shouldn't be penalized if that dumb hostess doesn't seat us on time."

"Don't worry."

"What do you mean, don't worry? You're talking five dollars more a dinner."

Marvin looked at Sheila helplessly, and she sensed his entrapment. I understand, she wanted to say, as she touched his arm in sympathy. She sensed the tension among the waiting crowd as the time reached six, though an announcement over the loudspeaker seemed to mollify the crowd.

"We will honor our commitment for the 'Early Bird Dinner' for everyone now in the restaurant," the voice said, with a touch of contempt.

When they finally were seated and their orders taken, Mrs. Shrinsky looked around the restaurant.

"There's Mrs. Morganstern. She just lost her husband last week," she whispered. "I'm surprised to see her out already enjoying herself."

"What would you expect her to do?" Marvin asked, looking at Sheila. She imagined that he was begging for her support, but she pretended not to notice.

"It doesn't look right, that's all I'm saying." Mrs. Shrinsky said. A waitress passed with a heavily laden tray.

"Sure they give you a discount. But look at the portions. You get what you pay for."

Their food came and, after more complaints about the size of the portions, Mrs. Shrinsky nudged Sheila's elbow.

"Watch how many leave with doggie bags. They also steal the bread, the pigs," she hissed.

Sheila picked at her food without appetite. The noise level of the restaurant heightened. Marvin remained silent, occasionally watching her through his clear blue eyes in their frameless lenses.

"Look, Marvin," Mrs. Shrinsky said suddenly, nodding in the direction of a departing couple. "Harvey Bernstein is getting better since his stroke, although he still drags one leg."

The harassed waitress came back to their table to take their dessert order. She reeled off the list of pies and ice creams by rote.

"Not for me," Sheila said. She had been watching a man at the next table masticating his food with badly fitting false teeth, and it had brought her to the edge of nausea. She had had to swallow repeatedly to keep down what she had eaten.

"She'll have chocolate ice cream," Mrs. Shrinsky said. "And we'll have one apple pie and one lemon meringue."

"No, really," Sheila protested.

"It's included," the waitress said.

"Don't worry," Mrs. Shrinsky said. "Nothing goes to waste."

Mrs. Shrinsky ate the chocolate ice cream, in addition to her pie.

Back in her apartment, Sheila turned on the stereo, but the music grated on her ears. Then she went to the telephone and dialed Birmingham information for the Holiday Inn. It turned out that there were three Holiday Inns and she dialed all of them, knowing that Bruce would note her extravagance when the bill came in. He always stayed at Holiday Inns, where he received a special discount.

"Twenty percent off. How can you beat it?" he told her proudly.

On her last call, when the clerk informed her that there was no Bruce Sonnenschein registered there, she lost her temper.

"You're full of shit," she screamed. "He has to be there."

"Did you try the other Holiday Inns?" the clerk said with annoyance.

"Of course, I did, you schmuck." She hung up the receiver angrily and paced the apartment, trying to calm herself. Was it rage or self pity? she asked herself. She passed a mirror and looked at herself.

"You're twenty-one years old!" she screamed, watching the tears spill over her lids and roll down her cheeks.

When she got out of bed the next morning, she was exhausted. Her mind refused to simmer down and, though she might have dozed, she knew she had not truly slept.

"You look tired," Mrs. Milgrim said, suddenly appearing in the doorway.

Sheila groaned, but she could not find the courage to be impolite. Besides, Mrs. Milgrim had a plate in her hands filled with bagels, lox and cream cheese.

"I thought maybe you'd like some bagels."

"I hate bagels," Sheila said.

"These are not the frozen ones," Mrs. Milgrim said, unperturbed. "Real water bagels. Mrs. Bromberg from across the street sent her husband ten miles to the bagel place." She placed the plate on the kitchen table and began poking around in the cabinets for the instant coffee.

"You went out last night with the Shrinskys?"

"We were the early birds."

"What did you eat?"

"I had the chopped steak."

"And a baked potato?"

"Yes, with the baked potato."

"And the sour cream and chives? I love the sour cream and chives."

Mrs. Milgrim sighed. "I don't go too often. It's very expensive." She smeared some cream cheese on half of a bagel. Sheila watched the woman's wrinkled hands shake slightly as she performed the act. The thin gold wedding band looked forlorn on her shriveled finger. She smeared some lox on a fork, pressed it over the cream cheese and handed it to Sheila. A bit of cream cheese lingered on a fingernail. Sheila felt her stomach retch.

"What did you have for dessert?"

Sheila put the bagel on the table and went to the bathroom, where she poured cold water on her face. She stayed in the bathroom a long time, hoping that when she got out, Mrs. Milgrim would be gone. But she was still there when she returned and the coffee had been poured.

"They have a terrific cheese cake," Mrs. Milgrim went on, revealing that she had been contemplating the Primero desserts. "My Eddie loved cheesecake. It was his hobby, he used to say. Cheesecake and Malox."

"You don't look so good," Mrs. Milgrim said suddenly, concentrating on Sheila's face.

"Maybe I'm coming down with something."

"It may be the water. Not like New York."

"The water?"

"There's a lot of things here that are very suspicious. Things spoil quickly. The milk is different, too. You got diarrhea?"

She couldn't stand it any longer. Rising, she forced a smile, feeling that it was making her face crack. I've got to get the hell out of here, she decided.

"I've got an appointment, Mrs. Milgrim."

"An appointment?" It was obvious that the explanation would have to be fleshed out with details.

"I'm meeting some friends in Fort Lauderdale."

"You're going to the beach?"

"Yes, to the beach."

"The beaches in Fort Lauderdale are not bad, although the water is polluted." Water again.

"Stay as long as you like, Mrs. Milgrim. Just let yourself out and lock the door."

She went into the bedroom, grabbed her pocketbook and, leaving a confused Mrs. Milgrim in the kitchen, raced to her car. She drove around for hours, coming home long after dark. Thankfully, the apartment was empty.

Bruce called her Monday night. She had phoned in sick and stayed in the apartment the entire day, bolting the door and drawing the blinds. There were repeated knocks on the door throughout the day. She had already begun to identify which knock belonged to whom.

Mrs. Shrinsky had knocked at least five times. Once she had actually turned the knob.

"Sheila, darling," she had called. She realized too late that they must have been confused by Sheila's car parked in its space.

"I called you in Birmingham," she told Bruce. Her tone was aggressive, although she had tried to compose herself beforehand. "I tried every Holiday Inn."

"What did you do that for?" He was annoyed.

"You mean a wife is not supposed to call her husband?"

"I didn't say that."

"Well then, where the hell were you?"

There was a moment of hesitation, a long pause on the line. In it, she discovered the full impact of its meaning. He could be lying.

"I stayed with a customer," he said. "What's wrong with that? I saved thirty-five bucks."

"Big deal."

"What the hell is wrong, Sheila?" She sensed his panic.

"Come on home and get me the hell out of this place."

"Are you crazy? I've got a million appointments. I'm about to close some big orders."

Her teeth began to chatter and she felt her throat constrict.

"I can't stand it here Bruce. I'm twenty-one years old. All they talk about here is sickness, dying and food."

"Food?" He seemed confused, giggling as if she had meant it to be some kind of a joke.

"And television." Her voice rose. "I can't stand it anymore." She must have conveyed the full impact of her anxiety.

"Baby, I love you," he said unctuously. It did not placate her. "We'll talk about it next weekend."

"You're coming home?"

"Of course." He paused. There was another long silence on the line. "You OK now?"

"Knowing you're coming home, I guess."

"Good. Look, keep cool. I'll see you on the weekend."

She wanted to ask him his itinerary, in case she wanted to speak with him. But he hung up before she had a chance to ask him. Despite her unabated anger, she imagined she felt better and the next day drew the blinds and unbolted the door. But before she could leave, Mrs. Shrinsky blocked her way.

"You want anything from the store?" Mrs. Shrinsky asked. She had managed to sleep and felt calmer. She was willing to believe that Bruce was telling the truth.

"No, thank you," she answered politely, fishing in her shoulder bag for her car keys. Mrs. Shrinsky hesitated at the door.

"You went somewhere yesterday?"

"Yes."

"You didn't take the car?"

"No." She hoped that her one-word answers would dampen Mrs. Shrinsky's interrogative impulse. Instead, they only stimulated her.

"You went with friends?"

"Yes."

"You buy something?"

"I didn't go shopping."

"You went to the beach?"

She felt her irritation grow, but she held back her temptation to fling an obscenity at the woman. "Go fuck yourself," she whispered to herself.

"No, I was picked up. I went for lunch." She regretted the words before they were audible.

"Oh." Mrs. Shrinsky paused. "Where did you go?"

"To someplace in Palm Beach. I forget the name."

"Expensive?"

"I didn't pay."

"Your friends must have money. Yes? They're comfortable?"

"Yes."

"And the food?"

"Delicious," Sheila sighed, slyly foreclosing on the next question. "I had the pate de foi gras."

"The what?"

"Chopped liver."

"Good chopped liver I haven't tasted here."

Sheila wasn't listening anymore. She started moving toward her car, waving when she reached it.

There was a minor disaster waiting for her at work. Some pipes had broken and flooded the dentist's office, and they had to close for repairs, which left her with a long afternoon free. Parking in another space a long way from her apartment, she literally sneaked inside, quickly changed into a bikini, took a blanket outside in the rear of the apartment, where neither Mrs. Shrinsky nor Mrs. Milgrim could see her, then lay down to sun herself.

"You'll burn up." It was Marvin Shrinsky's voice. He was standing over her, a folding chair in one hand. In the other, he held a tube of suntan lotion.

"You'd better use some of this. It's thirty. The sun will fry you."

The fact was that she had forgotten to put sun lotion on her skin. But how did he know that? she wondered. She wasn't exactly overjoyed at seeing him, but reasoned that it was better than being confronted by his wife. And he had always been a quiet man, conditioned by years of living with Mrs. Shrinsky.

He handed her the tube. She squeezed some of it into her palm and rubbed it into her skin. Then she turned onto her stomach and untied her top.

"Will you do my back, please?" she asked.

"Of course," he said.

"Thank you."

He bent down beside her, squeezed some lotion into his palm and smeared it over her back.

"The back of your legs, too?"

"I'd appreciate that."

She felt his hands gently running down her thighs and calves. She felt oddly aroused, closing her eyes.

"Feels good," she said. His touch seem to relax her.

She closed her eyes, as he continued to smooth on the lotion. After a while, he stopped, but she sensed that he was observing her.

"It's no fun growing old," he said suddenly.

"Consider the alternative," she said, offering the commonplace answer. He was silent for a long time, but she continued to sense his observation.

"I hate this place," he sighed.

"You're not alone."

"I feel like an alien," he said.

"You, too?"

He nodded and shrugged.

After a few more moments, she felt the heat penetrate her back, then turned abruptly to expose her front. She hadn't remembered that her top was loose and reached quickly with her arms to hide her breasts from view. She knew he had already seen her. She retied her top and sat cross-legged in front of him.

She met his gaze. His eyes were very clear and alert behind the lenses. Against the contrast of his white hair, his tan looked very dark. She figured he had more than fifty years on her.

"At least you can get out."

"I suppose I have that option," she sighed, with some degree of hope.

"When you're young, you still have options. Time is on your side."

"At least you have companionship," she said, feeling suddenly sorry for the man. "Being old may be no bed of roses. But being alone is worse."

"I suppose," he nodded in assent, but something seemed awry. "You could be old and alone, you know. Like Mrs. Milgrim." In his case, she wondered what was worse.

"I suppose she's driving you crazy, too."

"Too?"

"I'm sure my wife is no picnic."

"They mean well."

"I think you're too tolerant," he said. "But you are quite an event for them."

"Me?"

"For me, too," he said smiling. "When you get old, the principal entertainment is being a busybody."

"You mean a yenta."

"They're all secretly yentas. Their minds are like tabloids. Gossip, food are the most important things in life for them."

She laughed. It seemed a long time since she had laughed. She felt her top slip, but she did not adjust it and she knew he could probably see her nipples, which had inexplicably erected. Her eyes met his briefly. They seemed young, alert. He did not turn them away. 'I'm trapped in this old body,' they seemed to say.

His thrill for the day, she thought to herself, turning away and lying down on her stomach again. He was silent and she dozed. When she opened her eyes again, the sun had moved in an arc westward and he was gone.

Bruce arrived on Friday night, tired and irritable. Sheila had prepared him a dinner of steak and salad and had splurged on a bottle of good red wine.

"I had one helluva week," he said, chewing his steak. The wine made his cheeks flush. "Business is slowing. We could be heading into a recession."

"Just get me out of here," she said. "This was one lousy idea. They tell me I'm the principal event. I can't move without somebody watching me."

"Please, Sheila, not now. Don't hassle me now. I've had one helluva week."

"What about my week?" Was his week really as painful as mine? she wondered. He drank a glass of wine in a single gulp and poured another glassful.

"I'm in prison here," she said. He let his knife and fork drop from his hands. The handle of the knife made a clunking sound as it hit the plate. He finished another glass of wine. "At least you're free to do what you want."

"What's that supposed to mean?"

She felt the bloat of venom, ready to burst out of her.

"Do you sleep with other women on the road?"

She couldn't believe she said it as if it was at the forefront of her thoughts. The Birmingham incident had made her edgy and suspicious.

He stood up, walked the length of the living room, then back again. She was frightened. Had she gone too far? This place is making me crazy, she thought. Finally, he returned to the table. She refused to lift her head and look at his face.

"All I know is that I work hard, damned hard," he said. "I work to give us a better future. I work to make money, lots of money. I'm a salesman, and I live a traveling salesman's life. You knew that when you married me. Believe me, my life on the road is not fun and games. I make no apologies for it. I like it, and it does give me a sense of freedom. My work creates for me a life away from you, separated. In your world, think of me as out of country. But to me, you're home." He looked around the room. "This place is home. My real home is not on the road. What I do there, you must consider as a life apart."

There was something implied in what he said that rankled her. Is he saying that when he is on the road, he lives another life, a life of freedom? Is he saying that when he is on the road, he is beyond morality, not to be questioned, not to be judged?

"This place has got to me," she said, transferring her anger. "I do not feel at home here."

"Well then, look around for someplace else."

"You mean that?"

"Of course, I mean that," he said, stroking her hair. "We'll check with the office and see what these condos are going for, then we'll dump it."

The idea of escape placated her, at least through the weekend. They spent Sunday at the beach, then went out for dinner in Fort Lauderdale, got slightly drunk and had a good time together. It was like their courtship days. But then he was poking around in the dark on Monday morning, getting dressed, packing his bags. She lay there, listening, trying to hold back from thinking about the impending week. He hadn't mentioned selling the place again, she realized. When he bent over her to kiss her forehead in his ritual of farewell, she grabbed his wrist.

"I'm going to the office and put it on the market this week," she said. She could feel his arm stiffen.

"Don't make any hasty decisions," he said. "Just go in there and find out what we can get for it now."

"But suppose we can't get a good price?"

"Then it may pay to wait."

"But I can't wait."

He kissed her forehead again, sat down beside her on the bed, and held her in his arms.

"Cool it, Sheila. Cool it." He pressed her against him, held her for a moment, then released her and stood up.

"I'll call you," he said. She heard the door close and the car's motor turn over in the distance. He was off to his other life. She was sure he slept with other women on the road.

Burying her head in the pillow, she began to cry, her shoulders shaking, the sense of imprisonment too painful to bear.

When he was gone, she got out of bed and made herself a cup of coffee. The sun was just coming up. Suddenly, she burst into tears.

The sound of a familiar knock on the door startled her. So early, she thought, then got up and opened the door.

"You're crying?" It was Mrs. Shrinsky. Was she telepathic? For some reason, she actually welcomed Mrs. Shrinsky's presence.

"What's the matter, darling?"

She could not stop crying. Deep sobs wracked her body, and Mrs. Shrinsky reached out and embraced her. Sheila did not resist. Mrs. Shrinsky pressed her close, running a soothing hand up and down her back.

"It's all right, darling," Mrs. Shrinsky said. "What's so terrible?"

She calmed down, comforted, at least into restraining her hysteria, although involuntary sobs continued to convulse her.

"I can't believe this is happening," she said finally, gently disengaging and reaching into the pocket of her robe for more tissues. She sat on a chair and blew her nose.

"You had a fight?"

"Something like that," she said, trying to gather her thoughts together.

"A lover's quarrel." Mrs. Shrinsky folded her hands together and nodded her head. "Believe me, you'll have plenty of those. Plenty."

"I think he's seeing other women," Sheila blurted. Oddly, it seemed the only logical explanation for Mrs. Shrinsky's ears. Plural, no less. What else could she say? That she hated it here, hated her, even while accepting her gesture of comfort.

"Ahhaaaaa," Mrs. Shrinsky said, nodding, a knowing look spreading over her jowly face. Her eyes sparkled with what might have been acute joy, an idea that communicated itself to Sheila, even through her despair. It was the absolute pinnacle of yenta heaven, the role of advice-giver to a betrayed wife. Mrs. Shrinsky's Nirvana had arrived.

"With men, nothing changes," Mrs. Shrinsky said. "What is required is a little patience."

"Patience?"

"A man is a man," Mrs. Shrinsky said, pausing. Sheila imagined she could hear the purring of her inner works, winding up, setting its chiming mechanisms.

"It's not the end of the world. Maybe he has a nosh somewhere, a nosh here, a nosh there. But they always come back. They always come back. This I can tell you from personal experience."

"Your Marvin?"

She looked suddenly stunned. Then she laughed and shook her head.

"Not my Marvin," she said. "Not for years. But you'd be surprised how many friends of mine I've sat up the night with while they cried their eyes out, and I always told them the same thing. Patience."

"Patience?" Sheila repeated the words to herself, searching for some relevancy to her situation. Why patience?

"It'll burn itself out. It always does." She had the look of someone so authoritative, so wise, so knowing, and what she was saying seemed so meaningless, ludicrous.

Patience, Sheila thought, anger replacing her self pity. She felt a flash of venality. Patience meant time passing.

"But suppose it was your Marvin?" Sheila asked, her voice strong now.

"I told you. I'm long past worry about Marvin." Mrs. Shrinsky appeared confused by the question. "Even when he could, it probably would never even have crossed his mind." She smiled benignly.

Sheila felt a giggle begin. Then the tension seemed to drain and she stood up, feeling better.

"You all right now?" Mrs. Shrinsky asked, as Sheila busied herself by clearing the coffee cup from the table and rinsing it in the sink. She was thinking how quickly the information would spread and how soon people would be watching her with pity.

When Mrs. Shrinsky left, she dressed and, before she went to work, she stopped at the main office of Sunset Village and listed the condominium for sale.

"The market is not so good now," the agent told her.

"Just sell it," she said firmly. She felt her strength return. "I don't care what you get for it."

She realized her action might be futile because Bruce would have to sign the documents too, but even that inhibition could not dampen her will.

The office was open only a half day and when she returned to the condo, Mrs. Milgrim came by, salivating at the gossipy prospect.

"You had a fight?"

It was futile to protest.

"Nothing serious."

"I could tell you about men," Mrs. Milgrim said.

"Don't," Sheila said, curtly. She wondered if Mrs. Milgrim would catch her discourtesy. She hadn't.

"Could I tell you about men?"

"I really don't want to hear it," Sheila said. What could they tell her?

The historical gap was infinite. Actually, she felt like E.T., a different species on another planet. What am I doing here, she cried within herself.

"I'm going to take a shower," she said to Mrs. Milgrim. "And I don't need anything from the store. I don't need any solace. I don't need any pity. I don't need any advice."

"You're upset?"

She didn't answer, going into the bathroom and slamming the door behind her, listening, until she could hear Mrs. Milgrim's shuffling steps and the opening and closing of the front door.

When she came out, she sniffed. Mrs. Milgrim had left her trademark. Sheila squirted air freshener into the effluvia.

Then she got into her bikini and lay on the blanket behind the apartment, her body to the afternoon sun, waiting.

She could hear Marvin Shrinsky dragging his chair out of the screened porch, setting it up beside her. She looked up and squinted into his face.

"I've had one lousy weekend," she said.

"So I understand."

"And I'm getting the hell out of this place as fast as I can."

"Who can blame you?"

"I'm young," she said, holding down the edge of her hysteria. "I'm young. Look at my body." She started to undo her top strap.

"Please," Marvin said.

She got up and went into her apartment. He followed her. The screen porch led to her bedroom and she stood there in the center of the room.

"I'm young," she said again, removing the top and letting her breasts fall free. She held her hands under them.

"See," she said, her voice breaking. "Touch them."

He hesitated at first, reaching out finally, touching her nipples, watching them harden.

"Can I kiss them?" he asked.

"Help yourself," she said, feeling aroused. She noted the tell-tale bulge in his long shorts and thought of Mrs. Shrinsky's earlier comment about Marvin's absent potency.

"Would you like to, Marvin?" she asked, seeing the opportunity for a kind of weird redemption, a way to strike back at the enemies of her peace of mind.

"I'm a man wandering in the desert dying of thirst," he sighed. She pulled down his pants and discovered his youthful readiness.

"You've been hiding your light under a bushel, Mr. Shrinsky," Sheila said, leading him to her bed.

"From her," he sighed, demonstrating that he was, indeed, up to the mark in that department.

"And if she walked in right now?" Sheila asked.

"I'd be a legend in Sunset Village till the end of time."

When they were finished, Marvin kissed her on the forehead.

"Thank you," he said.

"It's my parting gift," Sheila said. "My statement for your wife and Mrs. Milgrim and Bruce for putting me in this prison. I feel like a free woman."

"I'll help you pack," Marvin said. "That's the least I could do."

TYING UP LOOSE ENDS

When his persistent chest pains were diagnosed as angina, Arnold Gold realized that he was, indeed, approaching the outer edges of his mortality. He was frightened at first, then surprised. For at Sunset Village, death was commonplace, and the Sunset Village theme song—the ambulance siren—was as ubiquitous as lightening bugs on early tropical evenings.

The knowledge that his flesh was expiring wrought profound changes in Arnold Gold. The doctor said he could live another ten years if he watched himself carefully, rested, and took his medication as prescribed. But, then, they always said that. Having just passed his seventy-second birthday, reaching his eighties in a reasonably together state seemed too remote a possibility to contemplate, especially when the pains stabbed at his chest.

The idea of confessing must have surfaced in his subconscious during the night after his visit to the doctor, because when he awoke the following morning, there was no debate raging within him. The decision was made; he would confess. He would tie up those last loose ends of his life.

He put on his bathrobe and went into the kitchen, where his wife, Rachel, was busy making coffee. They shared most household chores, and it was Arnold's job to make the English muffins. He put them in the broiler and watched them brown, pats of butter melting and running over their ridged surfaces.

"I'm about to tell you something Rachel," he said, looking at the muffins as he lifted them from the broiler with a spatula. "I'm about to make a full confession." He sensed that his wife hesitated briefly as she poured the coffee, but it did not deter him.

"I've been unfaithful," he said, finally turning toward her as he put the muffins on the small Formica surface where they had their breakfast. She continued to fill the cups with steaming coffee, then sat down, busying her hands with mixing the cream and sugar into her cup. She kept her eyes averted, concentrating on her task at hand. He knew she wouldn't look at him now, not directly, until he finished what he had to say. That was her way. She was a pouter, and her anger smoldered rather than erupted. He sat beside her, sipped his coffee, and started on his muffins.

"Just don't say anything until I've finished," he said, biting off a tiny bit of muffin and washing it down with coffee.

"Jam?" she asked, moving the jar of blueberry jam toward him.

"It started when I worked in the Vogue Shoe Store on Kingston Avenue," he said. "We must have been married seven years. Believe me, Rachel, I never looked at another woman until then. But you were having those terrible headaches and, let's face it, I had certain needs." He looked up briefly. She was sipping her coffee quietly.

"We're different, you and I," he continued. "You could take it or leave it—mostly leave it—but I was going crazy. She was Charlie Weinstein's wife. They owned the store, and Sherry Weinstein was helping with the books and the stock."

Arnold paused, spooning a pat of jam on his muffin. He noticed that the spoon shook as he felt a faint stab of chest pain. He wondered if he was getting another attack, but it passed quickly. He finished his muffin and washed it down with coffee.

"She seduced me. I swear it. Charlie was on a buying trip in Manhattan, so we were alone in the store, and while I was checking the stock in the back, she came over and grabbed me. At first, I pushed her away. She knew I was a married man. You remember, we once met her on the street. But she seduced me, and since you had started having those headaches and I couldn't go near you, I was busting."

They stood up from the table and moved the soiled dishes to the sink. Rachel rinsed and he dried. He didn't look at her, wondering if she was crying. Sometimes she cried quietly.

"It went on for six months. Then she started to get too attached, and I wasn't going to give up my family. There was no way that I ever was going to give up my family. You know that, Rachel. No way. There was a terrible scene when I quit. Charlie couldn't understand it. I was the best shoe salesman they ever had. My commissions were the highest of anyone in the history of the store. You know that. That was the year we bought the Buick. But Sherry made one terrible scene right in front of Charlie, calling me an ungrateful bastard for giving up the opportunity they had given me. I never told you what I went through, Rachel. I was so filled with guilt and remorse that I could barely stand it."

He felt a lump gather in his throat and his voice cracked, but he felt better for having said it. She might as well know everything, Arnold thought.

When they finished washing the dishes, he followed her into the bedroom and they began to make the beds, he standing on one side, she on the other. He looked up at her and saw her lips pursed tight, her eyes concentrated on the movement of the sheets and blankets.

"Hand me the pillow," she said. They tucked the bedspread under the pillows and rolled it above them, smoothing the sides.

"There was no chance that she was going to break up our marriage. All right, so you weren't very sexy and I was. That wasn't everything. After a while, you can get used to anything. I wish I could have gotten used to it. But then, remember when I got that job selling the Debbie line in Macy's. One day a woman comes in, a small Italian woman with long black hair. I'll never forget the first time. She came in and insisted that she wore a size three. She had very small, well-made feet, but when I measured her, she was actually a four. 'You're a four,' I told her. I mean, I knew women were vain about their feet, but there was no way that I could have stretched a three or a three-and-a-half onto her feet, so I told her straight out that she was a four. 'I said three,' she insisted. 'No way,' I told her again. But she was really insistent so I went to the stockroom and brought out a size three in two different styles and wrestled with her feet for a while. Maybe it was the way I handled her feet. She also was married and wore a ring, as I did. I would never pretend I was anything but married. It was an act of faith with me Rachel. An act of faith."

Rachel went into the bathroom to use the shower first, while Arnold vacuumed the apartment. As he passed the mirror, he shut off the vacuum cleaner and looked at his face. Over his lips was a thin film of sweat, which he wiped away with a tissue. This is the toughest thing I've ever done in my life, he thought to himself, sensing the anguish he must be causing her and wondering if things would ever be the same between them again. But he *had* to tell her. They had been married forty-eight years. My God, where did it all go? He wondered if he would ever make it to his fiftieth anniversary.

When Rachel had finished in the bathroom, he went in, showered, shaved, and dressed She was sitting in the living room when he emerged, stonefaced, reading the newspaper. It has to be said, he wanted to tell her, but he was afraid it would hurt her more if he put it that way. Better to be forthright. Just let it come out, he decided, steeling himself for the recriminations. "See what a damned liar your husband has been!" he wanted to cry out.

He picked up the shopping list, which they had prepared together the night before, from the top of the television set, and she followed him out to the car. He welcomed the idea of doing something that required being watchful and looking straight ahead. She sat beside him, silently, listening. Occasionally, he imagined that he could hear her sigh.

"Could you imagine? Her name was Concetta, and I used to meet her at her apartment in Greenwich Village about three times a week, before I got to work. It was on those days that I didn't start until twelve—only you didn't know that. I was crazy taking chances like that.

"Her husband was a garbage man, and he usually left the place at five a.m. She lived on the ground-floor apartment and always left the door open for me. She had a kid, a boy, but he was always in school when I got there. If there was any problem, she would simply keep the door locked and I knew to stay away. I liked her Rachel, I really liked her, but luckily she was a Catholic and there was no chance that she would endanger either of our marriages. I know I should rot in hell for what I did, Rachel. But what was I supposed to do? I wanted you. But you were having cramps, or headaches, or were too nervous or too tired or the kids had gotten you down. I'm not making excuses. I really wanted you to want me." He swallowed deeply and didn't notice the speed bump in the street, and they lurched as he sped over it.

"Be careful!" Rachel squealed as her head knocked the ceiling of the car. "Did you hurt yourself?"

"You'd better watch where you're going," she said, the words ejaculating in a hiss that revealed her pain and anger. I have got to tell her, he vowed, pressing on with his story.

"There's another thing I never told you," he said, the muscles in his throat constricting. "I don't know how to tell you this. It sounds so terrible, even when I say it to myself. But I masturbated a lot in those years. I couldn't help myself. I was young. I had needs. I used to think that maybe I was abnormal, a sex maniac or something. Sometimes I masturbated two, three times a day. Can you believe that? It made me feel dirty. How was I going to tell you what I was going through? Would you have understood?" He listened for some reaction, but none came.

"You weren't interested. You could take it or leave it—and you left it, mostly. I wasn't bitter. I respected what you felt and, after a while, I stopped pressing the point. Sometimes you would say it: 'Arnie, what's the matter? You getting old? You got a girlfriend?' Well, my girlfriend was Madame palm and her five sisters." How obscene, he thought, ashamed of the crude joke.

"It wasn't that I was a philanderer, Rachel. I was emotionally involved only twice." He hadn't quite expected it to come out that way. He paused as he searched the parking lot of the supermarket for a space. The traffic was heavy and they had to circle the lot several times before they found a place to park.

In the supermarket, they split the list and went their separate ways with their separate baskets, meeting, as they always had, near the first checker, where they unloaded the two baskets together.

"How are things with the Golds?" asked the checker, a large woman whose glasses slipped down to the tip of her nose.

"How are you Helen?" Rachel asked pleasantly, but with an edge that told Arnold she was putting on a front.

"You're looking good, Helen," Arnold said, as they waited for her to make the change and pack the bags, which they wheeled in a cart across the parking lot before loading them into the car. Then they headed back to Sunset Village.

"When they made me assistant buyer, they had a cashier at the store named Judy Farber. She was eighteen, a pretty little thing. I think I was thirty-six then, because I made a big thing about being twice her age. She would kid me a lot about it, calling me 'old man.' Imagine at thirty-six being-called 'old man.' We used to take our lunch hours together and, after we ate, we'd take walks down thirty-fourth street when the weather was good. I swear, Rachel, I wasn't looking for trouble. After Concetta, I had vowed that I would never be unfaithful again. Who needed it? I had you. I had our kids. I had a nice life. We had just moved to that new place on Empire Boulevard and had bought a lot of furniture on time, and I had to take another job to pay it off. You remember. I worked Saturdays at that shoe store on Flatbush Avenue. You used to tell me not to work so hard, and I used to say I had to or we couldn't pay these things off? Actually, its a wonder I didn't have a heart attack then."

He maneuvered the car through the Village gates, waving at the guard and slowing down to take the bump, then headed toward their court.

"I'm really ashamed of this, Rachel," he said, pausing. "She was a virgin. She lived with her family in the Bronx, and since we lived in Brooklyn, I couldn't see her very much at first. Neither of us had any money, and there was barely any way to enjoy any real intimacy. We necked and petted in the stock room, or in doorways. A couple of times, we went to the movies and sat in the last row. Christ, its embarrassing to tell you this."

Arnold was silent as he drove the car into their court and carefully edged it between the white lines of their parking space. They both carried groceries into the house and began to load them into the cabinets and refrigerator.

"I think you forgot the soda," Rachel said. He went out to the car and found the six pack of soda on the floor behind the front seat and brought it into the house.

"This cheese is moldy," Arnold said, sniffing a package that he was about to put in the dairy drawer of the refrigerator.

"I never saw so much spoilage in my life," Rachel said.

"We'll take it back tomorrow."

When they finished putting away the groceries, they went into their bedroom to put on their bathing suits. They tried to get to the pool before one o'clock each day, so as to get chaise lounges that would allow them to take advantage of the sun late into the afternoon.

While they changed into their suits, he began again.

"It wasn't until we discovered that a friend of Judy's had an apartment, a cold water flat in a brownstone, in the forties, that we really found a way to be together. It cost us $5 a week; her friend was really hard up. I used to get there at about seven o'clock every morning. You were always asking why I had to go in so early when the store didn't open until ten. Sometimes it was pitch dark when I left the house. Well, it was Judy Farber. You know, I can barely remember her face. I try sometimes and it just fades away. I was thirty-six years old, and she was a virgin."

He watched as Rachel smoothed her gray hair and wrapped it in a kerchief. Her profile was still sharply etched, though flesh had acccumulated under her chins and her jowls had fallen. As he studied her, she moved away to the kitchen and began making lunch.

"You want a tuna-fish sandwich?" she called from the kitchen.

"Again?"

"What about bologna?"

"Not too much mustard," he answered.

He put on his cabana jacket, slipped into his sandals and went into the kitchen. When she had finished making the sandwiches, he cut them lengthwise, put them on plates, and filled their glasses with ice cubes. Rachel poured the soda, and they sat down at the table.

"They say its kosher, but it tastes like goyishe bologna," Rachel said, through a mouthful of sandwich.

"It's not that bad," he shrugged, chewing slowly and washing it down with a gulp of soda.

"I'll tell you what was really odd about my relationship with Judy Farber," Arnold broke in headlong. "She didn't like sex that much either. Can you believe that? I would meet her every morning—nearly every day but Sunday—and two out of three times, she complained of cramps, or headaches, or feminine problems." He laughed, not looking at Rachel but knowing that her lips were fixed tightly again, the corners drooping. He wondered if her eyes had misted but dared not look into her eyes.

"'Maybe it's because I feel so guilty,' she would tell me. 'Well, how do you think I feel?' I would ask her. Me with a family, a wife, responsibilities. Actually, I hated being involved with her—emotionally, that is. You didn't know it, Rachel, and I doubt if you could possibly understand, but I thought I was going to go crazy. Besides, I was exhausted—holding down two jobs, getting up early every morning, fighting the subway crowds at night, and working all day Saturday. Not to mention that I was on my feet all day. I felt like hell. I looked like hell. To make matters worse, if that was possible, she wanted me to leave you and marry her. The pressure was unbearable, especially since I had convinced myself that I was madly in love with her. I know this is all confusing to you, Rachel. Actually, we came that close," he said, holding up two fingers sideways, with just an air of space between them. "That close."

He shook his head and the image of Judy Farber's face rose clearly to the surface of his mind for the first time in more than thirty-five years. Actually, he had seen her again a few years after their affair ended; she was married and had two kids in tow. And she had started to get fat. She gave him a big hello, with a wet smacking kiss on his cheek, as if he was some long-lost uncle.

Arnold and Rachel got back into the car and drove to the pool, finding that someone was occupying their usual place. Disappointed, they moved to the other end of the pool.

"So, we'll go home earlier" Rachel said, apathetically.

"Might be a good idea. There's a new movie at the seven-plex, with Jack Nicholson."

"We'll see," she said, smearing oil on her skin. He turned his back and she splattered some oil on him. Then she turned her back and he rubbed some on her. When she sat down, she pulled out her knitting and began to twirl wool through her fingers. He put a paperback book on his lap, a mystery novel. He liked mysteries, so much so that one side of his bedroom was literally piled high with a collection. But today, he kept the book closed on his lap.

"I vowed, Rachel," he went on. "I swear, I vowed that never again would I get involved with another woman. My family meant more to me than anything. You meant more to me. That might be hard to believe right now, but you did." He listened to the clickety click of knitting needles.

Occasionally, someone they knew would walk by and they would nod the requisite greeting. They weren't part of any particular group. Neither of them played cards. And Rachel wasn't much of a joiner. Besides, the yentas were too gossipy.

"I don't want to be in their pot," Rachel had said.

Arnold hadn't made any friends. But then he had never made any friends. Actually, he thought now, the only friends he had ever had outside of his wife and kids were women.

"Yet I didn't feel like a philanderer. It was as if your lack of enthusiasm about me, at least sexually, was a kind of permission. Only a man could understand that. Anyway, I vowed I would never again get messed up with any women, and I actually didn't for maybe ten years. Not that I didn't occasionally have a little nosh. There was always something around. Sometimes I even went with prostitutes. Look, I might as well tell you everything. Why should I leave anything out? But it used to scare the hell out of me that I might be picking up a disease. You would have killed me if I brought home a disease. You can't imagine how I worried. I was always worried about something. With Judy, I worried I would be making her pregnant. With the other women, I worried about bringing home a disease. Sometimes I worried that someone would tell you, and I don't think I could have taken the pressure in those days. I was very proud that I never once brought you home a problem, never once gave you cause to doubt my faithfulness as a good husband and a good father."

He wanted to reach out and touch her arm, but he held back. She continued to concentrate on her knitting, the needles clicking, her fingers working swiftly. He knew that she was listening, that she was agitated, by the extraordinary speed of her work.

"I can't even remember some of the names. Then, when I went to work for Gimbels, I met this woman, Dolly Schwartz. She worked in toys, and I met her when I went to buy a toy for Alan. There's poetic justice! I go to buy a toy for our first grandchild, and I meet Dolly Schwartz. She was good-looking, big and tall, with a full figure." He checked himself. Was it necessary to be so graphic, he wondered, remembering how much he had enjoyed the sight and feel of Dolly Schwartz's tits. They were so big and full, with huge red nipples, like little statues in a pond. He had buried his head in them, kissed them, sucked them. God, how could any man on earth ever forget Dolly Schwartz's tits? And how she loved to have them touched and looked at, how proud she was of them. He felt a rare surge in his loins. It had been a long time since he had thought of Dolly Schwartz.

"She was married." he continued. "But her husband was a traveling salesman and was away a great deal of the time. Her kids were all grown up and, to make matters more convenient, she lived only a few blocks from us in Sunnyside. And you were busy with Millie and the new grand-child. Remember, you were at Millie's house more than you were at home. All you could talk about, think about, was Alan. Not that I don't love Alan. But he and Millie were your whole life then. You used to make din-ner and leave it for me under a piece of plastic with a little note, 'Went to Millie's. Baby-sitting for Millie and Bob.' That's all right. I didn't care. Really I didn't. Nor am I blaming you. Frankly, I think you were tickled to death to get rid of me in those days. Remember all those executive meetings I said I was going to. We never had one. Our executive meet-ings usually were held before the store opened. Anyway, you didn't com-plain. You didn't have to worry about my dinner and you could spend more time with Millie and Bob and Alan. I really liked Dolly Schwartz, and she really liked me. We had a good time together. She was all woman. We even considered giving up our marriages."

"You think I'm terrible, don't you?" he said, pausing and, for the first time since they had been at the pool, drawing her eyes toward him. But they were quickly deflected when someone they knew approached her.

"You still on the sweater?" the woman asked.

"It's a cardigan. It's always harder to make a cardigan."

"Who is it for?"

"For Arnold," she said, pointing at him.

"That's one thing we got plenty of in this family," Arnold said. "Sweat-ers." When the woman left, Rachel began knitting furiously again. He picked up his paperback mystery, opened it, then closed it again.

"The thing with Dolly Schwartz actually lasted three years. It might have gone on longer but Millie and Bob were getting upset with your being overly possessive. Look, let's face it. That was the real truth. Why do you think they moved so far out on the Island? Bob told me. It wasn't that they didn't love you. You know how much they love you. But every night, Rachel? They had no privacy. Also, Sammy was already in med school, so that was that. Not that I didn't have those 'executive meetings' maybe once or twice a month, but, frankly, I didn't like the idea of leaving you alone at night. So I began coming home nearly every night, and Dolly wasn't too happy about that. So that was the end of Dolly Schwartz."

The sun sank behind the clubhouse, throwing their end of the pool into the shade. A few minutes later, they got their things together and drove back to their apartment. Rachel had defrosted some chopped meat and, while she took a shower, Arnold made the salad and formed the meat into patties. He made a good salad, sliding the garlic around the bottom and sides of the wooden bowl like he had seen the waiters do at expensive restaurants. By the time he finished the salad and mixed in the dressing, she had come out of the shower, so he went in for his. There was always just enough hot water for two showers. When he had dressed, the hamburgers were ready and the table was set, complete with little glasses of tomato juice on each plate. They always ate dinner at the dining-room table.

"Too rare?" Rachel asked, as he bit into his hamburger. He chewed it for a few moments, then held up two fingers in a sign of approval.

"That new broiler was a good choice," he said. They ate in silence for a while.

"You like the salad? That's the one thing about Florida. You can get the ingredients for a good salad."

When they finished their main dish, Rachel scooped out two balls of chocolate ice cream and served it.

"Dolly Schwartz wasn't the last of it," Arnold began again. "But she was the last where there was any danger attached to it. You know, as far as us breaking up. I don't think I really considered breaking up our marriage, Rachel. Not in my heart. I mean that. You were you and I was me. Sex isn't everything, although it seemed pretty important to me at the time. But people are different, and you can't expect to get everything in one package. Not that I was such a bargain myself. You used to tell me, 'Arnold, you're not so good in bed yourself.' Maybe you were right. I was no big deal.

After awhile, it became too much of a hassle and, by the time I was sixty, I finally figured out that it was ridiculous. Oh, there were one or two little knishes on those retailers conventions, but it wasn't the same. It wasn't that I felt old. Frankly, I felt that I was really being unfaithful. We were married nearly forty years and I was just beginning to feel unfaithful."

They finished the ice cream and did the dishes together. He washed and she dried. When all the dishes were put away and the apartment was swept, they drove to the movie theater. He showed the cashier his senior-citizen's discount card, paid for the tickets, waited in line for some popcorn, and they got into the theater just before the film rolled. They liked to sit up front, right in the middle of the big screen, where they could watch the huge characters parade before them, a hundred times bigger than life. They always held hands in the movies, but this time he was afraid to touch her. He had taken his pills before dinner but felt the pains begin as the picture progressed and he had to take another nitro during the movie. The pain then went away quickly.

"Did you like it?" he asked as they walked back to the car.

"Not as good as that other one we saw him in."

"Definitely not as good as that."

"Nothing he has ever done has been as good as that."

It was very dark now and he drove slowly, knowing that Rachel got particularly nervous on the road at night. She sat beside him tense and watchful. Concentrating fully on his driving, he didn't think about what he had confessed to her until they got back to their apartment. He sat alone in the living room while she undressed for bed. Had he told her everything? Had he left something out? He did not feel any special elation in the unburdening, except that he had, at last, wiped the slate clean, and that was worth the effort. Maybe he did censor things a bit, he thought. He had come very close to breaking up his marriage over Judy Farber and Dolly Schwartz, but he could not remember in any detail the reasons why he had rejected the idea. Surely, he could not have conveyed to Rachel the intensity of his feelings, the wrenching crisis of decision, the agonizing. It had all occurred internally, far from her field of consciousness, as if they had lived on different planets.

He got up and went to the bedroom. She was already in bed reading the newspaper. It was her habit to save the morning paper to read before she went to sleep. She had put a single curler in her hair and had lightly creamed her face. He put on his pajamas, picked up the paperback mystery that he had with him at the swimming pool and slipped in beside her.

He wondered what might have happened if he had told her about his escapades at the time they happened. Surely, that would have meant the end of his marriage. He wanted to ask her but didn't dare right now. It had never occurred to him that she might have known about these things all along, but that was another question he thought best to postpone.

For some reason, their marriage had survived it all. That was the enigma.

He couldn't concentrate on his book, so he closed it and put it on the night table beside him. There were other unanswered questions, he thought. Perhaps, she too, had a confession to make. He doubted if it would be as extensive as his own, nor could he imagine that she could ever have been unfaithful to him. He would forgive her, he pledged secretly, knowing that she had forgiven him.

She crinkled the newspapers, lay them on the floor beside the bed and, almost simultaneously, they pulled the light chains of the lamps on each side of the bed. He lay there quietly for a moment, hearing her sigh. Then he turned, moved his body close to hers, and slipped an arm around her, cupping one breast, toying with her nipples. He felt himself stir, an unusual feeling these days, but he knew its signals.

Through it all, he must have loved her, he thought, wanting to say it, just as he felt it. He was warm now, wanting, and the beat of his heart crashed in his chest as he drew her closer to him and let his hand slide down over her belly.

"I'm nauseous from the popcorn," she said suddenly. As always, he froze momentarily and felt his ardour sputter and cool.

"Shall I get you an Alka-Seltzer?" he asked.

"Its all right," she sighed. "I'll be OK in the morning."

He moved away from her and listened as her breathing became more regular and she dropped off to sleep. He must have followed soon after because the next thing he knew it was morning and the sun was streaming in through the spaces in the blinds.

HE'S GOING TO MARRY A SHIKSA

 When Heshy Leventhal first announced that he wanted to marry Pat Grady, his mother became instantly hysterical. He had, of course, expected the reaction, but the suddenness, not to mention the noise of her eruption, was beyond his most fearsome expectations.

"A Shiksa?" she screamed, the sound a shattering thunderclap in the family's small Brownsville apartment.

"Sha. The neighbors," his father cautioned, turning to his son.

"You're willing to disgrace us," he said, his small myopic eyes misting behind thick rimless glasses.

"A Shiksa?" his mother screamed again, repeating the word in an ever-increasing crescendo.

"I knew you'd feel this way," he mumbled. He had told Pat that, come what may, he would stand up to them. The promise reassured him, although his mother's wailing was enough to tempt fate.

"It's out of the question," his father said. His mother had collapsed in a chair, her shoulders heaving. She buried her head into the crook of her arm.

"Look what you've done to your mother," his father admonished. He had always chosen the path of quiet reason. He was a socialist. His father's words seemed to encourage his mother's hysteria, and her sobs grew louder.

"My mind is made up," Heshy said.

"You couldn't find a Jewish girl," his father said. He lifted his hand and pointed to the window. "The streets are filled with Jewish girls. You couldn't find one. One single Jewish girl?"

"It just happened, Pop," Heshy said, reaching out to touch his father's shoulder. The older man shrugged him away as if Heshy was deliberately communicating some disease.

"I love her," Heshy said. The words seemed hollow, almost foolish as they rolled off his tongue.

"Love!" his mother burst out. Her tears had slowed and he knew she was getting her second wind. She was not one simply to cry it out without words. "Love!" she screamed, looking at her son, her lips curling with contempt and sarcasm. "This pisher knows about love."

"We love each other," Heshy said quietly, remembering his promise to Pat, trying to withstand the powerful intimidation of the ridicule.

"And the children. What about the children?" his father said, still relying on quiet logic.

"We'll cross that bridge when we come to it."

"This is the son you raised," his mother screeched. He knew that, from now on, she would communicate with him through his father, as if he was not in the room.

"It never works," his father said. "They become Catholics. They'll take the children. They always take the children. And the Catholics will hate them because they're part Jewish."

"They'll hate him anyhow," his mother said. "She'll treat him like dirt," she intoned. "And it'll serve him right."

"You'll like her, Mama," he said. It was a futile remark, he knew, but his 'I love her' argument had little effect and he felt he should try a new tack.

"He says I'll like her. How could I like her? I don't ever intend to see her. I don't ever intend he should come into my house again. I would rather they rolled me into the grave this minute than see her. And I swear on my mother's memory, may she rest in peace, that the Shiksa will never come into my house, ever."

"I'm sorry you feel that way," Heshy said, feeling his own tears begin. A tiny sob stabbed at his chest.

"But I love you both."

"Love again," his mother screamed, the sound a thunderclap.

"I think you're crazy," his father said finally. He must have sensed that it was futile to continue a strategy of reason.

"This is 1951," Heshy said. "The world is changing."

"Nothing changes," his father said. "Not for Jews."

"When we let him drop out of college, it was our first mistake," his mother said, continuing to ignore him. The remark seemed an odd watershed in her hysteria. Actually, college was an enormous economic hardship and he had taken a job as a toy salesman in Manhattan. Pat had been the secretary to one of the bosses. Since then, they had always taken refuge in the argument that his dropping out of college had somehow addled his brains.

"I'm sorry," he said finally, knowing, as he had suspected, that it was beyond resolution. "My mind is made up." As he turned to go, he heard the cacophony of his mother's last reserve, the outpouring of a passionate frustration, plumbed from some powerful genetic undercurrent.

"You're not my son," she screamed. "You and your Shiksa died today. I curse you in my mother's memory." As he closed the door, gently, because he was leaving in sadness not anger, he heard his father's stern attempt to placate her. "Please, Dorothy. Don't say what you might regret."

Pat Grady's experience was not much different.

"My father threw me out of the house," she told Heshy when they met later. "He called you a bunch of Christ killers and dirty kikes. My mother kept crossing herself and saying that your people ate babies." Her eyes were swollen from crying and he held her tightly, kissing her cheeks, tasting the saltiness that lingered there.

"You they called 'The Shiksa.'"

"Just that?" She paused and brushed his hair back from his forehead.

"In their mouths, it was not a pleasant term. More like a curse." He smiled. He loved her and that was the balm to ease his pain. "So we're both orphans."

They were married in City Hall and, though he called his father inviting him to the brief ceremony, he knew what was in store for him.

"You're killing us, Heshy," his father said, the voice of reason barely recognizable. Heshy could imagine what the poor man was going through with his mother.

"And mother?" he asked. His mother was bound to inquire whether he had mentioned her.

The moved into a tiny apartment on the edge of Greenwich Village, deliberately choosing a more diverse neighborhood than the circum-scribed ghettos of Brooklyn and the forbidding suburban waspiness of Queens. The estrangement with their parents continued but they kept them informed of their lives nonetheless.

"I spoke to my mother today," Pat would report.

"And?"

"She's still babbling about going to Church and praying for my soul."

"Tell her it's one of our boys that's hanging up there on the cross."

"I'm sure she'd appreciate that. She refers to you as 'him.'"

"Better than kike."

"I could hear my father grumbling in the background. I thought I heard him say 'Jewboy.' She smiled and patted his arm. "But you know, I think she was glad to hear from me. I think if I said to her: 'Mom, I'm sick. Mom, I need you,' she would break her neck to get here."

"Did you tell her you were pregnant?"

"Yes."

"I told my father," Heshy said. "And the voice of reason prevailed."

"What did he say?"

"He said that now my troubles were just beginning."

When Marvin was born, Heshy dutifully called his parents. His mother answered the phone. He had not heard her voice for more than a year, but the fact she had picked up the phone seemed like a minor victory. He imagined that she might have been waiting for news, since he had informed his father about the impending birth. Her voice was calm, not without a touch of pathos. She had this ability to create an aura of pathos about her on the telephone. I will not feel guilty, he told himself. It was his private incantation and it had sustained him through this trying period.

"Ma?" There was a long silence.

"Who then?"

"You have a grandson."

He could hear a long sigh, then: "You want me to say Mazeltov?"

"Of course."

"Mazeltov."

"His name is Marvin, after your mother. His middle name is Patrick af-ter Pat's father."

"A regular Abie's Irish Rose." He detected her sarcasm, then the evidence of her repentance. Obviously, she knew she had gone too far. "He's healthy?"

"Eight pounds."

"You were nine pounds." He smiled, waiting for her to continue.

"And the Shiksa?"

"For crying out loud." He felt a sharp tug of anger. "Her name is Pat and she's the mother of your grandson."

"To me, she's still a Shiksa."

"She's the mother of your grandson," he said, enunciating each word slowly so that she would not miss his drift. Two can play this game, he thought. Now the guilt ball is in her court.

"Be that as it may," his mother said, but he could sense her grudging retreat. "At least," she said, drawing the line, "I hope he's going to be circumcised."

"He was already. The doctor did it." He decided to preempt her thoughts. "And no, he won't be baptized."

"Why not? They'll get him sooner or later." He decided to ignore the remark and, instead, said good-bye, deliberately cold and distant. He sensed that she wanted to continue to talk, but he decided that it was her turn to suffer the agony of guilt.

"My mother came to visit me," Pat told him while she was still in the hospital. She seemed glowing with happiness. A white ribbon was tied around her hair and little Marvin's red pinched face was nestled against her breast, greedily nuzzling the nipple. She looked down at Marvin. "She says he looks Irish and made the sign of the cross over him so many times, I thought she was the Pope."

"And your father?"

"He was outside looking into the nursery at the baby. But he wouldn't come in."

"Do you think he really looks Irish?" Heshy asked.

"Exactly like my brother Sean, my mother said."

"Poor guy. With a name like Leventhal."

On the day before Pat was to come home from the hospital, she told Heshy that his parents had been there.

"I saw them. I was standing by the window when these two older

people came in. I was standing right next to them and they were pointing and tapping at the window at your son."

"You didn't introduce yourself?"

"My knees were shaking. Besides, they were very upset. Marvin was
crying his lungs out and your mother complained to the nurse."

"Complained?"

"She insisted that the Leventhal baby was being ignored. The nurse
was fit to be tied. I heard her say: 'That stupid Shiksa nurse.'"

"That's my mother."

"And she said one more thing."

"Can I guess?"

Pat smiled and nodded.

"She said: 'Thank God, he looks Jewish.'"

"You got that right."

"She didn't stop to see you?"

"One dumb Shiksa was enough for the day. Besides, I hid in the bathroom."

A week after Pat got home from the hospital, Heshy's parents arrived
in their small apartment. Their visit was not spontaneous, requiring
some heavy negotiations and compromises on both sides between his
mother and him. Phone calls were exchanged and Heshy's reactions were
heavily laden with guilt. He knew his mother was sorely tempted to see
the baby and troubled in her heart that she was still allowing her pride
to dominate her desires. Naturally, his tactic was to make it appear that
she was responding to his entreaties.

"How can you ignore your grandchild?"

"He's only half mine."

"That is absurd," Heshy said. Finally, after a long exchange in that vein,
Heshy played what he sensed was his trump card.

"You want to deprive your own grandson of ever getting to know his
grandparents? Let it be on your head." It was a bullet to the heart. Two
days later, his parents came, laden with baby clothes, blankets, rattles
and teething rings.

"Just act natural," he told Pat. "No matter what. Chances are she won't
even acknowledge your name."

"As long as she doesn't call me Mrs. Leventhal."

"That's the last thing on Earth she'll call you."

"Or the Shiksa."

"In her heart, that will be your name."

The visit lived up to Heshy's expectations. His mother briefly acknowledged Pat's presence with a thin smile and turned her attention immediately to little Marvin, whose diaper she insisted on changing. Heshy could see his mother was happy and his father beamed and winked at Pat, when his wife wasn't looking. The high point of their visit was when little Marvin peed in his grandmother's face as she changed his diaper.

"Well, you've been officially christened," Heshy exclaimed. Pat kicked him in the shins, and Mrs. Leventhal ignored the remark.

"Boys do that," she said with some authority. "My Heshy did that to me all the time."

The important thing to both of them was that the ice was broken and the story of little Marvin peeing in his grandmother's eye became part of the folklore of their lives.

As for Pat's parents, they melted in a different way. It was Pat's father that could not stay away from his grandson, although he always visited during the day when Heshy was at work.

"I noticed there are a bunch of beer bottles in the ice box," Heshy said one day. "You feeding the kid beer?"

"You know the Irish and their beer. They start young."

"You're kidding."

"Of course, you ninny, it's for my father when he comes over to see the baby. He can't keep away from him." Heshy could see that she was pleased, and he was happy for the reconciliation.

"He calls him Paddy," Pat said.

"And me?"

"You've graduated from kike to smart Jewboy."

"I can just see him in the saloon telling all the micks about his daughter marrying this smart Jewboy."

"You're the smart Jewboy and I'm the Shiksa."

Perhaps it was the memories of those earlier days that prompted Pat Leventhal to continue to reject the idea of moving to Sunset Village. None of Heshy's mother's forebodings had ever come to pass. Actually, the fact that they were named Leventhal set the pattern for their lives. When the children were still in school, they moved to Jackson Heights. By then, they had had another child, a daughter. They had lived in the same apartment for thirty-five years. Heshy never made lots of money and often regretted that he had not gone to college. But he made certain that both his children graduated. They had a very small circle of friends and, although they did not practice any religion, they were "the Leventhals." It was rare that she was ever referred to as "a Shiksa." Even Heshy's mother ceased to use the term and, when Pat would joke that "she was just a dumb Shiksa," the older Mrs. Leventhal would counter with a strenuous rebuke.

"You must never say such a thing," she would say, and from her tone it was obvious she meant it. At the end, her last thoughts were whispered to her son.

"Be good to my Patty," she said. Remembering that always brought tears to his eyes.

Because they had so few friends, they knew no one when they finally arrived in Sunset Village. They learned immediately that it would be impossible to be alone, nor did they want to be.

"Make friends," Marvin had said. "Don't be standoffish."

The day they arrived and waiting for the furniture truck, their next-door neighbors, the Bermans, invited them in for coffee. Abe Berman was a big man who used to be a plumber and his wife, Sadie, was a tiny woman with a graveled voice and a cigarette always dangling from her lips. She was also, as Heshy observed from the force of her interrogation, a yenta, a dyed-in-the-wool yenta.

"You're from New York?" she asked, settling a squinty glare on Pat as she poured the coffee and offered a plate of brownies.

"Jackson Heights."

"We came from Crown Heights."

"We lived in the same apartment for thirty-five years," Pat said. But Heshy sensed that Sadie Berman caught the scent of something that needed corroboration. Besides, one couldn't mistake Pat's antecedents. It had been a long time since they had been subjected to such scrutiny.

"We looked at a place once in Jackson Heights," Sadie Berman said. "But there were too many goyem."

Both Heshy and Pat ignored the reference, looking at each other with understanding.

"You know," Sadie Berman volunteered, "there used to be goyem in Sunset Village. As a matter of fact, it started with goyem."

"Not now," her husband said. "Besides, they're more comfortable with their own."

Heshy felt discomfort, although Pat's glance told him that all was under control.

"I'm a Shiksa," she said suddenly. The Bermans looked at each other in embarrassment.

"Oi," Sadie Berman said quickly. "I said the wrong thing. I have a big mouth."

"That, I'll vote for," her husband said.

"I didn't mean to be a yenta," Sadie Berman said with what seemed to be sincere embarrassment. "There are plenty of Shiksas here, married to Jewish husbands."

"Why not?" Abe Berman said. "They make the best husbands."

"I'll say yea to that," Pat said.

"Nowadays, what does it matter?" Sadie said, sensing perhaps that she had bridged the awkward moment.

Later, when the moving truck had come and they finally settled down in their own bed, Heshy turned to his wife and hugged her.

"Well, what do you think?" he asked.

"I think that all Jewish men should marry Shiksas." She held him closely and he felt warm and at home in the strange new environment.

They were too busy to do much socializing during the first weeks at Sunset Village, their time taken up by decorating their one-bedroom condominium and learning their way around the area. Sadie Berman would come in occasionally with offers of help, but it struck them both as more of a bread-and-butter courtesy than a sincere offer.

Before long, Heshy was called upon by the leaders of rival Synagogues that had been established in Sunset Village. The representative of the

Orthodox took one look at Pat and politely left the apartment, but the Conservative, a Mr. Horowitz, an ex-lawyer, was determined to lead them to commitment.

"We have a number of intermarriages," he said pompously. "And our Rabbi has a great understanding of the problems attendant thereto." Obviously, the man had not forgotten his legal training, Heshy observed.

"I'm sorry, we're simply not religious," he said.

"Your wife did not adopt the Jewish faith?" Mr. Horowitz asked.

"No."

"Is she a Catholic?" Mr. Horowitz asked, lowering his voice as if Pat was not within earshot. She was puttering around in the kitchen, but Heshy knew she was listening.

"No."

"Well, then," Mr. Horowitz seemed to puff up like a giant bird, his beak pointed into the air. "What do you consider yourselves?"

"We're people," Heshy said. "We consider ourselves people."

Mr. Horowitz harumphed politely into his fist, gathering his dignity, until he could muster the courage to leave.

"Your fuse is getting short," Pat said, stroking Heshy's thigh.

"I know," he said, feeling not the slightest twinge of regret.

In the laundry building one day, he met Abe Berman, who was standing with a group of men. There seemed to be an odd sense of camaraderie about the group, a kind of cliquishness, that reminded him of his Brooklyn days when the boys hung around the candy store, something he had never done. Again, he felt the old envy, the wish to belong. Abe Berman came over to him, tucked an arm under his and dragged him to the group.

"My wash," Heshy protested.

"Who worries about the wash?" Abe said. "This is Heshy Leventhal." The men nodded recognition. He rattled off a series of names, nicknames which might have come from earlier days, "Natie, Solly, Izzie," One other man was named Heshy.

"That's what they call me," Heshy volunteered. "My family never called me anything else. My real name is Harold."

"His wife calls him Heshy too and she's a Shiksa," Abe said, imparting the information with some pride.

"How lucky can you get?" the man called Natie said. "The best, absolutely the best."

"I wanted to marry a Shiksa," one of the men said. "But my mother threatened to kill herself by throwing herself out of the window."

"Jewish women," another man said. "They've been put on Earth to torture us. Do this. Do that. Gimme this. Gimme that. Buy me this. Buy me that. You marry a Shiksa and they do for you."

"That's because they got a goyishe kop," a woman who overheard them interjected. She waved a finger at them. "Nothing like a good Jewish wife."

"In the next life, I'll take a Shiksa anytime," Abe Berman said. Heshy, feeling the discomfort of their remarks, went back to his wash, riveting his attention on the tumbling clothes. When he finished the laundry, he stuffed it into his bag and, without a word to Abe Berman, left for home. He did not tell Pat about the incident.

They began to go to the pool every day. Pat wore a big hat and large sunglasses, smearing her thin Irish skin with layers of creams for protection. Poolside was always crowded and there seemed to be an unwritten rule that one could stamp out his turf and it would, by silent consent, be their place. They made little effort to make friends, but could not shut out the chattering around them as they concentrated on their paperbacks and observed the people from behind their glasses.

A group of women sat near them, part of a regular clique of yentas. They were rarely silent as they replayed their card games of the night before and gossiped continuously about their neighbors, their past lives, punctuated by homilies and incantations. They agreed on little except, of course, their universal distaste and contempt for "goyem." When they discussed the outer world and its personalities, they were sure to extract an ethnic identification before pursuing the subject.

"I used to love Cary Grant in the movies," one of them might say.

"You know he's Jewish."

"Really?"

Actually, they were amused by most of the talk. But sometimes the conversation of the yentas took an odd direction, and Heshy would watch his wife stiffen and poke her nose deeper into her book.

"I don't know what's happening in the world," one of the women said.

Having run out of local gossip, their talk had turned to politics, and had drifted back to what was the central issue, always the central issue—Jews.

"I don't know what's happening," the woman repeated. She had a large face with heavy hanging jowls and pockets of chicken skin around her eyes. "Remember when Nixon was president? This Blumenthal married a Shiksa and became a Presbyterian. Schlesinger married a Shiksa and became a Lutheran. Henry Kissinger married a Shiksa."

"That's why he was so rotten to Israel," one of the women interjected. "Once they get their hooks into a man, that's the end of it."

"I don't know what they see in them," the first woman said. "When they get old, they all look alike."

"Like the Chinese," the second woman said.

"Ben Gurion's son married a Shiksa," another woman said.

"And look what happened to Ben Gurion."

"What happened?"

"It's too long ago. I forgot."

Heshy smiled and looked at Pat. She acknowledged his glance with a smile, but he knew that her amusement was tinged with sadness.

"A Shiksa is bad business," the first woman said. "They go after a Jewish husband and take everything they can take."

"And the children are always a mess."

"Always."

It was not that anyone was impolite, or even unfriendly. What was said with such passion never translated itself into personal enmity. But the idea, like a virus, was loose in the firmament of Sunset Village. The Shiksa was an alien. The goyem were never to be trusted. It is safer among your own. The Jews must help themselves. Under every goyem beats the heart of an anti-Semite.

"It can make you paranoid," Pat said one day after returning home from shopping. "People look at you and you can't help thinking that they know. 'There goes the Shiksa, Mrs. Leventhal.'"

"It's your imagination."

"I wish it were. I met the wonderful Mrs. Berman and we walked with our cart down the aisles. When I put in a jar of Polish sausage, I'd thought she'd vomit."

"You eat that?" she asked.

"And you said?"

"I said nothing. But I wanted to say: 'Yes, we eat that when we get too drunk to taste anything.'"

"You didn't?" Heshy laughed.

The knowledge that such an idea was loose was enough to inhibit their wanting to search out friends. So they kept to themselves. It was not what they would have liked and they viewed it as a failing in themselves.

One morning, just as they had finished their coffee and were preparing to wash the dishes, they heard a frantic knock on the door. It was Mrs. Berman.

Her eyes were puffy and red and she clutched shards of tissue in her hands. "I'm going crazy," she said. "I have to talk to you."

"Is it Abe?" Heshy asked. They dried their hands and sat down beside her on the couch.

"Not Abe, Danny." She looked up. "My son, Danny."

They waited as the woman gathered her strength, getting her breathing under control. She blew her nose. Her hands were gnarled, spotted with liver blotches, hard-working hands. On one finger gleamed an old-fashioned thin diamond wedding ring.

"He's getting married," she began, sighing, the pause tentative.

"That's wonderful," Heshy said, feeling the obligation to fill the void.

"Wonderful?" Mrs. Berman shook her head. "Not so wonderful. That's why I came to you. He's going to marry a Shiksa." She dissolved in tears. Pat bent over to comfort her with a hand on her back, looking at Heshy and shrugging. The woman recovered herself finally and looked at Pat.

"He said he's in love." Heshy remembered, smiling to himself at the woman's exaggerated sense of pain.

"Love," the woman said with contempt. The quick stab of anger, sobered her, and her tears dried. "I came here to ask a favor."

"A favor?"

"I want you to talk to Danny." Heshy was not sure who she was addressing. "Both of you," she clarified.

"About what?" Pat asked.

"I want you to tell him the truth."

"The truth."

"He'll only respond if he gets it from the horse's mouth. Not that it will make much of a difference, but at least it's a try." They looked at each other, but the woman was under control now, determined. "I want you to tell him how difficult it has been. The hardships. The problems for the children. I know you have children. The confusion. The suffering. I'm sure you can tell him about the suffering. No matter what I say, he pays no attention. You think I don't know how terrible it must have been."

She raised her head and looked deeply at them. Her pain was quite palpable and she was convinced of her logic. Heshy was tempted to show the woman the door, but that would have been impolitic, he reasoned. No sense making an enemy, he decided, his initial anger dissolving into pity.

"Of course, we'll talk to him," Pat said. The woman leaned against Pat and put her arms around her.

"I knew you would," she said. "I told Abe that."

"How is he taking it?" Heshy asked, disguising his sarcasm.

"Worse than me."

"Danny will be here tonight. I made him promise to come talk to us before he got married." She stood up and smoothed her house dress with her gnarled hands. "I really appreciate this," she said, moving toward the door.

"It could have been worse," Heshy said, as she opened the door, standing in the doorway. Pat stepped on his toes but it wouldn't deter him.

"She could have been black," he said. Mrs. Berman nodded in serious agreement and closed the door behind her.

"Black and Jewish," he called after her, completing the thought, knowing the woman could not hear him.

"I knew it was coming," Pat said. Heshy pointed after her.

"Could you believe it?"

"What will we say to the boy?" Pat asked.

"We'll tell him how terrible it's been," he mimicked. "The pain. The confusion. And we'll serve him polish sausages and beer and you'll sing old Irish ditties and talk about having married a white Jew, someone who couldn't possibly be in on the murder of Christ."

"You Jews are all crazy," Pat said, laughing. "My father was right."

But getting through the day was no laughing matter to either of them. Heshy felt the tension as the day progressed. They stayed home eschewing the pool, had a light lunch, took a nap, watched television for a while.

"What shall we tell him?" Heshy asked during dinner.

"I don't know." Pat admitted.

After dinner, following some mutual urge, they called their children. It wasn't their usual routine, because they exchanged letters frequently and spoke to them every other Sunday. They each chatted a while with their children, their spouses, their grandchildren, then, satisfied, hung up and looked at each other.

"Feel better?" Pat asked. Actually, Heshy had made the first suggestion to call but Pat had agreed quickly.

"Much."

Danny Berman arrived at about nine. He was neatly dressed, about thirty, with a bushy mustache. He was understandably nervous and his eyes darted everywhere but on their faces.

"I don't know what I'm doing here," he said. "It's all part of the treatment, I suppose."

"Your mother tells me you're getting married," Heshy began, feeling ridiculous over the inanity of his remark.

"You'd think I was about to join the KKK."

"I know what you mean."

"That's what I understand." He paused, sat down and crossed and uncrossed his legs. "Are you going to tell me horror stories?"

He must have realized that there was a touch of enmity in his remark. "Look," he said. "I'm here because I love them. But they're so far out in left field that I can't begin to make them understand." He stood up, his mother's eyes flashing in his sockets as he surveyed the room, a helpless search. "I've been living with her for two years. We love each other. It's a formality. That's all it is. We want kids."

"They know that?"

"Of course they do. And they know Charlotte."

"It's really none of our business, you know," Heshy said.

"You're telling me."

"And we really can't give you any advice."

"I know that."

"And we're seeing you only because we don't want to offend them."

"I understand."

"And we're not going to tell you what's right and what's wrong."

"How can you?"

"There is one thing," Pat interjected. She had been sitting quietly watching them, her face reflecting an uncommon troubled thought. They both turned toward her, feeling the pull of her emphasis.

"I don't really like Jewish people," she said quietly. Heshy watched her, startled, and the younger man looked at him, his eyes dancing in confusion. "They're too paranoid, too intolerant, too proud," she paused thoughtfully, "too overbearing, too sensitive, too outspoken, too holier than thou..." She paused again. I don't believe this, Heshy thought. Is this my Pat talking?

"I think they're too hung up on history, too masochistic, too emotional, too clannish."

Danny stood up, his feet planted solidly on the floor, posing in an attitude of instant combat, pugnacious.

"...too quick to jump to conclusions, too ingrown..." Her voice was calm. Danny looked at her, bug-eyed and confused. Heshy watched her, feeling the pull of old memories and his mother's warnings.

"And I don't like the Irish for the same reasons. And the Germans and the Poles and the Hutus and the Tutus and the Arabs and the Japanese and the Wasps and all the rest who think a drop of strange blood is going to water down the genes."

Danny and Heshy exchanged glances and smiled.

"Pat," he said, "you scared the living hell out of me."

"I meant to," she said. "And him too."

"I get the point," Danny said. "But will my folks?"

"Eventually," Pat said, "or else."

He embraced her, shook hands with Heshy and left the apartment.

Later, as they prepared for bed, Heshy wondered aloud.

"You think he'll marry the girl?"

She looked at him and kissed his cheek. "If he really loves her. Isn't that the test?"

WHY CAN'T YOU BE LIKE
THE SOLOMON BROTHERS?

The Solomon brothers were the very model of familial devotion to anyone in Sunset Village who observed them. To watch them going about their daily chores, shopping at the supermarket, visiting the clubhouse, playing shuffleboard, or simply taking a walk, one could not help but admire their solicitousness to each other.

Their neighbors, Lily and Bernie Morrisson, were constantly citing them to their two sons, who hated each other.

"Why can't my children be like the Solomon brothers?" Lily would lament when they would come to visit—individually, of course. Their wives also hated each other, although they shared a mutual dislike for their husbands' parents, the Morrissons.

It did not stop with the brothers and their wives, but passed down, like a genetic disease, to the grandchildren.

"We're one big happy family," Lily would sigh, weary with the undercurrent of family intrigue that such a situation demanded. When their sons would pay their visits to their parents, they would always be under pressure, since they invariably had told their wives they were off on a golfing trip.

It was all very confusing to the Morrissons.

"If only you were like the Solomon brothers," Lily would tell them. It became a perpetual refrain, and she did not observe how much it offended her sons, who restrained their anger at the example.

"Them again?," their son Harry would say, shaking his head. "My brother Sam hates me. He always hated me."

"We're the Morrisson brothers," their son Sam would say. "There's a big difference. My brother is a putz."

"Don't talk like that, Sam" Bernie Morrisson would interject. "Harry is a good boy. You just don't understand him."

"He's a putz."

"Brothers should love each other," Lily Morrisson would say, tears welling in her eyes. "If only you were like the Solomon brothers."

Sometimes they would ignore her.

"What did we do? Is it our fault?" Bernie would say after one or the other went back to New York. It had been their great dream for their sons to love each other, to stick together through thick and thin. It was their greatest disappointment in life.

"How come you're so good to each other?" Lily would ask the Solomon brothers when she and Bernie were invited into their neat little apartment for dinner. Most of the time, they kept to themselves, but because they were immediate next-door neighbors, Lily and Bernie had become friendly, not intimate, but friendly.

The Solomon brothers' apartment was beautifully decorated. Their living room was a medley of blues and greens, with chairs and couch covered with matching chintz. Original oil paintings reflecting the same color schemes hung on the walls. There also were a number of photographs scattered around the room showing the brothers, in various stages of their lives, smiling shyly into the camera.

In the background, there was invariably some landmark indicating that they had traveled in a foreign land. They apparently had traveled extensively. Both were small men, compact figures, and their clothes were immaculate, the creases in their trousers perfectly sharp, their sport shirts in colors that were always compatible to each other. And the food they served was exceptionally tasty, usually French. They were excellent hosts.

"It's always such a pleasure to watch you together," Lily Morrisson said one evening as they sat around the dinner table after a particularly delicious meal. Both brothers had assisted in the serving as if there were some special internal rhythm that made them compatible, like the workings of a finely tuned clock. They complemented each other. They responded to Mrs. Morrisson's remark by stealing a shy glance at each other.

"Our sons hate each other; they haven't even talked in years. It's horrible." Lily said.

"We can't understand it," Bernie said. "It's very unpleasant, especially now."

"Why now?" Mark Solomon said. He appeared to be the older brother, although they were so close in age it was hard to tell. He was bald but had let his hair grow long enough to fold it over his pate. The other brother, Isadore, had a full head of steel gray hair. He was never addressed as Izzy, always Isadore.

"Next week is our fiftieth wedding anniversary," Lily said, "so we've asked both of our sons down with their families and their children."

"How wonderful?" Mark said, clasping his hands and darting a glance at his brother.

"Marvelous," Isadore responded.

"It's going to be like an armed camp," Bernie said. "We insisted on it, though. And we booked a room at Primero's for a sit-down dinner. Believe it or not, Lily got them to agree to split the cost down the middle. I tell you, I'm not looking forward to it."

"I'm the one that insisted," Lily said. "Why not? We're a family. Why shouldn't both our children and their families come to celebrate our fiftieth anniversary. What's so terrible?"

"Even the children hate each other," Bernie sighed.

"But why?" Mark asked.

"Why?" Lily repeated. "Because why is a crooked letter."

"Maybe it's our fault," Bernie said. "We had them one on top of each other. Lily was an only child. To her, there was nothing worse than being an only child...."

"It was terrible," she interjected.

"So we had them close together."

"We thought they would be friends. We thought they would love each other. Anything was better than being an only child. From the beginning, we told them that they should love each other, stick together, help one another, be good to each other," Lily said, her eyes drifting from one

Solomon brother to the other. "Like you two." The brothers blushed and lowered their eyes.

"Maybe we should call the whole thing off," Bernie said, shaking his head. "Who needs the aggravation?" It had been a sore point of contention between him and his wife and he could see her lips purse in anger, although he knew she would hold her temper in front of the Solomon brothers.

"I'm sorry," she said. "A fiftieth anniversary is a family event. How many people live long enough to celebrate their fiftieth anniversary?" She looked at the Solomon brothers. "How long were your parents married?"

"Oh, they died early," Mark Solomon replied quickly. Isadore Solomon nodded.

"See," Lily said. "I'll bet you would have loved to be at their fiftieth."

"Oh, yes," Isadore said.

"Who needs the aggravation?" Bernie repeated.

"We won't be here forever," Lily said. "I'd feel terrible going to my grave knowing that they still hated each other."

"She thinks that the party will bring them together, that they'll suddenly discover what it means to be a family," Bernie said glumly.

"Why not?" Lily said, looking at Bernie with contempt, indicating the depth of their disagreement. "There comes a time when people must recognize that blood is thicker than water." She seemed on the verge of tears and Bernie tapped her arm, an obvious signal for them to leave. She stood up and hugged each Solomon brother in turn.

"If only my sons were like you," she whispered.

Making the arrangements for the fiftieth anniversary party was not without its problems, as little communication existed between the brothers, and their only point of contact was their parents.

"What motel is Harry and Mildred staying at?" Sam asked his mother on the telephone.

"I think the Holiday," Lily responded.

"You're sure?"

"Not absolutely. I think so."

"Well, I'll make reservations at the Ramada, but if Harry and Mildred are there too, Gladys will have a fit."

"So she'll have a fit."

"It's easy for you to say. You don't have to live with her."

"Thank God."

"That was uncalled for, Ma."

She paused a moment, gathering her thoughts, quieting her anger. It was the daughters-in-law that made matters worse between the brothers. It was those miserable bitches.

"Fight when I'm gone," she whined. "Not when I'm alive."

"Now you're starting that again."

"Wait until your children act like this. You'll have your own punishment."

"This is shit, Ma." Sam pleaded. "All I asked is what motel they'd be staying at."

"It's going to be some wonderful fiftieth anniversary."

"It wasn't my idea to have this party, Ma," Sam said.

"A family should be together at their parents' fiftieth anniversary," she said, pounding her fist on the telephone table.

"Take it easy, Ma. You'll get yourself sick."

"Good," she sighed.

When she hung up, she felt fatigued by the conversation.

"Maybe we should call it off," said Bernie, who had been listening.

She turned toward him, her eyes as cold as ice.

"If you didn't give up so easily, maybe they wouldn't be like this now. You should have insisted that they be like brothers." Her knuckles rapped the top of the television set.

"You're blaming me?"

"Who else?"

She tossed and turned all night and, in the morning, she called her son Harry collect at his insurance office. She had never done that before.

"You all right, Ma?" Harry asked with a show of genuine concern.

"Why shouldn't I be all right?"

"You scared the hell out of me."

"I had a question."

"I'm listening, Ma. But I'm in the middle of a meeting. Eight people are watching me."

"Will you be at the Holiday or the Ramada? I forgot."

"That's what you called me about?"

"Sam wanted to know."

"What did you tell him?"

"At the Holiday."

"Where is he staying?"

"At the Ramada."

"Good."

"I can't believe my own sons can act like this. I can't believe it. My daughters-in-law, I can believe. Two miserable bitches..."

"Not now, Ma, please. Not now."

"You both won't be happy until you eat my heart out. Two sons? Two schmucks."

"Maybe we shouldn't have this at all," Harry snapped. "I'm sure Sam feels the same way. Who needs it?"

"We're a family..." his mother began.

"Don't start, Ma. Please. Not now."

"Who do you think gets the heartache? Not you. Not Mildred. Not Sam. Not Gladys. Me. And your father."

"I'm hanging up."

"It's nothing but aggravation," she sighed, tears beginning. She blew her nose into a tissue.

"Why can't you understand? Sam and I can't help it if we're related. We just can't stand each other."

"I don't want to hear," Lily said, hanging up the phone.

"Is it necessary to aggravate yourself?" Bernie asked.

"I'm only a mother," Lily sighed.

At her weekly canasta game in the card room of the Clubhouse, Lily endured the constant chatter about children and grandchildren. It was common knowledge that her sons couldn't stand each other. Lily's lament was well-known to her friends. Sometimes, she imagined, they took a special delight in tormenting her.

"My Robert bought a house in Jamaica with my Sybil," Yetta Goldstein said, arranging her cards in her hand, not looking up. "One will use it for a month, and the other will use it for a month."

"It's a big house?" another of the players asked mechanically.

"Four bedrooms. And they have altogether five servants when they stay there. I have my choice of whether to go when Robert's family is there or when Sybil's family is there."

Lily held her tongue. She is doing it purposely, she thought. Whenever she stayed with one of her sons, the tension made it impossible and she had to find some pretext to leave earlier than planned. But even those visits had ceased years ago.

"We'll be gone soon enough," she invariably told her sons privately on those occasions, usually at the very last moment, when they carried her suitcases to the taxi.

But despite all that had happened and was happening, she was determined to go through with the fiftieth anniversary party. It was a matter of pride, she suspected, and she had already broadcast the impending event to her fellow canasta players and to the yentas who sat around the pool probing into the lives of their neighbors.

"You're still having the golden?" Minnie Schein asked. Minnie's was always the voice of impending doom. She was always the first one to announce a death or a disaster. She had been asking about the fiftieth since Lily first made the announcement.

"Absolutely," Lily said. "A fiftieth is a fiftieth. How many times does it happen?"

"You think there'll be fireworks?"

"Why should there be fireworks?" she mumbled, regretting her previous confidences.

But despite her bravado, she was frightened. A soup-to-nuts meal had been arranged, complete with anniversary cake and fancy service. At first, she thought she might invite the canasta players. Two of them were widows and the other was married, but she was frightened that if there was a blowup, they would tell the whole world.

"I've decided I'm going to invite the Solomon brothers," she announced to Bernie one night as they lay in bed watching television.

"To where?"

"Where else? The party."

"You think that's smart?" Bernie asked. It had reached a stage where he rarely referred to the party because it always triggered aggravation, usually ending with an attack on him. Somehow, when Lily was angry, all their troubles were Bernie's fault.

"I want them to see how brothers can be. Maybe they'll feel ashamed. Maybe a good example will make them realize the importance of being good and loving brothers."

"Maybe?" Bernie wanted to protest, but he held off. The example of the Solomon brothers had been flaunted for years and it had done little good. He also knew that the party had become a fixation in Lily's mind, as a kind of last chance, perhaps, to set the stage for a family reconciliation.

But when she invited the Solomon brothers the next morning, their hesitation was apparent. They looked at one another and she could see that they were uncomfortable.

"But you said it's strictly family," Isadore Solomon pointed out. "We'll feel out of place."

"Out of place?" she protested. "You're my neighbors, my dear neighbors. I want you to share our joy."

"But it's so..." Mark Solomon groped for a word.

"So personal," Isadore interjected.

"Please," she begged. "It's important to me and Bernie."

They hesitated for some moments more, watching each other.

"All right," Isadore said finally. She hugged them both.

"You're wonderful," she said. "If only my own sons were like you."

"I still think it's a rotten idea," Bernie said as he got into his best suit on the evening of the party. Both families had arrived and settled into their separate motels. Lily warned both sons to be on their best behavior when they telephoned to announce their arrivals.

"Nothing is going to spoil my fiftieth," she told them both firmly.

As she stood before the mirror applying make-up to her aged face, she wondered if Bernie wasn't right after all. "But we're a family," she insisted to herself, convincing the image in the mirror that she couldn't just give up on the idea of family.

"You know, I can't remember when the whole bunch of us was ever together." Bernie said.

"That's because it never happened."

"Sad," Bernie mumbled.

"If this doesn't work, I give up." Lily said.

"So they'll be together at our funerals," Bernie said, pinching Lily's upper arm.

"Don't be so sure the daughters-in-law will come."

"In the box, I won't worry, believe me."

Lily decided that she and Bernie would arrive at Primero's early, not only to check out the details of the dinner, but to be sure that they were there when the families started arriving.

Nothing good would come of the warring factions being alone together before the ice was broken, she decided. Luckily, the arrangements had been made carefully. In fact, Lily had driven the manager of Primero's to near desperation as she planned the menu, the seating arrangements, the flowers. She even ordered a dozen matchbooks with gold leaf lettering saying, "Lily and Bernie Morrisson, A Golden Wedding Anniversary."

Satisfied that everything was in proper order, they stood near the door of the private room waiting for their sons and their families to arrive.

Sam and Gladys and their three teenage daughters were the first to arrive. There was the usual fussing and kissing as the grandchildren submitted to Lily and Bernie's blandishments, fidgeting, obviously annoyed at having their lives disrupted.

"You look very good, both of you," Gladys said to her in-laws, making a great show of ingratiation. She was a large woman, grown obviously larger since the elder Morrissons last saw her, a matter about which she was quite sensitive. "I got fat."

"A sign of contentment," Lily said, smiling, determined to be charming. She noted, too, to herself, that the three daughters took after their mother and were already showing signs of their future expansion.

"Yeah, a contented cow," her husband Sam said sarcastically, revealing obvious tension between them.

"You look beautiful, Gladys," Lily insisted.

"Really beautiful," Bernie said, offering support.

My handsome son had to marry such a pig, Lily thought, hating herself for harboring such thoughts. But Gladys would not surrender to the obvious hypocrisy.

"I look at a Danish and gain ten pounds."

"If only you stopped at looking," Sam said. The tension between them had been at fever pitch as they drove in their rented car to Primero's.

Gladys had threatened to throw herself out of the car and Sam pulled over and opened the door.

"So, jump," he cried. "And I'll cut off your mother's allowance."

For years, he had provided Gladys' mother with a monthly stipend. The threat had calmed her, at least temporarily. But it had not shut her up entirely.

"Its all right for me to suffer, but you didn't have to inflict your guilt on the girls."

"They're part of the family."

"We didn't have to come," the oldest girl screeched. "Its no big deal."

"It is to me," their father said.

"Well, then you should have come alone," Gladys screamed. "Your mother hates me. Your brother hates me. His bitchy wife, Mildred, hates me, and those two retarded children of theirs hate me."

"You forgot someone," Sam said.

"Who?"

"Me."

They drove the rest of the way to the restaurant in silence. When Harry and Mildred arrived with their two sons, both wearing scraggy beards and blue jeans, Sam and his family moved to the other end of the room. Bernie eyed the boys with distaste.

"They couldn't put on suits," he whispered to Harry. But Mildred overheard.

"They're doing their own thing. There's nothing wrong with what they're wearing."

"She's belligerently liberated," Harry said, looking at his mother and shrugging.

"The boys look wonderful, wonderful," Lily said, kissing them both. One of them waved to the girls, who huddled in a corner.

"Hey Cozzes. Qué pasa?"

The girls turned away indignantly.

"Three fatties," Mildred mumbled. "And look at their cow of a mother."

"You promised, Mildred," Harry pleaded.

They had all come bearing gifts, which now were piled on the floor behind the two seats of honor. A waiter came and took their drink orders.

"Make mine a double martini," Mildred said, looking at her husband.

"Easy on the juice," her husband warned.

"How the hell do you think I'm going to get through this?"

The room was small, dominated by a table set lengthwise. Lily had put place cards in front of each plate, separating the two sons and their wives for obvious reasons. She deliberately placed her sons and daughters-in-law side by side on opposite ends of the table, intermixing the children. Next to each daughter-in-law, she left an empty chair for the Solomon brothers.

"What did you do that for?" her son Sam demanded. Harry came over to offer the same protest. The two brothers glared at each other.

"Why couldn't you put them together at the other end of the table?" Harry suggested.

"Who needs them?" Sam shrugged.

"What's the matter with you two? You don't even say hello to each other," Bernie said. They turned toward each other and shrugged.

"So, hello," Harry said.

"Big deal," Sam replied.

"You can't be nice just for a few hours?" their father said.

"OK. OK," Harry said. "We'll be nice."

"But we can't vouch for her," Sam said, motioning toward Gladys with his chin.

Mildred ordered another double Martini.

"I see she still gets tanked," Sam hissed.

"Talk about tanks," Harry shot back, nodding toward Sam's corpulent wife.

"Stop this at once," Lily said. "At once." She meant to keep her voice down. At that moment, the Solomon brothers arrived.

"And these are the Solomon brothers," Lily announced when she saw them walk shyly into the room, obviously uncomfortable. She grasped their hands and walked them around the room introducing them individually to every member of the family. They endured the ordeal bravely, despite the absence of either smiles or warmth from the family.

"So you're the famous Solomon brothers?" Sam said, watching them curiously. "My mother has mentioned you both many times."

"I hope favorably," Isadore Solomon said, looking at his brother.

"Favorably?" Sam said, downing his second scotch. "Did you come here by walking on water?"

Harry laughed, watching the Solomon brothers' confusion.

"My mother thinks you're twin Jesuses, is what he means," Sam said.

"You should learn from them," Lily said. The Solomon brothers looked at each other sheepishly.

"When are we gonna eat, Ma?" one of the teenage girls asked loudly.

"When they stop guzzling," her mother answered.

"The three little piggies," Mildred mumbled.

"Four," one of her sons said, poking his brother in the ribs.

"I see they're still retarded," Gladys snickered, and the girls giggled behind their hands.

"This was definitely not a very bright idea, Ma," Sam told his mother.

"No kidding," Harry said.

She put each of the Solomon brothers next to her daughters-in-law. On the other side of each of them was one of the grandchildren. Despite the politeness and good cheer on the part of the Solomon brothers, their dinner partners were not overjoyed. They protested.

"Why do I have to sit next to him?" one of the girls whispered, loud enough to be heard.

"Yeah, why?" one of Harry's sons said, also above a whisper. "I'll lose my appetite."

"See," the girl protested. "Even the retard objects." She started to rise.

"Sit down and shut up," her mother said.

The girl's lips puckered as she held back her tears and sat down again.

Lily and Bernie sat at the center of the table, one son beside each of them.

When everyone was finally seated, the conversation seemed to disappear and only the sound of silverware clinking against plates could be heard in the room.

No one spoke, as they quickly wolfed down the chopped liver course.

Bernie whispered to Lily: "See, I told you."

"Better quiet than argument," she said bravely.

But the quiet was shattered when one of the waiters dripped soup on Harry's wife, Mildred. She had been nursing her third double martini and the waiter urged her politely to move so he could place the soup on the table. She hadn't, and a few drops of liquid had fallen on her shoulder.

"Why can't you be more careful, you schmuck?" she cried. The waiter flushed.

"Mildred," Harry snorted. "No big deal."

"Not for you. I'm the one that got spilled on." The waiter pressed the damp spot on her dress with a napkin.

"Get your damned hands off me," Mildred screamed, elbowing the waiter in the stomach.

"She's two sheets to the wind," Sam said smugly. His brother glared at him, then turned toward his wife.

"I warned you, Mildred," Harry sneered.

"Warn shwarn. You don't think I can get through this without a couple of drinks."

"She can't get through anything without a couple of drinks," Gladys whispered to one of the Solomon brothers. But her voice carried and Mildred turned her venom on her.

"Well, old fat tits has got to put in her two cents."

"Christ, Mildred," Harry said, half rising from the table.

"You better shut her up," Sam warned. Harry turned toward his brother angrily.

"And you shut up old lard ass."

"Children," Lily screeched, her voice filling the room like a siren, jolting everyone to silence. She wanted to cry, but she lifted her chin bravely, although a single tear glistened in her left eye.

"This is our fiftieth anniversary. Why must you fight? Isn't it time that everyone stopped fighting?" She hadn't meant to make that speech until after dessert was served.

"You should show some respect," Bernie admonished. Both sons lowered their eyes in a pretense of shame for the benefit of their parents.

"It was a shitty idea," Mildred bellowed, her tongue thick, her hands fluttering in front of her, playing with a napkin.

"Will you shut up?" Harry shouted.

"She's plastered, Dad," one of their boys said.

"The least we can do is sit together and peacefully break bread on our fiftieth anniversary," Bernie shrugged, his eyes roaming the table. His look seemed to quiet everyone and they passed uneventfully through the soup course.

Then the waiters served the chicken kiev and vegetables. But Mildred, with a gesture of contempt, waved the plate away.

"Bring me another martini," she commanded the waiter.

"You'd better not," her husband said.

"I'll do what I damned please."

"Then you'll do it by yourself."

"Who the hell do you think you are?" Mildred said, rising unsteadily, hands on hips, glaring at her husband.

"Throw the broad out," Sam hissed.

"She's a disgrace," Gladys said, as their three daughters watched smugly.

"Sit down, dammit," Harry shouted. Mildred dropped back into her seat. A moment later, her head dangled over the table.

"Now you see one of the reasons why we have nothing to do with them," Sam said to his parents.

"That's bullshit," Harry said. "Besides, who can stand your arrogant superior selfish attitude." He looked at his mother. "He was always obnoxious, Mom. Always a son-of-a-bitch."

"I was a son-of-a-bitch?" Sam said incredulously. "If it was up to you, you'd screw me out of everything. Take, take. That's all you know." He looked at Mildred, her head on the table's surface, her hair spilling into the sauce of the chicken kiev. "You probably drove her to it."

"She's a damned good wife," Harry said defensively. "The tension got to her, that's all." He looked at Gladys. "Better than that fat-assed yenta you married, and the three little piggies."

"I won't sit here and take that," Gladys shouted, rising from her seat. Her three daughters, all sniffling, rose with her. The Solomon brothers glanced at each other with increasing discomfort.

"Can you die from this?" Lily said. She slapped the table, rattling the dishes.

"Enough!" she screamed, her face turning beet red.

"Just sit down," Sam said to his wife and children. Gladys looked at him with disgust.

"I will not."

"Yes, you will." She stood for a long moment, the daughters as well.

"We'll discuss this later," she warned, finally sitting down, the daughters obediently aping her action.

"You don't think they'd miss a meal, do you?" one of Harry's sons said.

"You see. You see," Gladys shouted.

"I'm disgusted with all of you," Lily said. "Monsters, the whole lot of you." She looked at her own sons. "Brothers? Some brothers. If I would have known how you both would turn out, I would have drowned you at birth."

"That's a disgusting thing to say," Gladys said.

"I know," Lily continued. "Look at my family, my wonderful family. Not one ounce of pleasure have I ever gotten from any of you. Not one ounce. Even on my fiftieth anniversary."

"Please, Lily," Bernie said.

"How can I leave this earth knowing that my children hate each other?" She looked into the faces of the Solomon brothers.

"Why can't they be like you two. Brothers who love each other." Her eyes searched the faces of her own sons. "Why is it that you can't be like them? Devoted. Loving. It's a pleasure to watch them together. And you two together are like animals, animals."

"They're not such great examples, Ma," Harry said.

"Not now, Harry," Sam pleaded.

"Somebody's got to tell them."

"Let it be someone else then."

"Why?"

"Come on, Harry. It'll only make things worse."

Both Solomon brothers had turned white. But Lily was ignoring her son's exchange, not noticing the increasing tension.

"I always dreamed that my sons would be together, through everything, helping one another." She looked at the Solomon brothers. "Like Mark and Isadore."

"They're gay, Ma. Fags. Fagales, Ma," Harry cried.

"Why can't you shut your fucking mouth?" Sam shouted.

"They're fags, Ma" Harry repeated. He seemed on the verge of hysterics. "And I'll be willing to bet they're not brothers." The Solomon brothers turned ashen.

"Not brothers?" Lily said, confused.

"Worse if they're brothers," Harry said. "That would be incest on top of it." He turned to the Solomon brothers. "Tell her, for chrissakes."

The Solomon brothers exchanged pained looks. Then Isadore Solomon shook his head and turned toward Lily and Bernie.

"We feel so bad for you both," Isadore said, with dignity.

"You're not brothers?" Lily asked.

Everyone in the room grew silent waiting for Isadore's answer.

"If you mean are we siblings," Isadore said, his voice wavering, but his dignity intact. He looked at Mark. "But we are brothers in spirit." Mark smiled and nodded agreement.

"And body," Harry said smugly.

But Isadore was not finished.

"Enough, Harry," Lily said, turning to Isadore. She nodded toward Isadore and he continued.

"We have been brothers in the truest sense for nearly as long as you both are married. We're friends, good pals and, most important, we love each other. We also respect each other, trust each other and depend on each other."

Mark nodded as Isadore spoke.

"I am sorry to say this but there is more love and brotherhood between us than can be found in this room." He turned to Lily and Bernie. "I don't mean you, Lily, or you, Bernie. And don't blame yourselves. There are no signs of brotherly love here. Your children are strangers to each other. They hate each other and their spouses and children hate each other."

"Advice from fags we don't need," Sam sneered.

"We came here for your sake, Lily and Bernie. You are very brave to believe in the fantasy that siblings must love each other." He looked at Mark and smiled. "We feel more like siblings than they ever will. And we choose to be recognized as brothers, the Solomon brothers." He sucked in a deep breath and sighed. "Thank you for inviting us."

They started to move out, just as the anniversary cake with fifty lit candles was being wheeled into the dining room.

"No, wait," Lily said to the Solomon brothers, as she took Bernie's hand and they stopped before the cake. "Help us blow out the candles," Lily said to the brothers.

They stood around the cake and blew out the candles. Then they all exchanged kisses and the four of them together left the room.

"Did you make a wish?" Isadore asked, addressing his question to Lily and Bernie.

"We always make the same wish," Lily sighed.

"As you can see it never came true," Bernie shrugged.

"So I made a new one," Lily said, squeezing Bernie's hand.

"Me, too," Bernie said.

"I hope I'm in it," Lily said.

"Who else?" Bernie chuckled. "I'm in yours, aren't I?"

"For a change," Lily said. "For a change."

JUST ONCE

The shuttle bus meandered slowly through the main avenue, halting at the stop stations to pick up other passengers. Rose sat in the first section, just behind the driver, and she could hear the motor cough and sputter as it revved up for movement. It was the principal form of transportation within Sunset Village, a godsend for those who didn't have cars and needed to get around.

She was off to the clubhouse for her Wednesday Mah-Jongg game and she had taken out her knitting, mentally counting the knits and purls for the beige socks she was knitting for her grandson, Kenny. It was hot, she would remember, although the movement of the shuttle bus created a light breeze that gently stroked her cheeks and rustled her hair.

The little folded note, on white paper, seemed to flutter to her lap and, looking up to see how it got there, she had seen his face, tanned, with a shy smile. The shuttle bus moved on, and, she remembered, she had turned forward with some embarrassment after she had observed what she imagined was a wink, as he stood where he had apparently stepped off the shuttle bus, looking after her. Perhaps it was a trick, she thought, looking at the folded note on her lap, then turning again to see his figure in the distance still rooted to the spot where he had disembarked.

Replacing her knitting in the bag, she fished for her glasses, found them, perched them midway on the bridge of her nose, because they were half-glasses just for reading, and opened the note. She read the words, gasped lightly, then looked around her to see if anyone had noticed what had happened, or was looking over her shoulder. It was purely a reflex, as the shuttle was half empty and the occupants seemed absorbed in their own thoughts.

"I think you're cute," the note read. She read it again, turned it over, as if searching for more words, then looked back to that spot where the man had been. But the shuttle had already turned into the broad street leading to the clubhouse, and another row of condominiums blocked her view of where she had seen him last.

"I think you're cute," she repeated to herself. "Cute?" Either the man had mistaken her for someone else or he was simply crazy. Some of these old men reverted to childishness as they grew older. She had heard enough stories about that and had observed some strange goings on to be able to dismiss such silliness as sheer senility.

"Me, cute?" she thought. She couldn't wait to tell the girls at the Mah-Jongg game. But when she got to the card room and slid into her seat at the table, she could not bring herself to say a word about the incident. Maybe it would be better to remain silent, she decided, although she made a mental note to tell her husband, Jake. But she could not get it out of her mind.

"You're not concentrating, Rose," Dotty Cohen said with her usual haughtiness. She was all business at the Mah-Jongg table and could tolerate no bad moves by others.

But the admonishment didn't help Rose's game. Her mind kept wandering, reconstructing the man's face, which was fading quickly from her memory. All except the wink. No, she decided, it was definitely not a tic.

She didn't tell Jake either, and when he dozed off in his chair in front of the television set, she looked at the note again. She had refolded it and put it in her change purse. Her fingers shook as she opened it and read the words again. She wondered what it meant.

Later, as she creamed her face in the bathroom, her eyes lingered over her image in the mirror. The lines spread out from the sides of her eyes and, despite the best efforts of her various pre-bedtime moisturizers, her facial skin seemed to her like the hide of an elephant.

"You're an old lady," she whispered to her reflection, although she admitted to herself as a sop to her vanity. "Maybe you don't look sixty-eight. But you also don't look cute."

She smiled, showing the evenly matched front capped teeth attached to the back bridge, which she removed and put into a glass, poured in the cleaning fizz and put it into the medicine cabinet for the night.

But when she got into bed, she still could not put the incident out of her mind. Years ago, in public school, they would pass little puppy love notes between them. There was a fat boy in the back of the classroom who dropped tiny folded papers on her desk; on them, in bad penmanship, were written what were gigglingly referred to later as professions of love. "I really like you," they would invariably read, under which would be a long uneven line of X's and one big "smack," which was the blockbuster kiss symbol in those days. She would show the note to her girlfriends after school, many of whom had received the same missives. She couldn't remember the fat boy's name.

She hadn't thought about that part of her life for years and was surprised to discover how detailed her recall was. It was nearly sixty years ago, she thought, proud of her memory and warmed by the recalled images. She imagined that she could even smell the pungent ink that half-filled the little inkwells while the faces of her childhood friends floated in her mind. Finally, flushed and happy that she was able to remember such pleasant things, she slipped into sleep.

She was still happy in the morning, feeling an uncommon lightness within herself that she could not understand. The apartment looked particularly cheerful to her, the furniture, the drapes, the little knickknacks that were scattered on tables and shelves, well-suited to their environment. Even the pictures of her children and grandchildren scattered throughout the apartment seemed to reach out, triggering even greater pride than usual.

The toast seemed crisper, the butter more delicate, the soft-boiled eggs perfect and the coffee the most delicious she ever tasted. Even Jake noticed.

"You're singing," he said, watching her move about the little kitchen.

She hadn't realized, putting her hand over her mouth to stifle an eruption of giggles.

"So I am," she said, not understanding how the tune had slipped into her mind. She had been singing "I'm in Heaven," repeating the phrase over and over again and humming the rest of the tune. After a while, she began to sing again.

"There you go," Jake said.

"I guess I just feel good," she said, kissing him on the forehead.

Later, when she went outside to sit on the lounge chair behind her apartment, she found herself breathing deeply, savoring the perfumed smell of the tropical flowers, flavored with the morning moisture. Even the sky looked incredibly blue to her. She resumed her knitting, but her mind wandered, and she found her thoughts again telescoped to her girlhood.

She met Jake while she was still in high school, Girls' High, taking a business course. Jake worked at his father's delicatessen, standing behind the counter in a big white apron that was stained with all the colorful residues of the appetizer section.

He was a born kibbutzer and flirted outrageously with the female customers. She remembered how important he looked behind the counter. The raised floor walk made him seem especially imposing. Their first date was a Sunday afternoon in Prospect Park. He took her to the zoo and they went rowing on the lake. She remembered that Jake had rolled up his sleeves, showing off his large biceps, which he seemed to be flexing perpetually. In those days, big muscles were supposed to devastate young ladies.

She was already in love with him by the end of the day, and she let him kiss her lips when he took her home, a very daring action, because even at sixteen she believed that girls could get pregnant if a man kissed their lips. One of her girlfriends assured her, however, that if you kept your lips closed tight—which is what she had done—nothing would happen. The idea of it provided much humor in the family for nearly fifty years, the telling and retelling of it, already passed down through two additional generations.

But she never told about other intimacies. They seemed so benign in today's world, she thought, reveling in the idea of her early naiveté. Once he had cupped her breast and she had been moved to near hysterics, frightening him, as if she had cried rape.

"You won't respect me," she whimpered.

"I love you," Jake assured her.

"You'll think I'm a loose woman. Then you'll lose all respect for me."

There was something magic in the concept of respect, she remembered.

One didn't discuss such things with one's parents in those days, especially hers. Her father was a tailor who took piece work home and worked on his sewing machine every night. Sometimes, in the night, she could still hear the whirring of the wheel and the staccato movement of the needle. And her mother was always cooking, cleaning, washing, sweeping, rarely stopping until she fell exhausted into bed. Sex, as a topic of conversation between parents and children, was unthinkable.

"I was dancing with Jake last night," she said to her friend, Helen, who lived in the next apartment. "Why does he have to carry such a big pen in his pants?"

"A pen?"

"I felt it rubbing against me. He got real mad when I asked him what it was. He said a pen. I wanted to ask him what he needed a pen for when we were dancing, but I didn't."

"You should tell him to leave it home."

"I did. I was real mad at him. I even told him he smelled of pickled herring."

"And what did he say to that?"

"He said what else was he expected to smell from, considering where he worked all day." She had lived with Jake nearly fifty years and, although he had not worked behind a delicatessen counter for ten years, he still smelled faintly of pickled herring.

They went steady for nearly a year before she learned what she thought then were the facts of life. A girl at school, Milly Katz, unraveled a bit of the mystery.

"They have this thingie between their legs."

"A what?"

"A thingie."

"Oh. You mean what they make number one with."

She had, after all, two younger brothers and she had seen them naked on numerous occasions, especially when they were babies.

"It gets hard sometimes."

"So?" That, too, wasn't much of a mystery. She had seen her little brother's thingies get hard sometimes, when they woke up in the morning. Theirs had poked out of their pajamas.

"Well, when they put their hard thingies in the place where we make number one, you have babies."

"Without kissing?"

"I think so."

"It sounds so yukky."

"I know." Milly made a face. "It's getting me nauseous just to think about."

When she realized that kissing alone would definitely not make babies, she and Jake spent long hours on the porch hugging and kissing and staring into space. She even let him put his hands on her breasts over her dress. Occasionally, she would see his pants bulge, which she thought disgusting. By then, she realized that he was not carrying a pen in his pants.

They were the first of their friends to get engaged. But even after he had given her a ring and she finally let him put his hand inside her dress, but over her brassiere, she still had only the vaguest idea of what sex was all about.

There was a battered musty smelling couch on his parents' front porch and after a walk, or a movie, they would come back to her place and lie together on the couch, hugging and kissing. A couple of times, she felt him shudder and moan and he had jumped up with embarrassment, telling her a quick good-bye and going home.

"Don't you feel well?" she would ask.

"I have to get up early," he would say, bending over awkwardly and kissing her on the cheek.

She, too, experienced strange and oddly pleasant feelings, especially when they were together and she found herself developing a compelling curiosity about what he had in his pants. By then, her friend Helen had gained greater knowledge and was able to provide additional information.

"White stuff comes out," she whispered to Rose after Rose had expressed some curiosity about what happens when the thingie goes into her.

She had already discovered the place with her fingers, although she couldn't believe anything thicker than a finger could go in there.

"That's what Kitty told me." Kitty was one of the Italian girls in her class. "She knows a lot about boys."

"You mean it comes out in a stream, like number one?"

"And Kitty says they feel a thrill when it comes out."

"Did she ever see it?"

"Plenty of times, she tells me." She put a hand over her mouth to be sure that no sound escaped. "She said she can make the boys do it by holding it in her hands and rubbing it. Up and down."

The idea of it excited her curiosity, and the next time she was with Jake the back of her hand felt his thing over his pants. He moved away, quickly mumbling something about "after we're married." It was then that she realized that marriage meant being naked with each other and doing things. After that, knowledge came swiftly as she questioned some of the older girls she knew, one of whom had recently gotten married.

"It hurts like hell," Harriet Marks told her. "Especially the first night when he breaks the hymen."

Hymen, she thought. She had an Uncle Hyman and, although she had a clear picture of what occurred, she was still confused about what she was supposed to do and what was supposed to happen.

They spent the first night of their marriage at the Prince Georges Hotel in Brooklyn, and she stayed in the bathroom for nearly an hour before she found the courage to come out. When she did, he was on top of her in less than a minute, trying to get his thing into her. It hurt like hell, just as Harriet Marks told her, and she was sore for the next three months. Also, the mystery was solved and it was no big deal, she decided. Later, after they had been married a few years, it got a little better in that department. Occasionally, she even felt a thrill herself.

That was a long, long time ago and she had never even entertained the idea of doing it with anyone but Jake. She didn't even do it that much with Jake. The whole idea of it eventually became boring, unimportant to their lives.

Sitting in the lounge chair, thinking about those early days, made her smile. Such innocence, she thought. Incredible! How the world had changed. Nothing was left to the imagination anymore. Why am I thinking about this? she wondered, but the memories continued to make her feel good.

There was more to it than just feeling good. She felt a heightened sense of perception and, later, when they went to the clubhouse to see an amateur play, she turned and searched the faces of the audience. But the face of the man who had sent her the note, who had winked, seemed blurred in her mind and, besides, many of the men seemed to look alike. All the old men look alike, her friend Minnie Halpern assured her.

Yet she persisted in her search, not admitting that this was her sole intention as she became more mobile than usual, spending more time in the clubhouse and the pool area. She even persuaded Jake to play shuffleboard with her, a game she usually detested.

"Slow down," Jake protested.

"I don't like to just sit."

One day as she sat by the pool, she set aside her knitting and, feeling drowsy, closed her eyes and dozed fitfully. Jake had stayed home to watch a television program and she had declined to participate in the usual yenta conversations that tinkled around her in the tropical air.

She might have been dreaming, though it was not clear, but something passed near her or over her; a shadow had come and gone. Opening her eyes, she saw his face again watching her from across the pool, a tall man with a heavy shock of white hair. His head moved, jaw thrust forward, in a kind of signal suggesting that there was something she must do.

Looking around her, she saw the white folded paper lying on her half-finished knitted socks. Her reactions were confusing; she felt that she wanted to grab for the note, but she was forcing herself to hold back. Her heart was beating wildly in her chest. She also wanted to smile at the man who continued to observe her at a distance, thrusting his jaw out— which she now knew was a signal for her to read the note.

With trembling fingers, she opened it. But it was not clear enough for her eyes to read and she had to dip into her knitting bag for her glasses. Turning her back to him, she read the note.

"I really think you're cute." The word really was underlined. The intensity of a hot blush increased the temperature of her skin, which was already warm from the sun. But she did not turn to look at the man again, although she was certain now that she had memorized his face. Yet she felt the urge to turn and smile, actually to wink back at him, but she resisted that, too. Instead, she picked up her knitting and, sitting awkwardly on the side of the lounge chair, resumed her stitching. When she did finally turn, he was gone.

But now that she had a clear picture of him, she found herself imagining him in various situations and in conversations. She began to daydream a great deal, sometimes as she sat at the table.

"What are you thinking?" Jake asked. He might have made the remark before, but it had just penetrated her consciousness.

"Nothing," she answered, resuming her eating.

It was incredible to experience such thoughts and feelings, she decided.

An old married woman like me. To have a secret admirer was something that happened in movies. She had already determined that she would never, never acknowledge the man's intentions, never stop to pass the time of day. And if she passed close to him, she knew she would have to turn away.

But the more she would try to deny him, the more his image grew in her mind. She wondered what his name was. He wasn't so bad looking himself, she thought, mentally comparing his looks with Jake's, He didn't have Jake's huge paunch and he still had all his hair. What a beautiful head of hair! Did I think that, she admonished, as she began to clean her apartment furiously, running the vacuum cleaner at a fast clip until even Jake began to notice her uncommon speed.

"Take it easy, Rose."

She slowed down her efforts. It hadn't helped much anyhow since she could not eliminate what was on her mind.

One evening, as she and Jake were coming out of another show at the clubhouse, he loomed in front of her, full face, a sliver of a smile on his lips, a brief wink, and thrust a paper into her hands. She clutched the note, tightened her fist around it, and continued to walk past him. It all happened in a split second. What surprised her most was that she actually abetted the action, conspired with the strange man. Her hand opened and closed as if she had expected the offering.

They rode the shuttle bus back to their apartment. Her hand was moist as she clutched the paper, and both her curiosity and anxiety were churning her insides. They had barely opened the door when she made a beeline for the bathroom and, locking the door, stood for a moment against it, calming herself, getting her breathing to function properly. Then she took her glasses out of her pocketbook and opened the note, soggy with perspiration. She had to read the note three times before she could believe its meaning.

"Please meet me by the water tower at 3 p.m. tomorrow. Please." Under the note was a P.S. "I think you're the cutest thing I ever saw."

She tried to urge indignance upon herself, to will it. The idea of it, she whispered. I have got to tell Jake, she decided, wondering what his reaction would be. She had been a good and faithful wife for nearly fifty years, fifty years. No other man had ever touched her and, even in her memories, she could not think of a single other man who had ever kissed her, although she vaguely remembered playing spin the bottle when she was a little girl, during which some of the boys had kissed her cheek. Nobody had ever, ever written her such outrageous notes; nor had any man ever gotten fresh with her.

She read the note again, refolded it and put it in her change purse, discovering that the other two notes also were hidden there. Why am I saving them? she wondered. Someday I might need the evidence.

She lay in bed that night unable to sleep, listening to Jake's heavy breathing that, she knew, soon would turn into deep, resounding snores. It had been her natural habit to drop off to sleep before the snoring began in earnest. Now, the opportunity had passed and the noise was deafening.

Slipping quietly out of bed, she wrapped her dressing gown around her and sat on the living-room couch. The note was still disturbing her. She could not get it out of her mind. It was not a question of her going. That would be unthinkable. She would feel ridiculous. What would she say to him? Besides, he might by a psychopath, although she did not feel that his face was that of a crazy man.

Just suppose, just suppose I did go, she thought suddenly, ashamed of the idea of it. But the possibility loomed, rose in her mind, like the beginning ripple of a giant wave, forming far out to sea. Nothing like this had ever happened to her. Finally, she admitted to some curiosity.

Just this once, she thought. What harm would there be in it, after all? The wave continued to form, and she felt its power, its urging, heard it crash inside of her. Just once, she thought, her face growing hot. She also felt some odd stirrings in her body, warm, pleasurable. Her nipples were erect. My God, she cried to herself, watching the hardness in the large puddle of her nipple.

There could be no question of sleep that night, and she stayed up, trying to concentrate on her knitting until it began to turn light behind the blinds and, for appearances sake, she slipped into bed beside the snoring Jake.

But in the full light of morning, her resolve strengthened again and she saw how utterly preposterous it was to entertain thoughts of meeting this man. Besides, the lack of sleep had given her a slight headache, enough to rationalize her not being able to make her regular Mah-Jongg game.

She called her friends and told them to get someone else to fill in. She wondered why she had made the call after Jake had left the apartment. She washed the breakfast dishes and cleaned the apartment, then sat on the lounge chair in back of the apartment and busied herself with knitting.

A light breeze rustled the stalks of Bermuda grass and she heard the insects buzzing in the flowers she had planted near the screen porch. While she knew she was having a conflict within herself, it did not affect her sense of up-lift. 'What could he possibly see in me?' she thought, feeling good about his interest, her curiosity expanding.

By the time the sun stood high in the early afternoon, she had decided to go. What harm would there be? Besides, it was quite possible that he was only fooling. There were a lot of old kibbutzers around Sunset Village who did things just for laughs. He probably wouldn't even show up, she decided, although the sense of anticipation stayed with her, rising as she combed her hair and dabbed on some light make-up.

She had never fussed with herself with such diligence before, rubbing in a little rouge, leaving a faint glow at the edge of her cheekbones. When she was finished, she smiled at herself, a contrivance, to see how badly her face wrinkled when she did it. I'm an old woman, she said with resignation, but secretly, inside herself, her body was stirring with feelings she had never had before, or, if she had, she could not remember them.

Jake had come home and was watching television when she left, presuming her to be on her way to her Mah-Jongg game. She felt too much guilt to say good-bye, but slipped out, holding her knitting bag, a permanent fixture, and headed in the direction of the water tower, which rose above the low barracks-like white building of her condominium section. It actually was a short walk, but she timed it to arrive later, slowing her pace as she got closer to be able to observe whether he was really there.

When she saw him, she stopped dead in her tracks, hoping he had not seen her, but her legs would not move in retreat and, for a long moment, she stood frozen, indecisive. The area around the water tower was completely deserted and he was leaning against the slats looking in the opposite direction.

She could leave, she knew. She had not been spotted. Her heart was pounding in her chest and she felt a sudden tightness in her stomach. Just once, an inner voice might have been telling her as she responded to a compulsion, urging her on, and she felt her legs carrying her forward. The sudden action made him turn, and he moved from his leaning posture and stood up as she approached.

A handsome man, she decided, as she came closer. It was an odd thought, quite without logic in her state of mind. New things were happening fast, new sensations.

"I didn't think you would show up," the man said. He was a good head taller than her and the lines in his tanned face were deep, as if he had spent years outdoors. He was smiling, showing even teeth. Probably implants, she thought. She imagined his age about the same as Jake's, late sixties, early seventies, but there was a more youthful cast to his features and his body had not run to fat.

"I figured maybe if I came, you would stop bothering me." She smiled thinly, as if it were a joke, then lowered her eyes.

"You've got to be thinking that I'm crazy."

"Aren't you?"

He was looking at her directly with an odd intensity. She felt a warm flush cover her body. Then, without contriving, she smiled broadly.

"I couldn't help myself. I've been watching you for a long time. Then, finally I couldn't help myself. I really think you're as cute as a button."

She felt herself relaxing, unwinding. She liked being here, liked this bantering.

"You're blind as a bat. I'm a grandmother six times over and I just looked at myself in the mirror. Besides, I'm married and have been for nearly fifty years."

"Big deal."

"It is a big deal."

He reached out, touching her arm, squeezing the flesh lightly.

"I've got seven grandchildren," He lifted his hands, folding three fingers of one hand, to emphasize the number. "Also a wife. And we've been married for forty-eight."

"It's a miracle," she said coquettishly, "considering that you're such a flirt."

"Me? A flirt?" He looked at her in mock innocence.

"What then? A masher?" She was surprised that she had not moved away when he touched her. His hand had lingered and she was conscious of it, deeply conscious of his flesh touching hers.

I'm the one that's crazy, she thought. What am I doing here?

"I may be old, but I'm far from dead."

"Who said that?" She hated any reference to death. He must have sensed the offense.

"I thought it would be nice to meet you face-to-face," he said, almost as if his confidence had wavered and he had run out of brashness. "Ever since the first time I saw you, I have not been able to get you out of my mind." He paused. "There. That's my confession."

He looked at her and rubbed his hand up and down her arm. Her eyes darted quickly to each side of her. The area was deserted and she let him continue to touch her.

"Anyway," he said, "I got you here. And that's what counts."

"So I'm here. So what happens now?" She regretted it instantly, knowing it was not what she meant. He removed his hand.

"I'm not so sure about that," he said, his smile disappearing. "I just know that I wanted to see you, that I'd like to see you from time to time."

"I know what you're looking at," she said seriously, hitting the nub of her own curiosity. "But I don't know what you see."

"I see a lovely, beautiful woman, a desirable woman, an exciting woman."

She felt a strange flowing inside of her, a life force, an aliveness that she had not felt before, ever.

"I'm an old lady," she protested.

"Will you please stop that?" he said with some authority. He had a sense of command about him, she observed, and she suddenly reveled in the idea of obeying him.

"All right," she said.

"Besides," he said, "I don't feel like an old man. Not when I'm around you. Not when I'm thinking about you."

She observed him in detail now, her eyes exploring his face. There was definitely a youthfulness about him, she decided. It was the hair, tight, curly, white. It was lovely hair. He must have felt her looking at him. Then he moved his other hand to her upper arm and applied pressure.

"I don't think I'm more than seventeen right now," he said. "I feel so damned good."

"Maybe eighteen." She felt quite good herself.

"Listen, I'm here with a sixteen-year-old."

"I'll be sixteen next month."

"So you're going to let me rob the cradle?"

It was madness, sheer madness. Suppose someone saw them. What was she doing here? Why was she liking it? She suddenly was frightened and stepped away from him, disengaging.

"What's the matter?"

"Suppose someone should see?"

"So they'll see."

"I can't believe this is happening," she said.

"Believe it."

"I really better be going." Her fright was real now.

"So, when will I see you again?"

"I don't know. Maybe we shouldn't." Who is this talking? she wondered.

"Look," he said, moving toward her, holding her arms again. She did not try to disengage. "Meet me tomorrow night." He looked toward the edge of the road. "Over there," he pointed. "I'll be in my car. About eight-thirty. OK?" He looked directly into her eyes. "Please."

Tomorrow night, she was thinking. Wednesday. That was Jake's gin night. "I'll see," she said after a long pause, but she knew he had taken it as it was offered, an assent. He released her, and they stood there for a time. She was happy, yet she wanted to cry. There was no making any sense about it.

Finally, she turned, feeling her heart pound heavily as she moved more quickly than usual. It was not until she put the key in her apartment lock that she remembered that she did not even know his name.

"So early," Jake asked, when she stepped inside the apartment.

"I had a headache. So I decided to come home for a nap instead of playing.

She went into the bedroom and lay down on the bed, but she could not calm herself. What has come over me? she wondered, touching those places on her arm that he had touched, reshaping his face in her mind. It wasn't until she lay there a long time that the sense of guilt intruded. How can I do this to Jake? she thought. But it did not linger long. After all, she had been a good and faithful wife for nearly fifty years and soon they would put her in a box and lower her into the ground. Surely, she must be allowed one, just one, different experience with another man, before they closed the lid. It wasn't the first time she had thought about it, she admitted. But it hadn't been for years, many years. What woman of her generation had not wondered the same thing?

Getting through the night and the next day was a chore. The hours dragged on, despite her determination to keep busy. She spent the day rearranging her closet, cleaning out the refrigerator, redoing her drawers, most of which was purely make-work.

"You're certainly ambitious," Jake observed. He spent the day dozing on the couch and reading the papers. Occasionally, he would watch television. She made an elaborate dinner, including a stuffed roast chicken and a big salad.

"I ate too much," Jake said, pushing the plate away after his second helping. She had barely eaten.

"Every time I eat too much, I lose," he said, as he kissed her on the cheek, and went out of the apartment to play gin. Quickly, she cleaned the kitchen and took a shower, poured on her favorite perfume, carefully combed her hair and made up her face.

"Some old lady," she thought. She put on her white slack outfit and let herself out into the soft night. She was too agitated to walk swiftly, afraid that she would perspire if she moved too fast.

The car was there, idling softly, and when he saw her, he opened the door. When she got inside, he turned off the motor and slid closer along the front seat.

"I was frightened that you wouldn't come."

"I'm here."

"And I'm happy you're here." His fingers crept along the back of her neck. She did not stop him, savoring his touch.

"There was something I wanted to ask you," she said.

"Ask, I'll tell anything."

"A small thing." She looked at him. His white hair seemed to glow in the dark and she had the urge to touch it, but she resisted. "Like your name."

He laughed, his fingers gripped her neck now. He bent over and kissed the side of it.

"You're beautiful," he said. "And I'm a complete ass. I'm Milton Sussberg." He held out his hand, which she took in hers, their fingers entwining.

"Pleased to meet you, Milton Sussberg. I'm Rose Lefkowitz."

"That I know."

"You're a regular yenta."

"I know where you live. I know your husband's name. I know you have three children, six grandchildren and you used to live in Bensonhurst."

"You are a yenta."

"And this Sussberg has a wife named Elaine, three daughters who all live on Long Island. I worked as a housing inspector for the city of New York for thirty years. I was in World War II. And that's all I got to tell." He bent over again and nibbled at her neck. She lay her head on the backrest.

"And I think you're cute," he whispered, his lips moving near her ear. She could feel the warmth of his breath.

"And I think you're crazy."

"I like necking in cars," he said. "I never necked in a car before."

"Who had cars in those day?" she said, his lips moving lightly over her cheek now, finding her lips, pressing against them. She felt her heart lurch as she returned the pressure and moved into his arms. Her hands caressed his hair now. I am dreaming this, she decided, not caring how it was happening, except that it was happening. Maybe it is a reincarnation. Maybe I am sixteen again.

"You're the most delicious thing I ever tasted," he said, his hands moving over her body, touching her breasts. He reached into her blouse and caressed her nipples over her brassiere. She felt them grow erect. Just this once, she repeated to herself. Just this once.

His hands reached behind her and he tried to undo her straps, but they were complicated, with at least six hooks fastening them together. She undid them herself, letting her breasts fall free, suddenly not ashamed of their sag. His lips caressed her nipples, and she felt excited at her body's response. And she continued to caress his hair.

"You're crying," he said suddenly. Tears of happiness had spilled over her eyes and down her cheeks, His hand had felt the moisture.

"I don't know why."

"Sixteen-year-old girls do strange things."

"Will you respect me?" The words had jumped out of her, dredged up from some long-forgotten pool. She giggled.

"Respect you?" He hadn't understood.

"Well I am sixteen," she said. Then he kissed her breasts again and she felt him moving her hand down to his crotch, and she felt his hardness.

"And I'm seventeen," he said, unzipping his pants and putting his erect member in her hands. It had been a long time since she had felt something like this. He was bigger than Jake, and she caressed the soft skin. Her eyes had become accustomed to the dark and she had the odd desire to look at it, something that she had never been curious about with Jake.

"You're not disappointed?" he asked, obviously noting her curiosity.

"You are seventeen," she said, kissing him again, continuing to caress him, feeling her own response as he fumbled with the catch and zipper of her slacks. She looked about her for any sign of movement, but the road was completely deserted.

"Maybe we should go in the back seat?" he suggested, and they quickly moved to the back. Then she removed her slacks, and he had pulled down his pants. They kissed again and what had briefly fallen rose again to her touch. It was all so strange, an odd fulfillment of an old wish. And she had not resisted, not in the slightest. The space was tight, the movement of their bodies awkward as they joined and she felt the opening of her body meet his member as it had never happened before, not with Jake, the only man in her life. There seemed an instant reaction as her body lurched and she felt her pleasure come instantly. My God, what is happening, she thought, feeling a wave of pleasure pound inside of her as she let out some odd primitive sound that she had never heard before. He too moaned briefly, and she knew he felt his own pleasure.

They lay joined for a long time, then he was the first to untangle himself and pull up his pants. She dressed again, too, feeling a strange contentment. Now I know, she told herself.

"It was wonderful," she said, when they had zipped themselves up and rearranged their clothing. She leaned back in the crook of his arm and, turning her head slightly, looked out of the window into the canopy of stars, clear and sparkling in the moonless night.

"I can't believe this happened to me," Milton Sussberg said.

"You're not a big philanderer?" She had not really confronted the question before. It was just another aspect of her curiosity.

"Me?"

"You mean you don't ever write notes like that to other strange ladies."

"Never in my life. I swear it." He kissed her forehead. "I saw you, found the courage and did it. That's all there was to it."

She wondered if she should believe it. But then, she wanted to. That would fit nicely. She was still happy, very contented now.

"You're quite a woman, you know," Milton Sussberg said. She lifted his wrist and focused on his watch.

"I better get going," she said, moving her hand to the door latch. Outside, he stood next to her. She looked up, directly into his eyes.

"It was wonderful," she said again, and he gathered her in his arms.

"When will I see you again?" he whispered.

"Again?" She was suddenly confused.

"Of course," he insisted.

"Why, never," she answered. "I'm a married woman. You're a married man. This is a small community. Surely, you didn't expect..." Her voice trailed off and he moved her away from him to get a better view of her face. He is very cute himself, she decided, reaching out and touching his hair.

"But I thought you said it was wonderful," he said. There was a note of pleading in his voice.

"It was."

There was the sound of a motor. A car was coming, and they stepped backward into the shadows. She bent over and kissed his cheek. Then she turned and moved quickly away. She did not look back, although after a while she heard the engine of his car start. When she reached the court where her apartment was located, she paused and looked up at the sky. Every star in the firmament seemed to be looking down on her.

"Wasn't I entitled to just once, God?" she whispered. She was not a religious woman but she felt, for the first time in her life, some connection with the universe. She held up one finger toward the sky.

"Just once," she said, like a child begging with all its charm and persuasion for a special favor. "Just once," she whispered again. She stood there, waiting, watching the stars.

Then she sighed, took a deep breath and, with a big smile on her lips and a great wave of happiness in her heart, she let herself into her apartment.

THE BRAGGART

It was not that Molly Berkowitz was intolerant of other people bragging about their children. She always listened patiently, with attentiveness, hiding her heartache and pain. Invariably, the braggarts talked endlessly about their successful children—doctors, lawyers, captains of industry, daughters who had either married well or made it big in the business or professional world.

She imagined that she hid her desperation well. What use did it do to trample on someone else's joy because of her own pain. In that sense, she felt herself wise. Besides, she was a widow and to criticize what to many was the single crowning glory of their lives might jeopardize her friendship with the group. And the life of a lonely, friendless widow in Sunset Village could be a true purgatory. So she held her tongue and bore her heartache as she listened to her friends recount the victories and glories of their children.

"My Barry opened another store last week. He called me and sent me another hundred dollars as a good-luck gift. He now has fifty stores." It was Emma Mandel talking, a never-ending avalanche of braggadocio.

"How wonderful," Molly Berkowitz would respond.

But Emma's story would set off a chain reaction as, one after another, Molly would be treated to a hurricane of repetitive one-upmanships from her group.

"My Joycie has become a full professor," Helen Goldstein would say smugly, tipping her nose skyward in a pose of superiority. You can't buy intellect with money, she seemed to be saying, requiring a blatant response from an unabashed materialist, usually Dolly Cohen, who, along with Emma, was one of her closest friends.

"My grandson Larry got his car last week, a Mercedes," she would say smugly. "All my grandchildren get a Mercedes when they pass their driver's test."

"How wonderful," Molly would respond, forcing a smile of shared joy.

"And when they're twenty-one, they get a trip to Europe for three months."

"How wonderful."

"And when they marry, my Bruce gives them a house in Scarsdale and sets up a trust fund for their children."

"Do they have children when they get married?" one of the women would interject, winking at the others, breaking the tension in Molly.

"They don't have children," another wag among the yentas would wisecrack—usually one of the other women who also bragged about her children. "They buy their children in Saks." Then, after a pause: "In the section next to better dresses."

"Wait. Wait until they get old. They'll have everything. There'll be nothing to look forward to."

"When their teeth go, they'll put in a false set with diamonds, so when they smile people should know how much they got." The women laughed.

"I couldn't picture anyone with diamond teeth."

"What's wrong?" Emma said. "If you've got it, flaunt it."

"Really, girls," Dolly Cohen would admonish them, although she was obviously secretly proud to emphasize Emma's point. "What is my Bruce going to do with it? Take it with him?"

"He might give it to you," someone said.

"I wouldn't take it," Dolly Cohen insisted. Pride was the only thing that made the bragging palatable, a vindication. Molly knew what pride meant. It was the source of her pain. Her children could hardly be bragged about. They were total failures, economically, and, it seemed, emotionally. Her daughter, Alma, was in the throes of a bitter divorce from her third husband, and her son, Harry, was a taxi driver in New York, scratching to make a living, not even owning his own cab.

Many a night she had cried herself to sleep thinking of their condition, wondering where she and Al had gone wrong. We worked day and night in the grocery store, she would rationalize, wondering if that had been the real reason, knowing in her heart that it couldn't be. They had always been present to provide advice and love to their children, who also helped in the store. What had they done to make their children turn out so badly?

Her mind spent hours dwelling in the past, groping through the early days, sifting and evaluating decisions that might have pointed them in the wrong direction. Where had Al and she gone wrong? They had always stressed education, and though they had been foreign-born, they had forced themselves to improve their English so that their children might not be ashamed of their accents. Al never did succeed in eliminating his, but that was because he arrived in America as a teenager, when his speech patterns were already fixed.

Al, a good man, devoted husband and father, was fifteen years older than she. She bitterly regretted not having been more forceful when Harry wanted to quit high school—at least that was the illusion she liked to live with. Actually, she had raised hell and invoked every tactic of persuasion she knew—hysterics, guilt, dire warnings, threats.

"Without education, you're a nobody in this country, a nobody," she had cried. And when that admonishment had no effect, she used other tactics.

"You're breaking my heart," she said, meaning it.

For Harry, the die was cast and Vietnam came as a welcome relief for him. He enlisted against her wishes. Molly could never erase that time from her consciousness, as if it were a trauma. Harry had gone to Vietnam and, although he was a military policeman and generally in the rear of the combat zone, she worried about him constantly. Perhaps, she thought, it was her worrying about Harry that started Alma down the wrong path. She had been a pretty little thing with genuine reddish-blond hair and green eyes and a figure that had matured earlier than her mind. She had, Molly knew, mistaken lust for adoration, even love, and no amount of explanation ever managed to get that point across.

It came as a shock to her to discover that her daughter was not a virgin at fourteen. It was during the war—Harry had been overseas two years by then—and Alma, a freshman at Erasmus Hall High School, seemed a normal adolescent. She would kiss her mother and father every day before she left for school, warming their hearts. She is a good girl, a wonderful girl, they told themselves proudly.

The explosion of that illusion seemed to mark the sealed fate of her hopes for her children. She had been busy with a customer when the telephone call came, the ring persistent from the back of the store. Surely a customer, she thought as she excused herself and rushed to answer the phone. An angry voice screeched into her ear.

"Am I speaking to Mrs. Berkowitz?" the voice snapped.

"This is Mrs. Berkowitz." Her heart lurched. She thought perhaps it was someone with word about Harry.

"Will you keep your whore away from my daughter?"

"What?" Molly was confused, yet relieved to find it was not about Harry. Obviously, this was the wrong number.

"I want you to keep Alma away from my daughter."

"Alma?"

"This is Mrs. Kugel, Marilyn's mother."

Of course, Marilyn, one of Alma's friends. She would remember what came next for the rest of her life.

"I work all day. Today I came home sick. I found them in my apartment. They were in bed with boys."

There seemed no logic in the conversation, in the revelation. Her Alma? There must be some mistake. Her tongue froze in her mouth.

"She has ruined my daughter. I saw them. I nearly vomited."

"You are mistaken," Molly managed to whisper.

"I saw them!" the woman shouted. Molly felt weak in the knees. Cold sweat poured from her armpits. Her little girl? It was impossible. Then Mrs. Kugel hung up.

The confrontation with Alma was the first of many, the beginning of an endless chain, always accompanied by tears and hysterics and, when Al was alive, with threats of "telling your father." Always, the confrontations ended with confessions, tears, and exhaustion.

"But why?" To Molly, this had always been the central question, the eye of the enigma. Was it something we have done? she wondered.

"I don't know, Ma."

"Is there something wrong, something missing?" It had seemed such a monumental sin in those days, and she had concluded that the sense of right and wrong was somehow missing in her daughter's make-up.

"I don't know, Ma."

At great expense, she had taken her daughter to psychiatrists, thinking she was being very modern and understanding, but it hadn't helped. Nothing helped and, as her daughter's promiscuity advanced and she became the talk of her school and the neighborhood, Molly had no choice but to accept the fact of her daughter's behavior.

What it had led to was three broken marriages, although she was happy that one of them had produced a lovely grandchild, a beautiful boy, gentle and polite, whom she had practically raised. And yet, despite all the heartache and disappointments and the obvious failures of her children, she still loved them and they still loved her. An emotional upset, invariably involving some man, always brought Alma running home to her mother. She was in her mid-forties now and although the cute little figure had thickened and the blond hair now required the help of dyes, she still retained, Molly thought, vestiges of attractiveness.

"I've botched things up, haven't I, Ma?" she would say when she had settled in at her mother's condominium after the drive from up north. Molly sat beside her on the couch holding her hand.

"You're still my daughter, Alma."

"Thank God for that. I'm gonna change, Ma. I'm gonna put it all behind me now."

"I know, darling."

"No. Really, Ma. This time I'm going to get it together." She would look at her mother and tears would begin to flood her eyes. "We haven't made you very proud, have we, Ma?"

She could remember then, the pain inflicted by her friends.

"Your kids are just a couple of losers," Alma would say, wallowing in self-pity, searching for the needed kind word.

"I have two of the sweetest children in the whole world," Molly would respond, watching the words soothe, like medicine.

"And I have the most wonderful mother."

It was, of course, her secret pride. And while she would not dare confess it to her friends, she knew that, despite their failures, her children still came to her for emotional repair. My children still need me, she told herself proudly.

Harry would visit her every few months, taking the bus from New York. He always arrived exhausted, more tired than the visit before, although he tried to put on a brave face. He was over fifty now, paunchy and bald, with deep black circles under his eyes.

"I look like hell, don't I, Ma?" he would say, as Molly watched him eat the chicken she had roasted in anticipation of his visit. His wife, Natalie, never visited, nor did Molly ever inquire why. Harry had enough troubles, she thought.

"A few days in the sun and you'll feel better."

"I wish I could live here permanently, Ma," he would confess, biting into the chicken like a man assuaging a terrible hunger. When he had finished the meal, he would light a cheap cigar and stretch out on the couch in the living room.

"New York's a jungle. I was robbed three times last month alone. Pushing a hack is like riding around in hell."

"You should do something else."

"What the devil else am I good for? I've got no skills. No education. And no luck. Ma, if Natalie didn't work, I couldn't make it. How's that for laughs? Some reward, eh? I fought for this goddamned country when they needed me. And now all I get is a good swift shove in the butt."

"Maybe you could find a job down here," Molly would say, searching for ways in which to comfort her son.

"Are you kidding?" he would say, closing his eyes. "What the hell would I do for a living?"

Before he left, Molly would always thrust a handful of money into his hand.

"What's that for?" he would say, staring dumbly at the bills.

"I can't give my son a present?"

He would put the money in his pocket and shake his head.

"I'm an old woman, Harry. What does it matter?" He would take the money, perhaps out of superstition, as if it represented some talisman, something to renew his hope.

She never complained of her children's failure to her friends, although she felt that they did surmise her pain and that their knowing did not prevent them from bragging about their children's success. Nor did it interfere with their friendship. Widows at Sunset Village had a great deal in common, besides the loss of their mates. They needed each other to ease the loneliness and help ward off the occasional bouts of despair.

One night, the telephone in Molly's condominium angrily intruded on her sleep. With a pounding heart and shaking fingers, she reached for the instrument and, gasping, mumbled into the receiver. There was no fear greater than a telephone call in the night with its urgent message of disaster. My children, she thought, and was secretly relieved when she heard Emma Mandel's frantic voice.

"Please, Molly. You must come," she cried.

"What is it?"

"Please, Molly."

Throwing a housecoat over her nightgown, she rushed out of her condominium and walked quickly to Emma's place in the next court. The night was warm and humid and the effort caused a thin film of perspiration to gather on her upper lip. A brief glance at the clock in her bedroom had told her it was three a.m. She was not surprised to see Dolly Cohen rushing from another direction, and they converged at Emma's front door. They nodded at each other and Molly knocked lightly. The unlocked door gave way under her knock.

Emma was seated in the living room, her ample body paunchy in its old-fashioned satin nightgown. A single lamp threw a yellow light over the room, dominated by an oil painting of her son and furnished with expensive antiques that he had sent her from all parts of the world. They knew the history of each item. It had been drummed into their brains through repetition.

She looked up at them as they entered. Her eyes were puffed with tears. A pile of wet tissues lay on the end table beside her.

"What is it, Emma?" Molly asked, understanding well herself this pose of despair.

"We're here, Emma," Dolly said, taking her hand in her own and patting it.

They sat down on each side of her as Emma dissolved into tears, her body racked with sobs as she struggled to catch her breath.

"We're here, Emma," Molly said, certain that her friend had just received a terrible emotional blow.

"Is it Barry?" Dolly asked. "Did you hear from your son?"

Emma managed to control her sobbing for a moment, time enough to shake her head in the negative.

"Are you sick?" Dolly asked. "Does something hurt you?"

Again, Emma shook her head in the negative. The questioning and the closeness of her friends seemed to soothe her. She gripped their hands and Molly felt the moisture of the tear-stained tissue. The tears rolled down Emma's cheeks as she sought to control the heaving in her chest.

"It's all right now, Emma," Molly said, squeezing her hand. "Your friends are here."

They waited while she slowly quieted down. Molly watched the pendulum of an antique clock move smoothly behind the glass in its base. She had spent many hours in this lavishly appointed room.

"Everything is genuine," Emma had often bragged.

"There, don't you feel better now?" Dolly asked, glancing at Molly and nodding. "She's better now."

"I could see she feels better now," Molly said.

Emma nodded, disengaging her hands and reaching for the tissue box beside her. With the clean tissue, she rubbed away the wet tears and blew her nose.

"I was lonely," she said, sniffling, her speech still interrupted by involuntary heavings in her chest. "I feel so—"

"Nonsense," Dolly said. "What are friends for?"

"I couldn't sleep and I was just sitting there in the dark." Emma's chest heaved again. "And I was so frightened."

"There's nothing to be frightened of now, Emma," Molly said. She knew the affliction, the sudden fear, the terrible onslaught of anxiety, as if a great black ugly bird were suddenly thrashing about in the room.

"It came over me suddenly. I felt I was going to die."

"Now that is silly," Dolly said.

But they all knew that was not being silly.

"I needed someone," Emma said. "I cried out in the darkness for David. My husband, David. He's been gone for ten years." The tears came again.

"It's all right now," Molly said, looking toward the drawn blinds, hoping for a sliver of light. The big black bird could not stand the light, could not hide in the brightness of the sun. She knew the terror that the night could hold.

"I wanted to call my Barry," Emma sobbed. Then she was silent for a moment, perhaps gathering her energy for the long wail that followed, a familiar sound at funerals. The friends reached out and held her hands again.

"I wanted my Barry," Emma cried. "If only I could have called my Barry."

"We're here," Dolly said.

"We're here," Molly repeated.

They watched her as she fought to control herself again. After a while, her chest stopped heaving and the wailing ceased.

"You should have called him," Molly said gently. "It would have made you feel better." She had always called her children when she felt frightened and blue and they would talk to her until she felt better and could poke fun at her silliness. And her children would call her when they felt the same way, at any hour of the day or night, sometimes collect, which she didn't mind.

"He'd think I was crazy," Emma said, recovering.

"But he's your son," Molly said, sorry now for having probed. For a moment she thought she had set her off again, but Emma was in control now, although vulnerable, her guard down.

"I used to call him," she confessed, her lips trembling, "but then I stopped."

"You stopped?" Molly was puzzled. She looked at Dolly, who turned her eyes away.

"He flew down a psychiatrist from New York."

"A psychiatrist?" Molly said, startled.

"He must have thought I was crazy."

"It doesn't mean you're crazy if you see a psychiatrist," Molly said.

"What did the psychiatrist say?" Dolly asked.

"Nothing. I didn't let him in the place."

"What did Barry say to that?"

Emma paused, crumpling her wet tissue and reaching for another. "He said I needed help and that I was foolish for not seeing him and that he had spent lots of money to send him down. He said the man charged seventy-five dollars an hour."

"My God," Molly said.

"It cost a thousand dollars," Emma said. The remark seemed to signal her returning strength.

"At that price, maybe you should have seen him," Dolly said.

"What was he going to tell me?"

"They are doctors, Emma," Dolly said. "Perhaps he might have helped."

"Like they helped Mrs. Margolies. Put her in an institution. I told him that all I wanted to do was talk to him, that it made me feel better."

"Do you feel better now?" Molly asked gently.

"Much," she said. She reached out and held her two friends by their hands. "It's so good to have someone," she said, the tears beginning again, rolling down her cheeks. But they were tears of gratefulness, not of fear. Molly felt her own tears begin.

"Look, now she's crying, too," Dolly said, her voice cracking, her tears beginning. They all reached for the tissues at the same time.

"We're making a river here," Molly said, feeling laughter begin in herself as she dabbed at her eyes.

After a while, Emma stood up. "I'm better now," she announced while walking to the window and drawing the blinds. Dawn had come. They could see the first pink and red signs of the rising sun.

"Now can we go and get some sleep?" Dolly asked. Molly nodded. The huge black bird had disappeared.

When she got back to her condominium, she lay down and looked at the ceiling. Then she picked up the phone and dialed her daughter.

"My God, you scared the hell out of me."

"I just wanted to talk to you. I just wanted to hear your voice."

"Sure, Ma," Alma said.

"I missed you, that's all. I was lying here and decided how much I missed you."

"Me too, Ma."

They talked for a few minutes.

Then Molly said, "It's long distance. I better hang up."

"You feel better?" Alma said.

"Much better." She paused for a moment. "I love you, my darling."

"Me too, Ma."

She hung up, lay quietly for a few moments, then dialed her son.

"Did I wake you?"

"Wake me? Hell no, Ma. I'm just going to sleep. Pushed a hack all night."

"Did you have good business?"

"Not bad, Ma."

"Wonderful."

"Are you OK?"

"I'm terrific. I just missed you, that's all."

"Great, Ma. It's nice to be missed."

"You be a good boy, Harry."

"I'm always a good boy."

"It's long distance, Harry. I just called to hear your voice."

"Sure, Ma, anytime."

She hung up and pulled the covers up to her chin, waiting for sleep to come. It arrived quickly and she slept soundly until noon.

AT LEAST YOU HAVE YOUR BINGO

 When Jack and Barbara Katz's first son was born, Barbara's mother gave him a $100 savings bond and Jack's mother bought a sweater. That wasn't the start of it, but it made matters worse.

"Only a sweater?" Barbara asked.

"What is that supposed to mean?" Jack replied.

"No sense belaboring the obvious," Barbara said. She finished giving the baby his formula and laid him in the crib. Then she went into the kitchen and began to busy herself with preparing dinner.

"You mean every gift has to be equal?" Jack asked.

"Not equal," Barbara paused and cleared her throat. "Necessarily."

"Necessarily? I don't get it."

He was really not confused. He knew what she meant. Barbara was an only child and her mother was determined to keep her under her wing. At first, he accepted the various gifts proffered by Barbara's mother as the due of newlyweds. Jack's mother, on the other hand, was not much of a gift giver, except on birthdays, anniversaries and other appropriate times. Nor did she have any desire to keep him under her wing. Boys are different, he decided. Their mother preferred that they fly on their own. Mothers of girls were apparently not so disposed. He had one brother and, therefore, little experience with the relationships between mothers and daughters.

He wasn't making much money then, although he had a good job as a bookkeeper with a dress manufacturer. It was mostly the food gifts that got under his skin.

242

"Things aren't that bad," he told Barbara when his mother-in-law left a big bag of meats and groceries.

"She likes to do things for us," Barbara said.

He let it pass, though it bothered him. Then it became a weekly ritual.

"I don't feel comfortable about it," he said.

"Don't be silly," Barbara said. They had only been married a few months and the little hurts were easily mollified by a bit of hugging and kissing. It continued to bother him, of course, but it wasn't until the first baby gifts that he began to understand what was happening. The $100 savings bond had been a link in an endless chain. Barbara's mother also bought them the crib, the baby dresser, the bassinet, an entire set of baby bottles and the sterilization equipment.

"How can she afford all these things?" he asked.

"She loves us."

"My mother loves us, too." he said, regretting the words. She looked at him with sarcastic disdain.

"You don't believe that?" He wanted to press the issue, but he held off. There was no doubt in his mind how his mother felt about him.

"The proof of the pudding is in the eating," Barbara said. By then, he was getting aggravated, and every night when he came home from work, the issue grew more and more magnified. They would eat their dinner in a state of nervous tension while the baby cried in the background.

"I think he's colicky," Barbara said, rushing off to the telephone to describe the symptoms to her mother. The Greensteins, Barbara's mother and father, lived a few blocks away, and any hint of disturbance in connection with the baby brought them rushing to Jack and Barbara's apartment. Mrs. Greenstein would lift the baby from the crib and pat his back until a few more burps would emerge. Then she would hold the baby until he fell asleep and gently replace him snugly in his crib.

"She's wonderful with him," Barbara would say.

"He's your kid. You be wonderful with him."

"She loves him, Jack. Would you deprive her of her pleasure?"

"You mean we had him for her benefit."

"I didn't say that." But she was quick to tears in those days. "At least one grandmother loves the child," she whispered between sniffles.

By then, the implication was quite clear, and when his parents came to visit on Sundays, Barbara would sneer at their fussing over the baby. Sometimes she became irritable and impolite, and his mother would call him the next day to complain.

"She certainly doesn't treat us very well," his mother would say. She, too, was quick to tears and her voice cracked easily.

"It's called the after-birth blues."

"I feel like I'm intruding."

"Don't be silly," he lied, hoping she would understand, not daring to explain.

Both sets of parents had been reasonably polite and affable to each other before the marriage. They were all on their best behavior. But after the marriage, that all changed. They had, for example, come to his parent's house every Friday night for dinner. It was obvious to Jack that these visits were a source of rapidly diminishing enjoyment for Barbara.

"Do we have to?" she said after the fifth visit.

"It's a small price to pay. Besides, it makes them happy."

"It's such a hassle to get there, and so ritualized. And, if you must know, boring."

"I go with you to your parents every Sunday. I wouldn't call it exactly a barrel of laughs. Besides, your mother spends nearly every day with you at the apartment."

His parents lived in Coney Island and it took more than an hour to get there from Forest Hills, where they had an apartment not far from Barbara's parents. It was, admittedly, a shlep, but there had been a tradition in his family for them all to get together on Friday nights. Not that they were religious. It was a regular routine of his grandparents' life, his mother's parents, and somehow it passed on to the next generation. Most important of all, his mother looked forward to it and worked hard to make a great meal.

One Friday night, Barbara absolutely refused to go to his parents' dinner. Jack had to call his mother and tell her that his wife was sick.

"But I made a delicious chicken and potato kugel the way you like it."

"You always do that, Ma."

"So I'll see you next Friday."

But Barbara refused to go on the following Friday and he had to make more excuses. In the end, they worked it out to come once a month and, by the time the baby was born, the Friday night dinners at his mother's house were a thing of the past. The baby became the prime excuse and there was little that his mother could protest when it came to that.

Mrs. Greenstein continued to visit daily, leaving just before he came home from the office. It was she who advised her daughter to quit her job two months before the baby was born.

"Your duty is to your child," she told her daughter. "I'm sorry, I don't agree with the way they bring up children today. Someday you'll go back to work. In the meantime, your husband's duty is to be the breadwinner and yours is to be a good mother."

Despite Barbara's devoting all of her time caring for her baby, Mrs. Greenstein insisted on helping her and often cooked dinner.

"What are mothers for?" she intoned on a daily basis.

"I see your mother's been here again," he told her. She was a good cook. There was no denying that. But it annoyed him that Barbara didn't make his dinner.

"I'd prefer you to make dinner," he said.

"I don't see what difference it makes. Your ideas are old-fashioned, Jack. If my mother wants to help, what's wrong with that? Where is it written that I also have to make meals?"

"I still like the idea. It makes me feel more like a husband than a son-in-law."

"You don't appreciate anything my mother does for us, Jack. I think you're damned ungrateful."

They would finish the meal silently, until the baby began to cry and the tension would increase, and he would wind up having to take an Alka-Seltzer before he went to bed. Why am I putting up with this? he asked himself. And yet, despite his instinctive misgivings, he felt some pettiness on his part and, in the end, tried to placate Barbara by enduring the situation. On the baby's first birthday, they had a party for him at the apartment and invited both sets of parents. Mrs. Greenstein gave him another $100 in a savings account and announced that she would add to it frequently.

"That will be for his college," she told them, flourishing the pass book then putting it ceremoniously into her pocketbook.

Jack's mother gave the baby another sweater, one she knitted herself.

"It's beautiful, Ma," Jack said, kissing his mother on the cheek. His father watched him, beaming. Mr. Katz was a quiet little man. He worked in a butcher shop and his fingers were always chapped from being in and out of the refrigerator. When he touched the baby, Jack could feel Barbara wince, as if his rough hands would somehow injure the baby.

She brought up the matter after the party.

"I wish your father wouldn't touch the baby."

"You think he'll contaminate the kid?"

"I think he'll scratch him."

"That's ridiculous. He never scratched me." She pouted for a while and, just before they slipped into bed that night, she said, "Well, at least he won't have to worry about college."

"Stop grandstanding," he mumbled.

When he received a respectable raise, Jack insisted that he and Barbara look for an apartment in Brooklyn Heights, which was much closer to his Manhattan office near City Hall. It wasn't easy to persuade Barbara to leave her mother's neighborhood.

"What about my mother?"

"What about her?"

"She'd die if we moved so far away."

He had secret thoughts about that, but he held his tongue, although the silence telescoped his message. Finally, in an unusual act of courage, he signed the lease to a Brooklyn Heights apartment himself, forging Barbara's name as well. He put down a two-months' security deposit.

"We're moving at the end of the month," he announced. He had stopped by a bar to give himself a bit of courage.

"You are. I'm not."

"The hell you aren't. Either you move with me, or we've had it. And I mean it." He could tell she was frightened. His threat took all the fight out of her and he felt quite proud of himself. By the time he arrived home from work the next night, she was resigned to the move. He knew, of course, that she had discussed it with her mother and his action must have frightened her as well.

Three months later, Barbara's parents moved to Brooklyn Heights. Not that distance had been much of a barrier to Mrs. Greenstein's daily visits. She would dutifully take the subway, changing three times, walking five blocks from the station to their apartment, always laden with packages.

When Barbara announced that her parents were moving around the corner from their new apartment, Jack resolved to have a heart-to-heart talk with his father-in-law and took off to visit him at the retail jewelry store he owned in Rego Park.

"Really, Dad, I think you should stay where you are," Jack told him. "First of all, it will take you more than an hour to get to work. Second of all, Ma is much too possessive of Barbara and the baby."

"You can't change people," Mr. Greenstein said. It was his favorite line. Jack liked him. Being in the retail business kept him working most of the time. He wondered if it was more by choice than necessity. Living with his mother-in-law must have been a rather trying experience.

"That's not very hopeful, Pop. She's ruining my marriage."

"Learn to live with it," his father-in-law said, with a sigh.

"Why should I have to live with it?"

"Because people don't change."

It went around and around like that for nearly an hour and after their little talk was over, Jack was more depressed than ever.

"You can't talk her out of it?" he asked Barbara that night.

"Why should I? I like my mother around."

There was no moving her. It was a conspiracy and he knew it.

"How would you like it if my parents moved around the corner?" Next to threatening to walk out, that seemed the most telling argument.

"I don't care where they move, as long as I don't have to see them. It's a free country."

"What did they ever do to you?"

"You mean for me? Not one damned thing. That's the whole point."

"How would you like it if I said that about your mother?"

"My mother?" She took a deep breath, like a baseball pitcher winding up. He was sorry he had started it. "My mother is a saint, the dearest

sweetest most wonderful woman in the world and my greatest friend.
Your mother is a selfish, egocentric, domineering bitch."

The fury of her response frightened him. The words were more of the
old refrain, but the venom with which they were delivered seemed to
have a sharper edge to it than usual. In fact, he sensed an air of finality.
For whatever reason, she hated his mother and, by inference, anyone on
his side of the family. He knew then that, unless he walked out on their
marriage, his options were few. Her mother would always be a thorn in
his side and Barbara would always treat his mother as a stranger.

The gauntlet was down, but he didn't pick it up, and life went on as
before.

They had two other children and, as it happened with their first child,
Mrs. Greenstein dominated the gift department. By then, his own parents
had been relegated to the role of pariah and when they occasionally did come
to visit, Barbara usually cooked up some pretext to assure her absence.

"She's gone to a PTA meeting, Ma," he would say sheepishly. "But she
did make dinner," he lied. He had made the dinner.

"You think I'm a dummy," his mother would say.

"No really Ma. PTA."

On these occasions, his mother would spend the entire visit crying,
and by the time she left, her eyes were puffy and red.

"What's wrong with grandma?" his oldest son would say.

"She has a toothache."

"Boy, it must really hurt."

"It does, booballa," his mother would say, hugging the boy to her breast.

"What did I do to her?" she would ask. It now was a regular part of
her conversation with her son.

"She's just busy," Jack would say.

"I can't understand it. Am I such a horror? I gave her a beautiful boy,
a good provider. What did we do to her?"

"Nothing, Ma."

He would curse Mrs. Greenstein in his heart. It was, he believed, all
her fault. She was the evil force in his life. She possessed his wife, possessed her mind. Not that it didn't have an effect on her body. She was
not as loving as she might have been.

But the only matter over which Jack and Barbara ever argued about was the in-laws. Both sides. They didn't argue about money. There were no personal jealousies between them. They agreed on all matters involving the children. There were no ego problems between them. Only the one issue.

"I'd like my parents to come over Sunday," he might tell her.

"Let them come. I'll be somewhere else."

"What the hell did they ever do to you?"

"Do we have to go through that again?"

"Well, then your mother can go take a flying fuck for herself."

"She doesn't care if you're here or not."

"Good. Because I don't ever intend to be here when she's around."

It was, of course, an idle threat. He had long ago stopped being around when his mother-in-law came to visit—which was most of the time.

Sometimes the conditions of his life would get him down, especially the effect it had on his parents, who seemed to have drifted out of his life, reappearing only to emphasize his own lack of courage.

"How come you don't call, Jack?" his mother would begin every telephone conversation. Then the tears would come, the accusations, all of which were correct.

"I don't see my own grandchildren. I don't see my son. My daughter-in-law thinks I'm worse than Hitler...."

"Enough already," he would say, his heart breaking, cursing his impotence. You can't make people love each other, he wanted to say. Even family. Especially family.

"Who can I talk to, if not you, Jack?"

"It's pure self-pity." It wasn't only that, he knew. He pitied her and he pitied himself.

"You'll have yours someday," she would say.

"That again."

"History repeats. Everybody gets their just rewards."

"You're wishing it on me." He knew that was true, but she could not help herself.

"What do you expect me to do?" he would say, when all attempts at placation failed. She had recovered by then and her logic had returned.

"There is nothing you can do, Jack. Nothing."

Time smoothed their acceptance. There was no cure for it. Their children grew up and had families of their own.

It was his father-in-law's second heart attack, compounded by his growing arthritis condition that brought them to Sunset Village. A new crisis loomed when Barbara insisted that he take early retirement and they move down South with the Greensteins. He was in his late fifties then and had put in enough time for a pension, but he resisted on principle. It was the same as it had always been.

"I owe it to them," Barbara said. "The doctor has urged them to go to Florida. Look, I'm their only daughter. They couldn't survive by themselves."

"But I don't owe them anything." he protested. The vehemence of his protests had softened with the years. He had simply removed the Greensteins from his consciousness.

Nevertheless, he was bored by his job, and the opportunity did exist for early retirement. The company was cutting back its personnel and allowing the older men to retire early. When the letter from the company making the offer arrived at his apartment, Barbara opened the letter and all the practical arguments collapsed.

They bought two one-bedroom condominiums, side by side, and Barbara and her mother continued to live as they always lived, while Mr. Greenstein failed steadily.

"Such a wonderful daughter," the yentas would whisper. "So devoted." He would hear them as he sat around the swimming pool sunning himself. At first, he spent lots of time alone, although occasionally he and Barbara would play canasta with another couple, the Epsteins, who lived in the condominium on the opposite side from their in-laws. That was on the days when Mrs. Greenstein was too tired to go to the clubhouse for the shows.

He had, of course, declined to participate in anything that included Mrs. Greenstein and, when she came into their apartment, he would always find some excuse to leave.

He never exchanged a single word with her, although he no longer revealed any open contempt. On her part, Mrs. Greenstein ignored him as well. He had, after all, never been a factor in her life. When she was not physically with her mother, Barbara was constantly on the phone with her. He had even shut that out of his mind and had long ceased picking up the telephone when it rang.

Only once did he raise the question with any passion. The management people had arranged an eight-hour inexpensive bus tour to Disneyland, and he thought it might be nice if he and Barbara went.

"It would be too much for mother," Barbara said.

"I didn't invite her."

"How can I leave her alone?"

"For one lousy day?"

"Go yourself then."

He felt the old passion rise inside of him, the inner constriction, the feeling of entrapment. Most of the time he had it under control. People never change, his father-in-law told him many times. It was a bit of essential wisdom. Why had he endured it for so long? It was a question that he never answered, for he refused to dwell on it.

He did go to Disneyland by himself, and he found that he was one of the few unattached males. It was the first time he realized how many widows were around. A Mrs. Ginzberg, who had been eyeing him as they lined up for the bus, sat next to him. She was a woman in her early sixties, well groomed, and with a typical nose for interrogation that seemed to characterize most of the people he met at Sunset Village. They wanted to know. So far he had been standoffish, perhaps shy, feeling his way around. By the time the bus was an hour out of Sunset Village, he had picked up the essential vibrations.

"So you're married?" Mrs. Ginzberg had said. Her disappointment was, at first, obvious. A slight tremor in her cheek betrayed a sudden anxiety and he imagined she looked around to see if another seat was available. But all the seats were filled.

Jack nodded. He was exhausted by the hour-long interrogation and was watching the flat Florida landscape move swiftly past through the large glass windows.

"Your wife is sick?" Mrs. Ginzberg asked. He could feel the cunning in the questioning. So she is getting down to the cream cheese now, he thought.

"In a way," he said, knowing he had put a touch of venom into the bite. Why not, he thought, looking at the woman.

"A terrible thing to go through," Mrs. Ginzberg said, the implication clear. "My Willy was sick for two years. It was terrible. Day and night."

"I know," he said.

"For better or for worse," she intoned.

"Mostly worse," he said.

"It must be terrible for a man," she whispered, moving closer to him. He felt her breath on his cheek and a brief movement of her leg against his.

"Good it's not," he said. She turned her full face toward him now and beamed.

"Well, at least today we'll have a good time."

They did, following the group leader around and standing in line for the rides just like the little kids. On one ride, they actually held hands. When he returned, he was tired. Inexplicably, he had agreed to meet Mrs. Ginzberg the next evening. Just a friendly little talk, she told him, especially since, as he had informed her, his wife was an invalid.

"We'll have tea at my place," Mrs. Ginzberg said.

"Why not?" he replied. What else did he have to do?

Barbara was already asleep when he got home and crept in beside her, sighed, and slipped quickly into a deep sleep himself.

"You had a good time?" Barbara asked at breakfast. She normally spent most of her time in the kitchen with a telephone glued to her ear talking to her mother. Jack had long ago stopped listening to their conversations. Occasionally, she would turn to him and ask a question, as if it signified some human contact with him. But she rarely interrupted the non-stop conversation to accept an answer.

Because she spent most of the day in her mother's apartment, he normally did not see her again until dinner. He had taken to spending most of his time around the pool when the weather was good. He did again that day, although he thought about his impending evening with Mrs. Ginzberg. A nice little talk, a little tea, he thought, perfectly harmless.

"You going to watch television tonight?" Barbara asked at dinner. It was a meaningless question. He knew she didn't care as she spent each evening with her mother.

"I'm going to play Bingo." The idea had come to him as he passed the clubhouse on the way to the pool. They had a nightly bingo game in one of the smaller rooms in the club.

"Bingo?"

"They have this nightly game. It looks like it might be fun."

"Good," she said. "I think Mama is getting too old to go out at night anyway."

"So you come with me?" he asked. It would be his last effort, her last chance.

"And leave Mama alone?"

He nodded and quickly left. Mrs. Ginzberg was waiting for him at her condo. "You came?" she said, opening the door. She was dressed in a hostess gown. She had applied her makeup carefully and put on a generous dose of perfume. She had a comfortable apartment, filled with pictures of her family, husband, children, grandchildren. All the faces seemed to be smiling back into the room, providing a kind of sunny glow to the small apartment.

"It looks like you had a happy marriage," he said, viewing the pictures, as she proudly pointed out the various people in the photographs and informed him of their relationships.

"It was fine," she said, but he detected a brief hesitation and pressed ahead.

"Was it all worth it?" he asked. She looked at him, patted his hand, then her arm swept the pictures in the room.

"Worth it? Who knows? Nevertheless, this is my life," she said. He wondered what she meant, but he looked at her with curious interest. She was a well-kept woman with a small figure. Age had thinned her legs and painted her face with deep wrinkles, especially around the eyes.

"My wife isn't really sick," he said suddenly, feeling the pointlessness of continuing the lie. It is lonely to lie, he decided. Who knew that better than him?

"She's a card player?"

"No. A daughter."

Mrs. Ginzberg looked at him, puzzled, then her face brightened.

"One of those?"

"One of those," he nodded.

They sat around and talked for hours. Then she made him tea and they ate cakes that she had baked. At eleven, he left.

"How was the Bingo?" his wife mumbled as he crept into bed.

"I like it. I really like it."

"Thank God. There's something you like," she said sleepily.

With the exception of the one-week period of mourning they spent after Mr. Greenstein died, Jack spent most of his nights at Mrs. Ginzberg's. The ritual mourning was a torturous time for him, sitting around with Mrs. Greenstein and his wife, while the old lady recounted the glories of nearly sixty years of marriage with Mr. Greenstein.

"He was wonderful. The best husband in the world." Mrs. Greenstein tearfully told all visitors, embellishing his father-in-law's traits as the week went on. Jack had pitied the poor man. He never had a chance. He had died on the day he got married and knew it. People never change, was his refrain. He had barely lived the life of a worm.

Once, he had dreaded his father-in-law's death, knowing that the aftermath would be a nightmare for him. On the night after he died, Barbara came into the apartment, put on her nightgown and bathrobe and took her toothbrush from the rack in the bathroom.

"I'm going to sleep in Mama's place," she announced. He had, of course, wanted to protest, but decided against it, surprised that it wasn't hurting as much as he had expected.

"She's very lonely and upset," Barbara said, lingering in the center of the room, as if the act needed explanation, perhaps surprised that he did not protest.

He slept alone that night for the first time in years, discovering that sharing the bed had nothing at all to do with feelings. It was merely an existence. But he bravely spent the week of mourning sitting with them in his mother-in-law's apartment, telling himself that it was out of respect for his father-in-law.

Actually, it was sympathy. The poor fellow would be forgotten as soon as his clothes were cleared out. And Jack's own children, who had come down for the funeral, were barely remembering who he was by the time the mourning was over. He suspected that that would be the way it was going to be for him as well.

"He was always such a quiet guy," one of Jack's sons said. "I don't think I ever said two words to him."

"Nobody did," another son said. "I hardly knew he existed."

They were nice kids, he decided, even if they didn't know their grand-father. What did they really know of their own father? He had literally run away from the house during their growing up. Even his wife berated him for that.

"You were never home," she said.

Home? Where was that, he wondered?

When the mourning period was over, he went back to his Bingo.

"He likes Bingo?" he heard his mother-in-law whisper to his wife.

"Thank God."

"It'll keep him busy."

He was able to snicker at their remarks by then and would arrive at Mrs. Ginzberg's house precisely at the time the Bingo game started, leaving when it was supposed to be over.

He felt comfortable with Mrs. Ginzberg. He liked her. Sometimes they played rummy. Sometimes they talked. But when she seemed to indicate a physical advance, he drew away. It had been a long time since he had any sexual relationship with Barbara. Desire had simply disappeared. Not that Barbara had missed it. Indeed, he imagined that she was thankful that she no longer had to endure him.

Now that Mr. Greenstein was gone, no meal in their apartment was ever served without Mrs. Greenstein's presence. She was at breakfast, at lunch, at dinner, and Barbara spent every waking minute with her. He said nothing, looked away when Mrs. Greenstein looked at him, ignoring her completely.

Barbara, of course, noticed everything in connection with her mother. And because there was no longer any pretense, she apparently felt secure enough to broach the subject.

"One kind word," she berated him. "Why can't you give her one kind word? After everything she did for us, after all her goodness?"

He decided not to answer any questions put to him on that subject. He had been reading the paper and now lifted it higher to block any view of her.

"You've got no heart, Jack," she cried. "No heart at all. The woman lost her husband. I'm the only thing she has in her whole life."

"Good for you," he mumbled. But her ears were sharp. She pushed the paper aside and stared at him, fuming.

"You're an ungrateful bastard," she said. He picked up the paper, smoothed it and began to read again.

"Bingo. That's all you know. Bingo." Barbara cried.

She slept in her mother's apartment a few times a week on a regular basis. He did not question it, but because there was only one double bed in Mrs. Greenstein's apartment, he could envision them, mother and daughter, locked in some maternal embrace. It seemed obscene.

"Do you think I'm normal?" he asked Mrs. Ginzberg one night. He called her Edith, her first name, by then.

"Normal?"

"I hate my mother-in-law," he said. "I mean I really hate her."

"So what's so abnormal?" She had a fine sense of humor.

"And because of her, I think I hate my wife and, maybe, because they both smothered them early in their lives, I may also hate my children." He shrugged. "No. I don't hate my children."

"I hated my mother-in-law," Edith announced. "But later I realized that it was because I was jealous of her, that she had more influence over Charley."

"Did she?"

"Yes."

"But that's wrong."

"What could I have done?" She looked at Jack. "What could you have?"

"I don't know."

"You could have left her."

"I did. In my soul, I left her. In my heart, I left her."

"But you're still with her, at least physically," Edith said. He knew what she meant.

"I'm getting older," he said. "I'm in the sixties." She had moved close to him and he let her kiss his lips and stroke his neck. He felt some vague stirrings, something he had not felt in years.

"We could try," she said.

"It doesn't hurt to try," he agreed. They kept the lights off in the bedroom and got into bed together. They hugged each other and she kissed him very hard and caressed him where he had not been caressed in recent memory.

"See," Edith said when they had made love successfully. "A good woman does a good job."

Later they lay in bed and talked and she told him that this was the first time she had been with a man in fifteen years.

"Did I feel like a sixteen-year-old girl?" she asked herself playfully. "A little bit, maybe."

"I know that I felt like a sixteen-year-old boy."

Occasionally, when Barbara would sleep at her mother's, Jack would slip off and sleep with Edith Ginzberg, but the tension of possible discovery made him restless and he decided it would be better to keep things going the Bingo way.

Once or twice a week, they would spend the entire Bingo time in bed together. Other times, they would talk, play cards, be with each other. It became a regular routine, and Barbara rarely questioned him.

She spent evenings with her mother, who was declining swiftly and needed much personal care. He ignored it entirely, even when his wife would justify her actions vocally.

"It's the least I can do. After what she did for us. I'm willing to sacrifice. I really am." It was a regular soliloquy, but it took on a new dimension as Mrs. Greenstein began to fail. She was reaching ninety.

"At least you have your Bingo." There was a note of self-pity in her tone, but he ignored her. The one thing he would never let her take away from him was his Bingo.

"Could you imagine her reaching ninety," Jack told Edith on the day after his mother-in-law's birthday. She was in a wheelchair and Barbara had ordered a birthday cake and had helped her mother blow out all the candles.

"You'll kill my mother," Jack said. "That's what I heard two weeks after my marriage. You'll aggravate her to death. Now she's ninety and I wish I had." Edith put a finger over his lips.

His Bingo nights were the happiest in his life, Jack decided. They weren't very cautious either and he knew that some of Edith's neighbors knew of his situation and looked at him curiously when he arrived at her apartment every night precisely at seven and left at eleven.

"'Here comes Mr. seven-eleven,' they must be saying," he said to himself whenever he passed one of her yenta neighbors on his way to her apartment.

"Do you think they'll tell?" Edith would ask.

"Who would believe it?"

Mrs. Greenstein died suddenly one evening at eight while watching "Murder She Wrote." Barbara was sitting on the couch, watching with her mother, as she did every night. She heard the brief gurgle and her mother's head slumped over her chest. If it hadn't been for the odd gurgle, she might never have noticed because the old lady often slept in that position.

"My Mama," Barbara cried. She knew the woman was dead and ran for the telephone to have Jack paged at the clubhouse.

"It's an emergency," she told the operator. "Page him at the Bingo. I'll wait." After a long five minutes, the operator's voice returned.

"I'm sorry, he doesn't answer the page."

"That's ridiculous. Did you page him in the Bingo room? My mother just died."

The operator repeated the paging process, but by the time she came back on the phone, Barbara had lost patience, knocking on the door of one of the neighbors. As always, Jack had taken his car to Mrs. Ginzberg's place.

"Please," she pleaded. "I must get my husband. My mother just died. He's at the Bingo."

Mr. Cohen, the neighbor, who also was watching "Murder She Wrote," responded to her plea and drove to the clubhouse. Because Barbara was too distraught, Mrs. Cohen volunteered to go to the Bingo room to summon Jack Katz. She returned in less than 15 minutes.

"He's not there," she informed Barbara.

"Not there?'

"I asked everybody. They didn't even know a Jack Katz. He's a regular, I told them. How could they not know him? You told me he played every night for two years."

"They never even heard of him?"

"Never," Mrs. Cohen shrugged.

"I can't believe it. I'm going myself."

Barbara's eyes were red with dabbing at her tears. She had left her mother dead in the wheelchair.

With Mrs. Cohen following, she burst into the Bingo room. Her hair was unkempt, her clothes awry, her complexion ashen. There were nearly a hundred people playing, listening intently as numbers were called and displayed on a big board in front of the room.

"Jack!" she screamed. People looked up from their boards, annoyed at the interruption. She strode to the front of the room and searched the faces in the crowd.

"Where's my Jack? Jack Katz. He's one of your regulars." She turned to the man who was picking little numbered balls from a cage.

"Never heard of him."

"Jack Katz," she cried.

"Never heard of him," the man repeated, turning his eyes from her.

"But he's been here every night for two years."

The man shrugged and she stood watching the faces of the people, ignoring her now, intent on the numbers that flashed on the board.

"How do you know he was here?" the man asked between picks into the cage. "Did he ever win a prize?"

She had been too anxiety-ridden to be rational, but the question stirred her sense of logic. No, she had never seen a prize. Along the wall, she noticed a vast array of prizes. The man watched her.

"We give them away every night."

"You better come along." It was Mrs. Cohen, gently nudging Barbara to leave the room, which they did finally when it was apparent that Jack wasn't in the Bingo room.

"I'll call the undertaker for you," Mrs. Cohen said, following Barbara into her mother's apartment. The old lady's body, ashen now, seemed solidly frozen upright in the wheelchair. Only her head had moved. Barbara sat on the couch and looked at the lifeless figure.

"What should I do now?" she asked quietly. There was, of course, no answer, and she collapsed in tears.

Jack arrived later than usual. He had had a wonderful evening. Edith and he had made love and he could still smell her perfume as he walked in the door of his apartment and reached for the light switch. Almost before the light snapped on, he felt Barbara's presence. She had been sitting in the dark. Her eyes were puffed, her face bloated.

"She died," Barbara said. "Mama died."

He knew he felt elation, release, but he did not want to add to her grief. Too bad for her, he thought.

"And you weren't at the Bingo. I had to call the undertaker myself."

"That's good," he said. "They took the body away?"

She nodded.

"Have you called the children?"

"No."

"I'll do it." He went to the table where the telephone was and put on his half-glasses.

"They didn't know you at the Bingo."

"They didn't?"

"You never go to the Bingo. You never went to the Bingo."

"They said that?" Jack asked, not expecting an answer. Actually, he felt no remorse or contrition. Nor fear. He just didn't care about her response to his absence from the Bingo room.

"Where do you go?" she asked. She was crying softly now and it was difficult to hear her words.

"To the Bingo," he said, turning toward her. "My Bingo."

He pitied her. She was alone now. He knew how it could hurt. He knew, too, that the nightmare, his nightmare, was over. Had he waited for this moment, he wondered?

"What will I do now without Mama?" she asked. She was thinking of herself, he realized. He went into the bedroom, took out a piece of luggage and quickly packed a portion of his wardrobe.

When he came through the living room, she was still sitting there as he had left her, crying lightly. She looked up with disinterest and indifference as she had always looked at him.

"Where are you going?" she asked. The reality of her mother's death, he could see, had not yet penetrated.

"To the Bingo," he said and, without looking back, closed the door behind.

"You need a suitcase for Bingo?" she asked.

He looked at his wife. He felt nothing. He wanted to laugh and made a joke.

"For the prizes," he replied. "I expect to be a big winner."

He turned and left the apartment without looking back.

An Unexpected Visit

Whenever Harold Weintraub drove through the imposing brick gates of Sunset Village, past the fancy colonial gatehouse, which could summon up images of verboten wasp country clubs, he would smile and shake his head. Under all these trappings, he told himself—the big showy clubhouse, the neatly clipped Florida grass, the little blue ponds and dredged canals, the gaily painted shuttle buses, the tricycles with their pennants crinkling in the breeze—lay, at least in his own mind, the unalterable fact that this was merely a dumping ground for aged Jewish parents of a certain working-class social strata. They were the Jews who never really made it big, a counter stereotype, a far cry from the usual "goyishe" perceptions of the rich kike who knew how to make all that money.

But this time through the gates, Harold Weintraub wasn't smiling, nor did all those philosophical musings interfere with his concentration on finding his father's condominium. They all look alike, he told himself with exasperation, as he maneuvered the rented car over the high slow-down bumps and squinted at the street signs. He hadn't even bothered to telephone his father, which would not be unusual in itself becase he hated to talk to his father on the phone, even under ordinary circumstances. The instrument had become a conduit of hostility, the conversations a frustrating exercise in noncommunication.

"Hey, Pop. It's Harold."

"Whoopee."

"How are you doing?"

"Three months, Harold?"

"You going to start again, Pop?"

"Three months?"

"If that's all you're going to say, I'll hang right up."

"I can't understand. A boy doesn't call his father for three months."

"Pop, it's long distance."

"When are you going to come down?"

"Maybe in February."

"That's what you said last February."

"I'm busy as hell, Pop."

"Sure."

"Really."

"Three months. Not to pick up the telephone."

He maneuvered the car into a court, then, noting the unfamiliarity, backed up onto the main road again. In the five years since his father had come down to Sunset Village from Brooklyn, after his mother had died, he had been here exactly three times, spending no more than four hours straining for conversation, until the atmosphere became stultifying and, he sensed, even his father had enough and was itching to get on with the rhythm of his life. There was a certain ritualization about each visit. The mandatory visit to the clubhouse and the pool to "show him off" to his father's cronies, male and female, all of whom resembled each other.

"My son, Harold. This is Mr. and Mrs. Schwartzman. Mr. Pomerantz. Mr. Berkowitz."

"So good-looking," he would hear one of the yentas whisper.

"A professional?"

"He's a toy manufacturer," his father would say. "You know the game 'Foreign Policy?'"

"Adult games, actually," Harold would say politely.

"A big shot," his father would say, jerking a thumb over his shoulder, happy in his moment, a kind of triumph, parading his progeny. "To me, they're toys."

Invariably, the conversation would drift toward his marital status, as if he were an old-maid schoolteacher, a familiar image for his father, who spent thirty years as a carpenter for the New York school system.

"All right, Harold, I'm sorry I asked," the old man would retort—the subject, Harold knew, was always on the surface of his father's mind.

"Actually, I'm living with a girl," Harold told him on his last visit. They had been walking along the edge of the road and the old man had stopped and turned his tanned face to his son, narrowing myopic eyes.

"Living with?"

"It's not that my honor is at stake, Pop. It's the accepted way. Neither of us want marriage. Believe me, it's better. When you can't stand each other any more, you split."

The old man shrugged. "Who knows? Maybe it's better."

They resumed their walk. Harold waited for the inevitable.

"Jewish?"

"As a matter of fact, no."

The old man shrugged again.

"A shiksa," he said, rubbing it in, thinking of how Janice's obviously Irish face would stand out like a beacon in this place.

"You can't find a nice Jewish girl and settle down?" his father said angrily.

He could see the old man's face flush beneath the tan. "I am settled."

"And children. What about children?"

"Who the hell wants kids?"

"There you may have a point," his father said, sticking a gnarled finger near his nose. Then the old man's shoulders sagged and they walked slowly back to his place without a word.

But he wouldn't go without an explanation, and when they got back to his father's place, he felt the need to say more.

"Pop"—he said it gently—"times have changed. It's different now. Freer. Women, too, want this kind of freedom. That's not to say that someday I won't get married and have kids. There's no need for commitment. Janice. Her name is Janice. We care for each other. We have a lot in common. She's twenty-six, with a great job. Hell, she even shares expenses. Look, I'll be thirty-seven on my next birthday. I've got time, lots of time."

"I got no time," his father said.

Harold remembered the conversation, even through his concentration, as he searched for his father's place, cursing the builder and his mass-produced look-alike two-storied product, the barracks architecture, the sameness. He parked in front of a small structure around which people were clustered. It was the laundromat. Eyes turned toward him. He was obviously an event. Men and women came toward him. He held out a piece of paper with his father's address on it, like a greenhorn immigrant lost in the middle of Times Square.

"About a quarter of a mile in that direction," a gray-haired man said. He wore a sour expression. A woman in a flowered house dress stood beside him.

"What's his name?"

"Weintraub."

"Weintraub. Weintraub," the woman mused aloud. "Harry Weintraub?"

"Morris."

"He used to be in the fish business in Philadelphia?" the woman asked. The gray-haired man rolled his eyes skyward and lifted his hands, palms upward.

"No. Morris Weintraub. The New York Weintraub," the younger man said.

"A quarter of a mile that way," the gray-haired man said, motioning toward the woman with his hand as if she were suffering from body odor.

"From Philadelphia?" he heard the woman ask again, as he stepped back into the car.

Kuchlefel, he thought, remembering an expression of his mother— Yiddish slang that meant a spoon in everybody's pot. Odd how that world still survived, in his mind, in these people. He followed the road slowly, watching for bumps, stopping while a train of tricycles passed, the older men and women chatting as they rode by, smiling like kids in organized play at a summer camp.

What the hell was he doing here? he wondered. In the middle of the week. Away from his office in the middle of the week.

He actually felt the compulsion to go at 3 a.m. as he tossed in bed, hearing Janice's even breathing beside him. He quietly slipped out from under the covers and padded to the living room, fished into the cigarette box, lighting up and inhaling, something he had not done for years. It went down harsh, and he stifled a cough.

"I forgot," Janice said simply. She had broken the news to him at dinner and he had felt the lamb chop turn to lead in his stomach.

"How can you forget?"

"Believe me. It's easy."

"It's like playing Russian roulette."

"Yeah," she said with heavy sarcasm. "God damned diaphragm. Ah diden know wad luv can do," she mimicked.

"How was I supposed to know?"

Her eyes misted. She reached out and patted his arm.

"It's my fault, kid. A stiff cock and my memory turns to glop."

"Jesus. It's not funny."

"I'm not laughing," she sighed. "No sweat. I'll have the thing vacuumed and that will be that."

"Our kid?"

"It's my body." She looked at him archly. "Hey, which side are you on? I'm the Catholic, remember."

"How long has it been?" He must have looked very serious, reflective. A brief frown, perhaps a sudden tug of truth, wrinkled her face like crinkled paper. Feeling his own embarrassment, he checked himself from making any further clinical inquiries. But it was too late. She had caught his drift.

"I'm four weeks over. The home test is positive. It's well within the limits of an easy abortion. It's just a few hours out of my day and a little rest, that's all. I'll take off Friday and be back to work Monday. So I'll louse up our weekend." They had planned a country drive. She chucked him under the chin. "Look, kid. It happens."

He took her in his arms and kissed her hair, watching his own face in the mirror behind her. He felt his unhappiness and pressed her closer.

"I love you," he whispered.

"Jeezuz," she said, moving apart and watching his eyes. "It's not the end of the world."

That was precisely the point of his own uneasiness. He sat up half the night and chain-smoked, mulling it over. My kid, he thought, picturing a young boy, perhaps as he had been. It was then that he thought of his own father and the gnarled workman's hands that he had clutched on endless walks through parks and zoos and parades and circuses. This is stupid, he told himself when dawn poked through the edges of the blinds and, smashing out the cigarette, he crawled into bed quietly beside her. She slept peacefully. Perhaps it didn't matter.

But the idea of it would not go away. As a faraway abstraction, abortion had always seemed right, attractive actually, because it foreclosed on the complication of unwanted progeny. It's an option, a choice, he told himself, arguing that it was a sensible approach to a biological problem. My God, he told himself, deliberately keeping himself stiff beside her, that's not the issue. It's my damned kid.

In the morning, he told her that he was going to go down to visit his father for the day. She looked up quickly, doughnut poised in mid-air, dripping coffee drops on the front page of *The New York Times*.

"He OK?"

"I think so. I'm feeling a little pang of guilt, I guess. Haven't seen him for nearly two years. It's a light week anyway. What the hell? It's only a day."

"Nice Jewish boys," she said sprightly, a broad smile breaking.

Was she as concerned? What did the abortion mean to her? He wanted to ask, but felt himself waiting for something, a message, a signal. It never came, only the brief rustle of the paper as she turned the page.

He followed the directions and finally recognized his father's street, confirming the numbers. Mr. Weintraub lived on the upper story of the two-story building. After parking the car, he took off his jacket and, holding the loop, swung it over one shoulder. As he stood before the green door waiting to rap the door knocker, he wondered why his heart was beating so fast. He'll go straight through the roof, he smiled, banging on the knocker.

He heard a movement inside, the shuffling, and the door was opened slowly. A gray-haired woman in a flowered house dress stood before him, waiting for a response.

"I'm sorry." He stepped back to look again at the number on the door. "I must have got it wrong somehow. I'm having a devil of a time finding my father's place."

"Who?" She seemed a little hard of hearing.

"Morris Weintraub."

"Morris?"

He heard a toilet flush and a door click open.

"You called me, Ida?" He heard his father's voice from inside the apartment. Then his father was beside the woman, looking at him, squinting into his eyes.

"Pop." Harold moved beside him and kissed him on the cheek. The old man grabbed his forearm.

"Harold!" He seemed beside himself with joy. He looked at the woman beside him. "This is my Harold."

He felt a long pause, a hesitation, as he stood in the center of the living room, knowing that his father was assembling his thoughts, preparing himself as he had seen him do over the years.

"This is Mrs. Schwartzman," the older man said, stumbling over his words. The woman's hands fluttered as she smoothed her house dress.

"I'll make some coffee." She moved into the little kitchen, visible through the lattice doors over the countertop, and busied herself with the coffeemaking, loudly enough to assure them that she was not listening.

Harold had, of course, drawn his conclusions instantly. The uncommon articles and photographs in the room offered confirmation.

"I was actually passing through on business," Harold said, noting that despite his tan, old age was setting its mask on his father's face.

"I hadn't expected..." Mr. Weintraub began looking through the shutters that separated the kitchen from the living room.

"I can see," Harold said, unable to hide his sarcasm, instantly regretful. Why should it annoy me? he asked himself. A twitch in his father's cheek signaled the older man's displeasure, a sign of his special kind of seething nature, which Harold observed in their early life together. They sat silently for a while until Mrs. Schwartzman brought their coffee and put it on the cocktail table.

"I promised the Fines," she said, forcing a smile. The smile was tight, too ingratiating. He noted that her lips trembled.

"No, really, Mrs. . . ." Harold said.

"Schwartzman," his father quickly said.

"I promised. Besides, you should have a little time together." She took her pocketbook from the top of the television set.

"You'll come back soon, Ida?"

He could see the extent of his father's anxiety now, feeling pity.

"I'll be back in a couple of hours. You know Molly. She likes to talk, and poor Sam can't talk back."

They watched as the door closed and the father reached for his coffee with a shaking hand.

"I would have explained," the older man said after he sipped and shakily replaced the coffee cup. "Who expected you to walk in like this?"

"I think it's terrific, Pop. I really do." He reached out and touched his father's sleeve. "Its just hit me too quickly." Dammit, he told himself. He was still annoyed. He still had not accepted the idea of it, but he was determined to keep that hidden.

"Better than being alone. Ida is good to me. She cooks good, takes care of me." He looked at his son and his eyes misted. "I was never happy alone, Harold. Look, your Mama and I were married forty years. She wasn't always easy to live with, but it wasn't so bad. That's the problem. Who goes first."

"Pop, if you're happy, that's all that counts." He was conscious of his own cliché.

But his father must have felt the lack of conviction.

He continued, "Your Mama was a wonderful woman, a wonderful woman." He paused.

Harold thought of the many times his mother talked about his father, privately, to him alone. "He's a good man, your father. He'll never make a lot of money. He's no ball of fire. Maybe he lets people step on him too much. And he takes it out on me when other people get him down." The words cracked through the mirror of time. He imagined he was enveloped in the softness of his mother's ample body.

But the older man's guilt would not let him be silent. "Alone is not so much fun, Harold."

"I'm happy for you, Pop. I really am."

"We have a lot in common. We never fight. Not that everything is always perfect. It wasn't always perfect with your Mama."

He looked at his gnarled, tanned father, shrunken by age, wondering obscenely, he thought, if they actually had sex, which brought him around to his own problem. He felt it harder now to broach the subject. Was it actually advice he was seeking? Or some kind of validation?

"Are you going to get married?" The idea had begun in innocence, but sounded treacherous when he said it. His father's alert brown eyes looked at him in confusion.

"Married?"

He was being observed as if he had just uttered a most preposterous remark, plumbed from the depths of stupidity and ignorance.

"And lose more on the social security?"

Harold could understand now how far out of their world he was, a traveler from another planet. "I didn't know," Harold mumbled.

"Sure you didn't know. How could you know?" At that moment, the sound of an ambulance's siren splintered the silence.

"You hear that?" his father said

Actually, Harold hadn't. Living in New York made his ears screen out the cacophony of sounds—horns, screeching brakes, shouts, screams, subway trains, sirens. Noticing now, he realized it was a kind of clarion.

"That's the Sunset Village anthem. The chances are that somebody is leaving this world."

"Why would anyone want to leave Florida?" he said, groping for humor. Harold knew he had botched things up by barreling in on them before his father was prepared mentally for the confrontation.

The older man smiled, sensing the break in tension. "You can get plenty of exercise just going to funerals," he said, laughing and lifting his coffee cup.

Harold did the same and sipped. The liquid was tepid. Looking about the room, he felt suddenly closed in. The air was humid, dripping with moisture, which made him note that the air conditioning was not turned on. Obviously to save money.

"Let's go for a walk, Pop."

The older man rose slowly and they walked into the bright sunshine, past the white painted façades of the barracks-like buildings. Looking into the windows, he saw dark interiors occasionally brightened by a lighted television screen. There was an appearance of cleanliness about the place, everything neat, properly trim and orderly, so different from the filth and hustle of Brooklyn, where they had lived. They had had a small apartment on the top floor of a four-story walk-up. Summers, with heat like this, they would actually all sleep on mattresses on the fire escape. He breathed deeply, felt the sweetness of the overscented air, the total absence of city smells. Where is my childhood? he asked himself, annoyed at the sentimentality but unable to control a tiny sob that bubbled inside and tightened his chest.

"Remember the times we used to go to Prospect Park?"

His father nodded. "Your mother used to say, 'Watch the frankfurters. He'll get a bellyache.' But we never watched the frankfurters and you never got a bellyache."

"I can still smell the elephants." We never talked much, even then, he was thinking, seeing in his memory the elephant's dusty parchmentlike skin. He joked to Janice that his parents never talked about the facts of life, or anything except protection. "Be careful of your stomach." "Don't get too cold." "Look on both sides when you cross." "Don't go near the bums in front of the candy store." "Beware!" "Be Careful" "Watch out!" What the hell could he possibly ask this man about his own dilemma? he wondered, feeling unable to form a single line of inquiry. They stopped at the curb while a group of tricyclists passed, their big bottoms perched on the smallish seats.

"It's a nice place here, Harold," his father said.

"As long as you're happy, Pop."

"I remember when you were a little boy, Harold." He said it suddenly, looking down at the asphalt.

"Ottisot?" He mimicked a small child. "You were always pointing. Once we were stuck between stations on the subway and you had to make a number two and there was no place to go, so you did it in your pants and stunk up the whole train." He chuckled and shook his head. "You were something."

Harold was struggling to form a clear picture of his father in those days. He had seemed taller, broader, stronger, but the memory was more tactile than graphic, a rough workingman's hand tightly grasped.

"Do you think about it... me as a kid... often?" He felt his tongue bumble. "Not being a parent, I just wonder, that's all." Would he see his defensiveness?

His father said nothing as they walked along the path that threaded through the grass. A puff of cloud passed over the sun momentarily, changing the coloring of the landscape.

"Think about it?" The father smiled and shook his head. "In this place, sometimes I wonder if anybody thinks about anything else. Every yenta in the place, male and female, brags about their children and their grand-children. You'd think we produced a race of rich geniuses. Not a bad apple in the barrel."

It was not the answer he wanted, Harold knew. But, of course, he had not framed the right question, the central question, because he could not quite find the right words.

"I've been a pretty rotten son, haven't I, Pop?"

The older man stopped and looked up into his son's face. His eyes suddenly misted.

"I said that?"

"I'm saying it, Pop."

"What right have you got to say such a thing?" They resumed their walk.

"I don't call. I don't visit often. I should be sending you more money."

"That's pretty terrible, Harold. I'll admit that. But a bad son? Not my Harold. A little neglectful maybe. But a bad son, never."

"So what is all that crankiness I get over the phone?"

"If I ask you why you don't call? Why you don't visit? What's a father supposed to say? It doesn't mean I don't love you."

Harold could feel him watching peripherally as they walked, embarrassed by the uncommon sentiment, knowing, he felt now, that he was sensing his son's inner turmoil, his doubts.

"It's also not because I don't love you, Pop."

"What's that got to do with your not calling and not visiting? That's a horse of a different color."

Words, but not communication, he was thinking, wondering why they never crossed that Rubicon, never been really inside of each other's heads. He thought of Janice again—the long, probing, existential "talking out" of themselves, the avalanche of words that rolled from unseen peaks shrouded in gray fog. And after all those words, did he really know Janice?

Janice who carried his seed, the seed of his ancestors. These were indeed oddball thoughts for him. The seed of his ancestors. Really.

"We used to take walks a lot together," his father said.

"Brooklyn in those days was a good place to walk."

"It was never boring."

The implication was clear and he did not pursue it. It occurred to him then why he could not frame the central question, the fulcrum on which both ends of the presumed advice might teeter. They simply had never transmitted meaningful things between them through words. What could he say? Hey, Pop, Janice is going to kill your grandchild on Friday. Or: I knocked up this girl, but don't worry, there'll be no fallout on me.

"Let me ask you a question, Pop," he finally said, stopping and digging the toe of his shoe in the carpet of trimmed grass. "You worry a lot about me?"

"Do I worry about you?" The older man smiled.

"Why do you always answer a question with a question?"

"Why not?"

"Seriously, Pop." Perhaps his father expected a smile and a chuckle, but he knew his face appeared anxious and that his father saw it.

"What else have I got to worry about?"

"A question again?" He paused. "Now you've got me doing it."

"I worry about you, Harold. I also worry about my health. You see such terrible things here. I worry about being alone. I worry about your Mama, wherever she is, she should only be happy. But, most of all, I worry about you."

"Why?" It was, he knew, the central question, boiled down into a single word and he knew before it had come what the answer would be.

"Because you're my child."

They resumed their walk in silence, passing a group of chunky women sitting on a bench, their legs crossed at the ankles.

"The yentas are inspecting," the older man said. "You should wear a sign saying, 'This is the son of Morris Weintraub.'"

"But that would take the fun out of it."

"Who cares?" the older man said. Beads of sweat had formed on his upper lip. "Let's go back."

As they walked, Harold pondered why he had come, why the idea of Janice's abortion had shaken him up. Why? That had been, in the end, the question. And he had received the answer. He felt the elation of resolution. It was as if his soul had been let out of its cage. The sky cleared; the sun, brightening and relentless, washed over them. He felt a burning on the back of his neck.

In the apartment, his father cleared the coffee cups and put them in the sink.

"Ida is very neat."

He remembered his mother, a blowzy woman, who always seemed to wear clothes that were stained. The dishes were always chipped, the silverware mismatched. She had been an abominable housekeeper, although neither he nor his father noticed it then. He reached for his jacket and threw it over his arm. His father was agitated by the sudden movement.

"So soon?"

"I told you I was just passing through. I wanted to see you is all."

The older man wiped his hands on his pants and came toward the son, who reached down and kissed his cheek, feeling the bristles against his lips. The father gripped his son's forearm and squeezed it.

"You're OK, Pop," Harold said. He felt his eyes moisten again.

"Be a good boy, Harold."

He started for the door and turned.

"And give Ida my love. If she's OK by you, she's OK by me."

"And next time, bring your girlfriend. Let's really give the yentas a megillah."

In the car, he felt lightheaded, joyous, and drove over the slow-down bumps too swiftly. His head bounced against the car roof and he laughed at himself and let out an Indian yell. No way they're goin' to do in my kid, he assured himself, trying to frame the way he would put it to Janice: Let's make it all legal, babe. Do the happily-ever-after bit. Jesus, he thought, what a lousy way to put it.

On the way home, he treated himself to a first-class ticket and let the flight attendant splash away with the champagne until he felt the warm inner glow that he imagined enhanced his feeling of celebration. He munched ravenously on the filet mignon.

"More champagne?" the flight attendant asked.

"Why shouldn't I?" he said, and giggled. Questions with questions. The flight attendant smiled, exuding plastic joy.

It was already dark and the champagne buzz dissipated as he reached their East Side apartment. He was still buoyant, and the brief anxiety that, once in New York, he would change his mind, had passed. He let himself in with his key, feeling the tension rise, knowing at once that she was already home. He could see the reflection of the bedroom lamp and the triangle shaft of light that it threw on the white shag carpet of the living room. He tossed his jacket on a chair and walked into the bedroom, where she lay, pillows propped, the *New York Post* on her lap, lifting her face to his. He sat beside her on the bed, kissed her on the lips, tasting, knowing he gave off the scent of imbibed champagne.

"I had a party on the plane," he said. "In celebration."

"Of what?"

"The two of us."

"No." He poked a finger and gently hammered at the tip of her nose. "The three of us."

Her eyes opened wide for a moment, then blinked.

"That's over," she said, shrugging.

"What's over?"

"It." She winced and he noticed that she was pale. "It has been eliminated."

"But. . ." He felt the airplane food begin to float in his stomach.

"Why louse up a weekend?" she said. "It was a good day for it. Why leave things hanging?"

He got up from the bed, turning his face quickly. He did not want her to see his pain. He walked into the kitchen, ran water from the tap, and drank two glasses swiftly. Perhaps, he thought, there was something inside of him he was trying to drown.

THE HOME

Sophie Berger's troubles began when she slipped on the bathroom floor and broke her hip. The pain was excruciating, but she managed to drag her body to the telephone in the living room and call her daughter in Miami Beach.

"Sandy, I'm lying on the floor in the living room. I fell in the bathroom and I think I broke something."

"My God, Mama. Hang up and call an ambulance. I'll be right over."

She called an ambulance, which arrived half an hour later. She also called her two best friends, Mildred Klepkes and Suzy Friedken, who ran over quickly. They were dressed to go out to the movies, the event for which Sophie Berger was preparing at the time of her accident. The two friends eased her to the couch and put a housecoat over her naked body. Then they gave her three aspirins, which helped Sophie a little, but she could tell from the swelling near her hip that something had definitely broken.

"They'll put me in a home now," Sophie cried, knowing that her tears were not necessarily a result of her pain. She could live with that, she knew.

"Don't be morbid, Sophie. It's probably only a sprain," Milly said, shaking her gray curls and tightening her lips.

"I know it's a hip," Sophie said.

"So it's a hip," Suzy Friedken said. "Sally Moskowitz broke her hip. And she's fine now."

"She was in a walker for six months," Sophie said.

"But she's fine now."

"She had a husband," Sophie said, hearing the familiar sound of the ambulance's siren, the Sunset Village anthem.

The attendants put her gently on a stretcher and began wheeling her out. She felt a needle prick on the side of a buttock.

"Call Marilyn and Leonard," she said to her friends. Then she looked up at the attendant and asked, "Where am I going?"

"To the Poinsettia Beach Memorial Hospital."

"Where else?" she whispered, feeling a softness descend as they put her into the ambulance.

She had been correct in her self-diagnosis. It was as if years of hypochondria had prepared her for this moment. When she awoke the next morning, she learned that they had put a pin in her hip and she would have to be in the hospital for ten days. Sitting beside her, silhouetted against the bright Florida morning sun, was her daughter, Sandy, who lived in Miami Beach. She vaguely recalled having seen her the night before as they wheeled her into the operating room.

"You feeling OK, Ma?" Sandy asked. Sophie felt her lips. They had taken out her false teeth and she imagined what her face must look like.

"I'll live," she answered, feeling the bare gums, hearing with distaste the slurring of her words.

"It's very common," her daughter said, moving out of the sun's stream, revealing her worried look, the brave-martyr expression on her face.

Sophie knew how she felt, pain and love and guilt all mixed up. She is thinking about the "home," Sophie thought, understanding.

"It's a vulnerable point in the anatomy for old people. But today with modern methods, they do wonderfully. Really, Ma. You'll see."

"You got in touch with Leonard and Marilyn?"

"Of course. They're both very worried. I told them I'd call as soon as I spoke to you this morning."

Mother and daughter talked for a while, mostly about the daughter's three children. Sandy's husband, Arnold, was a dentist and they lived in a fine house on DiLido Island in Miami Beach. Closing her eyes, Sophie remembered the details of the house, the large swimming pool, the sound of the children running through the house, Sandy's voice screeching after them while Arnold watched the football games. At first, they had invited her for dinner every Sunday and she had gone dutifully, hating to hurt their feelings. They would drive nearly two hours to pick her up, then two hours back. Usually, she would sleep over until Monday when Sandy would take her back to Sunset Village.

After a while, it became a big schlep, an annoyance that made her cranky and upset, although she tried to hide it from her daughter. I love them all, she told herself, but I have nothing in common with them. By then, of course, she had made friends and would much rather have spent the day sitting by the pool or playing cards or going out to dinner at Primero's.

"This is too much," she said to Sandy as they came through the gates of Sunset Village one Monday. She had wanted to say: 'Really Sandy, I am bored by this. I don't want to come. It doesn't mean I don't love you all. But you have your life and I have mine.'

"Really, Ma, it's no trouble," Sandy said.

"Maybe once a month. And you can always use the telephone."

"Are you sure, Ma?"

Sophie could see a hopeful glint in her daughter's eye.

"I'm fine, really." There was, she knew, a hint of whining in the way she said it, but she could not help herself. She could see her daughter was troubled, but what could Sophie do? She was what she was.

The result was that her daughter called her every day, sometimes twice a day. But Sophie was relieved from the Sundays. Now she came only for birthdays. On Passover holidays, she flew north to Leonard's house in Scarsdale, splitting her time between his and Marilyn's place in Greenwich. Apparently, her daughter Marilyn and her son's wife didn't get along. Not that anyone could get along with Leonard's wife, and visiting them, even on the holidays, was a source of terrible tension between her son and daughter-in-law.

"Why do you invite me if it creates problems between you and your wife?" she would ask when they were alone, which was often, because Leonard's wife suddenly became a beehive of activity whenever she arrived.

"You're my mother. I don't think any further explanation is needed." Leonard was a lawyer. He had always been very methodical in his habits and his language. Sometimes he talked too much.

"But if your wife doesn't like me, why punish yourself?"

"It's not you she doesn't like. Not you, per se. It's merely her way of getting at me."

"And what about her parents?"

"I detest them." He paused. "Actually, they're not half-bad, but as long as she treats you that way, I'm going to treat them that way."

She would look away from him in disgust—not that she didn't love him.

"Young people are crazy."

"I'm forty-eight."

After twenty-four hours in Leonard's house, she became restless and, although none of the tension erupted and her daughter-in-law would address her politely, she had no illusions about what disruption her presence was causing. Actually, her being in Florida had hardly changed anything, because she'd always spent Passover at Leonard's house, even when Ben was alive. What she dreaded most about visiting Leonard was the time of parting, when Leonard would attempt to foist a fistful of money into her hands or her pocketbook.

"I don't need it. I don't want it. You have your family," she would protest.

"Ma, the inflation. You could always use the extra money."

"Absolutely not."

She had the social security and Ben's small pension from the firm, and they had saved a few dollars. It was enough. Besides, it was important to be independent.

"You're being stubborn."

She sensed, too, that she might be being cruel to him, knowing he was tortured with guilt over the way his wife felt about her. What can I do? she thought, folding the money and firmly putting it back into her son's hands.

"Ma, please."

She would see his tears, remembering the small boy's eyes and the fear of the dark.

"I'll keep the lamp on," she would whisper, holding him in her arms and kissing him on the cheek. He would nod and turn away, embarrassed by his tears.

But if being at Leonard's house gave her "spielkiss" after only twenty-four hours, she began to feel her irritation the moment the door opened in Marilyn's huge Tudor-style house, in Greenwich's fanciest section. Marilyn was the dominant one in her home, overbearing actually. Although her husband, Marvin, was one of the merchandising world's most powerful executives, in his own house, he was constantly subjected to her daughter's withering criticism.

She liked Marvin more than Marilyn, and it upset her to see him being treated with disrespect. But Marilyn always had had a big mouth and had always been argumentative, surly, and obnoxious.

"I'm a bitch, huh, Ma?" she would say after some set-to with Marvin.

"I don't know how he stands you."

"I can't stand myself." She always wore loud, flashy clothes with heavy helpings of jewelry and make-up, even in the house. Her children also thought her ludicrous.

Sometimes Sophie would have to act as arbitrator in her daughter's domestic rifts.

"So I'm having this party on the eighth." Marilyn was always having parties. They were sitting in the dining room. The maid had just cleared the soup dishes.

"Now," Marilyn said, both hands thrust out in front of her, the forefingers and thumbs set in a circle, "why do I have to invite the Schwartzes?"

"Because they're my friends, that's why," Marvin said, his face flushing.

"They're tacky and boring, and after two drinks she thinks she's a femme fatale and starts pushing her boobs around."

"But they're my friends."

"Children," Sophie interrupted, suddenly discovering that she had become a kind of conduit for their communication.

"Why must I have to invite people that make the party miserable? They are two disgusting mockies."

"I grew up with Harry Schwartz. He's my friend. And that should be enough for you."

"All right then, I'll invite Harriet Silverstein."

"That whore?"

"See. See." Marilyn looked at her mother for confirmation of Marvin's hypocrisy. Sophie remained deliberately impassive.

"You forget, we nearly had a divorce on our hands. We found her in our bedroom making love to Sam Weintraub one Saturday night."

"Sam Weintraub would screw a wall. At least Harriet's amusing and intelligent."

Every meal at Marilyn's house progressed that way and caused Sophie's digestive system to run amuck.

"Sometimes, she's impossible, Ma," Marvin would tell her when Marilyn was out of earshot, which was not often. Even when she was, her voice reverberated throughout the house like a stereo system.

"Thank God she grew up and found you, Marvin."

"I don't know where it comes from."

"Occasionally, Ben lost his temper." Sophie knew that Ben had been placid, a giving person. She had worn the pants. What can I say? she told herself. She was of an age when she accepted her faults, surrendered to them.

"I loused up your visit again, right, Ma?" Marilyn would say, kissing her mother on both cheeks. Sophie knew she would be called four or five times a week to settle some dispute between them, although she rarely took sides and rarely, if ever, gave advice.

"Mama also thinks you're wrong," she would hear her daughter say at the other end of the phone, despite Sophie's scrupulous neutrality.

Sandy came to the hospital three times during the ten days she was there, but called frequently, as did Leonard and Marilyn. Her friends called her daily, and even though she felt the swelling go down and took her first hesitant steps in the walker, she worried about her future.

Sometimes they put her in a wheelchair and rolled her around the hospital corridors. It was a gruesome sight, the half-dead and the walking and rolling wounded. Many of them she knew by sight from Sunset Village, and she nodded to them as she rolled past.

Sometimes, she would see a casual friend come by on the way to visit a patient. Others she would deliberately avoid, like the henna-haired Molly Fine.

The hospitalization seemed excruciatingly long and she grew discouraged as she contemplated her future. Yet, she tried to assume a brave face. They must not think I am helpless, she thought, disgusted that she still had to use the bedpan.

When they brought her back to her condominium, Sandy insisted on living with her, sleeping on the couch. She filled the refrigerator and, patiently, with an air of mock cheerfulness, waited on her hand and foot. Sophie tried with all her strength to get out of bed alone, but it was a futile effort.

"Go home, Sandy. You've got a family," Sophie would plead.

"How can I leave?"

"Through the door."

Sophie could see she was torn and, pretending to be asleep, would overhear her whining into the phone, insisting to her husband that it was impossible for her to come home. A week after she had returned to Sunset Village, Sandy announced that her brother and sister were coming to visit for the weekend. Ordinarily, Sophie might have felt elation, but this time, news of their coming only fueled her anxieties. She thought to herself, 'They are coming for a convention to decide whether they should put Sophie Berger in a home.' She knew the procedure well. The children would come down filled with remorse and guilt that could be seen like chocolate on their faces. They would have interminable conversations about the future, even drive the victim out to see the "home" and meet the director. Most times they would succeed in their ploy, the victim would disappear into the "home," never to be heard from again, and they would put the condominium up for sale. Never, Sophie vowed. She redoubled her efforts to get out of bed by herself, impatient at the slowness of the old bones knitting. In addition, she had learned at the hospital that she was developing a cataract on her left eye, but she kept this condition secret. That would cook my goose for sure, she thought.

The couch in the living room opened up into a double bed, where both Sandy and Marilyn could sleep. They had borrowed a cot from Milly Klepkes for Leonard. She could tell they meant business by the fact that no one had planned to go to a motel for the night. She confided her fears to Milly while her children talked among themselves on the screened porch.

"They're going to try and put me in a home," she whispered.

"They'll never get me into one alive," Milly Klepkes said. There was a tendency to think first of oneself in Sunset Village.

"I'll take poison," Sophie responded, which was enough to shock Milly into facing her friend's immediate problem.

"I'll be glad to help if you need me, Sophie," her friend said with feeling.

"Don't worry, I'll holler."

On the first night of their arrival, the children of Sophie Berger sat around in her bedroom talking. It was the first time in years that they had been together, just the four of them, and despite her fears, she felt good about that. But Ben should be here, she thought.

"If only your father were alive," she sighed. "He'd be so happy seeing us all together."

"Daddy is with us," Sandy said. She was the youngest and had been very attached to her father.

"At least he protected me from the wrath of you women," Leonard said.

"You never had it so good," Marilyn said, sticking a finger in her brother's chest. She smiled at him, always the big sister. "If only you hadn't married that bitch of a wife, we could have been friends."

"Leave Cynthia out of this."

"Don't worry."

"She always does this, Ma," Leonard pleaded.

Later, after they had reminisced and discussed their childhood, which had been a happy one, Sophie believed, they broached the heart of the matter. She was ready and waiting, although the reminiscing had lulled her into a false state of security. The opening shot came from a predictable source, her eldest.

"The question, Ma, is what do we do with you?"

"With me?" Sophie asked innocently, feeling a sudden sharp twinge of pain in her hip.

"We can't put all this burden on Sandy just because she lives in Florida."

"Really, it's no burden," Sandy said, a moment too fast in her response.

"Don't be ridiculous. You have a family, a husband."

"Mama can live with me anytime she wants," Sandy said, kissing her mother's cheek.

"She can live with me, too," Marilyn said. "Ma, anytime you want you can live with me and Marvin. We'd love to have you, you know that."

"You make it sound as if I don't want her," Leonard said, taking his mother's hand.

"You think she would be happy living with that bitch you married?" Marilyn shouted. "I wouldn't have my mother degraded."

"She's got to stop about Cynthia, Ma. She's my wife and I want her respected."

Sophie listened, waiting for the ultimate suggestion, holding back her tears. She cursed her frail body, felt its humiliation. She had once been a big woman, a strong woman, the last to tire.

"I don't know what you're all worried about. In a few weeks, the hip will be good enough. Then I'll throw away the walker and start with a cane. The doctor said it's a long process, but you know, seventy-four is not exactly ancient. Not in this place."

Marilyn looked at her and shook her head.

"Seventy-nine, Ma."

"Who said?"

"Ma, this is Marilyn. These are your children. We know your age."

"You saw my birth certificate?" She had been so used to lying about it that the truth escaped her. She nodded her head, suddenly feeling old, but refusing to surrender. In six months, she'd be eighty. My God, eighty. Her mind was young. Her heart was young, she told herself.

"There are people here living alone in their nineties," she said proudly. They looked at each other, shrugged. Then Sandy bent over her and patted the pillows. They each kissed her in turn and left her in darkness.

But the way the condominium was constructed and the thinness of the walls made it possible for her to hear every word, despite their whisperings. She listened, alert to every sound, every nuance.

"For sure, she can't stay here," Marilyn said, her voice urgent.

"Maybe the hip will heal faster, but then what about the cataract?" So they knew about that. "We'll worry ourselves sick."

"Look, she's proud," Leonard said. "Maybe she should stick it out by herself for a while until she finally comes to the realization on her own."

"It's OK for you to say," Sandy snapped. "You're up there. I'm down here. I'm the one that will have to suffer for it. Already my husband is threatening me with divorce."

"Don't exaggerate, Sandy," Marilyn said. "We've had our problems, too."

Sandy sniffed loudly. "Shut up. You'll wake Mama."

She heard someone tiptoe into the room and stand silently in the doorway for a moment, then leave and close the door softly behind them. How could she blame her children? She thought of them when they were young but could not find any relationship between the little faces of their childhood and the reality of their adulthood. They were middle-aged now. Marilyn was well over fifty. Who were those people out there in the living room deciding her fate? Were they the screaming babies that she had once suckled at her breast, the helpless lumps of flesh that greedily took sustenance from her? They were definitely not the same people, she decided. And the woman who suckled them was a different woman. Her mind searched back to herself in that time, the tall buxom woman with the tight skin who could feel and enjoy the strength of herself.

"You work too hard, Sophie," Ben would say, planting the idea of tiredness.

"Who will do the housework?" she had always responded, the martyred woman, knowing now that she did not deserve her martyrdom. She had had the strength to endure. It was Ben who faltered. Ben was the weak one. But the voices persisted, as her attention drifted back to them.

"She's going to have to face it sooner or later," Marilyn said, with a tone of finality.

"The problem," Sandy said, "is an immediate one. She can barely make it to the bathroom, and only with my help. I have to help her out of bed. Can she go shopping? She needs help when she dresses."

"But surely she'll recover from the hip," Leonard said.

"You got a guarantee?"

Perhaps it was the reference to the bathroom that triggered the sense of her own indignity. In the hospital, they had viewed her body as an inanimate object, something to be pushed around and her private parts exposed, even explored by indifferent fingers. They had finally put a little sitting potty by her bed and watched her as she performed, like a child. But in her own home? How dare those people discuss her personal toilet problems. Over my dead body will anyone ever take me to the toilet again, she vowed, feeling the full impact of her indignation. She wanted to rush out of bed and into their presence screaming. Gripping the sheets, she balled the material up in her fists and calmed herself, listening again.

"If we can just get her to accept the idea," Marilyn was saying.

"Marilyn and her big mouth," Sophie hissed into the darkness.

"Look, we can afford the best there is. They're waited on hand and foot. We're not talking of a charity case. I think if we approach it right and not make her feel that we're putting her in a prison, she could be persuaded to accept it."

"Wonderful," Leonard said, his sarcasm obvious. "Who is going to tell her?"

"You're the son," Sandy said.

"Did that ever mean anything in this family? You've all always treated me like some sort of bric-a-brac. When did I ever have any authority in this group?"

"You should tell her, Marilyn," Sandy said. "You're the strongest."

"Since when?" Marilyn said.

"Well, you have the biggest mouth," Leonard chimed.

Sophie smiled, enjoying their discomfort.

"You know, just because I have a big mouth it doesn't mean I'm the strongest. You know how it is with Mama and me. If I say black, she says white. Marvin has more influence with her. Sometimes I wonder if she actually likes me."

"Mama?" Sandy said.

"What's the rule," Marilyn said, "that says a mother must like a child?"

"She loves you, Marilyn. She loves us all."

"Equally?" Marilyn wondered aloud.

"I never thought about it," Sandy said.

"Leonard was always the favorite," Marilyn said. "My Leonard this. My Leonard that. Little Lord Fauntleroy, Leonard Berger."

"You're exaggerating," Leonard said.

"Deny that you're the favorite," Marilyn pressed.

Sophie heard the long pause.

"See?" Marilyn said.

"Well, I was the boy," Leonard said.

"She still favors you," Marilyn said. "You can see it in her eyes every time she looks at you. My Leonard. My wonderful Leonard."

"If it was just up to me, she could live with us," Leonard said. "You both know that."

"With that bitch you married? I think she might wish she were dead," Marilyn said.

Sophie thought she was certainly right about that.

"She could live with me, too," Sandy said. "She knows that she's welcome in my house."

"Oh, she's welcome, but I don't think she'd want to be bored to death."

"Bored? In my house?"

"Bored, Sandy. Bored by your boring husband and your boring children. What do you want her to do, sit in the corner and twiddle her thumbs?"

Sophie smiled again. Marilyn might have a big mouth, but she knew how to put her finger on a situation. My poor Sandy, Sophie thought. Poor, boring Sandy.

"Am I glad I live in Florida and not near your big mouth," Sandy fired back.

"I didn't mean it," Marilyn said, her contrition filtering through the thin walls. "I was exaggerating to prove a point."

"Well, it's no exaggeration that Mama would not want to live in the immediate vicinity of your fishwife mouth."

"That I know," Marilyn said. "God, I'd love her to be near me. But she'd have a nervous breakdown in a week."

"That's for sure."

"So, what are we going to do?" Leonard said.

"We could get her a maid, a companion," Sandy suggested.

A keeper, Sophie thought. Never. She would be the laughing stock of Sunset Village. That was worse than a home, she felt. She wanted to shut off her hearing now, to tell them all to go away. Who needed them? Lifting her arms from under the blanket, she pressed them against the sides of the bed, straining against the mattress to raise the upper part of her body. The gasping of her breath drowned out the sounds of her children's voices as she raised herself with effort to a sitting position and slowly swung her legs over the side of the bed. Pausing, she caught her breath, gathering her strength and searching in the darkness for the sight of the walker, the outlines of which she could make out at the foot of the bed. Pressing down on her palms, she tried lifting her torso, moving sideways, inching her way in the direction of the walker. It took all her strength. She felt her heart beating in her chest as she strained the muscles of her upper body, compensating for the pain in her hip and the weakness of her legs. Sweat poured down her back as she paused to recover her energy. She heard the voices again.

"Look," Leonard was saying, "she is an intelligent woman. She knows the realities, the burden that she is putting on the three of us."

"Play to her guilt, right, Leonard?" Marilyn said with contempt.

"Well, she plays to ours," Sandy said. "That's why we're all here."

"Guilt?" Marilyn said. "I thought it was love."

"Are you saying that I don't love Mama?" Sandy asked, the pitch of her voice rising. "Who do you think has been taking care of her?"

"I didn't say you didn't love her," Marilyn said, turning to Leonard. "She's so damned sensitive."

"If you went through what I went through in the last few weeks, you'd be sensitive too."

"I didn't say you didn't love Mama," Marilyn said, her voice reaching the fringes of gentleness, but proceeding no further.

"I love her more than you do," Sandy said.

"I doubt that." The attempt at gentleness was gone.

"We all love her equally," Leonard said.

"What the hell does that mean?" Marilyn said.

The strain of her movement made Sophie gasp again. The voices became incoherent. Her progress was slow as she moved her body to the foot of the bed, every tiny progression taking a major effort and, with it, all of her resources. When she felt her endurance slacken, she rested, waiting for her heart to slow, her concentration to clear. I must not be discouraged, she told herself, taking comfort in even the most minuscule progress. She had, after all, traversed nearly the entire bed by herself. She suddenly thought of the story of the tortoise and the hare, which she read to them when they were children, feeling elation now as she looked sideways to measure the distance from her pillow.

"Well then, it's decided," she heard Leonard say. "We'll suggest it together, a kind of unanimous committee decision. Then we'll make arrangements to take her out for a visit. The one in Lauderdale, the Seaview. It's the best in the area, I'm told. And she'll still be close enough for Sandy to visit and we'll promise that we'll visit her at least three times a year. At least that."

"More," Marilyn said. "It's three hours by plane. No big deal."

Sophie reached the foot of the bed, reaching out with her hand for the walker, gripping its cool metal, then drawing it as close to the bed as possible to insure a firm grip. The crisis would come at the moment when she had to pull herself up, when for a second her arms had to support her full weight. She waited quietly in the dark room, her body poised at the edge of the bed with both hands on the metal frame of the walker. She knew that if she did not make it, she would fall, and they would hear the sound of her helplessness, confirming their worst fears. Her hands tightened on the metal frame as she closed her eyes, gathering her thoughts, and willed her aging body to give her this one victory. She tightened her eyes, feeling the backwash of tears and the quickness of her breath, a signal perhaps that her body was rejecting her will. Then suddenly the will exploded and she felt her arms tighten and her body lurch upward. There was a brief dizziness, a momentary faintness, and then she was standing, standing proudly. She stood there for a long moment, catching her breath and listening to hear if they had heard the inner explosion, the gasping breath, the beating heart.

When she realized that they had not heard, she arranged the walker before her and calculated the distance to the door. They would hear the light thumping, but she hoped that they would not notice until she had opened the door, an exercise that she knew she could perform. Pausing, she listened again.

"It's the only logical solution," Leonard said. "Otherwise, we'll drive ourselves crazy with worry. We must make her see that."

She moved cautiously, lifting the walker. She felt the strength return to her arms as she slowly moved forward, but had to ignore the twinge of pain in her hip.

When she opened the door, the light momentarily blinded her and she squinted into the room where they were sitting.

"Mama!" Sandy cried. "My God, you'll fall."

"Go on talking," Sophie said, taking a step, feeling her energy surge, the power of her victory. "I'm just going to the bathroom."

She felt their eyes on her as she quietly, but slowly, opened the door of the bathroom, maneuvering the walker ahead of her. When she was fully in the room, she pushed the door closed behind her, extracted herself from the rails and slowly moved her bottom to the closed seat of the toilet on which she sat for an appropriate time, smiling to herself, not listening to their voices anymore. The flush of the toilet when it came sounded like music to her ears.